A Respectable Life

Ann Foweraker

Art enthusiast, magistrate, village philanthropist and doting wife, Cordelia Steadman presents a picture of respectable country life. That is, until her past catches up with her. Even then, she thinks she has it all under control ... until she starts to receive the emails ... and the demands.

A psychological-suspense novel set in the tranquil Tamar Valley, Cornwall.

A Respectable Life
Ann Foweraker

ISBN: 978-1-909936-09-6

Paperback Edition 2016 Pendown Publishing
Cornwall, United Kingdom

Set in 11pt Gentium book basic

www.pendownpublishing.co.uk

Also by Ann Foweraker
The Angel Bug
Nothing Ever Happens Here
Some Kind of Synchrony
Divining the Line

Cover: NJM designs

Cover picture from an original in acrylics by Anthea Lay
'Hingsbury' 2015

A Respectable Life
Ann Foweraker

Author's Note

The village of Hingsbury does not exist, lovely as it is, you will not find it. If it did exist it would be in the Tamar Valley, about two miles from Callington and the same from Kit Hill on a 'newly created' ridge between St. Dominick, Ashton, Harrowbarrow and the slopes of Kit Hill. It, and all the characters within this novel, are figments of my imagination and do not relate in any way to any place, or any people.

It is also to be noted that, despite there being numerous novels called The Puppeteer, the title referred to in this book is not any of them.

The Windsor Free Festival and the Watchfield People's Free Festival, and within these The Freek Press, did exist, however, the bands White Lightning and Silver Linings did not.

My thanks go to the artist Anthea Lay for interpreting my sketch map of the village of Hingsbury and putting it into its setting for the cover design.

For those people who told me they love a map in a book - that map is provided overleaf.

Dedication:

To my parents; Win Foweraker for instilling a love of reading in me, and Frank Foweraker, for always reading and enjoying the stories I wrote as a child.

Map of Hingsbury

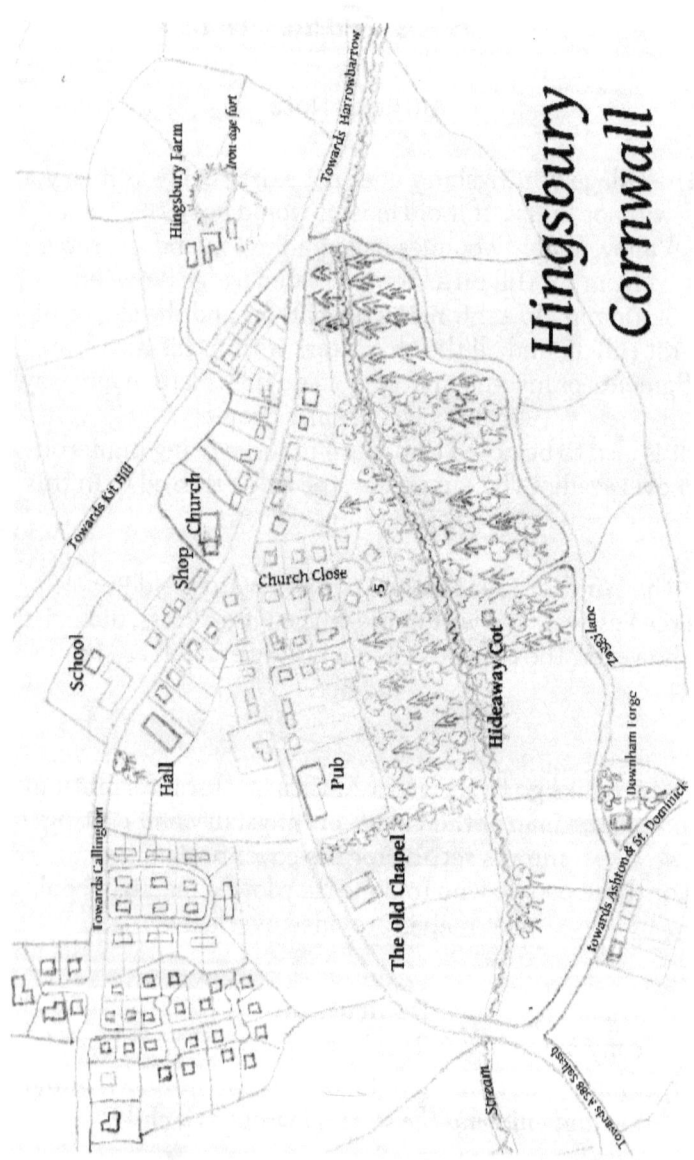

Part 1

Chapter 1

The morning the first crack appeared in Cordelia's carefully constructed life - was beautiful.

By breakfast the sun was already streaming into The Old Chapel, making the golden yellows and terracotta hues of her kitchen glow. Gerald, as usual, was sitting at the scrubbed oak table, his Times neatly folded back to read as he ate. He finished his toast and carefully lined-up his knife at a precise forty-five degree angle across his plate; Cordelia took her cue to pick up the teapot.

'Are you busy today?' his usual question at this point.

She smiled as she poured the tea, 'Fairly, I've a village welcome pack to deliver to whoever's moved into Hideaway Cottage and this afternoon there's a school governors' meeting, the one I told you about where we are changing our responsibilities for areas of the curriculum.'

'Good,' his usual response. He refolded the paper, picked up his cup and continued reading.

Cordelia glanced at the clock as she heard the letterbox clatter. The post was a little early today, she thought, as she left the table to collect it.

'Anything interesting?' Gerald asked without looking up.

'Not from the look of it,' she said, putting the envelopes down on the corner of the table and seating herself again.

Wednesday breakfasts were always nice and relaxed, the one day during the working week when Gerald didn't have to rush off to the office early. She thought again that he could retire in a few months, when he reached sixty, if he wanted to. That every breakfast could be this relaxed if he did; that they could go travelling, visit art galleries around the world, drink coffee at pavement cafés, explore ancient cathedrals ... that they could afford it and they had no one else to think about but themselves. They had not discussed it again since she suggested it last month to his shocked and baffled response – why ever would he retire now? He loved his work as an actuary. She picked up her cup of tea and began to sip, finding it hot, she set it back in the saucer and reached for the letters.

The first was from Age Concern, asking if she would be a collector in the village for the charity again this year.

'Age Concern, looking for collectors,' she said and put it down to reply to later, noting it had an email address she could use. The paper of the next envelope felt richer than usual, she turned it over. The name on the back, for return of undelivered mail, was that of a fairly local solicitor.

'Is it your court week?' Gerald said, 'There's a PCC meeting tomorrow and I need to be on time.'

'What?' dragging her thoughts back from the address on the letter. 'Oh, it's all right, I'm not sitting until next Thursday,' she pulled together a smile, but Gerald had retreated to his paper. Being a magistrate at the courts in Plymouth only meant one day a fortnight, but she always had to leave home early and returned late, usually meaning that their evening meal was later than Gerald liked it to be anyway, disastrously so, if he had an evening meeting to attend.

She smiled at him as he refolded his paper once more. Gerald, her rock, steady and stable, good looking in a sort-of academic way, a tall, heavy but broad-shouldered man who was fascinated by numbers. Theirs was a real case of opposites attracting; numbers for Cordelia were a puzzle – they jiggled around and meant nothing. Anything past primary level maths, embarrassingly, sent her mind reeling until even simple stuff could get confused.

She slid her unused butter knife under the corner of the envelope and slit it open. Inside, the paper was creamy and thick. She drew it out and flicked the page open. A quick glance gave her the same address but the letter began, Mrs Cordelia Steadman née Cordelia Springs.

Her maiden name leapt out and caught her attention – she rapidly scanned the rest of the letter. Her chest felt so tight she could scarcely breathe, feeling her world draining away, her fingers shaking, blurring the printing.

'Mr Maximillian Silver Springs – now Harris' 'born 25/05/1976' 'wishes to contact ...' She folded the letter, fumbled it safely back into the envelope and dropped it onto her lap. She quickly picked up the last unopened letter and tore it open.

'And this one's Save the Children,' she said, risking a glance at Gerald. He, deep in the financial pages as usual, appeared to have noticed nothing, for once a blessing. With one hand she held up the new letter, with the other she tucked the solicitor's letter under the chair cushion she was sitting on.

She read the advert from 'Save The Children' but her eyes saw a small chubby face with tight fair curls, as cherubic as any painted by Michelangelo. Maxie at four months, his pink fist gripping her own long blonde hair, squealing in delight as she jiggled him on her hip while dancing to the band her father played guitar with that last year together.

'That's your granddaddy playing,' Dee sang to Maxie, 'Wave to granddaddy, Maxie, wave.' Maxie, gurgled and squealed as Dee spun around, her skirts flying.

'You'll make him sick,' Margo said, reaching to take him from Dee, 'Come here lovely boy,' Dee passed him over to his grandmother and carried on dancing. That was the day the promoter spoke to the band at the end of the gig and everything looked great.

'I said, I'm off now.' Gerald was standing beside her.

'Oh!' she dropped the letter on the table, 'Sorry, of course,' she jumped up as he turned and walked to the door, just catching him up in time to take his kiss on her cheek and give one in return.

'Take care, see you this evening,' she said.

'As always,' he said with a smile that told her he felt reassured that everything was as it should be.

She watched his car disappear around the corner and hurried inside snatching the letter from under the cushion. She opened it again. Maxie. Maximillian – she'd just loved the sound of the name, taken from the artist Maximilien Luce, whose paintings were among her favourites at the time. The change of spelling on Max's birth certificate was an accident, the registrar spelt it that way, though it didn't matter to her then, or now, it was just the sound of the name. Silver, because she wanted to give him his father's name despite her mother's protest that you couldn't land anyone with a name that included Silver Springs. Dee had thought it sounded pretty cool though, and it was her choice, only her choice. She'd never dreamt that adding it would be a cast iron guarantee that a long-lost son had to be hers. After all a Max Springs, even with the same birthday, might have been a coincidence but never a Maximillian Silver. Would he look like his father?

Watchfield '75, The People's Free Festival; Silver Linings were playing as she passed stage B. He was tall, like she was, and slim with a long dark mop of wild curly hair that had a movement and life of its own. She watched as he played guitar, every nod of his head accentuated with the movement of his flowing locks. Dee thought he was beautiful from the moment she saw him, straight out of a Leonardo da Vinci sketch.

The set finished and Silver Linings loped off the stage. Dee started to walk away to get on with distributing her sheaf of Freek Press leaflets.

'Hey, freek girl, gonna write us up in the Freek Press?' the guitarist stood before her.

Dee blushed, not something she did often, 'No, I just help out, I don't usually write.'

'Go on, I'm sure you do more than that.' His smile was sparkling.

'I draw the titles but that won't help you much,' Dee laughed. 'besides – if you'd read it you'd know it's not about the bands.'

'I'll read every copy from now on, promise.' His eyes flashed wide and made her laugh again.

'I've got to post these,' she said, giving the papers in her hand a wave, 'see you,' and started to walk away. He followed, paced with her.

'Okay, where?'

'Okay, over there for a start,' pointing at a bit of fence with an old copy fluttering in the breeze. 'You play really well, I know 'cos Dad's a lead guitarist too, with White Lightning?'

'Yeah? What stage they on?'

'Tonight they're on A stage, Wednesday - Polytantric, Saturday back on A.'

Someone was shouting 'Ned! Hey, man – cummon!'

'That's cool, maybe I'll catch him.' He turned, shouted back, 'No sweat!' then back to Dee, a look right in her eyes, 'I'll see you around?'

Smiling, despite herself, 'Yeah, that'd be cool.'

Cordelia refolded the paper and put it back in the envelope, then took it out again and slid it into the roughly torn envelope from Save the Children and put it, together with the Age Concern letter, into her bureau. She cleared the table and loaded the dishwasher, screwed up the empty envelope and crammed it into the bottom of the kitchen bin. Resolutely not thinking about the letter, she collected a village welcome pack and left the house.

Chapter 2

I thought about her again today, only as a suitable character, of course. Though I wish I had bothered to listen when she came yesterday with the local welcome pack and introduced herself. Instead, I was too busy being annoyed that someone had disturbed me in my, quote 'secluded hideaway' pun intended.

I'm struggling. I admit it. It's not the first time I've had writer's block, but it is the first time that I have had people on my back demanding a manuscript, 'as per contract'. The hideaway is my agent's idea. He is fielding as much flak as he can, but my lack is his misfortune too.

I could blame him of course. I could say that to send a thriller writer into a rural retreat is not the way. He should have sent me to Moscow, or Beijing, or at least somewhere exotic. Truth is, he's just bought this holiday cottage and I was moaning on about being distracted – not letting on even to him that I was dry, uninspired, lost for plots and disgusted with myself.

I'm being harsh. I'm not lost for plots. I have the one that was pitched as the second novel, it's just that I don't like it anymore and I keep getting new ideas every day, perhaps three or four. Every day I rubbish each of them. They are not worthy. Hack stuff. I *now* have a reputation to keep up *'new thriller writer has a stunningly original voice'*

Ha! I almost pretended that I was Galsworthy, my agent, when I was forced to introduce myself, her patronising smile stuck on her face, openly asking for my name with her 'Welcome to the village Mr..?' How pathetic for an author not to be able to come up with a pseudonym on the spot, I stopped myself just in time and gave her one of the names I had been toying with for a character instead and added that I was only visiting. No way do I want anyone knowing who I am or what I do. Been there, done that, got the smarmy tee shirt. I need to concentrate.

I know, I'll find out her name by detection – that'll take me out of this funk. I need some ciggies – I wonder if the village shop has all I need.

Screw William Galsworthy, I bet he's never taken the 'five minute walk to the local shop and Post Office' he told me about. Bloody up hill and down dale all the way. Arrived with a sheen of sweat on me like I last recall from cross-country running at school.

I staggered into the shop and then had to stand like a spare part waiting while the scrawny woman behind the counter finished her gossip with some old codger who seemed to be just standing there, not buying anything. It gave me time to get my breath back at least. I couldn't see any ciggies on display but as soon as the old geezer said something like 'I must be off' I asked anyway.

'Twenty Lambert and Butler.'

'Good morning, I'm really sorry sir, we don't stock Lambert and Butler as nobody buys them.'

'Well, I do.'

She gave me a tight and tired smile, 'No one who usually stays in the village buys them, and I can't afford to keep any brands that don't all sell fairly quickly. I can offer you Sterling or Silk Cut, but Silk Cut only in tens,' she said turning and now I could see the range of ciggies behind her on the shelf, two brands plus rolling baccy.

'Oh, all right – I'll take two tens of Silk Cut,' I said, hearing the petulance in my own voice.

She reached round for them and smiling, placed them on the counter. 'Have you moved into the village, or are you just visiting?'

'Well, I'm staying for a while at 'Hideaway Cottage'. Do you know it?'

'Oh, yes. Just been sold to a gentleman from London, not you then?'

'Not me, I'm just staying there for a while.'

'Well, how long are you staying?'

This was beginning to sound like the rural inquisition. 'Perhaps six months.'

She smiled warmly, instantly transforming her face. 'Well, if you are here that long and would be sure to buy your Lambert and Butler's here I'd get a carton in for you, but we are talking ten packets.'

'Ah! Ideal.' Now she seemed happier, it was time to use the rural inquisition for my advantage. 'Perhaps you can help me with something else. A nice lady,' I cringed at actually using the phrase 'nice lady' but it would be the best use in the circumstances, 'dropped in the village welcome pack. I was a bit distracted at the time and didn't catch her name, tall, slim, blonde. To be honest I may have even seemed a bit rude and ought to apologise.'

'Rude - really? Well, that'll have been Cordelia Steadman, she often does the welcome packs. Lovely lady, does a lot for the village.'

'Really? What like?' Two can play at inquisitions.

'Oh, she's on the school governors, organises the annual art fair, helps out with just ever-so-many charity things, oh lots. If you go to the village events she's nearly always helping out. But then, she doesn't have to work you see, husband makes a packet, well, must do, the amount of money they put into converting the old chapel.'

'So they haven't been here long then?'

'Oh well, only about,' she glanced up to the ceiling for a second or two, 'twenty years, give or take.'

I suppressed a laugh. Twenty years was obviously 'not that long a time'. 'When do you think you'll have the cigarettes in?' I said changing the subject so that it didn't seem too obvious that I'd been fishing.

'Monday afternoon, Dave goes to the cash and carry on a Monday morning. Though if you want me to get them I'll have to ask you to purchase at least half of them up-front, I'm sorry, but I've been stuck with special orders before.'

Canny, but I also knew myself. If I had a hundred sitting there I'd end up chain smoking, especially if I got going. I had to keep my allowance to twenty a day, maximum.

'How about if I buy them all but you look after them for me? I don't want extra in the house to tempt me and the walk will do me good.' And I'd have a good excuse to mine this information hub whenever I felt like it.

I coughed up the money and had a quick look round, surprised by how much there was, and noted I could at least pick up breakfast cereals, milk and even a bottle of wine as the starter box of supplies I'd brought with me began to run out, no ready meals though. It looked like I'd be phoning out for fast food if I got to that all-out stage. No, *when* I got to that stage, no *if* about it – this had to happen. Perhaps all I needed was a kick, a bit of adrenaline, but not from the bottle, I already knew drinking alone would end badly.

The walk back to the cottage was actually quite pleasant, though it had to have just the same contours as the journey out. Strange. The quiet was odd too. Came and went as I moved through the lanes. Hardly any traffic noise, though I heard a motorbike revving away somewhere – and all around came gentle animal and bird sounds. When I got back to the cottage I made a coffee and allowed myself ten minutes sitting outside, listening.

I think I will see if I can meet her again, bump into her at a village event perhaps.

Chapter 3

Cordelia looked down at the torn envelope in her hand and stared at it. She had thought that by the time she got back from delivering the welcome pack she would have had some idea of what her response would be. She put the envelope down again and poured herself a coffee, strong and black. She took the envelope and the coffee through to the conservatory that overlooked the valley, the most peaceful room in a peaceful house and the place where Gerald most liked to be whenever he brought work home with him.

She took out the letter again and read it slowly and completely. There was no mistake. Her son had found her. Something she'd given up worrying about years ago. He wanted to make contact. It was couched in very careful terms, but she could tell he had questions he needed answering, and she couldn't blame him.

It would be so much simpler, safer, to just say no. Even as this thought passed through her mind she felt such a pang in her chest she knew she could not give up this chance, but she could feel the sweat prickle her hairline just at the thought of everything that could be destroyed.

The letter gave her options on how she could proceed. She could refuse. She could refuse, with an explanation. She could give permission for him to be given her address to write to. She could give an email address. She could give a phone number.

She opted for an email address. She reasoned that she could read it and take time in her reply and that Gerald would not see it. A phone call would be too random, Gerald might answer the landline, and her own iPhone was unreliable inside the house. It had to be the email. She noted that the letter could also be replied to by email, using a reference number and so, before her resolve left her, she flicked open her iPad and logged on to her email.

***

Her first thought on waking was: Is there a reply? Mouth dry, she slunk into the bathroom with her iPhone tucked in her wrap pocket. She heard Gerald go downstairs, then pressed the mail icon. There it was. Max Harris. She hit close immediately. Her heart was making her fingers tremble. She stared at herself in the mirror. Her eyes seemed wild, over-bright. She rubbed a wet flannel around her face, tied her wrap tighter and, slipping the iPhone back into her handbag in the bedroom, ran downstairs to put the kettle on.

Gerald was in the gym annexe doing his exercises as usual, she ran back upstairs, had a proper wash, combed her hair and brushed her teeth.

By the time he'd finished and was changed she had breakfast laid out just as he liked it, with a slice of bread poised to be put down into the toaster, juice a hand-span right from the cereal bowl, the muesli filled to the line, the milk jug placed top centre to the whole setting, teacup and saucer a hand-span to the right of that.

She poured her own muesli and spooned yogurt over it. As she stirred it in she wondered about the email, glad that Gerald would be gone quickly this morning so that she could get to it sooner.

'You all right?' Gerald asked, his face carefully arranged in concern.

'What?' But this was such an unusual thing for Gerald to say, she quickly realised her mistake. Usually she would chatter on about the coming day, or something that happened to someone in the village. She never really thought he took it in; he wasn't really very interested in the minutiae of village life. But silence, goodness, he'd noticed her silence. And as it was an early work day there was no paper yet to distract him, she should have been more aware, she would have to be more aware.

She smiled brightly, 'Oh! I'm fine, I was just working out in my head where I was going to put the sculpture exhibits this year. I didn't expect so many – we usually only have a couple – but that blacksmith who moved in at Downham, he's putting in three, and they are quite large, it seems, I have to go over there later and look at them.' She knew she'd reassured him when he stopped looking at her and resumed eating.

As soon as she had seen Gerald off to work, she opened the iPad and hit the email icon. Her hesitation was momentary, but she was holding her breath as she clicked on his name and the email opened.

> Hi Cordelia,
>
> Thank you for agreeing to communicate with me.
> You must be wondering 'Why now?'
> I know I could have looked before, but my adoptive parents were both so good to me I felt it would have been a betrayal of them to look before.
> Mum died recently (Dad died some years ago) and amongst her things was my adoption order - with my original name on it.
> I took it as a sign – I hope a good sign.

I would like to meet, but if this is not possible then, at least, I have some questions I hope you can answer.

The solicitors would not give me your address but they did say, perhaps unintentionally, that it was odd that you didn't live too far away, considering that I was adopted from a London borough.

A bit about me: I'm 39 (but you'll know that) I'm married with two children, a boy and a girl. I'm a teacher of Drama at Liskeard Community College.

Your turn.

Max

She read it twice. Again a choice. She could just opt to answer his questions by email. But he was so close. So close, Liskeard was only a dozen miles away for heaven's sake. She swallowed, her throat tight, aching. She put her hand to her mouth, trying to hold back the cry that was struggling to get out. Anytime, almost anywhere – she might have seen him. Oh my! Oh! Her eyes filled with tears. Her breath came in barely suppressed sobs. Her shoulders shaking, she reached out a hand and closed the iPad. She couldn't think straight. It was too much.

She walked into the conservatory and looked out across the valley. In the distance she could see the river glinting, in her mind she saw herself the day she told Margo.

She'd deliberately not let on that she'd missed her period. It was easy, her parents, as always, completely caught up in each other and in their lifestyle, so erratic, moving constantly from gig to gig, festival to festival. The clothes helped hide it too, her small wardrobe of clothes were all loose and flowing but she'd deliberately worn her looser clothes as her breasts enlarged and her bulge began to show. It didn't stop her being scared to tell them. There was a girl, at the commune they'd joined as winter approached, who had a small child, about a year old, brown-faced bright eyed, she carried her in a sling on her hip much of the time, crooning to the child as she worked around. Dee had chatted to her while they peeled vegetables together, made the baby laugh. Asked, casually, how hard it was to bring up a baby in a commune. Melissa had said it was easy, anyone would mind the baby if you had to go out, or if you were out of it, but the shrewd look she gave Dee made her back-off asking any more questions. She wasn't ready to let anyone know just then - the baby was still her secret, but now, nearly Christmas, it was time.

'Margo?'

'Mmm?'

'I've, umm, I have something important to tell you.'

'Okay, what is it? You have my full attention,' she said, still looking at her book.

'I'm having a baby.'

Margo's head flashed up, looked right at her, Dee noticed her mother's gaze flick down to her breasts, her stomach.

'How far gone?' she whispered.

'Long time,' Dee pressed the fabric of her dress down to show the bulge, 'about four months.'

Chapter 4

'William!' I said as soon as my agent answered the phone.

'Sean?'

'Of course it's me, who the hell else have you left in your hideaway? Huh?'

'Haha, well you sounded a bit odd,' Galsworthy said. 'How's the book coming along?'

'It must be your landline, do you realise that there's no mobile signal here at all? Not even outside the flaming cottage. I have to go right up the lane to the top of the hill before I can pick anything up.'

'Yes, well, that's why I have the landline, that and getting the internet.'

'Oh yes, have they heard of broadband here?'

'It *is* on broadband,'

'You could have fooled me when I was trying to do some research ...'

'Research? You said you'd done all your research ... that's what has taken you so long, remember?'

Caught! 'Just a bit extra. You know how it goes - no?'

'Sean ...'

'It's okay, really, it is all under control.'

'So what did you call me for?'

'Just wondered if you'd told anyone I was here? Or anyone here, who I was?'

'No, no, of course not. You were most specific. Why, has someone contacted you?'

'Nothing like that ...'

'What then?'

'Nosy parker in the village shop, it's like the inquisition. Thought I'd better check before I told them a load of old bull.'

'Oh, that's all. Fine, just don't make yourself sound too interesting, everybody knows how to google a name.'

'No problem, that's all. Speak soon.'

'And can you give me any idea of a first ...'
I put the phone down. He could call me back if he really thought it was worth it. He didn't. And now I knew I was clear to reinvent myself and, idiot that I've become, I hadn't thought of googling *her* name. I smiled as I opened up a new window on my laptop.

I didn't think there would be too many Cordelia Steadmans out there, and I was right. I found her quick enough, but was disappointed to find only newspaper reports with her name. I was hoping for a Facebook page, Twitter, LinkedIn at least. However, Mrs Goody-two-shoes had ended up in a number of press reports. Mostly to do with the Art Fair in the village, the school, a number of charity coffee mornings that, it seemed, were held at her home as the address was The Old Chapel. Logical name for a building that was just that. Ha! A nugget – she's a magistrate. Interesting. What else, nice posh lady, what else?

I tried Google maps to see if The Old Chapel, Hingsbury had a marker. It had! I zoomed in and dragged the little man down to have a look at street view. Not quite so in the back of beyond as this place then. When I'd tried to get a look at Hideaway Cottage from London it refused to go down the lane it is in. Not surprising really, it's the only house in it and it's a dead-end. But here was The Old Chapel. It looked really smart, barely ecclesiastical. No stained glass, instead huge clear panes filled the dominant arched window at the front. It was painted a discreet sandstone shade and the garden that was visible looked immaculate. I returned to satellite and zoomed out again to get an idea of the way from Hideaway to The Old Chapel. Hmm, not too far away, about as far as the shop was from me but in the opposite direction.

I opened a new document. Pasted the map into it. Added the bits I'd found about her in the papers. Gave the file a title. Okay, I know I'm not working on the book, but it feels like I'm doing something. What else can I add? There was one rubbish photograph of her in the paper. It didn't show the colour of her eyes, or the gentle wave of her hair. How old do I think she is? I need to see her again. I feel she's about my age, mid-forties? Hmm. I wonder if she has children, I can just see her with a couple of blond kids, all dressed in Boden. What do I want to find out? This is easier, I'll make a character list. *Name: Cordelia Steadman.* How middle-class can you get? Wonder if there are any middle names? *Age: height: eye colour: hair colour: Blonde. morphology: Slim. Occupation: Children: Interests: Likes: Dislikes: Where born: Parental Occupation: Marital status: married. Husband's name: his Occupation:*

I could fill in her occupation now, but I won't, I will confirm my findings first. This could be fun.

Right, now the new me. *Name: Jim Menteur,* let's hope no one has good French and a suspicious mind... she didn't blink when I gave it as my name so it's probably okay. *Age:* keep it simple, *45,* nobody traced someone just from their age. Ditto height, eye and hair colour, I'm not going to dye my hair am I? *Occupation?* This is harder. Why am I here? What occupation could I have that requires me to do nothing but sit in this building? Journalist? No, too close to author. Scientist? What do I know about science? Oh! This is ridiculous. I know, I could be a tax man – everybody would leave me alone then. Ha! No, be sensible. What... What.... What is the first rule of telling lies? Keep them simple and make sure they have an element of truth. *Jim Menteur is ... an English teacher, private school, currently marking exam papers and getting over a painful divorce.* Perfect! My messy divorce was over three years ago, just as I was writing my breakthrough novel as it happens, but I still have those memories to hand, and I used to be just that, a teacher at a private school, before I took the plunge. I'll risk using the same school. And marking papers keeps me busy indoors, in peace and quiet. I was into this now; I quickly filled in my origins, moving myself west to Bristol where I'd attended university, and my university to Reading, where I had grown up.

I scanned my new résumé. It fitted Jim well, I felt right in my new clothes, ready to engage with the village. Now, where did I stash the welcome pack, let's see what's on.

Chapter 5

Dear Max,

I want to meet you. However, this is extremely difficult for me. My husband does not know and it would be hard to tell him at this point. I am not saying it would not be possible at some time, but just now, impossible. I hope you understand.

I have given this great thought. I believe the school holidays start at the end of this week, would you be free to meet me on a weekday after then?

If so, I propose we have an initial short meeting somewhere neutral, in Plymouth for example.

If this is suitable for you, may I suggest I meet you at Smeaton's Tower at 1.05 on Thursday 31st July, I only have a half-hour lunch break but I hope it will be enough to see where we can go from there.

I do look forward to meeting you.

Dee

Cordelia pressed 'send', and only then released the breath she'd been unconsciously holding as she re-read the message for the last time. It had taken her so many drafts to write – and even now she felt it seemed a little stand-offish, the 'less than half an hour', mean, but it was the least problematic for her, no extra lies to tell about where she had been. Too late now, you cannot pull back an email from the ether, she told herself.

She glanced at the clock; where had the time gone? She needed to hurry as she had an appointment at the primary school as the new 'governor with responsibility for Humanities and Art', with the Humanities co-ordinator. Cordelia had an idea to propose and she couldn't be late as the teacher was fitting it into her lunchtime.

She ran from the house and jumped into her Clio. It was only a mile, but time was of the essence. Within minutes she was parking in the Hall car park and hurrying across the road to the school. She reported in at reception and was soon hovering near the classroom door, not wanting to disturb the teacher as she made sure all the children were lined up in the two groups, school lunches and packed lunches, ready to go off to the dining room. It was good; it gave Cordelia time to remind herself of the items she already had and the ones she knew of that might be available for free or, at least, very little.

'Walk, don't run!' Katie Small called after the retreating line of children, the ones at the back just beginning to jostle for position. 'Come in,' she smiled at Cordelia.

'Thank you, look, do eat lunch as we talk, I know what it's like.'

Katie shot her a look but dipped her head and picked out a pack of sandwiches from her bag under the desk, 'Thanks, so what are you thinking of?'

'I've looked through the syllabus, and I have an idea for making a collection of artefacts that the school could keep as a resource for supporting the topics. I know I can source some interesting items to fit with The Victorians, I have glass mineral water bottles, you know, the ones with the marble in the neck? And stoneware ginger beer bottles, one with a Callington maker's name, which would be even more interesting. I also have a Victorian bean-slicer and a cast iron shoemaker's last. Now if you think these are a good start and could be useful in the history work I can set about building this resource. What do you think?'

Katie finished chewing, nodding as she did so, 'Always interesting to have some real artefacts to handle and look at. What about funding though, I don't think we have anything left this year'

'No problem, I'm not expecting to pay much for the sort of things I'm looking for so I'll cover it. At the moment I just want to know if it really would be of use. You see, almost all my own historical knowledge came from looking at the artefacts first, and only then reading around them to put them into context. It all seemed so much more real to me that way.'

'Some children learn best that way it's true.' Katie smiled.

'What are we doing today?' a twelve year old Dee asked.

Margo was scanning down the museum information board. 'Looks like we'll study Egyptians today, it says they have a 'wide range of Egyptian artefacts.'

Dee loved the word 'artefacts', there was something other-worldly about the sound of the word, yet quite solid at the same time. Following signs she soon led them through to the Egyptian Rooms.

Centre stage was an Egyptian mummy, wrapped but exposed, standing in its sarcophagus.

'What does the word sarcophagus mean?' asked Margo?

'Ah, it means flesh and eating?'

'Well remembered, but in this case it is used to indicate that this case has the body inside it, like a coffin. Where did we come across this word before?'

'In that book about the Assyrians.'

'Good girl!' Margo beamed, 'Now what can we find out about this lot you don't already know?'

Dee started to look around and Margo found herself somewhere to sit and took out a book. After a while Dee returned.

'I know how they preserved the bodies.'

'Great. How?'

Dee settled herself beside her mother and began to tell her what she had learnt about the extraction of the brain and all the soft tissues, the funeral pots, the preservation of the flesh and the wrapping of the body. The occasional agreement from her mother was all she needed to complete the retelling.

'..... and they mummified cats too, those are some cats over there in those jars.'

'Cats? Why would they do that?' asked Margo.

'They believed they were spiritual and could help guide them in the afterlife. Who'd be a cat?'

'But it wasn't only cats they took into their afterlife. Some rich people had their slaves killed, or just entombed with them to serve them in their afterlife, or even wives.'

'That's awful!'

'That's how it was back then with their beliefs. Right, what else can the Egyptians teach us today? Is there anything here about the stars or about the building of the pyramids?'

'I'll go and see.'

'So you're happy that I go with whatever I can find? I'll start with the Victorians, but I'm willing to have a look at the other eras too.' Dee laughed, 'Though I can't guarantee original items for the Vikings.'

'If you could it might solve our budget problems.' Katie laughed too, 'An original Viking hoard of gold would probably do it; they are supposed to have come up the Tamar.'

Dee went home to get a bite of lunch herself, feeling happy that she might be able to make a good contribution to history at the school. As soon as she got in she opened her iPad, not really expecting a reply, but just in case, before she could move away she saw the new mail icon and tapped it open.

New mail; from him.

Chapter 6

I'm getting to know my way around this place. I zipped into the local town yesterday, picked up a few frozen and a few more ready meals at the Tesco there, and filled the car with fuel. A bit of a one-horse town really, a main street and that's about it, but sort of quaint at that. It did seem to have a few fast-food places if I get fed up with ready meals, Chinese, Indian, a chippy and some other far-eastern job - but none of them do deliveries, which is a bit annoying.

Buzzing since I started the detective work, I've got a new plot outline that I still like today. I can feel myself smiling at the thought of it. That is a good sign. I'll flesh out a few characters and if I still like it tomorrow I'm in. God I hope this is it!

I couldn't find the bloody welcome pack. I must have binned it the same day, it'll be buried under ready meals by now, stupid of me. Never mind, I'll get one of the sheets about the village from the shop. I already bought some ciggies in town but I'm sure I can find something to buy as an excuse.

This is weird, the walk to the shop is arduous, I arrived puffed out again, but the walk back is easy. Overall I feel as if I am walking uphill as often as down, both ways, but I can't be. The woman wasn't behind the desk as I walked in, but there was a shuffling sound behind a shelving unit. A glance round this revealed a man locking up the Post Office kiosk. He looked up at me, beaming.

'Sorry, I'll be with you in a minute,' he said and, going round the other end of the unit reappeared by the desk.

'Can I help you?'

'Ah, I wonder if you have any spare copies of the village newsletter? I seem to have mislaid mine.'

He looked surprised but pointed past me and said, 'Some on the shelf behind you.'

'Great, thanks,' I determined to make Jim into a more friendly bloke than I felt. Dredging up a name from my chat with the woman in the shop I tried, 'Would you be Dave?'

He smiled, 'Yes that's me, for my sins.'

'Ah, right, I thought the lady in here said you were called Dave.'

'Ha ha! This is where I say; that was no lady, that was my wife, boom, boom, Liz.'

I joined in his laughter. 'Good one. I'm new in the village, well, staying for six months at least ...'

'You'll be staying at Hideaway Cottage then.'

'That's me,' I said, hoping that the 'lady wife' had not been too damning of me, I held out my hand to shake, 'Jim Menteur.'

'Pleased to meet you, Dave Walley.'

'Likewise. I thought I might as well get into a bit of country life while I am here,' I said. 'Better than being shut up in the cottage all day and all night.'

'Work from home then, do you?'

'Well, I'm marking exam papers. Usually I teach at a big private school up country, but, well,' I pulled a solemn face and hoped that he would be as informative to his wife as she had been to him, 'Just gone through a bit of a painful divorce. Licking my wounds as it were.' This Jim persona was garrulous. I'd never tell another person this much about myself, let alone another bloke. Hope I wasn't overdoing it. 'So, this Village Fun Day tomorrow - what's that?' I said looking at the sheet I'd just picked up.

'Well, don't know if you'd like it, there's stalls and games up on the green, teas in the hall, a dancing display, five-a-side football and a bit by a local historic re-enactment society, Roundheads and Cavaliers, that should be fun. Oh, and there's a beer tent,' he finished with a grin.

'Beer tent sounds okay!' I grinned back, but wondered what she would be doing, but didn't dare ask as that would certainly get back to Mrs, and Mrs might think two enquiries a bit too much. 'What's the local pub like here then?'

'Okay, getting better now, it had a rough time when the brewery put a right weird couple in there. No idea why they were in the business at all, not a friendly pair. They've gone now, good riddance, but it's taking time to build back, the new couple are proper nice though, locals. I pop in most evenings for a swift half, about eight.'

It sounded like an invitation. 'I might bump into you one evening then, I must sample the local fare!'

He grinned, 'Good. Anything else, apart from the newsletter?' he said as the door opened behind me.

'Oh,' I said looking round, 'a pack of ten Silk Cut, until you pick up my Lambert and Butlers.'

'Ah, I won't forget, anything else?' he said putting them on the counter.

'Um er - a packet of Crunchy Nut Cornflakes, yes, and I'll take this,' I said placing a Mars bar on the counter.

My new friend Dave, told me the amount and I paid up, slipped the ciggies and Mars into my pocket and tucked the cornflakes and the news-sheet under my arm and left.

Notes on village characters:
Shop Keeper: Dave Walley, Mid fifties, Stocky, Hair: thinning, brown. Affable. Likes a 'corny' joke. Likes a pint in the local. Owns / runs village shop.
Shop Keeper: Liz Walley, Mid fifties, Scrawny, Black hair - too black - looks dyed. Sardonic.

Saturday may be my first chance to bump into her. The Village Fun Day is at the field beside the Hall. I came back from Callington that way, so I know where it is, just by the school. Jim is ready to be a social being. I can hardly wait.

Chapter 7

Dear Dee,

I am disappointed you can only give me half an hour at our first meeting. I have so many questions I want to ask, but maybe you don't want to answer them?

I am available this coming week, and so will meet you.

1.05 at Smeaton's tower on the Hoe, Thurs. I'll be the one carrying a copy of The Tempest.

Regards

Max

What did she expect, unbounded joy? She felt cold, a sinking in the pit of her stomach. Has she nearly wrecked this chance to meet him by being too cautious? But what else could she be. Gerald would not understand how she could have kept this from him for so long. And if he found out, what else would she have to explain? Her face suddenly flooded with heat, the skin prickling. It didn't bear thinking about.

"I long to hear the story of your life, which must captivate the ear strangely." The Tempest. Some things never leave you. She realised she hadn't even thought how she'd recognise him. She realised she was expecting to see someone she knew – someone who looked like Ned, or herself.

She hit reply; perhaps she could ameliorate some of the damage.

> Dear Max,
> Thank you so much for agreeing to meet me, I understand your disappointment, but I hope this is only an initial meeting, and we can work out a way to have a better opportunity for me to answer all your questions, and you, mine.
> Thank you for being so understanding. I am so looking forward to meeting you.
> "I long to hear the story of your life, which must captivate the ear strangely."
> Best
> Dee

She pressed send, closed the lid of the iPad and resolutely turned her thoughts to events coming up. The wait until next Thursday would be interminable, but she knew the best way to get through it would be to do something else, to direct all her efforts elsewhere. She'd had plenty of practice at that.

***

Friday morning and Cordelia had just finished reading the book club choice. Usually she had the book done and dusted in plenty of time, but since Wednesday she hadn't been able to concentrate on reading, her mind drifting off into the past too easily. She'd immersed herself in baking for the weekend all day on Thursday, and even that was not as organised or controlled as usual, with one tray-bake having to be heavily trimmed to remove over-dry edges where she'd forgotten to set the timer. So here she was rapidly skim-reading to the end. 'Betrayed' was a one-time winner of Richard and Judy's 'True-Stories', where a woman's best friend had almost completely ruined her family and caused huge psychological damage to her daughter. It was not the sort of book that Cordelia would have read from choice, but each person took it in turns to recommend a book for the group, so there was a wide variety. She sighed at the end, at the awful gullibility combined with loyalty and the twisted nature of some people's minds. At least it would get some discussion going, she thought. Putting the book down, she rang Marian, probably her best friend in the village.

'Hi, Marian,' she said as soon as the phone was answered.
'C'delia, all right?'
'Fine, I was just wondering if you were going to the book group this afternoon?'
'Yes, sure.'
'Would you like to pop round for lunch before then?'
'Ah! That sounds good! Oneish?'
'Yes, but, um, if you're not too busy you could come for elevenses too, we could catch up,' trying not to sound needy.
'Perfect! See you in half an hour then.'

Perfect, Cordelia thought, if anyone can keep my mind off Max it will be Marian, she allowed a smile to spread across her mind.

Cordelia had just put a bunch of sweet peas she'd picked from the garden in a delicately marked mauve Caithness glass vase and placed them on the coffee table when Marian let herself in the kitchen door, calling, 'C'delia?'
'In here.'
Marian bounded into the main room of The Old Chapel, a vast space, reaching full height and bright with light streaming through the huge windows. It was an impressive room, yet the furnishings that Cordelia had carefully selected made it seem relaxed and cosy. She had a dining area towards the back, nearest the kitchen, and a four-square group of two-seater sofas around the coffee table

making a convivial group at the other end. Everything had clean lines, there were no ornaments out, but four elegant glass-fronted cases, designed to echo the window shapes, contained a wide variety of objects, and the walls held Gerald's art collection.

'Sweet peas – lovely! Always such wonderful colours!' Marian said, as they returned to the kitchen where another vase of them stood on the table.

'You must take some, I can hardly keep up with them this year, and if you don't pick them you don't get more, so you'd be doing me a favour,' Cordelia said as she put the coffee on.

'Done!' Marian paused, 'So what's up?'

Cordelia looked up sharply, 'What do you mean?'

'Well, when I bumped into you on Wednesday you could hardly wait to be off.'

'Oh. Oh, sorry.' She fiddled with getting out the cups, spoons, milk, then looked up straight at her friend, 'I'd just delivered a welcome pack to Hideaway Cottage. The man there was less than friendly. It left me feeling quite out of sorts really, and I was waiting for an important phone call, so had to hurry back, I'm sorry I didn't mean to …'

'Silly, I'm not upset, I just thought you were!'

'Oh, well, perhaps I was, that man! He opened the door and barked 'Yes?' After I introduced myself and welcomed him to the village he just about slammed the door in my face.'

'Did he have a name?'

'Menter or Mentor. He was so rude. Jim, I think.'

'What was he like?'

'I really don't know. Um, tall, dark … scowling.'

'Haha, damn, I thought for a moment you were going to say tall, dark and handsome! Blow!'

'Oh, I don't think he's your sort, too much of a misery guts.'

'Some of us are getting a bit desperate. That's one problem living out here, you soon run out of likely candidates.'

'I thought you were seeing that Simon?'

'No, he turned out to be a 'ready for the pipe and slippers' type. What is it with some men, they turn sixty and all they want to do is sit about. I want a bit of fun!'

'Oh, was he sixty? A bit old for you?'

'Well, I had put down fifty to sixty. I think I'll change it to forty to fifty. Perhaps I need someone a tad younger than me, not older,' she grinned.

'And add they must be interested in sport, unless you've done that now?'

'No, I hadn't, I'm a bit concerned that 'interested in sport' may be a euphemism.'

'Good grief, no, surely not – how could you say you were really interested in sport, if that was so?'

'I don't know, there's a whole new language involved in this dating lark. Anyway, I don't want a couch footballer, as in interested in watching sport, actually, I don't want a footballer at all, can't bear the game. But I'll think about it, or perhaps I can add 'running half marathons' in my interest section, that might have the same effect.'

Coffee and lunch flew by and a much lighter-minded Cordelia went off to book club with Marian. There were only six members at Gill's when they had all arrived, and as soon as they were settled Gill got them started on the discussion.

'Today's book is 'Betrayed' by Lyndsey Harris as told to Andrew Crofts. This is a true story of a woman whose long-time friend from work, who had already drawn Lyndsey into her own web of lies about horrific secret abuse by playing on her loyalty and caring nature, then implicated Lyndsey's six-year-old daughter in such a series of events that Lyndsey was at risk of having her children taken away from her. Now, what do we think?'

'How could anyone spend their whole life telling lies? It doesn't seem possible,' Marian opened.

'I'm pretty sure this woman did, bad enough that she lied about her own life, let alone ruining the child's,' Toni said.

'Well, life can't be lived like that, you have to be able to believe people,' Linda said.

'She obviously had a mental condition, though,' Gill pointed out.

'I think it's called the 'soap opera syndrome', where they make their life into a series of dramas like a soap opera,' Cordelia added, not really wanting to discuss lying at all.

'We all lie,' Joan said, her voice low and steady, a retired research scientist, she tended to have less small talk than others and everything she said was like presenting a paper. No one interrupted her, 'In fact, there is the theory that the human brain developed exponentially to enable us to lie using language.'

'Well, I don't know about that, but I try never to lie!' Linda added, heatedly.

'On the contrary, you were asked 'how are you' when you arrived this afternoon and you replied 'fine', when actually you were at the doctor's this morning, were you not, and you told me then you'd been feeling rotten for a week.'

Linda flushed pink, 'That's not lying!'

'In the strictest definition it is, but I am not saying you are a liar, merely that the human race encourages many lies for us to get along with each other. We do not tell Aunt Maud that the present she gave us is hideous, nor that someone's baby looks like Winston Churchill, we tell lies to smooth society.'

'All very interesting Joan, but not this type of fantasising - this outright lying,' Toni said, not fazed by Joan's reputation for focused analysis.

'The maintenance of large elaborate lies is precisely one of the mechanisms I was referring to, but Gill is right, this woman had a condition.'

'So,' Gill said tentatively, 'Do any of you think you would have fallen for her lies?'

'They were a bit too extreme ...' Linda started.

Marian cut in, 'But well carried out – with physical evidence.'

'And the online presence was effective,' added Toni.

'And she built them up gradually, letting her friend into her confidence while undermining her friend's own self-esteem,' completed Marian.

'I *was* going to say, they were a bit too extreme, but just the sort of thing that someone might not want anyone but their best friend to know, so as the one trusted with the story, you might believe it,' Linda said a little sharply.

'Oh, sorry, I see what you mean,' Marian said.

Gill looked around the group, 'Cordelia?'

'Oh, I don't know. Loyalty came into it a lot. And asking people not to tell. It wouldn't have worked without both,' Cordelia said, feeling decidedly strange.

'See you two later for putting up the bunting?' Gill said to Marian and Cordelia as they parted.

'Six o'clock?' asked Marian.

'Yes, oh and can anyone bring a tall stepladder,' Gill said. 'If I remember there are a few places where we could do with the extra height.'

'Gerald and I can do that.'

'Great. See you all later.'

'Looks like we've got good weather for tomorrow anyway,' Marian said as she waved a goodbye and they walked down to the junction. From there, Cordelia walked slowly back to The Old Chapel, letting thoughts of lies and lying sift uneasily through her mind, and thinking about next Thursday and seeing her own secret.

Chapter 8

I've taken my Jim persona round all the flaming stalls, being amicable, he's won a bottle of shampoo on the tombola and nothing on the pick-a-straw or the 'electric wire' but not seen her yet. I scanned the table full of second hand paperbacks, and didn't see mine there. I'd have to have bought it if I did, just in case anyone recognised the author pic; though the shaven-headed, bearded guy on the back cover of The Stalker doesn't bear much resemblance to my current state. Bit rough around the edges, my ex would have called it, downright scruffy, my mother would have said. Jim's cultivating the 'designer stubble' look, it takes less maintenance than that fussy little beard did, and my curly hair is longer and a bit wild as I've just let it grow while I've been writing this novel.

The PA system announced the five-a-side football was just about to begin. As I can't stand football, Jim headed for the hall and a cup of tea and I suddenly realised that she was most likely to be in there anyway dispensing tea and cake.

The hall was surprisingly clean and fresh inside with tablecloths and small vases of sweet peas on every table. I saw her almost as soon as I entered. She was standing near the end of the hall talking to a shorter, slim, dark-haired woman. Jim headed for the tea counter and soon turned away with a cup of tea and a plate bearing a chunk of lemon drizzle cake. My mouth was watering with the scent of it. Jim hesitated and looked around, as if trying to see where to sit. I allowed Jim to look at her and start to walk in her direction.

Jim placed his cup and plate down on a table near the back of the hall, straightened and, putting on an apologetic smile, headed towards the pair of women.

'Hi, I, I think I owe you an apology?' Jim said. To give her credit, she smiled at me. Jim continued, 'Hideaway Cottage, you brought me a welcome pack and, ha, I wasn't very. Welcoming that is.'

'Don't worry,' she said with a small shake of her head.

'No! I mean it, I was like a bear with a sore head and I took it out on you, the only friendly face I had seen for a week. I was wrong, can we start again? Jim Menteur, pleased to meet you and thank you for bringing me a welcome pack.' Jim said, including the other woman in a glance as he did so.

'Pleased to meet you too, I'm Marian Wood,' the other woman stuck out her hand and Jim shook it, finding the grip surprisingly firm for a woman. I looked at her properly for the first time, a tight firm body on a woman in her forties, and dark curly hair that would be the spit of mine if I let it grow much longer.

'Marian,' I smiled at her, then looking straight at Cordelia, 'and, I'm sorry I really wasn't listening when you told me your name before.'

She smiled, held out her hand, 'Cordelia. Steadman.'

'Very pleased to meet you,' Jim said, shaking the warm, dry, long-fingered hand.

'Are you living at Hideaway permanently?' Marian cut in.

'No, well, I am only renting it at the moment, from the owner. I'm marking exam papers and ...' Jim stopped. I wanted to mention the divorce but felt it was a wrong move at this moment.

'Oh, are you an examiner?'

'No, just a teacher, doing a bit extra.'

'So you'll leave the village in September then?' Cordelia said, one eyebrow raised.

That caught me out - I'd been happily saying Jim was going to be here for six months.

'Well, certainly until then, but I have hopes of finding a post down this way, a fresh start, I have the cottage for six months anyway.' It was an instant inspiration that pulled Jim out of the firing line and set the landscape for further revelations.

In real life she was as attractive as my memory had told me, something willowy and vulnerable about her, but all grown-up and womanly at the same time. I find it so hard to pinpoint ages with women but I'd say the same as her friend, mid to late forties. Her eyes are a cool grey, but I bet they'd flash with fire at the right provocation. She's perfect for the Ambassador's wife.

'Nice to see you joining in the village activities,' Cordelia said. 'It's things like this that make a village.'

'Yes, I can see that. Is there a lot going on here then?'

'Well, depending on what you like, yes, there's lots on. Are you into sport at all?' Marian asked.

'Well, not football.' Jim smiled and tipped his head towards the open door, 'That's why I came in here. I suppose a bit. I used to play squash and I jogged, you know, round the school grounds.'

'Really?' the Marian woman sparkled at Jim. I may have made a mistake admitting to this somehow.

'Well, I used to.' Jim said, as I pulled in my stomach. Truth is I used to be a lot fitter, before the divorce, Angie kept my food intake healthy and moderated and I did jog a bit but I wasn't going to mention all this just now.

'Well, there's the local Harriers,' she said, 'if you want to take up running again, we run every Thursday evening, follow a trail, you know. It's a great way to get to know the local countryside, it's social and it's fun.'

'Oh. Really? I must take a look at that.' Jim said, even as I thought it was not the best thing to say, that Jim should have developed a sports injury or something.

'I could pick you up, take you to the first meeting if you like?'

39

I glanced at Cordelia, she was smiling, encouragingly, I wondered if she went too.

'Oh, perhaps then,' Jim said, 'that's very kind of you.'

'You'll have to excuse me,' Cordelia said suddenly, 'I'm needed,' and walked swiftly into the kitchen leaving me standing with the Marian woman.

'Don't let your tea get cold,' Marian said.

I turned back to it, cooling on the table behind me.

'I'll keep you company, if you like.' And we both sat.

'Thanks,' Jim smiled and I sank my teeth into the sweet sharp cake; delicious.

'Does Cordelia run too?' Jim asked after downing the almost-cold tea.

'Uh-uh!' she said with a shake of her head, 'C'delia tends not to go out much on her own in the evening, except WI, anything else it's with her husband. She dotes on him. Don't get me wrong, I love her to bits, but she goes over the top sometimes with the devoted wife thing.' Jim was wise to say nothing at this point, I was full of questions. 'And you wouldn't find Gerald on a run,' she laughed as the thought obviously amused her, but quickly smothered it, 'Sorry, shouldn't have said that,' and gave me a conspiratorial look.

'I'll not say a word.' Jim said, smiling back at her and raising a twinkle in her eye. 'So, what else is there in the village?'

'Depends what you like, as I said. There's an Am Dram, though they only do pantos so nothing going on there until September. What kind of teacher did you say you were?'

'English.'

'Oh, so you might be up for that then, if you are free?'

'Maybe, do you and Cordelia do that?'

'No, not my scene, get it, scene, and rehearsals are always evenings so ...'

'So everything is in the evenings? Apart from things like this?'

'No, no, there's a book group that meets afternoons, that's fortnightly, a social lunch group that has a meal and a speaker once a month, Pilates each week, umm, well, it's all in the welcome pack.'

'Well, yes, but knowing what is good is a different matter,' Jim said, whereas I was really still trying to find out about the habits and habitat of the 'nice lady'.

'Though I suppose you'll be working after August, but you might be interested in the book group? It would be good to have another man's point of view, there's only one man in the group and he's in his eighties and doesn't like most of the choices anyway.'

'I'm not sure yet what I'll be ...' Jim started, but Marian suddenly stood,

'Sorry, got to go and help, pleased to meet you. Do you want to try the Harriers?'

Jim hesitated as I couldn't make up my mind.

'Well,' she said, 'if you do, give me a ring,' and fished a card out of her bag and dropped it on the table.

I turned and looked after her as she disappeared into the kitchen and saw her join Cordelia at the hatch just as another woman left via the door. They were soon obscured by a short queue of thirsty customers.

A couple laden with cakes and tea moved away from the hatch and Marian caught me looking in their direction and flashed me a smile. I had picked up her business card and had been tapping the edge of it on the table while I thought; I now raised it in recognition of her smile, then turned it over to look at it. Greenwood Organic Skin Care, it said, Marian Wood, and a web address and phone number.

Maybe Jim would go for a run with the best friend, maybe she has more to tell me about Cordelia.

Notes:
Marian Wood: runs Greenwood Organic Skin Care, Best Friend (according to MW) of Cordelia. Dark curly hair, mid 40s? Fit (both senses) Runs. Slight northern accent. Married?

Chapter 9

'C'delia Steadman, you're a dirty liar,' Marian said, standing beside her in the hall kitchen.

'What?' feeling startled by the words.

Marian nudged her and giggled, 'Tall, dark and miserable you said. Well, I can only think you were saving him for yourself. He's a bit of all right. Could do with toning up a bit but, hey!'

'Well, I'll admit he's nicer than he was. I guess we all have off days.'

'What do you think? Married? Divorced?'

'I don't know,' Cordelia said, not caring, not thinking about anything else except seeing Max.

'It's all right for you,' Marian said, but Cordelia picked up the wistfulness in her friend's voice and understood that.

'Sorry,' Cordelia smiled at her friend, 'Well, if he's going to go running with you, I'm sure that someone will find out for you.'

'Hmm, if he does.'

'If he doesn't then he's not sporty enough for you anyway.'

'Ha! Hoist by my own petard!'

The rest of the weekend passed in a fog for Cordelia, trying only to prevent Gerald seeing that she was preoccupied in any way. Monday she did as she had said she would, and took herself to Downham to see the sculptures the new blacksmith wanted to enter in the Hingsbury Art Fair.

As she walked down towards the forge she spotted a huge dinosaur peering over the wall at her, it brought a spontaneous smile to her face, the first for nearly a week.

43

A huge, ruggedly handsome man in his thirties came forward to greet her as she opened the gate.

'Mrs Steadman?' he asked, brushing his hand across his leather apron and, presumably, deeming it clean enough to shake a hand with, offered it.

'Cordelia, please, well, I love your monster!' she said as they shook hands. 'Is he one of your exhibits?'

'I'm John, no, he's a bit big to move around, let me show you what I am thinking of.'

Cordelia was both relieved and disappointed; her mind had already placed the dinosaur outside the hall, peering through the tree on the corner of the playing field.

'These are wonderful!' The huge shark, about ten foot long made from bits of old plumbing, she thought she could recognise an immersion tank at least, and then the bird, like a pelican, again obviously made from metallic junk but totally transformed. 'I'm sure we can find room for these!' Wondering where, but determined to have them.

John looked really pleased. 'That's great!'

'I thought you said three?'

'The other's nearly finished; it's still in the forge – come and see.'

The change from the brightness of the day to the dimness of the forge took a bit of getting used to, the room smelt of heat and dust.

'Here she is,' John beamed, lifting off a dirty-looking sheet. There before Cordelia was a fearsome Medusa, her face made from a beaten dark metal, her eyes hollows and her 'hair' a seething mass of copper tubes of different bores, each ending in a head with silvery bulbous eyes and a gaping mouth complete with forked tongue.

'Oh my! Wow, she's impressive!'

'You like her?'

'I like her, she gives me shivers, but I like her. And I am sure I can find a place for her.' Imagining her set on a plinth where you would turn a corner round a display board and suddenly see her looking at you, and turn to stone in admiration! John just grinned.

There was no problem disguising her preoccupation that evening when Gerald came home, she described in detail the sculptures.

'I was wondering, I think they are so good, perhaps I might introduce his work to a couple of the galleries I know, particularly the Medusa. I'm thinking The Art Mill Gallery in Plymouth, I can just see them in the sculpture courtyard, and the New Craftsman at St Ives, perhaps? They may have the room. What do you think?'

'I wouldn't know; you know it isn't my sort of thing, anyway, you have always had a good eye for that sort of art, so if you like it, the galleries probably will.'

'And it might help him too.'

'Yes, why not?' Gerald said, almost absent-mindedly as he opened a book. Cordelia looked at the paintings on the wall, two for each year of their courtship, 1978 to 1980. Her, selling art in the Galleria Giovanni in the King's Road in Chelsea; and him, a careful buyer of precise, almost architectural, modern art.

It was only her second week working there when she first saw him in the Galleria Giovanni. He was tall, distinguished looking and, though not old, older than she was. She smiled brightly as he walked in, but almost immediately he turned away and walked over to a painting on the far wall. He stood looking at it for a long time, moved back and repeated his stare.

She was so new she was unsure whether to approach him or not, and had just decided to go and stand alongside him and pass a comment about the picture when he snapped round, nodded in her direction and left the gallery.

She smiled but her smile was soon subsumed in curiosity as she took up the same stance he had and looked at the picture. It was created from a series of horizontal and vertical lines. If she had to guess she would have said the artist dipped a ruler edge in paint and pressed it against the canvas, sliding it along to the end. The pattern was fairly regular, creating many rectangles and some squares, then there was something odd, something not quite regular.

She took a few steps back, the irregularity created a separation between two subtly different sets of spacing, the right hand being tighter than the left of the non-central irregularity. Too close and you didn't notice it, too far back and you didn't see it, but just so far and the scanning of the eye and the discernment of the spaces were optimal. She'd seen that painting every day for a fortnight and hadn't really noticed it before.

He didn't return to the gallery the rest of that week, nor all of the next, so she was surprised when he walked in again on a Wednesday lunchtime and repeated his performance, however this time, as he stepped into the more distant position she moved alongside him and said, quietly, 'The change is subtle, isn't it?'

He jumped as if he had thought himself quite alone. 'Yes,' he said, but turned and left the gallery.

She felt panicked, in case she'd driven a customer away, but to the minute two weeks later he reappeared, and this time let his glance fall upon her to receive her welcoming smile before examining the painting.

***

Cordelia was on her hands and knees scrubbing at the tiles in the entrance hall when Kevan Doige appeared at the door.

'All right missus?'

Cordelia scrambled to her feet. 'Hi Kevan, fine thanks. You?'

'Good, thanks. What do you want done today?'

'Lawns, and perhaps the edging on the path, if that's okay?'

'Sure,' he said, but stood there a moment.

Cordelia smiled uncertainly thinking he wanted to say something else, but he just shook his head and then moved off and down to the garden shed where the mower was stored.

Grateful to be left in peace Cordelia returned to her task, somehow the manual work was making her feel better, she always felt better when occupied.

'What do you want?' It was 1974 and the Windsor Free Festival. White Lightning, her father's band were playing, for free, they were living in an old campervan and mostly on the free vegetarian food provided. Margo and Johnny were also high most of the time. They'd been there for three days already and Dee was getting bored of just hanging out, people watching and waiting for Margo to have time for her.

Dee was standing at the entrance to the Freek Press tent.

'Well, I'm not sure, I just ...'

'Don't be such a bore Bongo, leave the girl alone, come in.' A woman with heavy dark eyeliner and auburn hair beckoned her. The bloke, lounging on a deckchair, grunted.

'Ignore him, I'm Jilly, what's your name?'

'Dee. I was wondering if I could help at all?'

'See, Bongo, she wants to help. Help is always welcome.'

'Help's cool.' Another woman, peering at what she was typing, added.

'We could do with help distributing,' Jilly said, 'it's only taking them out, putting them up every day, especially making sure every stage gets one pinned up.'

'I can do that!' Dee said delighted. For the rest of the festival she helped out with the Freek Press right up until the Thames Valley police swarmed through the site, smashed in the tent, broke up everything, splitting open Bongo's head when he tried to protect their Roneo machine. The Roneo was all right, Jilly said when Dee met her the next year at Watchfield, which was more than could be said for Bongo's head.

Thursday, up early, showered, dressed in the expected suit despite the promised warmth of the day, breakfasted and out of the door before Gerald; her day on the Bench. Thank goodness she was only one of the wingers that day, she thought as she drove in. Already she had a tightness in the pit of her stomach that made her feel queasy.

She parked and walked into the Magistrates' Court and on into the Retiring Room. Malcolm, the chairman for the day, and the other winger, Colin, were already at their court's table looking through the list of cases for the day. She liked Malcolm, he was a gentle man and though a retired insurance evaluator was not as cynical as Colin who ran his own IT business. Malcolm looked up and smiled. 'Cordelia, how are you today?'

'Fine,' she said, 'fine,' thinking of the perceptive comments from Joan at the book club. Social lies.

Chapter 10

I really couldn't make up my mind about the running thing ... it was Wednesday morning before I decided I'd give it a go. I'd been on a website and found out what it involved and found lots of assurances that it was an activity for runners of all levels, where they set courses according to the running speeds of the participants. Still I wasn't convinced, however, finding myself out of breath, yet again, as I reached the village shop on Monday to collect my ciggies, I decided that I'd give it a go, they say exercise stimulates the brain, and mine needs all the stimulation it can get.

Marian sounded delighted and offered to collect me from the end of Hideaway's lane, I didn't blame her for not wanting to come down to the house, the lane is a tight fit for my MG, mainly due to overgrown plants on the hedge-sides, but would definitely brush both sides of most modern cars.

The framework of the novel is building nicely. I have many of the characters sketched out now, and am building the back-stories for my main people. I'm in that in-between state, not ready to start writing but getting snippets of conversation and flashes of inspiration that tell me their motivations, and I am excited.

Jim's new friend Dave, from the shop, mentioned the pub again today so I think he'll have to go along. I've made him far too genial a bloke to turn down the unsaid offer twice, the only question is whether to walk or to drive? Odd thing is the pub is about the closest building to Hideaway, only problem is it is on the other side of the stream and up through the woods. I bet the local lads would know the way. As for me, is it turn left and go up the way past the shop into the village, or turn right to go up the other way, past

The Old Chapel? No prizes for guessing the route Jim is going to walk. Yes, he can walk, no chance of getting nicked by the local plod that way, that would never do, I bet they love to catch an incomer - watch him have a few then pop along the road to catch him out.

I found the route via The Old Chapel less steep than that via the village shop and did my best to walk slowly and steadily taking in my surroundings as I passed her house. The Old Chapel looked as impressive in real life as it did on the Google Street View. Her garden is neat and partitioned into areas, with trellises and arbours. Sweet peas swarming over one, roses over another. The grass is a beautifully cut sward with trimmed edges and a slate slab path. I did not see her, or her husband, though I noticed a dark blue Mercedes in the drive, and beyond that a smaller burgundy coloured car. His and hers I presumed.

The Plough was an ill-matched marriage between a rambling old house and a nineteen-seventies extension. The sign told me there was also a beer garden and car-parking round the back. Without the car I didn't need to go there, but I did, just to see if there was any track leading away into the wood and in the direction of Hideaway. There was a track, in fact more than one, but with no signage it was impossible to tell where, if anywhere, they would lead. Retracing my steps I entered the pub through the front door which stood casually ajar on this warm evening.

After the brightness outside it took a moment for my eyes to adjust to the dim light levels inside, but I soon saw Dave at the end of the bar, sitting on a tall stool and facing another man. He raised his hand to me, and said something to the other person. As I approached Dave stood up.

'Good evening, Jim, this here's Kevan. Join us?' and he reached round behind him and pulled out another stool.

'Glad to, good evening,' Jim said to Kevan, offering his hand and nodding. The man's grip was hard and firm and his hand calloused, I guessed this was a manual worker.

'What'll you have?' Dave asked.

'No, no. Let me. What's that you're drinking?'

'Thanks, mine's a Tribute and Kevan's on the Rattler.'

I caught the eye of the barmaid, a woman who might have been very pretty about ten years ago but hadn't changed her colour palette to accommodate her fading looks.

'Pint of Tribute, pint of Rattler,' I began, she turned and began pouring them before I'd even got the words out of my mouth. I looked at Dave, 'What would you recommend?'

'Depends, what do you like?'

I could hardly say a gin and tonic, not Jim's thing at all. No my man had to like a bitter.

'A bitter will do, for starters,' Jim said. And where the 'for starters' came from I don't know.

'Well, the Tribute's good, it's a Cornish bitter.'

Jim grinned, 'That'll do me then,' and I turned to the barmaid.

'Pint of Tribute?' she said.

'Thanks,'

'Jim's moved into Hideaway,' Dave said.

'Oh, really? Bolt hole away from it all, eh?'

'Well, it is certainly quiet.'

'It's a lovely little place,' the barmaid suddenly added, a sharpness edged her voice.

'Yes, yes it is.'

'Oh Betty, Jim's just renting it, no need for that,' Dave said.

'Renting it?'

'Yes, I'm just renting it for a while,' I said as I paid up. She shrugged and moved to the other end of the bar to serve someone else. 'Well, what was that about?'

'Betty and Geoff's daughter wanted to buy it, getting married next year to a local lad with a good job, and they were going to help out. Trouble is they couldn't quite meet the asking price and someone else could.'

'Ah!'

'Lot of the little places get bought for second homes.'

'Really, here?'

'Well,' Kevan said, 'that's what people do anywhere they like to go on holiday, and we are in an Area of Outstanding Natural Beauty.'

'Ah! Okay, I see the problem, Betty thought I was the one who'd bought Hideaway. I wouldn't like to be ... the owner when he does come to stay.' Jim gave a chuckle as I thought about the reception my agent would get at the pub in the future.

Kevan bought the next round and then Jim got a second round in, despite protests, but he insisted. Half way down this third pint Jim let my tongue run away with him.

'So, Kevan, what do you do?'

'I'm a gardener, do landscape work and maintenance, depending.'

'Is there a lot of call for that round here?'

'Loads, too many people take on a big garden then can't cope, so need a half-day a week to keep it all in trim.'

'I saw a pretty garden on the way here, The Old Chapel, sweet peas, roses, arbours, the works.'

Kevan grinned, 'Yeah, that's one of mine. Was doing the lawns there just today. You'd never guess what? When I arrived there was Mrs Steadman on her hands and knees scrubbing the tiles in the entrance hall.'

'So?' Jim said, while my mind whistled and wondered, fantasising over Cordelia on her hands and knees.

'Well, you'd think, someone with the money they've got would have a cleaner in to do that stuff, wouldn't you? I mean, I'm contracted for six hours a week for the garden, don't really need that much now that it's all in hand, but they insist so it can't be the money.'

'I'm going running with her friend tomorrow evening,' Jim said, to drag me away from my imaginings.

'Which one?' Dave asked.

'Marian Wood, she's taking me to a Harriers meeting.'

'I didn't know she did that,' Kevan said, his eyes lighting up.

'Know her well?'

'No, not particularly,' he looked into his pint, but I didn't miss his interest.

Notes:

Kevan (...) Gardener, Physically fit. Local man, forties? Soft burr to voice. Interested in Marian Wood

Betty (...) barmaid (owner) at Pub. Mid forties, dark hair, bit mutton dressed as. Husb: Geoff. (Pissed off at buyer of Hideaway)

Chapter 11

'Mrs Steadman?' Malcolm all but hissed. Cordelia snapped-to and passed the Magistrates' Court's sentencing guideline folder across to him, open at the correct page.

'Sorry,' she whispered. It was almost one o'clock and in her head she was already walking up to Smeaton's Tower and looking for him, she was both electrically alert and not focused, again she was glad not to be in the Chair that day.

The lunch break arrived and Cordelia gave her excuses for dashing away and left the building in record time. She started by walking but, as soon as she was out of view of the Magistrates' Court, she jogged towards the Hoe. By the time she could see Smeaton's Tower, the old lighthouse from the Eddystone rock fourteen miles off the coast of Plymouth now painted in red and white stripes and standing on the grass of the Hoe, she was slightly out of breath.

At first there didn't seem to be anyone, to be precise, any man, standing near the Tower, but as she came within a hundred yards a tall slim man walked round from behind the Tower, with something like an A4 book in his hand. He was casting his gaze around the scene, but before Cordelia had got within twenty paces his gaze had locked on hers.

She couldn't help herself, she slowed her pace, drinking in how he looked, comparing him with her memory of both his father and the baby she had last seen him as. His hair had Ned's curls, but the blond he was as a baby had given away to a hazel-brown. The book he was carrying was The Tempest, but she didn't need that to know who he was.

'Max?' she wanted to say more, but a lump rose in her throat and cut off her voice, she knew her smile was being squashed by the pain she was feeling, the ache of suppressed tears.

'Cordelia?'

'Oh, my God! You are ... you look ...' She sniffed and swallowed. 'It is so good to see you.'

'You said we only have half an hour,' he commented, sounding businesslike and it brought her up short.

'Of course, can we ...' she cast around and noticed a seat unoccupied a little way over, 'Let's sit over there,' she said.

They reached the seat and looked at each other again. Cordelia felt torn between her longing to touch him and her fear of doing just that. She sat, and he followed turning to face her as he placed 'The Tempest, a student's guide' down between them.

'I long to hear the story of your life, which must captivate the ear strangely,' he quoted softly.

'I, I know a lot of Shakespeare.' She smiled giving a little shrug, 'I know we have such a short time, so I'll come to the point.' He nodded. 'There is nothing more that I would like than to get to know you and your family, if you'll let me. I do have a difficulty with my own situation. My husband, Gerald, he's ...' she searched for the right words then remembered he was a teacher. 'Let's say he's a highly intelligent man who today would be identified as being on the autistic spectrum. He doesn't understand even social lies, let alone complete omissions. He would find it terribly hard to understand that I had not mentioned, ever, that I had a child, and very hurtful.'

Max was nodding, which gave Cordelia hope that they could work through this together somehow. 'So,' she continued, 'until I can find a way to explain myself to Gerald I cannot openly say you are mine.'

'That's it, is it? All self. Probably all you ever thought about, yourself, not me, not where I was or who I was with. Not whether I was okay ... or not.'

55

'No!' Cordelia gave a little cry, so intent on explaining the reason for the clandestine meetings she had planned she had forgotten to ask him anything. She found she had clamped her hand over her mouth. Pulling her hand away and dropping it as a fist into her lap she looked him right in the eyes. 'What is the most important thing you want to ask me? Here, now?'

His gaze was steady and penetrating, 'Why did you give me up for adoption?'

She felt herself sit back with surprise. 'What were you told?'

'That my mother gave me up for adoption, only that.'

Cordelia bit her tongue inside her mouth, the feeling of pain controlling her instant reaction to cry. She swallowed. 'No, no I didn't 'give you up', you were taken from me. You were just under six months, a happy, healthy, loved and loving baby. Social Services took you away 'for your own good' was what they said. Huh!'

'What was wrong with you then?'

'Nothing. What was wrong was that your grandparents and I were living in a squat in London when ... when the ambulance had to be called. Amongst other things they did, one of them notified Social Services that there was a very young mother with a baby in those 'unsuitable' surroundings. They swooped at one o'clock in the morning. There were all sorts of promises of your return if circumstances were better, but nothing ever happened. By the time Margo, your grandmother, was in a fit state to fight my corner it was too late, they said, the adoption process was going through and there was to be no contact, no information, nothing, in case, in case I tried to abduct you. So, no, Max, I would never have given you up, I loved you so much, you were all mine and you were all I had.'

Max had now sat back too, his face telling Cordelia that he was trying to understand what she'd just told him. 'Young?'

'Sixteen.'

'Living in a squat?' His voice resonated with incredulity and she could tell he was reassessing her in light of this information.

She tried to smile. 'It was the nineteen seventies, and, well I have so much to tell you, but let's just say your grandparents were living an alternative lifestyle,' she gave a half laugh 'That sounds such a weird sentence.'

He smiled and shook his head, 'Yes, yes, it does. Doesn't sound simple.'

'No, Max,' she couldn't resist saying his name, 'not simple, then or now, but this is why I hope we can meet in secret for as long as it takes to tell everything and for me to work out how to tell my husband.'

'What's your plan?'

'Are you free at all this summer holiday to meet me frequently to talk. I can only offer an hour or so each day, but it can be any day of the working week, and every day of that if you want.'

'Well, we're off on holiday for a fortnight near the end of the holiday, but these first weeks are clear.'

'If I tell you where I live you must promise not to try to come and see me at home.'

Max shrugged, 'Okay.'

'I live in Hingsbury.' She could see that he'd heard of the village. She unfolded a piece of paper that she took from her bag and indicated a point on a printed-off map. 'If you could pick me up from here.' The map showed Hingsbury, and the point was on the zigzagging lane that ran across from Downham Forge junction to the junction with the main village road. There were no houses shown alongside this road, and only one down a short lane off from it. 'It is a passing place, but one where the road is already wide enough for two vehicles, so it won't matter stopping there. Make sure you get the right one, the second one, the passing place on the first bend is just that, not wide enough to stop in,' she looked up at him. He glanced up from the map.

'And then what?'

'Then we whiz off up Kit Hill and talk, and then you can drop me back at the same place.'

Max was silent for a moment. 'It seems very complicated.'

'Please, Max.'

'Well, I'll see how it goes. What time?'

'I thought ten would be a good time?'

'Fine, I'll see you tomorrow.'

'Oh! Tomorrow,' she hesitated, but one look at his face convinced her. 'Tomorrow, good, I'll be there at ten.' She glanced at her watch, almost half past.

'You have to go?'

'Yes, I'm due back in ... What will you tell your wife?'

He looked straight at her, his grey eyes bright, 'The truth, of course.'

Chapter 12

I've encountered tractors on the road between Hideaway and the junction with the village when I've walked it but I've barely seen a car so when I saw one approach I guessed it would be Marian, however, at first glance I thought it was a delivery van. My mistake, when she drew up it was one of those cars that look like a van from the front but with windows down the sides and her business card reproduced on a sign on the door.

'Great evening for a run,' she said in greeting. It was, I guess, dry and warm but with a little cool breeze sliding along the valley.

'Thanks for the lift,' Jim said. 'You'll have to take charge of me this evening, I've never ... harried before.'

'Ha ha! Harried. Ah, no problem, in fact, I'll run your route with you if you like?'

'That would be great, if it's not spoiling your fun.'

'No problem,' and she was smiling as she weaved the car around the series of blind bends that the little back road consisted of.

About half an hour later we arrived at a long shaded lay-by near a village called Upton Cross where Marian tucked her car in tight against one of the cars already parked there. All around there were lycra-clad people doing stretching exercises or chatting as they jogged gently on the spot. Before we even got out of Marian's car another had snuggled up tight behind it, I wondered how anyone would get to leave.

'Got to park tight,' she said, as if reading my mind, 'we'd not all get in to park otherwise, and we all leave at about the same time, except the hare, his car's up front so he'll be off to set up the pub before we all get back. Come on,' and she got out. I realised I was not really dressed for this. I'd figured that a tracksuit would be fine and I had a decent pair of trainers from before. These people seemed to take it a bit more seriously. Never mind, I thought, Jim did not profess to be good at this, and if I needed to do more I could get some kit.

Within a few minutes Marian had introduced me and got me signed up.

'All right, Jim?' said a vaguely familiar voice. I turned to see Kevan, from the pub the night before.

'Oh, Kevan. Hi, I thought you ...' but he cut me off.

'I thought I'd give this a try, good exercise they say.'

'Yes it is,' Marian said, beaming.

Jim tried to take control, 'I take it you know each other already?'

Kevan held out his hand to Marian, 'Not really, Kevan Doige, I've seen you at Mrs Steadman's.'

'Yes, I know, nice to meet you properly Kevan. Are you new to Harriers, I don't recall seeing you at a meeting before?'

'Yeah,' he gave a rueful smile, 'you can tell, can't you? Not quite dressed right for it,' glancing down at what could only be described as a football kit; singlet and shorts, but with trainers.

'No, it's fine, you are both fine. There isn't a dress code, we just end up wearing what is best for the job in the end,' she said. 'Would you like to run with us then?'

'That's good of you,' he said and his eyes were sparkling. Mine would have been shooting flames if they knew how, so much for gently eliciting information about Cordelia while we ran round the course.

Marian took Kevan away to get him all signed up. I'd been watching the others and was just thinking how much I fancied a ciggie at that moment, when they returned.

'Oh Jim, you should be doing some warming up,' she said as they arrived looking very cheerful as if they'd just shared a joke. 'Never mind, we'll do it together,' she said and proceeded to show us how to stretch our calf muscles and thighs, and shake them loose, and jog a little on the spot to warm up. Not that I needed instruction. I've seen enough sportsmen doing their warm-ups, but one look at Kevan told me he was used to a warm-up routine anyway, so perhaps the football kit was for something he still did.

There was a whistle blown and everyone sort of came to attention. Group names were called and banks of runners sped off in what I can only describe as a jolly manner. In no time Marian was chivvying us to get going, and having negotiated the road we clambered over a stile and set off at a pretty good jog through rough woodland. The bank fell off steeply to the left and there was a set of steps cut into it but we trotted straight along the top, following the arcane symbols made of sawdust.

It wasn't long before the trail began to lead downhill but, what with the fallen logs to climb over and the slippery leaves underfoot, I was soon puffed, I wanted nothing more than to slow down, stop even, and take a breather, but a quick glance across at Marian, chatting, yes, chatting as she ran with Kevan, who was talking back, made me put some steel into Jim. I could see that Kevan was out to get Marian's attention, and I felt Jim had prior claim. Never mind, I told myself, it was Jim who had the lift back and perhaps that would be all the time I needed anyway.

Let's be honest, it wasn't bad, except the last bit, back up those steps I'd noticed in the beginning. By the end of the run they might as well have been a vertical ladder for all the help they gave my aching thighs, I kept putting my hand down to try to give myself some leverage. What was worse was noticing that Kevan was making light work of it, and keeping pace very nicely with Marian.

By the time Marian's Berlingo was released from the press I had gained my breath back and cooled down a bit.

The pub was just down the road and so within half an hour we were ensconced and enjoying a well-deserved pint.

'So, Marian,' Jim said, 'Greenwood Organic Skin Care, what's that then? A franchise?'

'No, it's not.' She sounded none too pleased that Jim had thought this, I don't know why. 'Greenwood is my own make; I make everything from pure natural organic ingredients.'

'Oh, that's you is it? My sister loves your stuff,' Kevan said in an admiring voice. I shot him a look, if he saw it he didn't show it.

'Sorry for being dim on this,' Jim sought to soften his words, 'What does that mean, have you ... designed the mixtures and have them made up to sell, or what?'

'Yes, I've designed the mixtures, as you put it, but no I don't get them made up. I like to be sure the ingredients used are as specified, so I make the products too. I have a little workshop in my back garden, if you must know.'

'So you're an entrepreneur,' Kevan said, and received a beautiful smile in blessing. Jim was not doing this well at all.

'In a small way, it does me. I sell on the internet and to specialist shops. Once in a while I'll take a stand at a relevant show, like the Holistic Health and Beauty at St Mellion Golf Club coming up in September.'

'Very impressive,' Jim said, hoping for a blessing. His reward was a smile of sorts but somehow her face also said that she thought he was being patronising; perhaps I was.

'So Kevan, what do you think? Are you going to give Harriers another go?' Marian asked as we stood outside the pub ready to go.

'Sure, I enjoyed it. Enjoyed the company too,' he said, eyes firmly on hers.

'That's great! Perhaps we can share lifts between us, seems a waste of resources to travel separately. What about you Jim, coming to Harriers again?'

'I'd love to, well, yeah, sure, um bit of a problem with using my car for three of us though, an MG, back seat's more like a little shelf,' he laughed deprecatingly, but I was secretly pleased to mention my pride and joy.

'An MG! Well - that takes me back,' Marian said, 'but I should be able to squeeze in there still, used to in the old days. So, next meeting ...'

'I'll pick you all up,' cut in Kevan.

'Great, here's my card, give me a call by Wednesday and we'll set it up. See you Kevan, come on Jim, we'd best be getting back.'

'So did you really enjoy it?' Marian asked as we drove away.

'Well, tell you the truth, I'd have enjoyed it more if I was fitter,' Jim said, 'I seem to have let myself go a bit since ...' he left it hanging in the air.

She flicked him a glance 'Since...' she prompted.

Jim sighed, 'Since the divorce. I'm over it now, really, just trying to make a new start. That's why I'm here. I have exam papers to mark, but at the same time I'm looking for a new teaching post. Sorry, don't mean to burden people with my heartache stuff.'

'No, don't worry at all,' she said her voice all soft and sympathetic. 'What happened?'

'Angie, my wife, my *ex-wife*, ran off with a journalist where she worked. Last to know, as always, painful that.'

'You don't have to tell me. Been there, got the tee-shirt,' Marian said, and Jim suddenly felt a lot happier, a rapport had been struck.

'Oh?'

'Except in my case it was so clichéd that it would make you laugh. His secretary.'

'I'm sorry, it's a blow whomever, whenever,' Jim said, his voice softening. She turned to glance at him, he hung his head in a meditative manner, hiding the smile he felt tugging at his lips.

I had to get the conversation back where I wanted it, I had recognised that we were near Callington, which meant only ten minutes from drop off, and I'd been letting Jim do all the soul-searching.

'And your friend, Cordelia, you were saying she 'plays the doting wife' is that because she's worried about him straying?'

'C'delia? No, I just think that's the way she is, and that's the way he is. Bit strange, very set in his ways and not a social chap but C'delia makes up for that.'

'No children then?'

'No, no children, they only have themselves to please, well, that's how C'delia puts it. I think she has a mother somewhere, but I know her father died when she was fairly young.'

'They told me in the shop she does a lot of stuff for the village and for charities.'

Marian shot me a glance, I think this has to be the last comment I make about Cordelia today.

'Yes, yes, she does, she's plenty of time to use up, not working and all, yet she loves to be busy.' She was silent for a while, and I, full of questions about Cordelia and daring not to ask any more stayed silent too, until we were in the village.

'Jim, don't take this the wrong way.... I may be picking up the wrong signals here ... but ... can I say, leave C'delia alone.' She turned off the main village road and into the end of the twisty lane, and concentrated on taking the bends, pulling up sharply at the top of Hideaway's lane. She turned to me, 'Sorry if I sounded a bit blunt. She's my best friend and while she is sometimes irritatingly perfect I wouldn't want it any other way, and I'd hate to see her ...'

'Oh! Sorry. I really didn't mean anything by my questions. It's just I only know you, her, Dave and now Kevan. I was only trying to make conversation,' I injected as much hurt into my voice as I could.

'Well,' she paused, 'in that case, I'm sorry, I don't know, I obviously did pick up the wrong signals.'

Jim gave her my best winning smile, 'Perhaps I was trying to hide my interest in another woman altogether,' and raised an eyebrow in query and went on before she could react. 'Thank you so much for this evening Marian, perhaps you'd like to come out just for a drink, or a meal one night?'

'Oh,' she gave a relaxed smile, 'yes, that would be nice, perhaps we can talk about other things that interest us then.'

I was just setting out for the village shop and my day's consignment of ciggies when I saw her. She was on foot and walking fast. My Ambassador's wife. Ha! Chin a little stuck out, marching, eyes forward, I'm sure she didn't see me coming up the side lane.

She seemed driven and I'm curious about people, that's what makes me what I am. I followed, discreetly, at a distance, always a step behind being seen if she did pause long enough to turn her head.

Chapter 13

Cordelia changed what she was wearing twice after Gerald left for the office. She couldn't do much about the impression she gave when she'd had to be in court, casual wear was not allowed and there had been no time spare to change, but today was different. Her first choice had been discarded as being too smart, too formal. She wanted to feel more like Dee than Cordelia, like the mother of the baby he was when he was snatched from her. He would want to know more, she could tell. She hadn't thought things out enough before meeting him that first time and when asked the question she'd told him the truth, but if he wanted details, would the truth drive him away? At ten to ten she left the house and started along Downham Lane, past the farm cottages then turned left into Zaggy Lane, she knew she'd left plenty of time but the thought of him leaving because she was a minute late drove her to walk fast.

London, this was it, the break they'd been waiting for! White Lightning were playing as support band to Hawkwind at the Hammersmith Odeon. Hawkwind had heard them at Watchfield and again at Stonehenge and liked what they heard. If it worked out then they'd go with them on tour, the promoter said, not much dosh up front, but plenty to come.

In the meantime the band had used its contacts from the free festivals and was staying at a squat in Hammersmith, big fancy building, about fifteen regulars and then the band and hangers-on. The bit of money up front meant they were partying. Margo had commandeered a small room for themselves, saying the baby needed a bit of quiet. It wasn't too much bother, everyone was so laid back about it; the guests were welcome, especially as they'd brought the gear for a party.

Dee was singing to Maxie, rocking him in her arms as she got him off to sleep. She'd made up a safe area for him, boxed in by the walls, her body on the mattress and her bag at the foot. She felt his breathing slow and snuggled him down, lying there next to him, still singing softly. It was early yet, about eight, she thought, but in parts of the house there was a commotion. She could hear raised voices and someone was wailing. She kept on singing, 'How many roads must a man walk down ...' The door burst open, 'Get him in here!' Margo was screaming, 'God, get him in!'

Two men half carried her father, Johnny, into the room, letting him collapse, fitting, onto a mattress. Margo fell to the floor bedside the mattress, trying to hold down his flailing arms. Dee was up now, standing, panicked.

'What? What is it?'

'I don't know, he was fine. Tripping, but fine, then he suddenly flipped.'

'And Billy,' one of the blokes said, leaning against the door, his eyes glazed.

'Billly what?'

'Billy's gone flipped.'

'Shit! Fuck! He's stopped breathing!' Margo wailed. Maxie started crying, his little voice rising to a shriek. From somewhere in something she had read Dee brought up the instructions for mouth to mouth resuscitation. 'Can we give him mouth to mouth, Margo? Margo?'

'What? Do you know how?'

'I, I can try. Margo, can we call an ambulance?'

'Fuck, yes! You,' she pointed at the only guy left in the room, 'call a fucking ambulance.'

'What?'

Dee recalled she should check for a pulse. She tried to find a pulse with Maxie's wailing pulling her thoughts away. There was still a pulse. 'Clear airways' came back to her. She began by tipping his head back and he took a breath! Margo had run from the room, Dee guessed to find a phone box and call an ambulance.

Margo returned. 'He's breathing now,' Dee said, trying to ignore the wailing from a scared Maxie, 'Help me tip him on his side.'

'Yes, yes, oh, good girl,' and together they levered the twitching unconscious form onto his side. They had just stood when another racket preceded the ambulance men. Some of the usual squatters were trying to prevent them coming in and others of the band were arguing and dragging them into the room.

'Can't someone shut that kid up?' one of the ambulance men said, trying to look into Johnny's eyes. Dee went to Maxie and picked him up, jiggled him, then sat down and put him to the breast as the fastest way to soothe him. In minutes they had given Johnny a check-over and decided he needed to go into hospital. They left and returned with a stretcher and had just got him on it when one of the usual squatters came and asked them to look at Billy. While one ambulance man went off, the other stood by Johnny's stretcher his eyes raking the room, taking in the mildewed corners, the holes in the ceiling, the mattresses on the floor, the heap of their belongings in the corner and returning time and time again to Dee and the baby. She half-turned away under his gaze.

The other man returned and grasping the handles said, 'Cummon, we've got two to take now,' and they picked up Johnny and, with Margo following, left the room.

The car was there, a silver family car, she didn't recognise the make, but there was just one man sitting in it; Max. She smiled brightly as she approached and went to the driver's side first, said, 'Hello' through the window, 'we need to go back the other way, can you turn here?'

'Sure,' he said, and she stepped round to the passenger side and got in. He manoeuvred the car in a three point turn and headed back the way he'd come in.

'Straight across at the crossroads,' she said, 'this road will take us towards Kit Hill.'

A few minutes later they were climbing the steep track up Kit Hill Country Park and Dee, seeing one of the smaller side parking spaces was empty of other cars, suggested he pulled in, their view facing out across the valley into Devon. The engine noise faded away and they sat back, the antithesis of lovers, each leaning back into their own corner of the front seats, half facing each other, half facing the view.

'How are you?' Cordelia asked.

'Okay, haven't been able to stop thinking about what you said though.'

'Of course not. I've been thinking too. I want to know about you, but it's only fair you have all your questions answered first.'

'Thanks.'

'So where do you want to start?'

'Okay, thanks.' He stared out of the windscreen for a few moments, then turned to face her, his eyes bright, 'Was I wanted?'

'By me, yes, you were. Okay, you weren't planned, you were an innocent mistake by a young couple in ... love at the time.'

'So, he, my father didn't want me?'

'He, Ned de Silver, never knew you existed to want or not want you. I don't want you to think badly of me Max, or of him. Really. We met at a Music Festival, he was in a band, I was with your grandparents, your grandfather was in a band, that's why we were there. Ned was eighteen, just, I was, well he didn't really know how old I was, I may have seemed older as I knew my way round the Music Festival scene better than he did, it was my third year touring them with the family, but I was just under sixteen and besotted with him. He was my first love and though I was grown-up in many ways I was naïve too. They were different times.'

'Didn't you try to contact him?'

'Yes, but by the time we did it was too late. The only number I had was for his parents' house, and they had moved. I always hoped I'd meet him at another festival but ...' she closed her eyes, her voice strangled.

'But?'

Cordelia heaved a sigh, 'But we stopped going to any of them after your grandfather died, and after he died was when the Social Services snatched you from me.'

Max was silent for a few moments, staring out at the view. Cordelia looked at him, remembering what she could of Ned, looking for his likeness. She had one photo of him, of them, she remembered the White Lightning's roadie taking the photo. He had always thought of himself as a bit of a David Bailey, getting down into awkward positions to get an unusual angle. He'd caught the two of them sitting on the bonnet of an old Jeep, leaning into each other, obviously happy.

'I have a photo of him,' she said. 'Your father, and me. Would you like to look at it?'

He turned sharply to look at her and nodded. She slid the four by four inch colour photo out of her bag, the colours looking a little weird despite not having been exposed to light for years, and passed it over. He stared at it, brought it closer to his eyes, then a little more distant, as if trying to focus. She knew the feeling, she'd taken a magnifier to it more than once. Yes, you could see him, get the gist of what he looked like, but she always wanted more from the picture and she, at least, had a memory to help fill in the details.

'You could probably find him now, with the internet and stuff,' he said.

'Possibly. But would it be right?'

He looked up at her again, his eyes narrowed with anxiety.

'You were right to find me, I knew you were ... there, somewhere. Ned doesn't. Besides, I was never quite sure if that was his real name. The others in the band laughed

70

when he said his name was 'de Silver'. I'm pretty sure the Ned was right, but the band was called Silver Lining, unless it really was *his* band, it's a bit unlikely. This is the fifty-something me talking, I didn't see it then, of course.'

'Hmm,' he mused, 'if it was 'de Silver' it'd be easier to find than plain Silver.'

'If it was Silver at all, as I said.'

'Well, at least I know why I have such an odd middle name.'

Cordelia smiled, 'Sorry about that, I wanted you to have his name but there was no way I could have him on the birth certificate back then, without him being around.'

Max smiled back at her, his face, his eyes showing the first signs of understanding and warmth towards her. She hated to break the spell, but time was running out.

'Time we were going back, I'm afraid, but we've plenty of time to catch up. Monday all right for you?'

'Monday? It seems so far away. Can I ask you one more thing before we go?'

'Okay?'

'What did my grandfather die of?'

'Perhaps not now, it's not that I don't want to say, I just want to put it in context.'

'But you said you were living in a squat and, well what happened?'

'He, it wasn't instant, he took some adulterated drugs. Scrambled his brain, he actually died about four months later. That's why the adoption process was on its way before ...' Cordelia found herself struggling to hold back the tears. He put out his hand and rested it on her arm. It felt like the biggest hug in the world.

Chapter 14

I followed her, taking care to make sure I was always a step behind being seen if she'd turned her head. She didn't. I masked my own shape by walking close to the hedge, half hidden by trailing foliage and if I caught sight of her, I'd slow. As I turned the second bend I saw her cross the road and when I peeked she was speaking to someone in a car tucked in a lay-by, it looked like a man. I stepped closer to the hedge, so all I could see was the edge of the outline of the car through the leaves. I heard the engine start and prepared to appear to be just walking up the road, but the sound wasn't right, and when I stepped away from the hedge it was to see the car driving off in the other direction. Cordelia was nowhere in sight. She must have gone with the car and this really interested me, why would she meet someone out on this road rather than be collected from home?

The book is going well now, my characters are filling out and, as they start to perform, the story is coming to life. I have the story arc mapped out as I see it and need only to build in the sub-plots to keep the action moving forward. I was feeling so chuffed with myself I almost rang William to tell him, before remembering that I was supposed to just be finishing off the novel, not writing the whole damned thing. It would be nice to have someone to confide in, though I think that may have been one of the straws that broke my marriage, Angie never did have much time for my whining, as she called it, when I got stuck.

It's Saturday and I still can't get that woman out of my mind. I wonder what she was doing. I suppose she may have come across someone lost and offered to show them the way. Unlikely, but possible, she seems the sort to go out of her way to help.

Jim is taking Marian out for a meal tonight. He made me phone up on Friday evening, or was it me wanting to be able to quiz the best friend again? She agreed but didn't recommend the local pub, though she said the food was 'good enough' she'd rather go somewhere else. We're off to another pub it seems, called 'The Springer Spaniel' sounds a bit made up to me but at least I don't have to get poshed-up for the jaunt. Jim's picking *her* up this time, the MG being eminently suitable for the trip. All I have to do is turn up at the right door. To my surprise she said she lives in a close of modern houses opposite the Church. I had her down as a 'house with character' person but at least I shouldn't have trouble finding it.

Number 5, Church Close, this is it, I thought, looking at the small pale-cream detached house I'd just pulled up beside, and if I needed confirmation, there was her Berlingo in the drive. I eased myself out of the car and was halfway up the path when the front door opened and she emerged. Suddenly I felt that Jim ought to have tried a bit more with his attire, the chinos might pass muster but the tee-shirt under jumper was a tad under-smart when she'd gone to the trouble of a dress and high heels.

The Springer Spaniel was a surprise; a cross between old-fashioned pub and nice restaurant. Now I could see I really should have made Jim spruce up a bit. Too late to worry about that, he'll just have to be extra charming to make up for it.

The menu offered such treats as gravadlax or game and bacon terrine to get my mouth watering and at half the price you'd get them in London and I decided there and then that Jim was not going to hold back. He ordered the Terrine and followed it up with the locally sourced sirloin steak, while approving Marian's choices of the sliced cured salmon gravadlax and the local pan-fried scallops. He boldly ordered wine for both of them, a large glass of the Pinot Grigio, white, for her and a smaller glass of the Sangiovese del Rubicone for himself, as we were driving.

'Tell me a bit more about your business,' Jim ventured, while we waited for the main course to be delivered and while I worked out how I could possibly ask a question that would tell me why Cordelia would be picked up in a car in the lane.

'Well, I packed in my job and moved down here,' she looked at me with her head slightly on one side as if listening to something, 'and I decided I'd try working for myself and set up the business. I was already interested in organic products for skin care, so took myself off on a course, invested some of my ... divorce settlement, and bob's your uncle, Greenwood Organic Skin Care was born,' she smiled brightly.

'So what was your job before? The one you gave up,' Jim asked, and I congratulated myself on not commenting on the divorce.

'Bio-chemist, working as an analyst in R and D for Reckitt and Benckiser, used to be Coleman,' she raised her eyebrows. I did a quick re-assessment. No country bumpkin this, organic stuff or not. 'Enough to turn anyone organic, certainly for something you put on your skin,' she concluded.

'Ah! I can see why you make your own ... mixtures,' Jim said.

'Yes, exactly. But what about you? You said you were looking for a post, any luck in the job market down here?'

'Well, to tell you the truth,' Jim said, as I lied through my teeth, this is where telling half-lies really helps, 'I rather missed the boat. No one gets a job in teaching over the summer vacation, everyone is away. I've applied for a couple, but don't expect to hear anything 'til nearer September.'

'Oh? Where are they?'

Damn! 'Um, gosh, I've looked at so many, I can't remember the names just now,' Jim gave her my best abashed smile, and caught the eye of a waitress to ask for another glass of wine for Marian, as hers was well on the way down even though it looked large enough to hold half a bottle.

Main course over, we were offered the dessert menu and I'd got no information for my money whatsoever, I daren't be too obvious after the warning shot she gave me, it had to be subtle. I eyed the sticky toffee pudding, but when Marian said she'd just have a pot of tea, if I didn't mind, I thought of my waistline and ordered that and a coffee for myself.

'So, is there any good walking around here, or walking groups?' I asked, thinking that was one legitimate reason for Cordelia to be out walking.

'Well, not in Hingsbury, but there is one based in Callington, and one in St. Dominick. Are you interested in walking?'

'Hmm, sort of. What days do they go out, do you know?'

'Oh, not really. I think the Callington one is a Tuesday, not sure. St Dominick's is a weekend thing. I can find out for you,' she said eagerly.

'Ah, yes, thank you.'

'How shall I let you know?'

'Oh, yes,' I did a high-speed debate about the wisdom of giving my mobile number out but went with it, 'if I give you my mobile, not that it picks up at Hideaway, but a text will get to me when I go out, thanks,' I said and recited it as she put it into her phone.

'That's fine.'

As always the journey back seemed much quicker than the one out and we were soon outside her place. I leapt out to do the gentlemanly thing of opening the car door for her, but she was out before I got round there.

'Would you like a brandy or something? You should be able to drive round to Hideaway without any trouble,' she said.

'Well,' I said showing a small reluctance, while the Jim in me was raring to go, 'Thanks, yeah, that would finish off a perfect evening.' We stepped towards the door, she put her key in the lock then turned to face me.

'Um, a brandy is not an euphemism, you understand?' looking up at me in the moonlight.

I leant forward a little, she picked up the signal and tipped her face up, I planted a light kiss on her forehead. 'Understood,' I said and as she turned and finished opening the door to let us in, I smiled to myself at the expression of puzzlement that had flitted across her face.

Her house was neat and tidy, with a purple and silver theme running through the accessories, though not the walls or floor, these were new-house neutral. She came back through the kitchen door with two sparkling brandy glasses in her hand and went to a retro sideboard bringing out the brandy.

'Do sit down!' she instructed, glancing at me to make sure I did before she poured the brandy, then bringing it over to where I'd sat on the sofa. She handed me the glass then sat at the other end, 'Santé!' she said with a smile. I hoped that was the limit of her French and gave her a Spanish 'Salud!' back, as she took a huge swig of the brandy. I glanced round the room trying to pick a subject to talk about and my eye fell on a pile of books on a side table beside the armchair.

'What are you reading,' I said, indicating the books with a lift of my head.

'Oh, that's the book group pile, I like to get ahead, even though it means I need to make a few notes so I remember what I thought at the time.' She got up a little quickly and scooped up the books, bringing them back and sitting closer to me, the pile of books between us.

'Oh, this is the one we've just finished,' she made to cast it onto the coffee table; I reached out to take it from her, my hand landing upon her hand. We drew the book back together, I took it from her but placed it back on the pile as her eyes were fixed on mine and it was time to forget all about books for a while.

Chapter 15

Cordelia had explained to Max how he could drive out the other end of the lane after dropping her, and turn right then turn left to get himself back to the A388, and watched as his car disappeared round the bend ahead of her. She walked slowly now, back the way she had come, feeling like a different woman, the tears she'd never shed for her father flowing down her face. By the time she reached home she had pulled herself together and, grateful she'd met no one on the road, went straight to the bathroom and took a shower.

Refreshed, she got out her plans for the Art Fair and tried to organise the entries so far by the area the individual artists would need to display their chosen works. She sighed, no matter how hard she tried there would always be the artist who changed their mind and brought a much larger canvas along, or suddenly only had two left when they were down to bring four. She sighed again; she could not concentrate on art at the moment. Her interest, indeed her expertise, if you could call it that, had been gained the same way that her love of history and ancient artefacts had and, usually, it enthused her.

As they were always on the move, Margo had used art galleries, museums and libraries as Dee's classrooms. From the age of eleven they visited art galleries of all sorts around the country, wherever they ended up, depending on the gigs that White Lightning managed to get. Never in one place long enough to sign up to any school, or to be caught by any truant officer, Dee learnt on the move.

Margo liked looking at art, but knew little about it, she knew what she liked when she saw it, as do many people, but Dee was moved by pictures, liked to read the bits of information about the pictures, and took time to read about the artists when she had time in a library. Some of the neo-impressionists gave her a great sense of calm, though Margo said she didn't much like them. She saw her first Maximilien Luce painting, a beautiful evocation of pollarded willow trees, in the Glasgow Museum gallery on a cold winter's day. She liked to say the name, Maximilien, it sounded grand. The second one she saw in Blackpool at the Grundy Gallery; she recognised the style even before she got close enough to read the name. Just as well she had an eye for art, it had been her saviour all in all.

Dee was working as a barmaid in The Belvedere Arms, close to Virginia Water and full of young things with silver spoons and plums in their mouths. Her ear was well trained from years of hearing her mother imitate accents and voice mannerisms, for the amusement of others as well as when required for a role, and she was adept herself through playing the game with Margo.

The group closest to the bar had come in laughing and gave their order of drinks without even looking at her, as if anyone who served behind a bar didn't deserve acknowledgement at all. The lager was being tricky, frothing up and needing to settle so, accurately mimicking their accents and cadence, she told the lad paying that she'd bring it over when it had settled; that made him look.

She sashayed over with the tray of lagers and set them down. She felt his eyes on her as she walked back and slipped through the gap to return to her place behind the bar. They talked loudly, as the braying packs often did in Dee's experience, one of the girls alternating between excited laughter and a whine. Dee learnt that this willowy girl was getting married and that meant she was giving up her job, but the art gallery she worked for insisted she find a replacement, and that was so unfair.

'Not seen you here before?' the lad said when he returned to the bar to order a second round.

'I've not been here long, just filling in until I can land a better job. Daddy insists I earn a living, but really, what can one do?'

'I'd have thought there're better jobs, yah?'

'What, for someone with Art and History? Bit rare around here.'

'Art? Fancy that, hey,' he turned away, 'Antonia, Antonia!' The girl with the brilliant engagement ring flashing on her finger looked up. 'Come here, come on, this might be just what you want.'

Antonia sauntered over, 'Yah?'

'This is. What's your name?'

For once Dee used her full name 'Cordelia.'

'This is Cordelia and she has a degree in Art History and no proper job, what do you think of that?'

'I don't know? What?'

'Idiot! You need to find a replacement – Cordelia here is perfect for it, aren't you?'

'Yah, I might be interested,' Cordelia said in her best imitation. The girl looked at her.

'Really, where did you study?'

'Oh, did you do Art History too?'

The girl flustered, 'No. I just wondered, I need to tell Giovanni, he owns the gallery.'

'No problem. I can go for an interview any time. Just give me the gallery details and I'll contact him,' she passed a pen and one of the pub's cards to the girl, blank side up, 'You can say you've found a replacement and that Cordelia Springs will contact him.' She could feel her heart beating hard and was aware there were now other customers waiting and she'd have to go and serve them. She looked at the lad, 'That'll be one pound twenty,' she said and while he fished out a note and some coins she wrote her name on the back of another of the pub's cards and passed it to the girl so she wouldn't forget, picking up the card with the details of the gallery on it and tucking in her pocket before going to serve the waiting customers.

It wasn't until much later when she got back to her bedsit that she looked at the address on the card. London, for heaven's sake, the damned gallery was in London. She'd assumed it was local, and had spent the busy evening imagining an interview where her knowledge of Art would shine through and she'd get *taken on regardless of her dress style. She could hardly go for an interview at an art gallery in London in her work 'uniform' of black skirt and white blouse, and the rest of her wardrobe hadn't moved on much from when she'd walked away from Margo.*

The address was in The King's Road; even that sounded posh. Never mind, she'd have to go, she couldn't keep on as she was, running two low-paying jobs and still not making much more than she needed to live. She looked at her savings, could she afford at least one nice dress to go to the interview in, as well as the cost of travel, there and back? She really didn't want to resort to what she still thought of as 'the other way' for something so trivial, even though she'd had to once before.

The thought brought a blush to Cordelia's cheek, how did she ever do that?

Chapter 16

I woke up in a foul mood. Well, so did Jim, he'd convinced me we were in with a chance of a leg-over but a good snogging session turned sour when Marian started going on about smoking. I mean, I've not kept it a secret but my aftershave and mouthwash must have drowned out the 'stench', yeah, that's what she called it, of cigarette smoke, until we got up close and personal. I should have known, as a fitness freak she was bound not to smoke herself, but the lecture, that came straight from the chemist side of her, who knew all the names of the chemicals they put in the 'death-sticks' and what they do to your system. She might have been more convincing if she wasn't half-cut and if my mind hadn't been sited somewhere in the region of my groin at the time.

Never mind, even that little episode has added to my arsenal when it comes to understanding my quarry, it seems that I 'need to quit before I try the dating market again' as 'no thinking woman would take on a smoker' and 'not one of her friends in the village smoked'. When I told her I could quit, her face was all sceptical, so I explained I had quit before, only taking it up again due to the stress of the divorce. This mollified her a bit, but not enough, I was out of the door before the witching hour. Seems any later would ruin her reputation 'There's no place like a village for gossip,' she added as she pushed Jim out.

I *had* quit before, and I *had* taken it up again when the divorce was going through, and when I was writing some of my best, as it turned out. A bit like the actor who having randomly dropped a book then placed it on top of his script before giving one of the best performances of his life, goes on doing this little ritual for evermore before stepping on the stage, I associate having a cigarette on the go with that wonderful state of being when the words just flow from the fingertips, the smoke curling up into the eyes, perfuming the atmosphere of the story. Giving up now, in the full flow of writing would be exasperating, but a small voice told me it might be the only way ... or was that just the Jim side of me still hoping? Perhaps I'll try cutting down to ten a day and smoke mainly while I'm writing.

'Sean?' my agent's voice sounding tentative over the phone line, publishers have probably been putting the frighteners on him again.

'Oh. Good afternoon, William. What can I do for you?'

'Oh Ha, ha – just the usual?'

'Checking up on me, eh?'

'Well ...'

'I can report that it is going well, and I am right in the zone.'

'Well, you certainly sound ... more positive ... different. How about if I take a run down to ...'

'No!' I snapped. Last thing I need is Galsworthy interfering. 'Not a good idea, I must not be distracted at this point, I'm sure you understand.'

'Well, fine, I mean, and how's the cottage?'

'Ideal, I never see a soul.' An idea struck me. 'Though your garden is a sight – jungle more like, I can hire you a gardener to hack it back if you want?'

'Oh, really? Well, yes, hadn't thought about that yet. I suppose that would be a good idea.'

'Right, I'll do that for you. Anything else?'

'Um, no, though an estimated date would be useful.'

I was tempted to prevaricate, but something made me say, 'Oh, tell the bastards they can have the first draft by the end of August.' When it came down to it I should have that done easily as long as everything kept running as it was.

'Really? Oh, that's good, I'll let you get on.' I could hear the relief in his voice and smiled to myself.

***

A fine drizzle so far this Monday morning but I set off to fetch my ciggies, as the walk is part of my ritual now, even though I hadn't quite run out having only smoked a dozen yesterday. I'll have to ask Dave if they can get me packs of ten next time. The steep bit up to the top lane left me a bit breathless but I kept a good pace as it wasn't a day for hanging around. As I rounded yet another bend in this narrow lane I saw the silver car pulled in the only place wide enough to park and still get two cars past, just where it was on Friday when she got in and it drove off.

As I walked past I tried to glance casually in the car to see who was in there, but as the driver was on the side against the hedge I could only see the person from shoulders down, but it looked like a him, not a her. I ventured a quick turn of the head as I neared the next bend, as if to check there was no car behind me, hoping to see him full face. The fine rain gathered on his windscreen formed an effective barrier to seeing him, but instead I caught sight of a well-wrapped hooded figure as it appeared round the previous turn. Now I was really interested. I wondered if they would pass me before I got out of the lane and where to stand so I could get the best view of the car's occupants. I had an idea, but before I could get into position I heard the car approach and just had to step to the side I was closest to. The windscreen was being wiped and between sweeps I got the impression of a youngish bloke, thirties perhaps, the passenger's head was turned away, hood held up. Why did I think it was her? Perhaps I just knew.

I glanced at my watch. I always take my walk at around the same time, but I'm not meticulous with the timing. Tomorrow I would be. Tomorrow I will make sure I am at the top of the lane, where any car would have to stop for the junction, so I can be sure.

Chapter 17

Cordelia chatted brightly on Monday morning, trying to disguise her excitement and her anxiety knowing that within a few hours she'd be talking to Max again. She was fizzing, her muesli felt more crunchy in her mouth, the juice sharper and sweeter at the same time, Gerald, slower than ever. Yet in reality it was just a normal Monday and Gerald was spot-on time leaving, as she noticed after she received his kiss, waved him off at the door and turned to look at the huge railway station clock that hung from the mezzanine wall.

As on the previous Friday, Cordelia left the house early enough to make sure she'd be at the lay-by at precisely the right time, however this time she had on her riding coat with hood to keep off the persistent mizzle. The coat was a bit warm really but this, typically Cornish, cross between mist and drizzle could soak you through just as effectively as proper rain. As before, she walked, keeping an eye on her watch and adjusting her pace, head down to keep her face dry. As before, he was there, but this time the sight of him sitting in the car, turned round already, waiting for her brought a rush of emotion, so that by the time she'd reached him the tears were flowing down her face and she had to brush them away with her fingertips before opening the car door to get in.

'Hi,' she managed to say, her throat so tight she felt she would cry out loud if she had to say more.

'Hi, okay?' he said, turning on the engine and putting it into gear. She nodded in reply and he drove them along the lane.

As they rounded the bend Cordelia saw a walker and instantly flicked her hood back up and looked away from his gaze. Max drove past carefully then accelerated towards the junction.

'Someone you know?' he asked as she dropped her hood down and relaxed again.

'Not really, newcomer, but, well ...'

Max said nothing but his mouth was a set line.

'Hingsbury Farm,' he said as they passed it and the huddle of cottages opposite it on the road, 'and Hingsbury, is there a Iron Age fort around here?'

Cordelia swallowed, this was safe ground, 'Yes, not much to see, but it's up on the end of the ridge, ditch and bank, half of it with trees along it, and small outer enclosure, all on the farm so not really accessible. Farmer will let you go and see if you ask though, depending what stock he's got grazing there. Are you interested in history?'

'A bit, it's just Joshua went to Cadsonbury last week with the school and he had me looking on the map to see where any other bury's were around Liskeard.'

'Ah, yes, almost anything with bury in it would have been named for one of those, not many as good as Cadsonbury though, some got ploughed up and levelled way back and there's not much to see.'

'This area was off my map, but I wondered anyway.'

There were hardly any cars up on the viewing point when they arrived, not surprisingly, as the drizzle meant that they sat as if in a cloud.

'Why don't we just meet up here?' Max said, 'If you might be seen by locals being collected?'

Cordelia smiled, 'Two cars next to each other, with a couple sitting in one, now that *is* suspicious, and, well, my car might be recognised.'

'Oh? Special?'

'Not really, just, Gerald bought me a personalised number plate on my fiftieth. Not really my thing, but it was thoughtful and imaginative, for him. CS 100, so quite recognisable,' she sighed. 'So, what would you like to talk about today?'

Max seemed to tense up, then, not looking at her, said, 'Tell me about my grandparents, your parents. I've been mulling over what you said, alternative lifestyle, what did that really mean?'

'Let me tell you a bit about them first, then you might understand it better.'

'Okay.'

'You know I had to smile to myself when I read that you were a Drama teacher – you know what they say about hereditary skills jumping a generation. Well, your grandmother was an accomplished Shakespearian actress, she did many other roles of course, in fact, mainly other roles, but she was good. She had an excellent ear for voices, and mannerisms, we'd play games of imitation, I even became quite good at it. We'd also trade lines from Shakespeare, you know, one would start and the other had to complete the line. That's why I wrote that line from the Tempest I sent you, it jumped out of my memory.

For the first eleven years of my life we lived fairly conventionally, except that we spent the winter season at one place and the summer at another. I changed primary schools twice a year, occasionally I actually returned to the same one a few years down the line. My mother was the main breadwinner and we lived in short lets, my father doing odd jobs, often round the theatres, and picking up backing with local bands, playing pubs and clubs. They made a living; I knew nothing else and was happy.'

'Well, fairly unconventional, but not unduly so ...' Max started, now looking at her.

She smiled, 'Until eleven. They had made some kind of pact, she'd follow her dream until I was eleven, then he'd follow his. He'd played backing and odd bands for years, but he was a talented songwriter and lead guitarist, he wanted to form a band and take it somewhere. That's when we took the really alternative route. He'd met great people all over and pulled together three other players to make White Lightning. They were good, well everyone said, they just needed the breaks. By the time I was thirteen we were doing every festival where they could get to play, paid or for free, just to get known. We were at the Windsor Free Festival in seventy-three and again, when the police smashed it up, in seventy-four, we moved all over the country, living in our Bedford campervan. We were at the Peoples Free Festival in Watchfield the following year when Hawkwind played – and that's where Hawkwind heard White Lightning play, the first time. They liked what they heard, so when they heard them again at Stonehenge the next year, well, that was White Lightning's big break, that's why we were in London.'

'No schooling?'

'No schooling. Instead Margo would take me to any museums and art galleries local to wherever we were. Oh, and especially in winter we'd spend a lot of time in the warmth of libraries. I got used to saying I was home educated if anyone asked.'

'I see what you mean now. Why did they do it? I mean, I can't imagine dragging my two around the country?'

Cordelia sat still for a while looking out of the window into the mist, and into the mists of time, analysing what she knew for the first time through much older eyes. She turned to Max.

'They'd do anything for one another, go anywhere, be anything. I think they loved each other more than anyone else, and that included me. You know I've never really thought this through before, but that was how it was. It explains a lot.'

They both sat in silence while each thought about what they had said and heard.

Feeling defensive, Cordelia broke the silence. 'They were both very talented and artistic people, and, even if they didn't bring me up conventionally, I still learnt nearly everything that I needed in life.'

Max gave a wry smile. 'I was just wondering what my life would have been like if I'd grown up with you. I mean, how did you move from that, to how you live now? I've Googled you, good works and village events, Art Fair and charity fund raisers, the epitome of middle-class conformity.'

'Oh! Well, to be Googled, oh my. Yes, well, Max, that really is another story for another time,' she smiled to take the edge off her words.

'Okay, I guess we'd better go back, are you okay for tomorrow?'

'Yes, same time?'

'Agreed.'

The rain had stopped by the time Max dropped Cordelia in the lane.

'Take care,' he said as she climbed out of the car.

'You too,' she smiled and closed the door, watching as he sped away and disappeared round the bend. She took a deep breath. What to tell and what to leave out, that was going to be the real question tomorrow. How did she get to be living like this?

Chapter 18

As beautiful as it is around here, and I must admit it is, in the rain it is as miserable as anywhere else, and by the time I got back I was thoroughly wet and sweaty to boot as it was really quite warm. By rights I ought to have jumped in the shower but the sight of my quarry, I am sure it was her, looking decidedly furtive had given me such a buzz my fingers were itching to get words down so I threw off my coat, lit up and settled at the computer. Two hours later I surfaced, rewarded myself with another cigarette, made myself a coffee and zapped a ready meal to eat at my desk. I wasn't about to get distracted while I was so much on fire, despite the Jim part of me hinting he'd like to get close to Marian again and that a quick phone call wouldn't hurt.

My most productive day yet! Okay, I really won't know until tomorrow when I scan it, but I know I have made progress. The target is under observation, contact is about to be made, and that is the next high on the story arc, that should get the pages turning. I smiled to myself and put a CD on the crappy music system William had dumped here, and turned it up high. Metalica's 'Enter Sandman' blasted out, no one to complain, no one to hear but me and none to see as I swung into a celebratory air-guitar stance, just for the hell of it.

I decided to reward myself with a trip to the pub and a bit of banter, might only be Dave up there, but what the hell - I deserved it – and I'd eat there too, slightly better than living on ready meals. About seven, after a quick shower to freshen up, I set out to walk to the pub as the weather had changed to warm and dry by mid-afternoon and as I might as well, after all, then I don't have to worry about how much I drink. As I walked I breathed in the tranquillity, it eased the tightness my writing had created within me, the tension from the situation my characters were in. At the top of the short steep lane up from Hideaway Cottage I decided to take what I have mentally named 'the Chapel route', past her house. Everything in the zigzaggy lane was freshly washed and glittering in the late sun.

As I reached The Old Chapel I noticed their cars were parked in a different order, the smaller car nearer the road. I smiled to myself, CS 100, how pretentious, a personalised number plate – but no doubt about who owned it. I had barely any time to consider whether this was of use to me when a man came round from the side of The Old Chapel and headed for the Merc.

'Evening,' I risked cheerfully. He looked sharply in my direction, a big bloke, tall, squarely built.

'Oh! Evening?' he replied, there it was, the hint of a question in the uplift of the tone.

I stepped forward, offered my hand. 'Name's Jim Menteur, just moved into Hideaway Cottage.' He responded to the offered hand with one of his own.

'Pleased to meet you,' he said, 'Gerald Steadman,' but without a smile. I let the small silence hang there for a moment, but soon realised he wasn't going to ask me a follow-up question so had to plough on myself if I wanted to get him to expand.

'I'm just walking up to the pub, don't suppose you'll be along there later?'

He harrumphed, 'No, not really, not on a weekday.'

'Ah, of course not, I'm er, I'm a teacher, holiday you know,' I said to make sure he understood I was not some kind of wastrel with nothing to do on a weekday. 'Ah! Steadman? I think it was your wife who brought me the welcome pack.'

He harrumphed again and glanced round behind him as if looking for his wife. 'Very probably,' and pulled a tight sort of smile, as if he'd just remembered he ought to.

So much for striking up a relationship with the husband to get closer to her. 'I'll be getting along then,' I said, 'good evening.' At which point *she* came round the corner saying, 'Can't you find it?'

She hesitated momentarily then came on, 'Oh, hello' she said with a smile, 'I wondered why Gerald was taking so long.'

'Sorry, I'm afraid I distracted him.'

'No problem,' to me, to her husband, 'did you find it?'

'Not looked yet,' and he opened his car and reached down into the foot-well, retrieving a mobile phone. 'Here it is,' he smiled properly and went over to stand, proprietarily, beside his wife. She glanced up at him looking happy. I felt like harrumphing.

'I'll be off then,' I said casually and began to walk away with a small wave of my hand.

'Bye, Mr Menteur,' she said.

'Jim,' I called back. 'Do call me Jim.'

Dave was there already, ensconced in the corner seat at the bar, reading a paper. He looked pleased to see me and waved me over immediately. I picked up the menu as I passed and dragged a stool out to sit on. By the time the barmaid was free, a youngster this time, and came over, smiling, to take my order I knew what I wanted to eat.

I wondered if I could get some more information out of Dave about the delectable Mrs Steadman by asking him about the husband, but my prying questions soon showed me that he really didn't know a lot about him, other than what he had already told me and the fact that he was also a churchwarden. I drank deeply and wondered if that told me anything new about her but I decided that being a church-goer seemed to fit the rest of her profile so it really made little difference.

Dave had placed the newspaper that he'd been reading on the bar, with one finger I turned it so I could scan the page.

'What do you think about that then?' he asked. The article was about the ease of acquiring a drone, complete with camera, that you might use to spy on your neighbours. 'I've seen them used on surfing events but I thought they cost thousands,' he added.

Dave didn't look like an archetypal surfer so this surprised me but I made a 'go-on' sort of noise to see what he was getting at.

'Seems you can buy them cheaply now and people are getting upset, like you could send it over your neighbour's garden when they were sunbathing or such,' he actually coloured up a bit, his neck flushing. I wondered at where his imagination was taking him. It wasn't long before mine took off. I flicked the newspaper with my finger, dismissing it.

'They like to stir people up a bit.' I smiled, 'Another bitter?'

He smiled and nodded, 'Proper Job, thanks.'

I wasn't sure if it was the type of beer or the usual Cornish acclamation, so I just asked for two more of the same and the glasses were soon replaced, followed by my meal. I went home satiated in beer and grub and ready to pursue a new line of enquiry.

Jim, or the drink, wanted me to walk back the other way from the pub, past the close where Marian lives, drop in and see if she was up. I determinedly turned the other way, can't be doing with distractions while the words are flowing ... and perhaps that sort of tension was helping too ... there is a sexual frisson, between the spy - the Puppeteer - and the Ambassador's wife, developing in the story.

***

I left the house early the next morning. My plan was to collect my ciggies and stroll back, aiming to be loitering around the junction at the time I expected the car to come out of the end of the lane. I was all of a jitter in the shop. I had no idea that being just that bit earlier meant I'd hit the 'rush hour' putting me in a veritable throng of people all picking up their papers and having a gas about the day. Main comment of the day was 'better weather today, nice to see the sun again' as if it had been hiding for a week or more – rather than just one day.

All in all it took longer than I expected so I was hurrying when I noticed a silver car flash across the junction ahead. I slowed, pacing myself, counting, working out how long it should take for the car to make the pick up and turn round, working it out carefully as I wanted to be strolling up to the junction just when they had to pause.

Chapter 19

'You could have been a little more friendly to our new neighbour,' Cordelia said as they walked back indoors.

'Really, I thought you said he was only visiting or something? Not likely to become part of the village is he?'

She sighed, 'That's not the point, but never mind, he is a bit strange I suppose, moody.'

'Hmm? Not like you to pass judgement. Talking of which, we have an extraordinary vestry meeting on Thursday, it's your extra court day though isn't it?'

Cordelia sighed again; everything seemed to be such a bother at the moment, most of the time her mind was filled with memories and Max. 'Oh? I'll prepare a cold supper and leave it for you in the fridge. Good job you mentioned it, I'll be able to pick something up on Wednesday.'

Next morning, after Gerald had gone off to his office and all the clearing and tidying had been done, Cordelia glanced at her watch, for the fourth time in almost as many minutes. If she left now, and walked slowly, she should be at the meeting place at the right time. At least the sun was shining today, so there was no need for the coat. She picked up her bag and, with a quick glance around the kitchen, headed for the door. Just as she was pulling it closed the phone rang. She stood there frozen for a moment, the door half-closed, the phone ringing. What if it was Gerald? She stepped quickly back in and snatched up the phone saying her number rapidly.

'Cordelia? Thank goodness. Please, can you help?' Gill's voice sounding panicked.

'What's the matter?'

'It's my father, well, it's...' Cordelia heard a breath being taken. 'I had asked for a carer to mind my father while I go to the hospital, but no one has turned up. If I don't go now

95

I'll miss my appointment and I've been waiting so long. He likes you. Is there any chance you could come and sit with him? The carer may turn up any time, please?'

'Sure, of course, I'm on my way,' Cordelia said, her heart beating wildly. She put the phone down and left the house, scrabbling in her bag for her car keys.

As soon as she pulled up outside Gill's door it flew open. 'Thank you! Thank you!' she said, her car keys clutched in her fingers even as Cordelia climbed out of her car. 'He's in his sitting room, quite calm at the moment. You have my mobile number?'

'I do, you go, don't worry.'

Gill ran to her car and was reversing out before Cordelia closed the door to Gill's house. She stood there a moment listening, then fished out her iPhone and wrote a text to Max. 'So so sorry! Last min emergency. Please forgive. See you tomorrow?' and pressed send before quietly looking in the sitting room door to check on Gill's father.

'Who are you ? What are you doing in my house?' Gill's father, Walter, said peering up at her and starting to push himself up from his chair.

'Hello Mr Jones, It's Cordelia, from the Chapel.'

He squinted his eyes at her and relaxed a little, settling himself back down in his chair, 'From the Chapel,' he said.

'Yes. Would you like a cup of tea?'

'That'll do,' he said, 'and don't forget the biscuits.'

Cordelia smiled and turned toward Gill's kitchen. She was soon back with his cup of tea, one for herself and a rich tea biscuit. She knew he wasn't supposed to have too much sweet stuff and that he was always angling for more.

He picked up the biscuit and turned it over in his fingers as if inspecting it, 'Huh!' he grumbled before snapping it in half and dunking one piece unsteadily in and out of his cup of tea and into his mouth before it dropped.

Cordelia heard her iPhone beep and fished it out. A text message from Max. She opened it. "Damn! Okay."

She wondered why she was staring at the two small words and feeling desolate. But that was it, it hurt as if she had abandoned him, let him down ... again.

'Get out! Devil! Devil!' Walter snarled. Cordelia hadn't been aware of him rising in his chair or that he had his walking stick handy, now raised as if to hit her. He lunged at her, stumbling as he did so. For a second she didn't know whether to try to catch him or fend him off. Instinct cut in, she dropped the phone on the chair as she leapt up, grabbing the stick and supporting his elbow almost at the same time. He shook and struggled, seeming much stronger than his frail frame suggested.

'Mr Jones, Walter! It's me – from the Chapel. From the Chapel!' she said, her voice rising even while she thought she ought to keep it calm and low.

'From the Chapel?' his struggles eased.

'Yes, from the Chapel. You know me.'

'Ah, God bless,' he subsided and she guided him back to his chair, easing his stick from his hand and laying it down on the floor beside his chair.

'Yes,' she said, 'God bless. God bless,' and thought again how strange the mind was and how lucky she had been to have found out beforehand that he thought of her home as still being his childhood place of worship and took her to be the Minister's wife, or something, at least someone who was good and not to be feared.

'I'm back!' Gill called as she came into the house a few hours later. Cordelia jumped up and went into the hall, raising her finger to her lips.

'He's sleeping,' she smiled at Gill.

'Any problems?'

'Oh, no, no, only when my phone went off, he didn't like that.'

Gill coloured up. 'Oh! I forgot to say, sometimes, not always, but sometimes he takes against them, usually something about being the work of the devil. I have no idea where he has got the idea from, but I always leave mine in a different room, it's easier. Sorry, I should have told you.'

'Don't worry, you hardly had time to say anything. Did it go okay?'

'What? Oh yes, thank you. Well, I hope so anyway,' Gill said, slightly turning away.

'Good,' Cordelia said, though she was picking up both anxiety and an unwillingness to talk about it from Gill's demeanour.

'Have you time for a cuppa?' Gill asked, turning back to her.

'Sure,' thinking that the only thing she had on her agenda for the day had been lost anyway and, perhaps, Gill wanted to talk after all.

'I was in for a biopsy, breast biopsy.' Gill said as she set the tea down on the coffee table in their living room, 'and, I'm sorry, I exaggerated a bit, I haven't been waiting long … it just felt like it, and I didn't want it put off. And, well, it's so worrying.'

'Oh! Gill, don't … It really wasn't a problem to come round, and any time is a long time when it's something like that. How long before you know?'

'Not long, thank goodness.' She sighed, 'All I've been thinking is how we'd cope with Dad and everything if, if …' her composure broke, her lips turning down, shaking her head to cover the words she couldn't say, her hand coming up to cover her mouth.

Cordelia slipped from her chair to reach out and hug Gill, feeling her friend's thin shoulders shake within the circle of her arms. 'It'll be okay, and even if it's not clear it will be early enough to deal with, you'll see.' She felt a huge breath being taken, the shaking subsided. She leant back a little to give a space. Gill forced a brief smile and a nod.

Cordelia slid back into her own chair, but kept a hand on Gill's arm for a few moments more.

'You're right.' Gill said, 'Don't say anything will you? To anyone.'

'Doesn't George know?'

Gill shook her head, 'It's complicated. I'll tell him if I have to.'

'Gill ...'

'No, I don't want to worry him too.'

'But surely that's what ...'

'No.' Gill cut in, 'It is better this way. Promise?'

'Of course,' Cordelia said, understanding in her own way.

Chapter 20

Wednesday morning Cordelia could barely wait for Gerald to be out of the house; after missing Max the day before she was so anxious to see him. For once she wished that every day was an 'early to the office' day. She knew that he would leave spot-on time as usual, but time seemed to drag. It wasn't as if she could do anything else until the time came to meet Max, but holding herself in check, making sure she followed the usual pattern of their lives was proving difficult, especially when she wanted to think through what she would say to Max, and what to omit, yet still be honest with him. He'd asked how she'd come to be who she was now, but that story was complicated. There would be things she couldn't bring herself to tell him.

When Johnny had died, without really regaining consciousness, four months after that dreadful day, it was as if Margo had woken from some kind of daze and looked round to find she still had a daughter... but no grandson. If wasn't as if Dee hadn't pleaded with her to help. The day they came and took her baby her mother barely said a word, while Dee fought and cried, eventually believing them when they said she could visit. The only problem with that was they didn't tell her where, and when she found out how to find the local council children's services they told her that she couldn't see him, not yet, not until the court decided if Maxie was in any danger.

'Danger? What do you mean danger? I'm his mum for Christ's sake! Please, please, let me have him back. I miss him so much,' her mouth pulling itself into anguished shapes, her voice coming out all strangled.

'Miss Springs, control your temper or I will have to call security.'

'I'm not in a temper. I just want my baby back!' Dee cried, louder than she intended, feeling panicked.

'Miss Springs, please understand that we can do nothing until the court has ruled. My advice to you is to get your mother to come to the court and make your case,' the woman smiled, her face tight with the effort.

The court sat and ruled; Margo didn't go. Dee did, but wasn't allowed to speak. She heard the evidence of the 'disgusting, unhygienic and depraved conditions' the child was being brought up in, of the fact that she was an under-age mother without proper parental support. Dee broke the rules and spoke out but her anguished cries and demands for Maxie to be given back seemed only to have hardened the court's resolve. They decided that both she and her circumstances were not fit to bring up a baby.

Two months later Johnny died. Margo did try to get Maxie back from social services then. Too late. Being adopted, they said. Dee never knew whether her behaviour that day sealed his fate, for they were notified when the adoption went through a month later and were warned of dire consequences if they tried to find him. No information about his adoptive parents was given and no communication would be permitted, now or in the future, as they believed him to be an abduction risk.

That's when Dee left. Just rolled up her few clothes round Maxie's favourite toy, took what money she could find, stuffed it all in a bag and left. She walked for miles, hitched a lift with a young woman driving an old Morris Minor, and slept in a bus shelter in the suburbs overnight, wearing almost all her clothes to keep warm. Next morning she walked again, her feet aching, the February cold and damp getting through to her bones, always heading away from London.

A car slowed up, though she'd given up sticking her thumb out to hug her clothes closer to try to prevent the constant shivering. It trailed behind her a bit, and then accelerated to be beside her, the window wound down.

'Want a lift?' a bloke's voice. She didn't even look towards him, concentrating on getting one foot in front of the other.

'Suit yourself,' he said and revved up, pulling away. She looked up as she heard the car brake hard. It stopped and he got out and came walking back towards her, his hands held open in appeal.

'Look, I'm heading for Windsor. Really, you look all done in. What can I say – just a lift? Am I going the right way for you?'

He was nice looking in a scruffy way, much like most of the band members, and his car had seen better days too. Something about him was familiar and comforting and, as she really didn't care if she lived or died at that precise moment, that was enough. All her world had been taken from her, what was there left? Windsor? She remembered Windsor, it was pleasant and leafy there, before the bust-up. That'd do.

'Okay,' she said and walked with him the little way to the car and got in.

She could tell him all this, possibly, so far. Would she admit to having kicked up too much of a fuss, to having blown the chance of contact? She thought she might, he needed to know how much she wanted him back but needed to understand that it was different back then, Social Services far more high-handed, far more likely to disapprove of alternative lifestyles and young mothers. It was hard to remember that it was only later that year that the 1977 Housing Act came in with offers of flats for unmarried mothers - when they had to help, rather than just take the child away. Such a long time ago; people forgot what it was all like then.

He said his name was Byron. So she called him Byron, 'Thank you, Byron.'

'It's cool,' he said as he peered through the rain that the windscreen wipers were having trouble shifting, leaving wide arcs of water with each sweep. He pressed the radio button, the car filled with music.

'Like music?' he asked after a couple of tracks.

'Yeah, some,' she said. Just then Hawkwind blasted through. 'Oh!' she gasped, her eyes instantly filling with tears.

'What is it?'

'Nothing,' she reached forward and pressed the button for off – pressing instead a button for change of station. Hawkwind died to be replaced by some fancy classical piece.

'What the hell did you do that for?'

'Sorry, Hawkwind has bad memories for me.'

'That song?'

'No, the whole thing ... my dad was going to play with them, support band, when he ... died,' she whispered.

'Shit!' Byron whispered back, and held his tongue for most of the rest of the journey.

'You are entering the Royal Borough of Windsor' read the sign. Byron broke his silence.

'So, Dee, where you going to stay?'

'Not sure yet,' she said, realising that she hadn't enough for even one night of B and B.

'Well you could crash at our squat, if that's not too rough for you?'

'A squat? Ha, are you joking?'

'No, and you don't have to come, I can drop you off here if you like,' he said slightly snappily.

'I virtually grew up in squats, that or festival camp sites, thanks, Byron.'

'Oh, all right then!' He grinned at her, 'let's go home.'

That squat, in the Dedworth area on the outskirts of Windsor, became home. Everyone was supposed to bring something into the squat in terms of cash, food or fuel. She did none of these things, instead her bed was guaranteed by sharing Byron's; and as it was 'his' squat nobody complained. No foolish accidents now though, he'd taken her to a Family Planning centre and told her to ask for the pill and even administered it to her, telling her she was such a dumb blonde she probably wouldn't remember. When Byron wasn't out on his rounds, servicing his clients with their

103

dope orders, he spent a lot of time on a steady high. Free dope and a breaking heart make good bed fellows. He kept her high, she kept him happy but she remembered crying a lot, when no one else was around to see - especially Byron. She remembered sitting for hours just listening to music as daylight came and faded and being told to light candles. Candlelight still affected her, even now.

There were two other couples and another bloke, each with a room and the shared kitchen and bathroom. It was almost civilised compared to some she'd stayed in with her family. At this squat Byron had managed to get the water back on, and no one came to see about it as there were no bills or meters for water, but they had no electricity, as he said that nicking that would only bring trouble on them. Each evening they made a decent wood fire to cook on, mostly from broken pallets that one of the others brought back from where he worked, and had an inventive range of cooking pots to cook in. They bought cheap white candles by the dozen and had them stood in old bottles all around the place.

Then Byron started taking her with him when he collected new consignments of dope from London, and she realised that the day he picked her up he must have been on his way back from collecting. He also took her to meet some of his clients, saying it was always good to have a back-up, in case he was unable to get out to deliver to them. Then he started sending her to the local drop-offs instead of going himself, saying he was off-colour, or just couldn't be arsed.

Six months or so she stayed there, with Byron getting more possessive and more demanding the longer she stayed. One day in early September she woke up and knew it couldn't last. That it mustn't last. That she was actually worth a lot more that just being Byron's old lady and his decoy.

Perhaps, even this episode in her life she could relate to Max. She could say that she had undergone some kind of breakdown. It was true, she'd felt helpless, hopeless, and useless, looking back now and taking on the role of armchair psychiatrist, it was obvious.

She left the house, timing herself as usual. She rounded the last bend and saw the car waiting for her and found herself breaking into a wide smile as she hurried up to reach him quicker.

Chapter 21

I had turned around and wandered up and down a few times before I heard a car coming and headed briskly back towards the junction. Perfect timing, I reached the turn just as the silver car pulled up. He looked to be in his thirties, glancing both ways at the junction before accelerating across. But there was no passenger. I'm sure it was the right car.

Even when I fail it fires the creative juices. It's wise not to have the protagonist or the antagonist get their own way all the time, it heightens the tension, makes the novel less predictable. That's what I need, that's what the new thriller writer with the *'stunningly original voice'* needs to do.

I am not sure who is the protag and who the antag to be honest. The Ambassador's wife is key, but she is not really the protagonist, she is the target. We are in the antagonist head in this story, he is the person we are following. This is playing outside the rules, rarely does the main character turn out to be the baddy; the reader will be waiting for the twist that makes him the good person. Well it won't come. That's the twist. I think it's genius, the story is holding together well and the tension is building nicely.

I've been on the internet too, Googling the drones Dave was droning on about last night – pun intended. He was right, quite cheap really, and reasonable pictures, video even; makes me think that no one is safe from paparazzi anymore. Found them on Amazon, got it sent as a gift to William Galsworthy, here, just in case the postman is a chattering kind.

I realised with a jolt it was already Tuesday and I hadn't put that call into Marian that I promised Jim I would. He's been quiet since I realised it was good for me to be in a heightened state of tension all round. However, I am a realist; I knew I ought to call her before she took against Jim, especially with that Kevan sniffing around. Even so it was after eight in the evening before I pulled my head away from the computer and took myself up the lane to call her, thinking as I did so I could probably just about shout to her across the valley if we had arranged it.

'Marian!' lightly and with a smile in my voice. 'How are you? Been meaning to ring.'

'Hello Jim.'

'Really, really sorry. Don't know where the time has gone, deadlines for marking and all that.'

'Didn't notice, been rather busy myself, away at a show, only just back as it happens.'

'Ah.' That squashed Jim! 'Oh? Where was that then?'

'Exeter, two-day health and wellbeing show. Always a good show for my business, I stay over with a friend up there.'

'And was it?'

'Brilliant, I have a number of decent orders plus some bookings to follow up.'

I know nothing about business – what do I say now to sound as if I do? 'Brilliant, will this mean expansion?'

'Expansion? I thought I explained I wanted my products made under my control.'

'Yes, but, well maybe ...'

'Never mind, I'm bushed. Was there something you wanted?'

'Um... Harriers! Yes, harriers.'

'Not coming then?' she said, and I could hear all her scepticism in her voice.

'Of course I am, I was just wondering if it is all set up, the lifts and such?'

'Not yet, Kevan should be calling me tomorrow, then I'll call you, okay?'

'Text me, remember?'

'Oh yes, I'll text you. Probably be the same sort of time anyway as the distance to the venue is about the same.'

'Great, thanks,' I finished lamely.

'Okay then, 'til Thursday!' she said and clicked her phone off even as I was saying my goodbyes, much to Jim's annoyance.

***

Next morning I was inspired. I woke early and even before I ate breakfast I had to fire up my computer and get writing. I kept half an eye on the clock though as I was determined to see if the silver car turned up again, and if it did, find out whether my target was, indeed, the mystery passenger. It was touch and go whether I had time to eat breakfast or not before I went so, in the end, I stuffed a slice of bread in the toaster and, after quickly slathering some butter across it carried it with me, munching as I went. I wasn't going to risk the hold-up at the shop this morning; I'd go there after. This time I planned to walk towards the shop, turn and wait at a point where I knew I could observe the junction but not be obviously loitering; sitting in the bus shelter.

Sure enough, I saw the silver car flit across the junction. I rose and sauntered towards it determined to be at the optimum point at the perfect time. And I was, and there she was, smiling and animated, and even looking in my direction as she looked my way for traffic. I pretended not to notice her, or the car, sauntering along with my hands in my pockets.

Gotcha!

I dashed back to the shop and picked up my ciggies, I could hardly wait to get back to Hideaway. I had things to write and things to do. The words flew – masses of red squiggly lines crawled across the pages as my fingers went faster than my brain, leaving a trail of spelling errors. I would go back over them later, right in the white hot furnace of creation I could only try to get the whole lot down as fast as possible. I wrote right through lunch and only drew breath and sat back at about three. I stood and stretched, realised I hadn't even stopped to light up again once the first ciggie had burned itself out, mainly in the ashtray. I put the kettle on and looked out of the window. Another beautiful day out there, I thought, gazing at the bank of trees opposite.

The kettle boiled, I made myself a coffee and took it outside. If I stared I thought I could see tracks in between the trees, it wasn't the impenetrable scrub and brambles I had imagined. I slurped my coffee and returned indoors. I had seen some boots somewhere and sure enough there were a pair of brand new Hunter wellingtons by the back door. I tipped one up and grinned to see the size was one larger than my own. Bingo. I grabbed his Barbour too, it was a bit tight but would do to keep the brambles from catching. I slipped on the boots and grabbed the, also new, walking stick that leant against the radiator by the back door. It was as if William had bought a few archetypal country items and left them here to add to the atmosphere. I could just imagine someone telling him, 'You must have a pair of wellingtons dear boy, Barbour, flat cap and a stout walking stick ... can't look like a townie, got to blend in,' and him scuttling out to get one of each.

The stream was a bit deeper than I had expected, but I managed to get across without the water getting in over the top of the boots. It was a good thing I had the walking stick, not only did it stop me falling when I slipped on the stream-bed's slimy pebbles, but it was also excellent for beating down the brambles and nettles that blocked my way on the bank.

I made my way up diagonally through the trees so that I wouldn't be seen, though it was extremely steep. I felt sure that the bank of the stream would be visible across the fields from the cottages up by Downham farm as I had seen, from the little bridge, that there was only a field between the cottages and the stream. At the same time I had also noticed that the trees stopped just before The Old Chapel, giving it a clear set of lawns down to the stream.

Inside the wood the foliage wasn't half as thick to get through, the brambles that managed to survive were thin and straggly, hardly any nettles, just thin grass, a dock-leaf-looking thing and a few other plants I did not know the names of, but which didn't hamper travel. There were tracks in here but, by the look of them, mostly wild animal tracks. I walked along until I could see The Old Chapel through the end trees but still remain hidden in their shelter.

Perfect. I turned and worked my way higher to where the walking was more on a level, determined now to see if there was an easy way through the wood to the pub. As I came up the valley side and it levelled out I came across a couple of frequently used tracks, with the unpleasant dog walkers evidence of both dog excrement and, worse still, bagged dog excrement! I followed one of these paths and there was the back of the pub. Obviously some people just popped through to walk their hounds on the higher more level part but didn't venture down the really steep part of the wood towards the stream.

Having sussed out both The Old Chapel and the pub I made my way straight down, or as straight as I could without falling, to see if I would emerge opposite Hideaway as I had predicted. I had to use trees for support and zigzag down to prevent falling, but made myself go three right followed by three left to keep basically in a straight line. As the stream glinted through the trees I looked up. There it was; Hideaway. Perfect. I managed to get back across the stream much more easily too as I noticed, from my slightly higher vantage point on this side of the stream, a set of large stones set in the stream bed off to my left and sort of lined up with the front door. They were still under water but were only covered by four inches or so, obviously there by design. As I stepped up onto the bank from these I realised there was a stone edge to the bank at that point too, perhaps marking the stepping stones, but which was currently completely covered on top by moss and grass.

I felt like I had been on a jungle adventure, the adrenaline was zinging. I grabbed myself something to eat and returned to the keyboard, no time to lose!

I can't believe how productive I have been today. If only I could have managed this before when I was supposed to be writing, I'd be sitting pretty now, relaxing over revisions already. The Puppeteer is upping the ante, putting our lovely Ambassador's wife on the spot and I'm contemplating a little upping of the ante myself. Just thinking about this is like an amphetamine hit, I just need to bottle this feeling and release it into my system as and when I need it.

Chapter 22

Cordelia was up early as usual for a court day, formally dressed and fairly focused. She'd explained to Max how it was that she had to miss this day with him as she couldn't do her usual day at court she was doing this one instead. He said he fully understood that she had to keep doing all her usual activities, he even seemed relieved, saying he'd been meaning to take Josh and Megan on a day out anyway.

He'd said he understood about her breakdown too. Sat there gazing silently into the distance until she asked if he was okay. He said he'd been imagining what it must have been like for her, imagining having Megan taken from them when she was only six months and how he would have felt, or how Heather would have coped. He totally understood, he said, it was enough to force anyone over the edge. So this morning she felt she could attend the court room with full focus and a clear conscience.

'Bye,' she called to Gerald. He, as usual, came hurrying through to give her the obligatory kiss at the door. 'Your supper is in the fridge, I'll see you after the vestry meeting,' she smiled up at him.

'Good, thank you, have a good day,' he said standing at the door as she walked round to where the cars were parked. She raised a hand as she passed and smiled at Gerald, dear Gerald, as she drove off towards Plymouth.

She was sitting with the same pair of magistrates from the week before, which was unusual, but it turned out that they also had reasons to change their court week. Colin was taking the chair today, and Malcolm and Cordelia were to be the wingers. Colin, looking all officious, was studying their court list as she arrived, but Malcolm noticed her and, standing, welcomed her.

Colin remained seated and smiled a little grimly. 'Lot on today Cordelia, hope you're on top form.'

She smiled tightly, 'Of course Colin.' Trust him to have recalled her little lapse from their previous session.

'What we have today are two shoplifting cases and one possession of drugs for supply - and soliciting.'

'Soliciting?'

'Yes, she's a prostitute and had an over the top quantity of drugs on her.'

'Alleged,' Malcolm muttered.

'All right, alleged.'

'The case just says 'supply of banned substances', where do you get the other bit from?' Cordelia said quietly, her mind doing unpleasant flickers.

'I happen to know she's been cautioned,' Colin muttered.

'Not relevant,' Malcolm said, his face stern.

'Well, we'll see won't we?' Colin returned to the list. 'Who is going to take the Sentencing Guidelines today?'

'I will,' Malcolm said quickly, his eyes on Cordelia who had gone a little pale. 'You okay?' he whispered to her when Colin strode off to see what was holding their clerk up.

'Um, just a sudden wave of ... nausea.'

'Do you need to go home, we can have someone else called in, you know.'

'No, no ... it will pass,' she said quietly. 'Thank you for taking the Guidelines today,' she gave a weak smile.

'No problem,' Malcolm smiled at her. 'No problem.'

The shoplifting cases were pretty straightforward. In each case the items had been found on the person of the culprit as they left the stores. One of whom they had seen previously on the same sort of charge. The other was kitted out with a special coat that had pockets into which she expertly slipped one item while holding another up to herself at a mirror. The coat alone was a mark of guilt, the fact that it was stuffed with items of expensive lingerie was conclusive.

Windowless, the court was stuffy by mid-morning, and it was all she could do to stifle a yawn as they reached the lunch hour, and she wasn't the only one, she'd noticed one of the prosecutors shielding his mouth to hide a yawn more than once.

No rushing to the Hoe this time, today she needed fresh air and to be alone for a while, so she walked swiftly past St Andrew's Church and around to benches opposite the County Court building to eat her cheese and tomato wrap there; away from the rest of the Court regulars.

She sat in the sunshine but could not stop her mind flitting back to that dark time; to how she got away from the squat. These memories were just too close to the surface, both what she'd already told Max and the flashback from earlier colliding inside her.

After everyone else had left the squat for the day, and even though she was supposed to be the one staying in, just in case someone came to repossess, she washed, plaited her hair and tied it back, sorted out her least creased clothes and set off up the town to see if she could get a job. She trailed round all the stores and cafés finding only two with 'assistant wanted' signs. She went into both. In both she was given short shrift, told that the position had been filled.

It was getting late, it had begun to drizzle and most of the shops and cafés had closed. Disappointed, she thought she'd just try some of the restaurants as they were just opening up, before heading back out of town. Right at the top of town, along a cobbled street opposite the main gate into Windsor Castle, she saw a 'waitress required' notice. The place was open so she climbed the worn stone steps and entered. The waitress rushed to her as she appeared in the dining room doorway.

'I'm sorry,' she said, 'we're closed. Closed at five-thirty, just waiting for some customers to leave.'

'I'm not, not a customer. I saw the advert in the menu board.'

'Oh, right, hang on, stay there,' she said and went to a box affair in the wall and called down it.

After a moment a rotund man with a florid face puffed up the stairs, bringing with him the scent of food, making her stomach squeeze, reminding her she'd not eaten anything since a slice of bread at breakfast.

'For the job?' he asked.

'Yes, I wondered, can I apply?'

He looked her up and down. 'Waitressed before?'

'Not as such.'

His eyebrows raised. 'No experience? Then I can only offer you a pound an hour. Hours are ten to four; I'll give you a week's trial.'

'Oh! Thank you.'

'Starting tomorrow - i you turn up dressed appropriately, black skirt, white blouse, no exceptions, clean and tidy every day.'

'Oh, right, tomorrow?'

'Yes, tomorrow, or don't bother.'

'Thank you,' Dee said, glancing in at the waitress, noting her starched white blouse and knee-length tight black skirt worn under a small frill-edged white apron.

Dee left The Nell Gwynne and walked in the fine rain towards the castle then crossed the street. As she stood there wondering how on earth she was going to get the money for the clothes she became aware of a man looking at her. A visitor, had to be, he was an oriental of some kind, Chinese? Japanese? He must have noticed her glance, as he then came forward.

'Lovely lady, I want you make love to me?' he said. Dee had trouble working out what he meant.

'Lovely lady, make love, I pay, make love not war, peace and love,' he said again.

'No,' Dee said her voice coming out small as she realised what he was asking for. She turned and began to walk away, but he scuttled up behind her catching her up, 'Please, lovely lady, I pay, I sad here, all alone, I pay.'

Two skirts and two blouses, how much would that be? A small voice whispered in her mind's ear.

'How much?' she heard herself say.

'Ten pounds?'

She began to turn away.

'I make it twenty, twenty five!'

Twenty five, good grief, nearly a week's wages, and the chance to get the job too. But, it's prostitution. Was it any different to what she did every night - just for a bed in the squat? The scent of food cooking in the Harte and Garter Grill at the hotel wafted over her, making her stomach contract again.

'See here, I am a respectable lady, you will buy me dinner first, over there,' she said using one of her mother's imperious voices and pointing at the hotel.

'Excellent,' he said, 'my room there too, come lady, come.'

The wine waiter was as snooty as hell, even though Dee gave him her best posh voice, she felt he could read the situation only too well. The food was good, she had not eaten as much meat in the whole of the past week, and the dessert, she had insisted on a dessert, now playing for time, was heavenly.

All too soon she had finished it, she sipped the glass of wine making it last. She could tell Wan, as he'd asked her to call him, was impatient. In truth she had got cold feet and was wondering if she could make a run for it. She swallowed the last of the wine; he caught her eye and gave a satisfied nod. As she stood she felt the effect of the half bottle of wine and rested her fingers on the starched tablecloth for balance. No, she wouldn't run out, she'd do this; she needed the money to get her started on her new life...

'Hello? Cordelia,' a shadow fell across her as Malcolm stood in front of her. 'Time we were getting back in.'

'Oh! Thank you! I was off in a world of my own,' she said rising and walking with him back towards the court.

The girl was young, seventeen, the precise age that Dee had been. Cordelia shivered. How many times had Byron sent her out to meet his clients, how often could she have been the one picked up? Colin had been right, the prosecution were throwing everything at the girl, saying that she had been observed on a notorious stretch of road approaching cars and talking to the men who sat in them through the windows. Classic soliciting behaviour, and, the prosecution averred, she was offering both drugs and sex to the men.

The defence said it was noted that she didn't leave with any of the men, nor was she observed passing anything to, or receiving anything from, the men in the cars. She was also dressed in jeans and a high-necked top. She was, in fact, trying to get information from the men about the whereabouts of a friend of hers who had 'gone on the game' to pay off debts. Lisa had been stopped once before, and been given a verbal warning, but she insisted she had just been doing the same thing – asking questions.

As to the drugs, well she completely denied it. Said she did not have, nor ever had, any drugs on her person. The drugs had been found in the car. The smart looking man had said that she dropped them in the car as soon as she noticed the policeman coming towards them. There were no fingerprints on the bags, neither his nor hers. It was his word against hers.

'Is he up for possession too?' Cordelia whispered to Colin. He shrugged. 'Is he?'

'Not relevant,' he snapped. Cordelia caught Malcolm's eye, and indicated with a flick of her head that she wanted to retire for a discussion. She wrote a note – in large letters - and placed it before Colin. 'We need to retire to discuss this'

Colin pushed it forward on the table, but not before Malcolm had read it. He turned to Colin. 'I agree,' he whispered, 'we need to discuss.'

Colin's 'tut' was audible. 'The Bench will retire,' he announced and stood briskly, his whole body language saying that this was a nonsense.

As they entered the retiring room and the door was closed but before they had reached their table, Colin wheeled round 'What is it? Why is it relevant? We are dealing with *her* case. What has happened to the man is irrelevant.'

'Do we know if he is even being charged?'

'It's not relevant.'

'Nor is something you claim to know that wasn't presented by the prosecution, though explained away anyway by the defence.'

'Well ... '

'I want to know if her friend has been reported missing, and if so when and what has been done about it.'

Malcolm came and stood by Cordelia's shoulder. 'Cordelia is right, in that this is all very one-sided, but it is also not relevant to what has been put before us.' Colin looked pleased until Malcolm continued. 'However, on the evidence presented, the prosecution do seem to think we will just take his word over hers - and that is not proof beyond reasonable doubt. We will have to find her not-guilty.'

'What? We can't just acquit, the press will have a field day on that, won't they?' Cordelia and Malcolm just looked at him. 'Oh, have it your own way, waste public money why don't you?'

'Colin, we are not here to save or waste, we are here to try to make the right decisions,' Cordelia said.

Colin looked at Malcolm, and his shoulders sagged a little; he was outnumbered. He led them back into the court to proceed to acquit.

Cordelia drove home feeling sad. The memories dragged-up by both telling Max about her life and then compounded by the girl's case in court were reminding her of such a troubled time. Yet, it was precisely at this time that she had changed, became focused, started making something of herself, reinventing herself as a new person.

Chapter 23

I can hardly believe it. The drone arrived today. Well, when I say arrived ... I headed out as usual for my ciggies and as I passed the fancy French-style letterbox William has stuck in the hedge at the top of the lane, there's the corner of a card sticking out of it. I had the key, I usually carry it to check on my way back, but instead I tried to wriggle it out from the jaws of the slot. With a bit of pushing of the rat-trap flap, it came out, in one piece. It was one of those 'we tried to deliver but you were out' cards. Tried to deliver my arse, took one look at the lane and gave up I suspect. Now, it seemed, I had to go to a 'hub' on the outskirts of Plymouth to collect it or to try to rearrange delivery – which would probably result in yet another card! Wasting my time, I muttered to myself as I meandered along the lane, phone clamped to my ear. It is actually called Zaggy Lane, according to Dave – would you believe it – after I've been calling it zig-zaggy lane to myself since I got here!

Just as well I phoned, the item would not be back at the hub until after one, I was told. I told them that no attempt had been made to actually deliver the item as I had been at home and the note was stuffed in the letterbox at the top of the lane. This was greeted with the response that I should have notified them that the access was difficult and they would have sent it in a smaller van. My fault – hey?

By the time I reached the shop I had decided I was going to send the drone on its first mission that very evening and that put a spring in my step. By the time I reached the top of Hideaway lane again I had looked through my text messages, amongst a few other random texts from friends and acquaintances, there was the message from Marian saying, 'Same time, same place for Harriers'.

Damn, I was torn, I wanted to get out there and try out the beastie, but Jim wanted to go running with Marian, to keep his options open. I recalled I'd promised to hire a gardener for William, so with that in mind I shook myself and looked for the running kit. I found it where I'd cast it after Harriers last week, festering in the corner of the utility room. To be honest it now reeked. I had meant to get it washed, but I hadn't run out of clothes yet so I hadn't been to a laundrette.

More time wasted, first I looked up sports shops in Plymouth, as I had to head into there anyway, then I scrolled through some sites looking for the kind of kit that the other Harriers were wearing, but taking note that until you had the fantastic thighs, abs and biceps, there were certain styles that were best avoided. I found something I thought might work on a middle-aged, not-so-fit bloke and noticed the only shop stocking that make was in the city centre. Just my luck, why couldn't it have been on the outskirts of the city where the 'hub' was?

As I had to wait until after one o'clock to go to the 'hub' I hit the city centre first, not a place I had ventured to before. 'All Sports' was on Armada Way which, I discovered, was a wide boulevard cutting across the main streets and running straight up to the famous Hoe. I spent more time than I usually would selecting the right kit. I even tried it on. Happy, or as happy as I could be, I bought an extra top to go with the shorts, top, socks and proper running trainers.

I decided on a whim to walk up to the Hoe. That's when I saw her, sitting all alone in the sunlight, opposite the Crown Court building. It was so odd; that I even noticed her, that she should be there on a day when I was, that it was really her. I drifted across the way, pretending to read an advertising hoarding for 'The Bugle Boy' on at the Theatre Royal, and watched her surreptitiously from a distance, the general ebb and flow of people walking between us forming an effective camouflage. A man came and stood in front of her and within a moment she stood and went off with him back the way I'd come, turned down past the Guildhall and disappeared. I followed at a discreet distance, who was she going off with now? It was obviously an older man than the one she met in the car.

Not far past the Guildhall and the Church all became clear as the entrance to the Magistrates' Court came into view, and I instantly recalled Dave's wife from the shop telling me she was a magistrate. No leverage here then, I thought and returned to my walk up to the Hoe.

Later, I found the 'hub' place remarkably easily, and felt pretty smug to have the drone nestling in the boot, but even more amused about having seen her out in the wild, dressed in a suit, all alone and looking vulnerable.

I felt a bit of an impostor in my proper running kit when Kevan and Marian picked me up as I soon clocked that he was still in his football kit, though his looked washed and, even, pressed. His car was a surprise too, I had expected something utilitarian, a bit like Marian's. None of that, this flaming gardener drove a classic car, an immaculate Mk2 Jag! I was filled with envy, thinking 'Morse'.

'Hop in,' he said cheerfully, I opened the door, admiring the burgundy sheen of the paintwork, mirrored by the burgundy leather seating. I slid in, the leg room tighter than I expected, belted up and sat back. Kevan drove off sedately.

'You all right in the back?' Marian said, glancing back at me.

'No problem, it's not for long is it,' I said, 'unless Kevan's going to drive like a granny all the way,' I chuckled.

He caught my eye in the rear-view mirror, 'You've got to drive for the other idiots on these back roads,' he said. At which an 'idiot' came flying round the blind bend ahead and it was only because Kevan was able to pull in and stop quickly in half a passing-place, no more than a shallow curve in the hedge, that they avoided a collision. It would have been mirrors at the very least.

I sat very still for a moment, realising that I had flown round that precise bend earlier that day in just the same way. And my MG was my pride and joy as much as Kevan's Jag was obviously his.

The meeting this time was at a place called Gulworthy, somewhere just on the other side of the Tamar. The terrain was woodland and paths of rubble bulldozed through a decaying nineteenth-century industrial landscape. We gathered at the end of a long and very rough track. I was willing to bet that Kevan had wished he'd not driven his pristine Jag to the venue. I was glad it wasn't my MG. Random chimneys stood out amongst the firs, whole head-high heaps of rubble that were once buildings just sat there, sections were cordoned off. I clambered out and we all ambled over to register. Marian gave me an appreciative look as I began my warm up.

'Taking us seriously then,' she said warmly. Jim's libido did a little flip, until I realised the 'us' referred to the Harriers. Down boy! Though not the tightest version of running shorts these were still too revealing for Jim to show that his hopes were rising.

'Well, sometimes it helps motivation to be in the right kit,' I said, and couldn't help letting my eyes flicker over to Kevan in his footy kit.

Marian ran with us again this week, saying that it was only fair. I really didn't like the track work, too much uneven rubble, but out into the woodland was much better. I was getting the hang of the symbols too, Marian would say what they meant as we came to them, not too difficult, most of them were 'this way', 'not this way' and 'choice of routes' where different levels of runner diverged or intersected.

Again, Kevan was able to talk and run and I overheard him ask her out to Sterts on Saturday, whatever that is, I heard him mention Cajun, so it might be a restaurant, whatever, she seemed pleased by the idea and agreed. The Jim side of me found this annoying, that they could chat so easily as they ran along, even though I felt we were making better shift of it this week than last, not feeling quite so out of breath nor quite so drenched in sweat. There was no doubt about it, I was looking forward to a pint or two afterwards!

'Kevan,' I said to get his attention, his body was tilted away from me and toward Marian as we filled in the end of a long table, him and me side by side, Marian at the end, other runners crammed in around the rest of the table. He leant back a little which opened him up to me, 'My landlord has asked if I could engage a gardener to tidy up a bit around Hideaway, would you like the job?'

He seemed a bit surprised. That was good, put him off his stride. 'Regular?' he asked.

Damn, 'Well, I'm not sure ...' I began, but what the hell, William could always sort it out later, 'Yes, I reckon he'd need that, after all he's not likely to come down and do it himself.'

'Ah! I'm pretty booked up for regular hours, I could do you a good clear up if it needs it, I'd just work a Sunday to do that, then perhaps an hour every second week? Sorry I can't offer more, see what he says.' He wrote his phone number down on the edge of the beer mat and passed it to me.

'Sure, that's good, he asked me to find someone reliable.'

Kevan nodded and took a draught of his non-alcoholic beer.

I'm not sure that I achieved the scenario Jim wanted from this exchange, played out in front of Marian. I had imagined I'd come across as the employer and he just the servant. Instead I ended up feeling like the go-between with him condescending to help out. Damn.

'Are you going to give the book club a go tomorrow then?' Marian said to me.

Am I? I had forgotten about it, hadn't even read the book she'd leant me, but then I don't read novels while I'm writing in case I pick up someone else's voice, and the little bit I had looked at was a nightmare – such a strong voice it would worm its way into any mind. However I hadn't forgotten my delight at finding some group where *she* would be and I could observe her for a longer period of time.

'Sure,' I said, 'where does it meet again?'

'Gill's place, right beside the school. Two o'clock.'

'Great, see you there then,' I grinned, flashing a 'hold that' look at Kevan, I was willing to bet he wasn't a great reader.

They dropped me off at the top of Hideaway's lane and I tottered a little worse for wear down it in the dark, realising that I ought to carry a torch with me when I went out around this place as dark was really dark, unless the moon was out and shining brightly, which it wasn't.

I tossed the kit in the corner of the utility room with the other one and made a mental note to get to a laundrette before next Thursday, to be hanged with doing it myself, I was too busy.

Not being able to talk while I was running was a boon in itself, once I stopped Jim muttering on about Kevan getting on too well with Marian, I could let my mind work on the next steps. A little venture into poison-pen or blackmail would bring the next phase to a head, I decided. I imagined ways for the message to be untraceable; too often finding the perpetrator in novels was narrowed down by a purchase of a specific magazine or newspaper, or the 'fingerprint' of a particular printer. My character had to be aware of these pitfalls, had to be clever yet blinded by his vision.

Chapter 24

Friday was another beautiful day and it lifted Cordelia's spirits to think that Max had probably had a great day out with his children. Just thinking about them made her want to see them, meet them, hug them. With a quiet ache in her heart she knew she was going to ask him to let her see some photos. She'd held off as long as she could, feeling that she owed him so much more than he did her.

She didn't intend to leave early, but she was out of the door five minutes before she needed to be and must have walked quicker than usual as a snatched glance at her watch told her it was still only ten to ten. Deciding she'd just have to walk further then turn back, and suddenly hoping that man wasn't about again today, she rounded the last bend and saw the car. Putting on a spurt she reached it, tapped the door and climbed in, beaming 'Morning,' at Max as he started the car and pulled away.

'How come you were early?'

'I have no idea,' he said, 'just happened.'

'Ha, me too. Good day out yesterday?'

'Yeah, thanks, we went on the Bodmin steam railway, Josh liked it at least.'

'Oh, not Megan?'

'Not quite her thing, and she's a bit old for the farm play area at the other end, but we had a good day out together.'

'I'd love to see photos of them you know ... and of your wife. I'd love to be able to picture you all,' leaving the unsaid wish in her heart; she'd love to meet them all. Max didn't answer and she felt crushed.

When they had settled the car in its usual place Cordelia began to tell Max about how she had started to change her life. She merely said she'd got a job as a waitress, he asked no questions, oblivious to the problem she had faced and

125

the lengths she had gone to in desperation to get this new start.

'After a while working that job, which didn't pay very well, I managed to get a second job too,' she said, saying nothing of how hard it had been to keep the first job, that giving up half of her wages was the only way Byron would wear her being out most of the day; saying nothing of how she'd cleared out of the squat one day when Byron had gone up to London on a collecting trip. She had painstakingly saved enough to rent a room in a house, not even a bedsit, just a room and had paid a month in advance. She'd managed to get a second job over at Virginia Water in a pub where the hours worked in well with her restaurant hours and, as soon as she was due to start there, she took her chance and left the squat.

He had come looking for her. He'd turned up at the restaurant one day, effing and blinding, but Mr Howard had turned him out, threatening him with the law if he so much as hung around. Mr H even gave her a lift back to her new home, out at Old Windsor, just in case Byron was lurking about.

She did tell Max about her bluffing her way into getting recommended for the job at the Gallerie Giovanni in London, but not how she managed to pay for the journey and the quality clothes she needed for the interview in London, she had tried to blot that out of her memory and didn't want to even touch that part, it didn't belong to her, not then, certainly not now.

'And that's where I met Gerald, he was one of the customers at the gallery, and we just hit it off,' she concluded.

'And you just happened to move down here?'

'That was Gerald, he always wanted to live down here and his firm had a branch in Plymouth, so he applied and, it seems, they liked to keep him happy, even back then. He's a partner now of course.'

Max sat back. 'Of course. All neat and tidy, and a quiet life doing good?'

'I try,' she smiled.

'I'll bring the photos next week,' he said.

Yet again Cordelia found she'd not read the book club choice all through before the meeting. She skim-read the last few chapters as she ate her lunch, it was an entrancing book if completely mad, she never quite knew what was going on, what was true and what fantasy. It appeared to be making a point, but allowed itself to get dragged hither and thither on its way. Or maybe it was only because she was not concentrating properly at the moment.

'I've invited Jim,' Marian said as they walked together towards Gill's house. 'I lent him my copy to read last week and last night he said he was coming.'

'But I thought he's only around for the holidays - isn't he?'

'Maybe, maybe not. Seems he has rented Hideaway for six months, and is looking for a post down this way. And he came along to Harriers again last night.'

'Oh! I see, all right,' Cordelia said, giving her friend a conspiratorial smile.

'And so did Kevan.'

'As in my Kevan? Kevan Doige?'

'Yours! Yes, and you know, he's a bit of alright. Shy I think, but at least he doesn't smoke.'

'And Jim does?'

'Mmm.' Marian laughed, 'masks it well but close-up, you know, yuk.'

'Oh? What gossip have I been missing?'

'Nah, went out for a meal, little snog and – yuk! End of that ... but we talked book club instead. He's an English teacher so likes reading and I thought it'd be good to have another man in the group alongside Harold.'

They arrived at Gill's door and were greeted and joined the others around the table, all chattering about anything except books. Marian made sure she took a place with an empty seat left beside it.

'Hope he won't be late,' Marian said, glancing at her watch.

***

Saturday morning Cordelia had arranged to pop into The Art Mill Gallery with some glossy photos she'd taken of the Medusa to show Fraser Kane, long-time acquaintance and the owner of the gallery, who was down for the weekend. She'd already rung him, preferring to deal with him rather than the less flamboyant and more cautious manager, and was hoping to persuade him to come back with her and see the actual exhibit.

'I'm off,' she called to Gerald. He came striding through from the gym annexe where he had been going through his stretches.

'Fine, see you at lunchtime.'

'Or before if I can get Fraser to come out, I'm planning to ask him for lunch,' she said quickly. She noticed the strained look come over Gerald's face, but he pulled a tight smile and went with her to the door, giving her a kiss and standing at the door as she rounded the building to the car area. She knew he didn't welcome having company in the house while he was there too, but one at a time was usually okay, perhaps it was because Fraser was like a crowd of people just on his own.

Cordelia pressed the button to open the door, swung herself in and put the key in the ignition, it was only then she saw it, a piece of paper trapped under her windscreen wiper. She got out again and carefully lifted the blade to release the scrap of paper. It was folded in half but when opened out appeared to be a rough heart torn from a sheet of white paper, on it, in letters cut from a magazine or something gaudy and shiny-surfaced, were the words 'I KNOW'

It felt like a jolt of electricity so sharp she let the paper slip from her fingers, in a frantic motion she tried to grab it before it drifted under the car. She missed it and was leaning right down, trying to reach it without actually kneeling down on the gravel, when she heard Gerald's voice.

'You all right, dear?'

'Fine,' she said, her voice sounding snappy as her fingers just reached the edge of the paper. She drew it across the gravel and scrunched it in her hand as she straightened. 'Fine, just dropped something as I was getting in.'

'Oh! That's all right then, thought you might have had a problem with starting.'

She slid into the car, dropped the scrunched-up note into the passenger foot-well and straight away twitched the key to start the car. It broke the silence and she beamed up at him, finding reverse and driving out.

'I KNOW' What did that mean? And why on a heart shaped piece of paper? And in cut out letters, it was just too weird, like something from an Agatha Christie. Who on earth would have left that? What did they know? What was there to know?

She'd been living her life so much in the past recently that all sorts of things flashed through her mind, all of which belonged to the girl she left behind when she stopped being Dee and became Cordelia. Think! Ah, someone might have seen her and Max and put two and two together and made five – but the only person she knew who had seen them was the visitor in Hideaway, Jim, and why would he do that? He hadn't shown any interest in her at the book club meeting, just in Marian, and it wasn't as if he knew her, she could have been meeting anyone – he wouldn't have known it was her son. No he wouldn't, no one would know that, but he might think he was a ... a... lover? Still, what would it be to him? Is that why it was in a heart shape? She drove on autopilot into Plymouth bringing herself up short when she almost missed her turning off the main road.

'Fraser,' she beamed and held wide her arms. It was the only type of greeting he understood.

'Caro Mio,' he responded in an educated Scots accent as he took her arms and brought her in close to kiss her twice, once on each cheek. The Edinburgh way of pronunciation was, he'd tell you, exactly how English should be spoken, with every syllable sounded, but insisted on peppering his English with snatches of any other language he fancied, pronounced in just the same way. 'How good to see you again. What is it you have brought me?'

'You too, and I am hoping to drag you off to my lair in darkest Cornwall to see it. Lunch as an added inducement.'

'Oohch my sweetie, I'm all tied up today, as it is, if you hadn't rung you might not have even caught me.'

'Oh, never mind, I have a plan B, I've brought you some proper photographs to look at.'

'Then follow me to my lair,' he beckoned. 'Two proper coffees in here, pronto!' he said to one of the assistants gracing the gallery, looking just as ornamental as Cordelia once tried to be.

Once comfortably ensconced on a sofa in the manager's office Cordelia withdrew the photographs. 'He's only just come into my area,' she said, 'but he has a good eye and there is something extraordinary about the pieces, as if they have a life of their own. This is my favourite.' She passed the photographs of the Medusa one by one, three angles, good lighting, a ruler included in the photograph to give scale.

The coffee arrived and the assistant caught sight of one of the photographs.

'Whoa, that's ... creepy, they look like they could move any moment,' she said.

Fraser stared at her and she turned crimson and backed away.

'But she's right, Caro, they are ... not creepy ... but effective.'

Cordelia smiled. 'I've a video moving round it, if you'd like to see it,' she made to draw her iPad mini from her bag.

He shook his head, 'How much would he want for this?' he asked, holding a photograph up and staring at it.

'I won't tell you - what would you pay?'

'Caro Cordelia, you know we work on commission.'

'Yes, of course, but I am out of touch with London prices, what could you sell it for in London?'

Fraser looked at two of the photographs again as if weighing them up. 'If it looks as effective in real life, this could go to ... twenty.'

'So after your cut he'd get ten thousand?'

'If he was a patient man and would guarantee never to make another I could at least double it,' Fraser shrugged. Of course if he got a name for himself his prices would rise.'

'Of course,' Cordelia smiled. 'So you'd be willing to take it on if he agrees?'

'As long as it has the same resonance with me that its photographs do, and knowing you, it will.'

'Thank you Fraser, I knew I could trust your instinct.'

She was feeling a real buzz but as soon as Cordelia was back in the car she noticed the small ball of paper in the passenger well, and a feeling of dread washed over her. She had to find out who it was from, and what they were going to do with what they thought they knew.

Cordelia stopped in a lay-by before she reached home and picked up the ball of paper. Carefully she smoothed it out. She looked at it from all angles, as if it were a piece of artwork. She noted the rough cutting-out of the letters, the colours and the texture. Some edges were now curled up, and she could see that there was writing on the back. She lifted an edge trying to make out the words in small type on the back without tearing it off. It looked familiar, a type

131

face and colour combination she recognised. She put the note between two sheets of paper and returned the paper to her photograph file and her file to her bag. She'd try not to think about it too much over Sunday, it was too risky to even get it out to look at, she'd wait and take it apart Monday, after she'd seen Max.

Chapter 25

I reached the deep passing place spot on time, there was no silver car waiting so I expected to see it at any minute. I exited the lane and headed for my bus stop perch. Five minutes, ten. No silver car. Now, I knew that she was in Plymouth yesterday, so perhaps they were not meeting today either, I reasoned. I put it out of my mind, I had other ideas bubbling away, I intend to provoke her into making a mistake, I hope. I wish I could hack into her emails and text messages like my antagonist does with those of the Ambassador's wife.

I also have a great idea for the drone, only problem is I should be writing not playing with that, however I must get to know how it works in daylight, as I hope to make my maiden flight this evening. It took me most of my morning and was a bit tricky, but the video it took of me operating it wasn't half bad, especially once I got it to slow down and even hover around a bit.

I read the blurb of the book club choice, I read a few reviews of the book on Goodreads, including a couple in the one and two stars sections, I found a couple of good observations and skimmed until I found at least one to reference in the book, sticking a post-it on the page. I was done and dusted in about half an hour. Feeling smug I revved up the MG and whizzed up towards the school.

When I knocked it was answered by one of the women I'd seen before at the village day, helping out in the kitchen, while I was chatting to Cordelia and Marian. She beamed at me and was effusive in welcome. They were all in the dining room sitting around a large oval dining table. Cups of tea were already in front of most people and I was offered tea or coffee myself before I sat down next to Marian, as she indicated when she saw me enter, and opposite Cordelia, a huge platter of cake and biscuits between us on the table.

Gill put my coffee and a small plate and serviette down in my place, to match everyone else, and sat down herself.

'Welcome everyone, and especially our new member, Jim, who's coming along while he can,' she smiled at Marian. 'Our book today is The Goldfinch ...' and we were off. I said little, keeping my comments to those I had prepared, and they were well received as being very observant. The rest of the time I observed ... carefully ... storing away fine details for my own use.

As we were packing up, the general chitchat rising in volume, I turned to Marian, 'I wonder if you'd like to come to the theatre with me, I noticed Bugle Boy is on at the Theatre Royal and I've been meaning to catch it.'

'Oh, that sounds lovely, what night?'

'It's a Tuesday, the nineteenth that is, and I thought we could have a bite to eat first?' I said, not knowing anywhere suitable but supposing there must be somewhere.

'Okay, that's very kind of you, give me a ring when you know for sure.'

Put that in your pipe and smoke it, Kevan, Jim smirked inside my head.

It was about half past eight in the evening before I considered that the light was fading enough, about the time people were turning lights on in their houses, making outside seem even darker. I tucked the drone in a plastic bag and, attired all in black except the green Hunter wellies, slipped out of the back door and across the submerged stepping stones to the other side of the stream.

Once through the thick undergrowth along the bank I walked carefully along inside the wood, shielded from view by the same undergrowth. Only when I got near the end of the bit of woodland, bordering The Old Chapel gardens, did

I start to climb up the steep incline. I didn't want to go as far as the level ground for fear of meeting a dog walker, so I stopped at a spot where I could lean against the trunk of a substantial tree and unpack the drone.

From here I had a clear view of The Old Chapel, lights on both upstairs and down. I estimated that it was only a hundred yards from my hiding position to the windows, and hunkered down to get the drone ready to fly. I knew I had to be very careful in the beginning; I had to get it to fly through the gap between overhanging branches and luxuriant undergrowth, brambles dotted with blackberries, nettles and what-have-you, forming a natural sort of hedge up against the wire fencing surrounding the garden.

Up...up... forward.. SHIT! The drone crashed, whining unhappily, into a clump of nettles. I turned it off and dropped the controls, snatched up the stick and gently parted the plants to try to extract the drone unharmed. I could reach it ... just. My fingers had almost closed around a strut when it dropped deeper between the stalks. My sudden lunge caused a whiplash nettle to swipe my face, and my hand brushed along a stem as I, at last, managed to get hold of the thing.

The stings already beginning to throb, I set up the drone for another try. At least this time I had a better window to aim for, the parted nettles lining up with the high spot in the overhang, it was now a wider and deeper slot to fly through. The drone took off ... I made it hover and then aimed for the gap ... it went through a treat and was soon zooming across the undulating lawns terraced out of the steep valley-side, sounding like a strimmer in full flight. I started watching the monitor as I could barely make out the drone as it neared the Chapel. Up... up... I suddenly had to veer it away as the window came rushing towards the drone .... along back ... around. It's a good thing I'm into video games; I think that is the perfect practice for piloting something like this.

Okay, back toward the lit window, pull back and hover. Gotcha ... this must be their bedroom. Big double and ... whoa! Wow, can't believe it ... there she is ... come in carrying something ... laundry? Perhaps. Video running? Check. Perfect.

A small peeping sound warned me that the battery was running low. I knew it was a small capacity, it was a compromise on price, but the time had gone so quickly. I pulled the drone back as the conservatory was below these windows, and then allowed it to drop to head height, looking in through the conservatory. No one about, but I could see rooms lit up beyond through the interior glass doors.

'Time to come home to Papa,' I murmured as I pulled the drone back and turned it for a headlong flight back to me. I got it through the gap but, concerned that it might hit a tree, dropped it a bit quickly and the damned thing landed in the nettles again. As if to mock me, the throbbing of the first set of nettle rashes flared up again. I retrieved the drone, with just a small brush of my wrist against the nettles, and checked it over. All seemed good. I carefully packed it up into the box and put it back in the plastic bag. Time to go home. I hadn't gone more than a few steps when I heard a voice.

'Good evening,' all jolly, not a voice I recognised. A liver and white spaniel burst out of the undergrowth behind me and scampered round my feet. 'Blackberrying?'

'Oh, Yes,' I called back, grabbing hold of the ready-made excuse I waved the bag a bit, 'not enough to make it worth it though,' I added, I didn't want a stampede of locals looking for juicy blackberries. 'and getting too dark now,' I added as it seemed a bit late to be out blackberrying to me.

'Tonto, here boy, sorry,' he called as the dog almost tripped me up.

'Don't worry,' I answered cheerily, glad to see the dog run straight up the steep slope and lead his owner away along the path. Close shave! I'd only considered the walkers; I hadn't thought about the flaming dogs. I will have to be better prepared next time.

I got back to the house without any further sightings, changed swiftly and set out for the pub, taking the chapel route to scope out the lie of the land, her car nearest the road, good. I arrived just before last orders, and ordered a pint. As I made the pint last, I read one of the local papers, The Cornish Times, amazed at how little actual news there was in it. Headline for the week concerned a fundraiser from Saltash completing his John O'Groats to Lands End ride, and showed him cycling through his home town.

It was quite dark by the time I left the pub, taking the chapel route home as planned. I'd learnt my lesson; I had a torch with me this time but didn't use it until I was well past The Old Chapel, I didn't want to be seen.

I imagined her finding the note and wondered what her reaction would be, if there was anything for her to actually be worried about, anything she was hiding, as her body language and her behaviour suggested to me, then I hoped to push her into making a mistake. I would have written more, but I think those words are enough to prick a guilty conscience and anyway the letters just weren't there on the special-offers sheet from the local Co-op that had been stuffed in the letterbox a couple of days ago. I had smiled as I cut them out – it would be impossible to track down one person from goodness knows how many people that had one of those adverts delivered to their homes in the past week - even more anonymous than a newspaper or a magazine. And the torn paper heart – ha! Genius or what? All done with loving care and wearing thin surgical gloves. I'd thought of everything.

No sign of them again today - though, it is Sunday ... perhaps they don't meet over a weekend anyway, after all her husband would be around wouldn't he? Why didn't I think of that before?

Chapter 26

She was going to tell Max about the note under her windscreen wiper. She had to tell someone. Two nights in a row her sleep had been disrupted by a sudden feeling of falling, and always into a black pit. She needed someone to give her a rational explanation, and there was no way she could talk to Gerald, nor even Marian. There was only Max.

After Gerald left for work she peeled a couple of letters carefully from the 'heart', using the time honoured method of steaming until she recognised the paper it came from. It had only been last week that an advert from the Co-op had come with the rest of the mail and that had these colours, besides, one of the pieces had an edge attached that read 'o-op'

'I'm not sure we can carry on meeting like this,' she said as they pulled in and stopped up on Kit Hill. Max stiffened. 'Look.' She held out the paper heart. 'I found it tucked under my windscreen wiper on Saturday morning.'

He took it from her and she dropped the loose letters into his hand. 'I peeled those two off – I was trying to see what the letters were cut out from. It was a Co-op advert, delivered with the mail last week, I think.' And all of a sudden she felt a bit silly, after all what did that matter, who wrote it and what they thought they knew were the only things that mattered.

'I KNOW, odd?' he said balancing the loose letters in their places

'Yes, and,' she let loose a sigh, 'not sure what it means, is it a threat? Or is it a poison-pen type of thing?'

'Or blackmail,' he added.

Cordelia looked sharply at him. 'Surely not?'

'Whatever it is, if they mean to do anything they will have to contact you again. Could it even not be for you? It looks rather childish, the heart and all, perhaps kids have been messing around and someone thought it funny to stick it on your car.'

Cordelia considered this for a moment; it didn't really seem that likely, although she would have welcomed this idea. Yes, the heart was rather childish, but it could indicate aspects that the words didn't mention.

'Do you want us to change our routine? It's no problem.' Max said smiling, 'I always felt it was a bit cloak and dagger.'

'Not enough cloak and dagger it seems. I could swear that no one has noticed us except that visitor, you know the one at the junction. And that's only because he is staying at the only cottage along that lane. I have no idea why he'd have anything to say about anything though.'

'So, do you want to change?'

'I haven't been able to work out an alternative just yet, we'll see,' she said firmly.

'All right. Anyway, I've brought them,' he reached into the glove box in front of her and pulled out a wallet of photographs. Cordelia could not stop the tears that suddenly filled her eyes.

'Oh! Thank you,' she said, as Max started to tell her who was who, as if she really needed to be told.

'Thank you,' Cordelia said, 'It really does help. I can see how much Megan takes after Heather, but I see you in Joshua.'

'Yes, that's what most people say, though Megan is brilliant with language and such a mimic, so they tell me that comes from me, but maybe it really comes from your mother?'

Cordelia smiled, remembering how Margo could take off someone's accent, even their mannerisms in an instant. 'That does sound like her.'

'Margo, is she? I mean, she's still alive isn't she?'

'Yes, very much so.' Cordelia thought, yes, swanning around on the Isles of Scilly with her 'beau', as she called the rich widower she'd taken up with. Good luck to her.

'I wondered, would it be possible to meet her?'

Cordelia froze. How would she be able to manage that?

'I ... I don't know, I'd have to talk to her.'

'Okay, let me know. I have never met a grandparent - not properly, both my adopted parents had lost theirs before I was old enough to know them.'

'Oh.' Cordelia sat very still. Would this be the time to ask? Was it too soon? 'Is there any chance I could meet ...'

'Joshua and Megan? In time ... I would need to prepare them first.'

'Oh,' she swallowed, as tears filled her eyes again, 'Oh, that would be ... I just can't tell you, how good.'

Cordelia walked slowly back to The Old Chapel after Max had dropped her off. She wondered how dependent her seeing the children was on Max seeing Margo. The way it had come out it was as if the two were interconnected. Margo!

She had kept Gerald's and Margo's contact minimal over the years. That first time it had been difficult enough. Cordelia had met Gerald's doting parents and knew just the level of social standing they were expecting their beloved son to marry into.

She'd reinvented her family in her head already before her interview for the gallery, perfectly aware of the sort of employee the owner was looking for, connected people of the right social and economic standing, she'd added interests in the Arts to their portfolio, so it hadn't been difficult to answer convincingly when faced with his parents' interrogation.

'So, Cordelia, what was it you said your parents did?' as if she'd already mentioned it and they were just wanting to be reminded. Maybe Gerald had said something to them already.

'My father, before he died, was in the music business, production, you know,' she smiled, as if making music were the lesser skill and being a 'producer' the higher one. 'And Mother,

well you know, good works and all that. Involves herself in the Arts a lot,' Cordelia replied, keeping her tones to the well modulated and rich Ascot variety. 'But of course that's only recently, my whole life has been peripatetic,' she loved that word, 'following my father's business career, here, the States, Germany ...' she'd trailed off.

'Such an exciting life then,' Deirdre, Gerald's mother, had said, looking really interested. 'I would so like to meet her, your mother, sounds as if she and I would get on well,' her smile small and tight. Cordelia was sure that Gerald would not be getting their blessing without this further level of investigation.

'Of course, but Mother's not in the country at the moment, she's off – travelling,' Cordelia said on impulse, hoping to put off the invitation she could see forming in Deirdre's mind.

It was Gerald, though, who had pursued the matter, he said he wanted to meet Cordelia's mother. Cordelia suspected Deirdre of pushing the agenda, but she could see that if she were to further her relationship with Gerald; Margo would have to be met. 'My dear Gerald', as she had begun to think of him, the fonder she became of this gentle, if a little unusual, man, The problem was, of course, that she had no idea how to contact Margo as the girl that was Dee had walked out of Margo's life when she'd walked away from her in London, what seemed a whole lifetime ago. She wished she'd told Gerald that Margo was dead as well, it would have made life simpler, but no, she'd told the truth, and now she had a problem. She was glad she'd said Margo was travelling; it gave her time ... time to try to find her.

Chapter 27

Okay, so I've got this bit of video and she would know it was her bedroom, and then of course she appears. I've looked at it a number of times, she is definitely carrying laundry but starts to turn towards the window just as I veered away, perhaps she heard the drone. What I do with this clip depends on what happens next. What I need is her email address. That shouldn't be too hard to get, not as she's such a busy bee organising things in the village, I bet it's out there somewhere already. I just need to research and find it.

'Cordelia Steadman email' I typed into the search engine ... and within a minute or two, after a couple of false starts, there it was. 'Hingsbury Art Fair: For more information, or to apply to exhibit, contact Cordelia Steadman at c.steadman@theoldchapel.co.uk'. Now all I have to do is make a new, untraceable, email address for myself. This is something my antagonist did ages ago; I logged in to one of the sites I had him use, one I'd already done the research work on for accuracy, for him. Now, what to call myself, I wanted her to open the email, I didn't want her to delete it as soon as it arrived.

I couldn't make up my mind so I went to make myself a coffee. While the kettle was taking its time boiling I ran back and brought up my novel, an idea having just struck me. I forgot the coffee, I forgot the open request for a user name, I lost myself in the book again.

It was three hours later when I emerged from the book. I was actually sweating. My antagonist was nearly caught, just because he cut a corner and got too close to his quarry, letting himself get sexually interested in her, rather than just seeing her as the tool to get to the Ambassador. I had that extraordinary, but so exciting, feeling of being inside someone else's head, yet having my mind taken over by something almost outside myself as the words rolled out onto the screen. I shivered. Coffee, I was making coffee.

When I returned to my computer with coffee and a couple of biscuits I noticed the open server and restored it to full screen. A name? Perhaps one she already knows so she would be more inclined to open it. Ha! I know, kill two birds with one stone. I couldn't stop myself laughing out loud as I typed in *K.Doige@hotmal.com*. It was clever how it worked. Saren was a new combination, a suite if you like, composed of The Onion Router, or TOR, and 'anonymising' via an offshoot of AnonEmail. Once within Saren you could use any name of the major email providers but you dropped just one specified letter and it became one of these undetectable emails, bounced all around the world's servers before it popped back into your designated email on your computer. No one really looks past the @ on an email address it seems, everyone just reads what they expect to see.

In the subject line I put 'I KNOW' ... I felt sure that would get her attention. I was grinning like a fool, excited beyond reason. I was about to attach the video and press send when something stopped me. I ought to see what effect the note had first and, if I was right about the weekend being a no-meet time anyway I ought, at least, to hold off until Monday night. I closed the screen and returned to my novel.

I ate late and went to bed early. It didn't make for a restful night, but I woke with a brilliant idea. I would have to leave a little early, but it could be worth it. I packed up the little drone and carried it on my route to the shop. I kept checking for other walkers and kept my ears open for the sound of a car but I was about half an hour earlier than I usually was so felt fairly safe. Just opposite the wider passing place I nestled the drone in the hedge, it was quite secure, sitting on top of the Cornish stone hedge but hooked in behind some of the hedgerow shrubs growing from the top of it. I used the monitor to make sure it was pointing right at the passing place, and that anything within that space would be recorded. Avoiding the lens, I draped a piece of fern over it, masking its outlines completely. I walked up and down, checking the drone could not be seen from any angle. It seemed well hidden. I walked past the passing place, and saw myself on the monitor screen do the same. I wished for a motion sensor ... but knew I would just have to sit and wait and press record as soon as I saw the car.

I had thought the bus shelter would be ideal, except there was someone waiting for a bus. I really didn't realise that there was a bus due at around this time, but then again I was a bit earlier than usual I supposed. Instead I wandered past gazing at the screen, pretending it was a large phone, I even mimicked using it as a touch screen, as if reading off emails or something. I had almost reached the shop when I saw the car arrive on screen; I pressed record as it did a neat three point turn and settled into the bay. He's done that before! And I have a good close-up picture of his face as he performed the turn, I couldn't wait to get this on the computer to enlarge it.

The bus passed me and I glanced back, saw the person waiting get on and the bus move off. I returned to the bus stop and the shelter. I turned off record for the moment, not wanting to run out of recording space at the wrong time. Suddenly there was a movement on screen, and it was her. I pressed record. She walked right up to the car, seemed to tap on it and get in, I could see she was animated and the car took off almost immediately. I saw her face full-on as she instinctively turned to look back as they pulled out, in case another car was coming along Zaggy Lane. I stopped recording and hunched back into the bus shelter, not wanting to be seen at all as they crossed the junction.

Is it wrong of me? I want to know where they go, what they do? How long they are away. The MG is a hopeless car to follow someone in, far too recognisable. What I need is something nondescript, or, ha! something like Kevan's. Would she know what he drove when he wasn't working? Possibly? Or possibly not? I shall find out what he drives for work, that'd be easier to hire than a Mk 2 Jag! I looked for the beer mat and found it in the pocket of the shorts mouldering in the utility room. I gathered the running kits up, went upstairs, hauled out all the washing I had piled in the linen basket and shoved it all into a large bin-liner. I phoned Kevan from the landline, it rang an inordinate number of times then clicked into voicemail, 'Hi, you are through to KD Garden Services, please leave your number and message after the tone and I'll get back to you.'

Bother, I was hoping to talk to him directly, never mind, 'Kevan! Jim here, can I come and talk to you about you doing work at Hideaway?' and then left the land-line number.

I had just gathered my car keys and some cash when the phone rang.

'Hi Jim, sorry about going to voicemail, I was mowing.'

'No problem, where are you? I'm just going out and thought we could talk about Hideaway, face to face as it were.'

'Can't we talk on the phone? Or I could pop down, let's see, Wednesday evening?'

'No, no, don't bother, um ...' Damn! What was I thinking?

'I'm up at The Old Chapel, if you really want to see me now?' he sounded perplexed.

Perfect. Off the hook! 'Wednesday evening will be great, actually, probably best you see the place to see what needs doing.'

'Okay, see you Wednesday evening.'

I grabbed the bag of washing and jumped into the MG and whizzed up the lane, far too fast, going in the direction of The Old Chapel. I only needed a glimpse of his vehicle; a white van with green writing on the side, to know I was on to a winner.

The laundrette said they would have my stuff ready by late this afternoon, but they didn't mind if I left it until tomorrow, I didn't want to waste any more time today, I had things to do. Back home I googled 'van hire', and found one in Launceston that looked right. The van hire firm has a dark blue logo and writing that might be mistaken for green at a glance. I called them and arranged to hire a small white van similar to Kevan's that afternoon. There was nothing for it, I would have to leave the MG up there for the time I needed the van, but they said I could leave it in their compound, which was reassuring. Armed with my driving licence and credit card, my own one, in my real name, not my author name, I set off. I returned a couple of hours later, having even collected my laundry en route, with a reasonable facsimile of Kevan's van.

As I uploaded the recording from the drone I realised I was relieved that they were still meeting, despite the note. Either this is innocent or she has not taken the note seriously. I watched the video carefully. He looks to be late thirties, early forties, definitely younger than her. Toy boy? He's good looking; I'll give her that. I realised I have his number-plate. Now, my antagonist has all sorts of contacts, he could find out in a trice who owned any car just by the plate. Shame I can't, but it would be so useful. I'll have to try my new plan instead.

This video is much better than the other one for putting pressure on. The other one is a bit creepy, really. I won't delete it though, it still might come in useful. I'll attach the new video to the email, but not tonight, my game plan has changed, and I don't want to frighten them off too much, yet.

Chapter 28

Back home, Cordelia tried to get on with arranging the Art Fair. She still had a few things to sort out, though all the basics were in place as she had done this for so many years that she booked things like the lighting equipment and the display boards as soon as the previous art fair was over. The publicity was all organised though there were the final press releases to send out and the roadside banners to set up. No, it was, as ever, the artists who kept her on her toes right up to the last minute.

Her inbox had at least three artists with change of size requests. Two should be easy enough she thought as the changes would just mean that their own area would be that bit more crowded than she liked. How she wished for the generous spaces that the Gallerie Giovanni provided. The Gallerie had been created out of an old spacious house, and so it had many rooms, all interconnected as most interior doors had been removed and some even widened, which gave masses of hanging space. The main walk-in off the street was the only part that been completely opened out, with just a small counter at one end and the rest of the space used to display the larger and more eyecatching paintings and sculptures, designed to draw the customers in.

In the village hall she had to arrange a framework of boards in a flared crenellation design in three long rows to give maximum hanging areas and surprising spaces in-between for the smaller sculptures, with larger spaces near the ends for others. So the third artist, asking for a new space twice that of the one he'd asked for originally, was going to be a problem. He'd attached a photograph, he probably knew after all these years that she could be influenced by the actual piece of art when being asked for the impossible. The painting was full of rich colours, a meadowland up close, as if you were lying on your front, raised on your elbows, peering through the rich tapestry of wild flowers, grasses and mini-beasts all both close-up and blurring into the distance, lit by a clear blue sky above. Cordelia sighed, the colours reminded her of another painting, nothing so pastoral, but one which lit up the Gallerie at the time when she was working out how to find Margo and trying to do just that. It drew her back to that time, to that difficult time.

...

At least she was in London, she thought, and the last time she saw Margo that was where she was. Cordelia made herself go back to the Haringey area where the last squat they had been in was. It was a year later but it was the only place she knew to start out with. She half hoped that it would all have gone, all been demolished. That is what the signs said on the empty ones. 'These properties are scheduled for demolition' and a picture of the housing block that was going to replace them, all glistening blue and white.

The terrace of houses was still there, now all sealed up, some with concrete blocks with 'Danger' notices pasted on them, others still with boards and corrugated iron. Number seven still had corrugated iron and it was obvious to her that it was still occupied; the corrugated sheet hanging from a central nail that meant it could be swung aside to gain entrance.

She'd taken the trouble to dress down, was wearing the only set of clothes she had kept from the 'bad days' as she thought of them, a once pretty turquoise dress, long with panels of velvet and fringing on the sleeves. She slipped in through the door, calling out as she did so, 'Hello, welcome all?' the usual password that told people that the incomer was a 'native', someone used to living in squats. 'Good man' someone called from further in, and Dee stepped further into the gloom. The hall was lit by squares of light coming through from back rooms with windows that had been unblocked, and she walked from patch of light to patch of light along the bare boards. Eventually she came to the old kitchen, from where the voice had emanated.

The woman sitting there looked up and beamed. 'Dee?' she said, 'Dee!' It wasn't her mother, but was the next best thing,

Annie, attractive in a wild animal way, slightly mad, a long time squatter, long time groupie, super communicator and such a useful person when you were looking for someone. She rose up and came to Dee, arms outstretched, and drew her in. 'How are you?'

'Good, Annie, getting my life straightened out.'

Annie nodded.

'I need to find Margo, any idea where she might have gone?'

'Ah! Margo, she was here, yes, up to about a week ago,' Annie looked hard at Dee, 'She kept hoping you'd come back you know, that's why she stayed so long.'

Dee waited, her heart aching almost to the core, but at the core was a point of rage that would not soften.

'Do you know where she is now?'

'Up in the world! She's working, got a super role as Lady Macbeth at the Aldwych Theatre. Left us and bought herself into some proper digs.'

'Where? Do you know where?'

'Sorry, Dee, I don't know, but you could always catch her after a show,' she looked at Dee. 'She'll be happy to see you, don't worry, she loves you.'

'Oh Annie,' Dee said, her voice catching as tears filled her eyes, 'I've missed her, I need,' she swallowed , 'I need to see her, I'll do that.'

'You're not in trouble are you?' Annie came over all concerned.

'No, not at all, I've got a job, I've found a lovely man, and he'd like to meet Margo.'

'Well! That's lovely. Good for you, if that's what you want.'

'Yes,' she looked at Annie. 'Not for everyone, I know,' she said, worried she'd upset this strange, beautiful woman somehow. 'And thank you, thank you, I really thought it was going to be impossible to find Margo.'

'Margo!' Dee called as she saw her mother exit the stage door of the Aldwych Theatre two nights later. Margo wheeled round, stopped theatrically in her steps, looked at Dee and then rushed to her, throwing her arms around her.

'Dee! Oh, Dee!'

'Margo, can we talk,' she said, pulling herself away.

'Of course my little love, we were just going for a supper, it's all booked but I am sure we can squeeze you in,' turning away to the others still coming out of the door. 'It's my daughter, just come back, Dee, she's coming with us.' A few turned and smiled, one man came over smiling. Margo smiled up at him, 'Justin, meet Dee, my daughter.'

'Pleased to meet you,' Justin said, lifting Dee's hand and sort of nodding to it.

'Hello,' Dee said, 'I'd just like to talk to Margo.'

'Nonsense, come with us, you can talk over supper,' and he took hold of Margo's hand, and hers again, and led them away.

'The problem is he wants to meet you,' Cordelia said above the hubbub of chatter, thespians winding down, still fuelled by adrenaline from the show.

'I don't see a problem, what's the problem?'

'Well,' Cordelia said, feeling slightly ashamed that she'd lied about her mother to Gerald, she could see how it would look to Margo. 'Well, you have no idea, he's so, so,' she had trouble finding the words to describe the status and level of class she felt he came from. Not upper class, but on the fringes, or they thought of themselves on the fringes. They 'knew' people, socialised with the right sort, went to the opera and the ballet, never down the pub.

'Snobbish?' Margo suggested.

'Not Gerald, no, but his parents, yes. With some right to be, I think.'

'Cordelia, my dear,' Margo put on her best patrician voice, 'if they are trying that hard then they are not the top quality people, let me tell you, they don't care who they talk to.'

'But I told them ...'

'What?'

'I suggested that you were of independent means ... just doing good work with interests in the Arts, oh, and that you are travelling at the moment,' Cordelia managed to smile at this. Margo laughed, her lovely laugh, the one full of fun.

'So I can act, if this boy means that much to you Cordelia, I owe you that much. I can act, if nothing else.'

'But what if they've seen you on the stage?'

'I hope you are not saying I look like the Lady M. even without the make-up,' she chided with a smile, 'and I use my own name as my stage name anyway, don't I?'

Cordelia had totally forgotten that, if she ever really knew, she'd been only eleven when Margo had given up her stage work. Her maiden name; so she must be Margo Tremayne to the world, and Gerald's parents need not be any the wiser.

'But, of course, we'll have to meet somewhere suitable. The Ritz for afternoon tea would be suitable, I could suggest I was staying there after my travels,' Margo continued.

'That would be perfect, thanks.'

'However, there is a bit of a problem with money. I have none, well, barely any, just paid up for digs, the show's only been running a week, no fancy clothes to speak of at all, and I'd have to at least offer to pay for the tea, even if your Gerald ended up paying, I'd have to have some in case ...'

'Oh!' Cordelia thought hard. After her lodgings and living expenses she didn't have much money either, possibly enough for tea at the Ritz, certainly not enough for something nice for Margo to wear to fit her role.

'Um, how much do you think you'll need?'

Margo pulled a moue, 'A hundred should see it covered, I can be careful over the dress,' she said, as if making a great sacrifice.

'So, if I can get that much, when can I say you'll meet Gerald?'

'You choose dear, I'll need a week to get the costume, now, tell me the exact lies you have told so that I do not put my foot in it.'

Cordelia agonised over whether she could, just one more time, make the money by selling herself again. She shuddered at the thought. She realised that when she felt she was worth nothing it had been easier to give herself away, to sell herself, now it felt wrong, demeaning, but she couldn't think of another way to raise the money in a short time. If she gave Margo all she had saved, that had taken her months to save, she still needed another fifty pounds.

London seemed a more dangerous place in the shadows, far more organised and scary, and too close to home, you never knew when you would bump into someone you knew or someone who had visited the Gallerie Giovanni, a big place but a small world. No, Windsor had proved to be the right place before, busy with tourists but easy-going, less frightening. Still scared, but determined, she bought a ticket and took the early evening train to Windsor on Saturday, telling Gerald that she had to visit a friend.

She was not dressed as a whore, she was dressed prettily, but in her bag she had two Durex. She wandered aimlessly up and down near the railway station, near the hotel, across from the castle. After half an hour she was approached. A heavily made up woman who looked to be in her thirties, dark hair piled in an old fashioned beehive, miniskirt, tight jumper, high heels and bomber jacket, came right up to her, invading her personal space.

'What game you playing?'

'Sorry, pardon?'

'You, prancing up and down. This is my patch, what you doing?'

'Patch?' Cordelia felt the heat run up her face but played the innocent.

'You don't fool me, clear off.'

'I'm ... I'm waiting for someone. He's late.'

'Right, yeah, right,' she said, but backed off a bit. 'I've got my eyes on you,' she said miming with her fingers from her eyes to Cordelia's.

Cordelia walked away from the railway station towards the junction with Peascod Street and hovered on the street corner. She was going to have to go home; she was feeling very wobbly after her run in with the woman. She leant against the wall and closed her eyes for a moment, gathering herself, trying to quell the shaking.

'Are you all right?' a male voice asked her.

152

Her eyes snapped open, a smartly dressed man in his forties was looking down at her with his head slightly on an angle, she straightened. 'Yes, thank you, I just felt dizzy for a moment.'

'You shouldn't be hanging around here,' he said, 'someone might get the wrong impression.'

'Sorry,' she said, as if it had never been her intention, 'but I'm waiting for someone.'

He looked at her intently. 'Really? That's a pity, I was looking for someone, thought it might be you,' he raised his eyebrows, 'I've been watching you, you've not looked at the time once. You're not waiting for someone.'

Oh! Right! Cordelia looked down towards the railway station, the woman was looking straight across at her. The guy glanced in the same direction, 'You're much prettier. I've a room in the Hotel here,' he nodded to the Harte and Garter. 'How much?'

This was it, her whole body trembling she pulled herself up straight, 'A hundred.'

He stepped back, 'What do you think you have down there, a gold mine?'

She looked at him keeping a straight face.

'Seventy, and you're on,' he said, 'but it better be worth it.'

She glanced at the woman again, then back at him. 'Eighty?' She swallowed.

'Desperate? You got a habit?' he reached out quickly grabbing her arm, turning it up? She snatched her arm back.

'No!'

'Good, 'cos I don't do druggies. Seventy or forget it,' he made to move away.

'Okay,' she heard herself say. He turned back, his smile nothing to do with being nice.

She had no idea really. The previous times it had been perfunctory. This man was different, wanted to know what she thought she was doing, getting undressed so he couldn't see. He wanted a performance, he said, he'd paid for more than a quick fuck. He hadn't paid anything yet, she realised, and said so. He laughed, peeled off seventy and put it on the cabinet beside the bed, the far side. She started again, undressing slowly and facing him, though actually looking past him at the money on the cabinet. When she'd finished he stripped off quickly and lay on the bed, she snatched a durex from her bag and, palming it, walked as seductively as she thought he wanted her to, over to the bed, climbed on and went to straddle him, ready to put the durex on him.

'Uh uh,' he shook his head, 'you can forget that for now, you can start by sucking me off.'

At least she knew what that meant, Byron had taught her that.

She moved to the side, realigned her body to bring her head down near his groin. She tried not to breathe his scent in, acrid and stale, as she opened her mouth. As her lips closed on him he knotted up her hair in one hand, put the other on the crown of her head and forced himself deep into her mouth, lifted her head, dragging it up by her hair and forced it down again, rising to fill her until she could barely breathe, forcing her head up, down, up, down, then holding her head tight to his groin, his hips thrust high, her nose blocked by his flesh, until she gagged and struggled for breath.

She felt him laugh as he released her, let her breathe and then made it happen all over again, her hair screaming at the roots, her eyes full of tears. He lifted her head off again as she almost choked but this time slammed it down on the bed as he shifted away. Holding her head down forcibly he swivelled onto his knees, only letting her head go as he grabbed her from behind, holding her tight with one arm wrapped round her hips and finding her with the other hand, forcing himself in, fucking her from behind, her face pressed into the bed, her tears soaking into the cover. She heard him grunt and grunt and grunt and shout 'Yes!' Still holding her tight he slapped her rear, hard, and pushed her over onto what had been 'his' side. She crawled off the bed, her legs shaking, she stood thinking, hoping, it was over.

'Where do you think you're going?' He raised himself up on one elbow, 'You ain't earned it yet. I need a bit more attention, yeah?' He indicated his flaccid cock, 'for seventy quid.'

'What? What?'

'Well, you can suck my balls, lick my cock, use your fucking imagination; I'll be good to go again in no time.'

'Oh right, okay... um...'

'Come on then, get a move on.'

She grabbed the money from the cabinet and raced round to her clothes, snatching them and her bag in one swift move - he was off the bed and tumbling after her as she reached the door, naked. She flicked the lock and snatched the door open and ran out, clutching her clothes to her she ran for the end of the corridor where she could see an exit sign. His bitter laughter rang down the corridor behind her, 'Bitch!' he shouted and she heard the door slam: he hadn't followed her. She reached the door to the stairs, looked through, then stood just inside the doors on the landing and dropped the dress over her head. Worried someone else would appear at any moment, or that he'd come after her once he'd put clothes on, she just stuffed her bra and pants in her bag along with the money and ran her fingers through her hair to straighten it as she walked down the stairs. She didn't look at anyone in the lobby as she went out, turned and headed toward the railway station, feeling dirty as she felt his spunk seeping out of her, running down her inner thigh.

The other woman was just getting out of a car as she reached the station. She turned and looked Cordelia up and down, a sneer on her face.

'Had a hard time, have you? He's a bastard that one, you were welcome to him,' she laughed and, preening, teetered off.

Cordelia decided to call Margo, talking would be the best way to find a solution. This time there would be no hiding the difficulties, she'd lay all her cards on the table.

Chapter 29

I have planned things very carefully but I hope they continue with their meetings as usual as I have only hired the van for two days. I do not want Kevan to see it down at Hideaway when he comes.

I know that every time I have spotted them, or even the car with only him in it, it has driven right across the junction. This means that I could reasonably expect them to do the same next time and therefore I could pick up tailing them from a position further up that road, one less conspicuous than the junction itself. I checked on the map, there is no real turn off until it hits the main road, but there is a farm track just past the short row of cottages opposite the farm entrance, which might make the perfect place to wait. If I park far enough back then the side of the van will be hidden from view, yet I'll easily see them go past and follow. I took the Google man for a walk along the road; it looks perfect, as long as the farmer doesn't want access to the farm track.

Next morning I was buzzing, I couldn't wait to get going, I had the drone packed, and my camera, and my pack of ciggies and, as I'm on a stakeout, a half packet of biscuits. I feel as if it ought to be doughnuts, isn't that what cops eat on their stakeouts? I picked up William's Barbour and his flat cap as part of my disguise, but I think it'll be a bit warm for the jacket. I was grinning like a fool to myself as I drove out of Zaggy Lane and straight across. Wearing the cap, I feel like a van driver delivering something; unobtrusive, invisible.

I spotted the cottages, pulled up and did a neat reverse into the mouth of the track. Only it doesn't look like the track on the Google maps, this one has been made up with a proper road surface. I sat there for a moment wondering if I have the right place or not. From behind me I heard a noise and glanced up at the rear-view mirror, a car had appeared and was coming up behind me and I was blocking the way. I pretended I was just turning and immediately engaged gear and drove forward looking to turn out. At that moment the silver car whizzed down the road across my bonnet. I pulled out left and paused on the road side. The car behind me in the lane pulled out and round me, I could feel them looking at me, but I pretended to be consulting a map or something, by picking up the hire invoice and peering at it.

As soon as the road was clear I reversed back into the gap. Now that I looked it seemed that the track went round the back of the cottages, so I kept half an eye on my rear-view mirror in case anyone else wanted to come out. I was in luck, after a couple of minutes the silver car flew past again, two people in the front. I revved up and pulled out, and just about caught them up enough to see him indicate right as he reached the main road. I followed as closely as I dared, ended up three cars back, but I kept him in view. He took the turn up towards Kit Hill, so did I, even though this placed me right behind him. I slowed, trying to keep him just in view, no mean feat as the road arced over making the viewing distance quite short. I lost sight of them momentarily, just before a sign for Louis Tea Rooms, pointing off to the right. I still hadn't caught them up by the time I reached the entrance so I slowed and checked they were not driving down to the parking area there. No sign of them, so then I had to accelerate to try to catch up again. I was going a bit fast when I noticed the turn off to the Country Park, it's not well signed, but I glanced to my left and there was a silver car, heading up the narrow roadway. I hit the brakes but stopped way past the entrance. It was too far to reverse back, so I drove on down the road looking for a place to turn, ending up at the crossroads where I made a tricky U-turn.

How many routes were there up there? Could I risk dawdling? I'd already lost time. I roared back to the entrance and turned in. I set to trickle up the road, looking in any side turnings as I went.

There was a car park half way up, off to my left, the tops of some cars showing, I turned in quickly, bouncing in the ruts, and turned again to the higher level. I circled this, sending up a cloud of rubble dust and, seeing no silver cars, exited immediately continuing up the road. Further up, off to the right, a smaller parking place appeared, and in it a silver car. I decided to dawdle past and verify that it was them.

Sure enough, correct number plate the lot. They were occupying opposite corners of the front seats, as if they were having a row, not a tryst.

I carried on driving up the hill and found the next space to park in. I got out, drone in bag, and walked down towards their car park. Once I was in sighting distance, but not in their view, I turned down another lane and stepped off this into the gorse scrub. I set up the drone and got it to lift off. The wind was a bit tricky, it wavered and yawed but eventually I got it stable and aimed the drone in the direction of the car. I was going to have to do this all by monitor, I didn't want to be seen.

The picture showed the car sitting all alone, I turned the drone towards it, I was going to try swooping up at it, so they would have very little time to see what it was. Record on, I flew the drone from a low position towards the car then, as the grille and number plate loomed large, pulled back, buzzing up the screen and over the roof. My jubilation at having managed this without mishap almost caused a mishap as I let the drone continue too high, almost going into a loop. Just in time I veered it away in my direction, stabilised and got it back to land not ten foot away from me on the track. I gathered it up just as a couple walking their dogs materialised from, goodness knows where, further along the track.

I walked back to the van and put the drone away, fetching out my camera. I wondered if there was any way I could get a decent still shot. I headed down towards them as before, but used the cover of the scrubby line of trees and some big rocks to give me cover as I crept closer. After a quick glance around to make sure no one was watching me, I aimed my lens through the trees and focused on her, side view, sitting in the car and pressed the shutter. I didn't think the lens would pick him up too, but who knows?

She turned suddenly, looking my way; I ducked down, pretending to be focusing on something on the grass. All she should have seen of me was the top of the cap. I backed off, and turned away so she could not catch a glimpse of my face, I even changed my walk as I went, giving it a bit of a roll. Oh I was good, I thought. I had enough so I returned to the van and set off, as long as they didn't get a perfect look at the van I was not worried now if they saw it drive down the hill; I was a random van driver visiting this hill. What a view as I drove down, I really ought to get up here when I'm not so busy, it looked magnificent. I drove past the silver car at a tidy pace, deliberately not looking their way, and drove the short distance back to Hingsbury feeling on fire. I couldn't wait to get back to the computer.

Looking at the video and the pictures had to wait once I was back. My mind was in overdrive, the next chapters were reeling themselves out before me, I just had to get down to it and capture them on paper as fast as I could. I came to, starving. It was half past five and I hadn't eaten anything, or smoked more than the one cigarette, since breakfast. That cigarette sat mostly as a column of undisturbed ash in the ashtray beside the computer, just looking at it made me want another so I lit up and went to heat up a frozen meal.

I am so close to the ending now, another ten thousand words should see it done. I can hardly believe it myself. I have never written so well or so fast. The antagonist has got the Ambassador's wife just where he wants her; she'll do anything for him to preserve her secrets. I smiled. Well, I knew now that my quarry has a secret too, no longer just an interpretation of actions and body language, she was guilty of something and it was time to up the pressure in both scenarios.

After I had eaten I downloaded the video from the drone and the pictures from the camera. The video was okay, I would have to edit it, leaving barely half a second, but in which you could see them in the car, his eyes following the motion of the drone upwards, hers looking at him.

The stills from the camera were better in their way. I had set it to take a series of seven shots in one second, so the pictures show her side view - nothing of him, her side view - him leaning forward so you can just make him out, her turning to look in my direction - his face showing clearly as he leans forward. He must have been the one who noticed me, which figures if he was looking towards her as she was speaking.

I decided that the stills are the best to send. It keeps the notion of the drone's existence out of the picture, as it were, which might be useful later. But what to do ... send her that last picture? What might her reaction be? Would her reaction help me or hinder? I went for a wander in the garden, swishing the long grass with my foot as I did so. It really needed cutting. Shall I? Shan't I?

Chapter 30

The conversation with Margo had been surreal.
'Margo?'
'Who is it?'
'Cordelia - Dee.'
'My goodness, you are still alive then?'
'Please, not now. Something remarkable has happened.'
Margo laughed.
'Seriously, remember Maxie?' her voice breaking as she tried to say his name.
'Our Maxie? Our lovely boy?'
'Yes. Oh, he's found me. He's lovely, a teacher, he's got two children.'
'What are you saying?'
'He's found me! Contacted me, we've talked, and ... he wants to meet you, but we have to do it without Gerald knowing.'
'Bugger Gerald, always tiptoeing round that man.'
'He doesn't know about Max, not about any of it.'
'About time he did.'
'NO!'
'Don't shout at me, I'm your mother, remember.'
'Sorry, Margo, listen. I can't possibly explain this to Gerald, I can't it would ... it would ... destroy us.'
'Nonsense, after all this time he'd just have to take it on board.'
'If you think that you really do not understand Gerald. We can do this, can't we? We can arrange to meet Max somewhere, you and me. That's all he wants, just to meet you. Nothing more.'
'What do you mean nothing more? I thought I heard you say he's got children.'
'Well, yes, but what's that got to do with it?'
'Oh I see, all about you? You don't think I'd like to know Maxie and his children too?'

'No! Of course, but well ... well, I don't know, that'd have to be up to Max. I haven't seen his children yet,' Cordelia said her voice near to breaking again. Damn Margo for wanting it all now, why couldn't she have been more interested when it really mattered. There was a silence from the other end of the line. Cordelia was just about to ask if Margo was still there when she spoke.

'All right, I can come to the mainland next week. I'll get a room at The Holiday Inn by the Hoe. Arrange with Maxie a day you can both come to meet me.'

'Thanks, I'll be in touch.'

'What's he like?'

'Lovely, so lovely.'

Cordelia was early again on the Tuesday morning, as if she couldn't keep herself away from telling him as soon as possible. Max, however, was not there early, so she'd backtracked to almost within sight of the cottages at Downham and re-walked Zaggy Lane to the meeting place. This time he was there and she broke into a run to reach the car and get in as quickly as possible.

'You're not late,' he said as they drove off.

'I know, but I've been waiting, just round the bend,' which she thought was rather how she felt at the moment. 'Margo will meet with us next week, she's going to take a room at the Holiday Inn up by the Hoe. Is that all right with you?'

'Yes, that sounds good, what day?'

'She's left that up to you, she's really only coming over for you, she's not got anything else in her diary.'

Max nodded. 'Okay, how about Tuesday? Does that suit you?'

'That's just about perfect for me, later that week I'm busy setting up the Art Fair,' Cordelia smiled.

'So, tell me more about Margo,' Max said as the engine made its strange wheezing noises as it cooled. The view was spectacular this morning, the sky bright, the hills luminescent in the brilliant sunshine but the valleys wreathed in a magical mist.

'Margo. I told you she was an actress, a Shakespearian trained, good actress, didn't I?'

He nodded.

'After Johnny died, after I'd walked out, and after she got her head together, that's what she went back into. The time I found her, after I had met Gerald, she was playing Lady Macbeth, I went one evening, on my own, to see her. She was magnificent, I felt so proud.'

'On your own?'

'Well, yes, especially after Gerald had met her, I couldn't let him find out she was an actress. It wasn't what he thought she was.'

Max was looking at her in a strange way now. 'You mean Gerald doesn't know anything about your family, your ... upbringing?'

'No, he ...'

'All your life, your married life, he's not known anything. Not just about me, about everything?'

Cordelia took a deep breath, but no words came. She felt the impact of Max's comment, the criticism within the questioning.

When she found her voice it was small and distant, 'I had reinvented myself. I told everyone the same story, the one I had told when I got the job at the gallery. Once I was in that role I couldn't back out, I couldn't suddenly change.'

Max was silent for a while, 'How on earth do you keep it up? It must be a strain?'

She laughed, 'No, not really, this is me now, that is my history, I half believe it myself.' She turned to look at him full face. 'It is only now, meeting you, telling you the real past, now it has become strange,' her hand drew a dividing line down her heart, 'as if I am two people inside.'

163

After arriving back from seeing Max, Cordelia felt restless. She realised she hadn't heard from Marian since her date with Kevan, so decided see if she was free.

'Hi, Marian,' she said when Marian answered, 'are you busy?'

'No, perfect timing, as usual! Just finished bottling a sample batch of shampoo.'

'Oh? Is that a new line?'

'As it happens, yes, I had a couple of queries for shampoo so I thought I'd research and have a go. So, this is the first batch for beta trialling. Been trying it out for the past couple of weeks on my own hair and I like it. Want a bottle to try, feedback required as usual?'

'Of course, sounds interesting. Might be the only thing left in my cabinet that isn't Greenwood's,' she said, smiling. It was so nice to be able to support someone not just because they were a friend but because their products were simply the best. 'Would you like to come round for lunch?'

'Oh well, now that sounds like an offer I can't refuse. Half an hour or so? I ought to clean up here first.'

'Suits me, see you later.'

By the time Marian knocked on and entered the already open door, Cordelia had got together a fresh goats' cheese salad, decorated with bright blue borage flowers from the garden, with a side dish of hot tiny new potatoes tossed in mayonnaise and sprinkled with fresh chives.

'In here,' Cordelia called from the conservatory.

'One Lemon and Jojoba shampoo,' Marian said placing a small bottle on the table.

'Wow, it looks good enough to drink,' Cordelia said as the sunlight struck through the pale golden liquid. She picked it up and put it on the bookshelf behind her.

'And that looks nice!' Marian said eyeing the lunch.

'Tuck in,' Cordelia said, feeling glad she'd asked Marian round.

'So, how did it go at Sterts?' Cordelia asked as she served herself with a plate of salad.

'Mmm, this is lovely,' Marian said, and rested her fork down. 'You know it was really good. What surprised me was - that man can dance!'

'No! Well, there's a surprise,' Cordelia beamed.

'Like I said it was a Cajun band, but I had no idea there would be dancing, but they'd set up at the back of the stage area – leaving that big half moon for dancing. Just as well, it was hopping with people almost from the word go.'

'It's a concrete stage isn't it?' Cordelia said, trying to remember.

'You're telling me! Absolutely no give, and I was wearing going-out shoes with no bounce in them. My knees were sore Sunday morning from the jarring! But it was fun!'

'Bit of a dark horse our Kevan then?' Cordelia grinned at her friend.

'And not a bad kisser either,' she winked. 'Just a bit shy, you know, he's a really nice guy, and pretty fit too, even though he's into football, and you know what I think about football, at least he plays it, not just talks about it. In fact, he doesn't.'

'Doesn't what.'

'Talk about it, he says it's just for a run around with the lads, after all he really doesn't need it for the exercise does he? You must have noticed his muscles, well, all that gardening, and with his shirt off,' Marian pretended to fan herself.

'Trust you to notice.'

'Makes a nice change, is all I'm saying. He's really sweet too, explained how he's dyslexic, and that's how he ended up gardening, just like Jamie Oliver but with gardening instead of cooking. And he's not stupid, got a good memory, he's very observant and he's even learning spoken Spanish.'

'Marian Wood, are you smitten?'

'Might be, might not, anyway it's all feast or famine, Jim's asked me out again, wants to take me to the theatre, seems there's a play he's been wanting to see and it's on at the Theatre Royal.'

'Better than Simon-pipe-and-slippers-man, though, isn't it?

'Oh, do not get me wrong, I'm loving it!' she laughed.

Chapter 31

Wednesday morning I took the van out again, I wanted to check that they followed the same routine, went to the same place, I thought it would be useful to know for the future. This time I pulled in up the road to the village, parked up just past the bus shelter. As soon as the car swept across the junction and away I was on their heels, though dropped back a bit as soon as I recognised their route, heading for Kit Hill again. I bowled up the hill as if I did it everyday of my life, but this time the car wasn't in the same position, there was a blue car there instead.

Cursing the fact I had not checked any of the lower car parks I continued up the hill, right to the top and turned in the larger car park there. As I wheeled round I spotted the car in the corner, two spaces beyond a red Volvo, but without any occupants so I wasn't sure it was the right one until I got close enough to see the number plate – it was. Only then did I scan the surrounding area, my eyes drawn to the towering chimney. There, standing by a block and looking away at an angle from the car park, luckily for me, stood two people. I recognised her. She's quite tall, but he's a lot taller, I saw him lift his hand and point at something in the distance, but before they turned and got a good look at the van I revved up and drove off. No chance of sneaky photos today. They must be getting bold to be seen together like that, and that sent sparks running through me.

When I got back I was so on fire that I almost didn't stop off for my ciggies, but did, leaving the van a bit down the road so Dave in the shop didn't see it. I was a little annoyed that I almost got too close to them on top of the hill, if they'd been looking my way they'd have seen the van and perhaps the writing on the side too well; the whole point of having a van like Kevan's is for it to be mistaken for his, not identified as different. Anyway, not much time lost and my suspicions confirmed, all in all I was still on fire by the time I returned to Hideaway. The computer beckoned.

Contact has been made and the Ambassador's wife has been given her ultimatum; she is desperate, she is under pressure, she will bend to the will of my antagonist. I find I am grinning as I type, enjoying the power that he has over her. Now would be the time to take advantage of her, if he wasn't so disciplined. But is he that disciplined? I let the hint of sexual tension rise through his interior dialogue. God! I am enjoying this.

I caught sight of the clock. Shit! That's never the time! Four-fifteen, and I have to get that bloody van back to Launceston by five. Shit, shit, shit! I grabbed the keys and ran out of the house, didn't even bother locking up.

I rolled the MG down Hideaway's lane and turned into the parking area. I had a momentary shock, it was as if the van was still here! Then it dawned on me – it must be Kevan's. And it was, he climbed out at the same time I did.

'Sorry, man!' I said, coming over all jovial. 'Had to pop out, hoped to be back before you turned up.'

'No problem,' he said. 'I just dropped in on my way home. Had a walk around, been a bit let go hasn't it?'

'Yeah, I have no idea what it was like before he bought it, but nothing's been done since, it seems. He's good for whatever you can do, but said he'd like a once a week if possible.'

'I'll do a big clear, might take two Sundays though. Then I will see how things go. I can only do the one hour every second week at the moment, really, pretty booked up.'

'Well, no skin off my nose, I'll just tell the owner.'

'Okay, then. See you on Thursday?'

'Oh, yes. How did the Cajun go down then? Bit fiery, eh?' I said remembering their conversation last Harriers meeting.

'Great, great band. Do you like Cajun music?'

Music! Thought we were talking food here. 'No, not really my style, a bit ...' I tried to find a word to describe something I knew little about, yet wanted to sound knowledgeable, 'bit, hillbilly isn't it?'

'Good dancing music, Marian loved it,' he grinned, and I could see that he recalled his evening with pleasure. Damn the man, how had the evening ended, that's what Jim wanted to know, how much pleasure was had?

'Right, I'll see you on Thursday, then on Sunday for the big clean up,' I stuck out my hand to shake hands and dismiss him.

He turned the van and drove away, I went in and got myself something to eat. Jim was nagging, what about Marian? What about her and that Kevan bastard? What are you going to do about it? I knew I had a date set up with Marian, but Jim still nagged at me, showing me the smug look on Kevan's face when he'd said how much Marian had enjoyed the dancing; smug.

I tried to get back into the plot, get the writing flowing again, but Jim kept turning my mind back to Marian. I decided it was time to put a spoke in his wheels. I would send the email to Cordelia, that would sort him. Let's see where her loyalty lies, will she alert her best friend? Will she panic and give me more ammunition?

I had the email address set up but when I looked at it again I wondered if she would see through it? After all, if I was a bloke like Kevan would I put my name to what was, essentially, a threatening email, or, at the very least, a bit creepy? I looked at the name and decided he'd have disguised it. Perhaps just his initials? K. D.? Or perhaps reversed, D. K? K. D? I tried them out loud. Dee Kay? Kay Dee? Kay Dee! That even sounded like a woman's name, though was phonetically his initials. I liked It!

I set up another email address through 'Saren'. Kay.Dee@hotmal.com.

As before, I put 'I KNOW in the subject line and just the same in the message. I attached the photo, the last one from Kit Hill, showing both him and her clearly, together in the car. I checked it all again. Would she open it? Jim nudged me, get the bastard, he smirked. I pressed 'send'.

Chapter 32

Wednesday turned out to be such a beautiful day, sunny and clear from the word go. Cordelia couldn't wait to see Max as it was the day he was going to start telling her about his life.

'Let's walk a bit, can we?' Max suggested after they'd been forced to drive up higher when there was a car in 'their' spot halfway up the hill.

Cordelia weighed up the possibilities, far more likely to be noticed sitting together here at the top with no view to admire from the car park, rather than a swift passing glance on the way up. Whereas two people just looking round the chimney on top and gazing at the view is easily understood. After all she'd innocently brought many guests to this point to show them the panorama stretching from moor to moor, almost coast to coast.

'Yes, why not?' she beamed and they both exited the car and headed up to the base around the mine engine chimney that marks the top of Kit Hill.

'I've been meaning to ask, have you had anything else, after that weird heart thing?' he said as they stood, the warm breeze blowing into their faces.

'No,' she smiled. 'No, it seems you were right, it was just someone playing games or something after all.'

'Good.' He walked over to one of the blocks marked with the distances and the places you could see on a clear day. They looked towards Bodmin moor, glowering blue grey in the distance.

'I have no memories of you, or anything from then,' he said, his voice quiet.

'I didn't expect you to, you were only six months old,' she reached out and touched his hand.

He smiled at her, 'I just feel I ought to have known something.' She shook her head. She wished with a deep

171

ache that he had felt something, somehow known, but realistically it couldn't be, and was better that he hadn't.

'I think I was about nine when they told me that I was actually adopted. I'm not sure quite why they told me then. I do remember that there was a bit of a flurry, someone else said something at Christmas, too much drink perhaps, and there was this shocked silence. Very shortly afterwards Mum and Dad explained that they were 'lucky enough' to have adopted me when I was a young baby.' He shook his head. 'I remember feeling worried, if this news meant that I had to leave, if I had to go away. When they assured me that nothing had changed, that nothing was going to change, just that I knew now, I felt relieved and easily put it at the back of my mind.' He started to walk away towards the next block with the view-markings on them. Cordelia followed.

'Perhaps they picked just the right time? Just the right age.'

'Possibly,' he shook his head. 'Just trying to imagine saying something like that to Josh, he's nine now, it must have been so hard for them.'

'Where were you living then?'

'Stevenage, we moved down to Plymouth just before I moved up to secondary school,' he said, pointing towards the city on the horizon, the sea glinting beyond it.

'So you've been around this area since then?'

'Yes, apart from the time I went off to Uni in Southampton.'

Cordelia closed her eyes and shook her head. So close all these years. She and Gerald had moved down at about the same time that Max would have been ten. They had first lived in Plymouth, near Gerald's office, then moved out to the chapel six years later, after they had it converted, and that was over twenty years ago.

'See you tomorrow,' Cordelia said as she left his car, feeling both happy and sad, having learnt so much about him and recognising how much she had missed. As she walked back along Zaggy Lane she realised her overwhelming feeling was of relief. If his tale of upbringing had been bad, she knew she wouldn't be feeling anything like as happy as she was. All in all it had been a quiet upbringing, his adoptive parents being quite a bit older, in their forties, their own parents dying during his early-years, before Max really knew who they were. The husband worked for the County Council and his wife was, in Max's early-years, a homemaker but later a librarian with the mobile library. They liked to go cycling and they liked the theatre and they brought their son up to enjoy both these activities, and both had become life-long loves for him.

Gerald's car was in the drive when she got home, it set her heart racing. She prepared herself to say she'd been out for a walk and delivering a welcome pack and headed in.

'Gerald?' she called.

A sound from upstairs, a drawer closing. 'Up here,' he said.

'Are you all right?' she said, going up the stairs, stepping into a darkened bedroom.

'Shocking headache,' he said, 'wouldn't go, eventually I just had to give in and come home.'

'Oh, poor you. What have you tried?'

'Two lots of paracetamol already, not touched it. I think it might be a migraine, though I've never had one of those before. It's affecting my vision.'

'Oh? That does sound like a migraine. Does the bright light make it worse?'

'Not worse, just, dark is better,' Gerald said, easing himself onto the bed. 'I think I'll just lie here for a while and see if it goes.'

'Sounds like a good idea, do you want anything? A cup of tea or a cold drink?'

'Not now, later maybe.'

'I'll leave you in peace then,' she said, backing out of the room and closing the door gently.

She put the kettle on for herself and got some lunch together. The rest of the day had to be focused on the Art Fair, everything had to be ready for the following weekend and she still had to finish the final layout. She ate, checked on Gerald again and began. Pieces of paper with the artist's name and size of picture on, and a large chart that she used from year to year, gave her an overview. When she was happy that everyone had a space and that the mixture of pictures would give the best experience to the viewer she began to transfer all the information onto a plan on the computer.

By the time she had done all this it was getting late, past six and she was surprised that Gerald had not come down yet. She crept up the stairs and opened the bedroom door. Gerald was lying on his back snoring. She withdrew quietly and returned downstairs, packing up all her pieces and tidying everything up. She prepared a meal then returned to the bedroom and gently woke Gerald.

He sat up and touched his head warily. 'Doesn't hurt so much now, at least,' he said. He tried to get up, but sank back down. 'Hmm, bit wobbly,' he tried again and managed to stand. Unsteadily he made his way across the room and out onto the landing, semi-shielding his eyes from the bright light.

'I'll turn the lights down in the kitchen' she said, darting ahead of him.

'Do I look all right?' Gerald said as he sat down and turned his face towards her.

'Yes, why?'

'My face feels a bit funny, like I've been laying on it in a strange way.'

'Smile,' Cordelia said as a test to see if someone had recently had a small stroke flagged itself in her head.

Gerald smiled.

'Looks okay,' Cordelia said thoughtfully, 'but perhaps we ought to make an appointment with the doctor tomorrow.'

'Really, for a migraine?'

'Just in case it wasn't a migraine,' she said as she set food before them both.

Gerald had gone up to bed and Cordelia decided to just check her emails before she joined him. The top one was yet another from an artist and she was ready to be firm and decline any last minute changes, only to find it was merely an invitation to a first night of a different exhibition. Next two were junk from Amazon and then the words 'I KNOW' leapt out at her in the subject bar of the next email. She stared at it, her body fizzing round the edges. The sender was Kay Dee. Dee, her own pet name! Kay, a woman? Did she know anyone called Kay? She clicked on the bar and the email opened.

Subject line 'I KNOW' ... text inside just the same, plus a photograph. The 'preview' showed her the side window of the silver car, even in thumbnail she could recognise herself and Max. Despite herself she clicked on it and it bloomed huge, no doubting the couple in the car. She recalled the man they'd seen. His shambling gait as he shifted away; she shivered. She snatched at the mouse and pressed delete. Immediately panicked and fumbled around to find the 'trash' to reinstate it. She couldn't just ignore it, it wouldn't go away. She sat there feeling cold, her hands pressed to her face. They would have to stop meeting. She had to warn Max.

Chapter 33

I made sure I was out early enough to see the silver car flit across the junction if it did. Ensconced in the bus-stop I kept my eyes firmly in the right direction, but no silver car appeared, in fact no cars crossed that junction at all. I waited past the time I should have called it quits then slowly walked up to the shop, with many quick glances back just in case. What did I expect? If I were in their shoes I'd have stopped meeting .... or changed the meeting times and venues. That's what I would have done. Did it matter? I still had all the ammunition I required, plus now I knew it really was not all above board, there was something to hide. With this thought I cheerily entered the shop and greeted Dave.

I wandered back to Hideaway half thinking about what to do next about Cordelia, with Jim nudging me about seeing Marian. Well, that part was simple, we were going running again tonight and I'd be able to firm up our date at the theatre in front of Mr Green-fingers, ha! Bugle Boy happened to be the poster I pretended to study while covertly watching Cordelia outside the Court House. I've always had a penchant for the Glenn Miller story, I'd heard good things about the previous tour and women are supposed to love musicals anyway. Two birds with one stone. I decided to book the tickets when I got back and a nice restaurant too, an absolute clincher, Jim smirked.

Coffee made, ciggie on the go, opened up the computer and headed for search, only to see the email icon flashing. Okay, I'd just have a quick look. Okay! It was from Cordelia. I could hear my heart, it was thumping so hard; the reality of many a thriller cliché. What had she written?

Who are you? Why are you doing this?

That was it, no accusations, no pleading, no dear Kay, no signing off as Cordelia. I was a bit disappointed, but what did I really expect? I went into my Saren account and typed....

> Never mind who - for now
> Just to see the supercilious smile slide off your stuck-up face – for now

... and hit send. That should screw her. The adrenaline was pumping, I drew deeply on the cigarette and setting it to smoulder in the ashtray called up the chapter I was working on.

My antagonist has got the Ambassador's wife just where he wants her. She will do anything for him to prevent him telling the Ambassador. He's decided to test her because he knows she must be completely bent to his will before he gets her to betray her country. I've decided, he's going to be both disciplined and undisciplined. The Ambassador's wife is directed to a meeting, in a hotel room. She has been told she must meet a man there and do whatever he says. It will be my antagonist. He has let his fantasies get the better of him and has rationalised it as making her completely his. Though she'll have to pleasure him it will be his undoing.

I almost missed the time for the rendezvous for Harriers. I think it must be doing me some good, that and the reduction in smoking, as I ran up the hill to the top arriving just in time and not too out of breath. However, not only had I not made my theatre booking but I was still at a loss for a good place to eat before the production. This was only made worse when Kevan suggested Marian might like to go with him to a jazz gig on Saturday at somewhere that sounded like Southall, but turned out to be South Hill. She grinned and accepted straight off. Without my preparation I just had to keep quiet and let Jim nag me all the way there and back.

***

It's not the same, not being able to spy on her going off with her secret lover. It had become part of my wind-up mechanism. I did make sure I was around at the right time, just in case yesterday was a one off. It wasn't. There wasn't even a reply from her on the email.

I opened up my work and tried to write. I sat staring at the screen for a long time before I realised I needed the buzz to get writing, and she hadn't provided it. I trawled through the photos and video clips I had of her. Perhaps I'd send another one; perhaps that would provoke a response. I loaded up the video that showed him turning the car, stepped it through frame by frame and snapped the one where he is full face, just about to turn the car around. I went back to my Saren account and attached the photograph. I almost didn't put a subject or text, but went with 'nice pic' for both and hit send. All Right! I was feeling alive now, even without a reply for her. I was ready to seduce the Ambassador's wife, or rather, make her my sex-slave, seduction per se not being required in the circumstances.

The phone ringing dragged me out of the Antagonist's bed. He's a bastard. She's done everything he asked yet has remained somehow aloof and separate. It has irritated him beyond reason.

'Yes.' I snapped.

'Hello? Sean?'

'William! What is it?'

'Just,' he gave a little nervous laugh, 'just a social call.'

'Social? You mean you are checking up on me, well you needn't bother. I can confidently say you can have the manuscript next ... Thursday.'

'Oh wonderful.'

'Now get off my back. By the way the gardener's going to slash the place into shape at the weekend.'

'What, oh, of course, and ...'

'I'll be moving out the following weekend, as soon as I've delivered the manuscript.'

'Really? Don't you need to stay there, where it's peaceful, to do the edits?'

'Shit, no, why would I stay in this dump. You haven't told anyone where I've been have you?'

'No, of course not. You said no one should know.'

'Well bloody keep it that way, won't you.'

'I'll look forward to reading the manu ...'

I put the phone down; I needed to write.

Chapter 34

Max would understand, she was sure of that, but he hadn't replied to her email last night so she was on edge from the moment she woke. She lay there waiting for Gerald to get up, which he did, promptly at his usual time. As soon as he started downstairs she grabbed her iPhone and checked her emails. No reply. Agitated she jumped out of bed, wrapped a gown around herself, darted down to set breakfast and put the kettle on. Gerald was doing his usual routine of exercises so she dived back upstairs to shower and dress. Fifteen minutes later she was back at the breakfast table, wearing a light summer dress with her damp hair clipped up out of the way, pouring boiling water into the teapot,

'How are you feeling this morning?' she said, covering the pot with a teacosy.

'Fine, no headache, nothing. I don't think we need bother the doctor.'

'Well, it wouldn't hurt.'

'No. If it happens again I'll go, I think it was just a bug or something.'

'Possibly, but, really ...'

'I said, no,' his voice firm but accompanied by a tight smile. Cordelia knew this reaction, it meant Gerald had made his mind up and when that happened it took an earthquake to change it, she gave a little shrug of acquiescence.

Gerald left for work spot on time, and as soon as Cordelia returned to the table she flipped open her iPad. A reply at last:

> Hi Cordelia,
> Bad news! What would anyone get out of doing this to us?
> Better not reply to it, it would only encourage her.

Any idea who it is?
I agree, we should miss meetings until we know what's going on - though you know telling Gerald would stop all this nonsense!
We can catch up when we meet Margo on Tuesday, but keep me informed if you get any more.
Love Max

Immediately she wondered if the Kay woman would find them in Plymouth, but just as quickly rejected the idea. This must just be someone who had opportunely seen them together and was making mischief, the email equivalent of a poison pen letter.

She poured herself another cup of tea. As she sipped she saw the camera man again in her mind's eye. A shiver of ice then fire flowed through her, she stood, feeling her face flush hot. This was not just some random observer, some busybody, this was deliberate stalking. Suddenly she felt very exposed, glancing around her own kitchen as if someone was watching her even now. She tightened her arms around her body and ran up to the bedroom; sat on the bed, somehow feeling safer there.

Think! Think! Who could it be, and why? Damn, Max was right, she should never have replied. It was like those internet trolls you heard about; the advice there was never reply. She gazed off into space, trying to see all their last meetings from a different point of view. Had there been anyone around at the same time as their meeting that she, even vaguely, recognised? Not at the pick up? Not on Kit Hill? Yes, on Zaggy Lane, they had passed Jim, but he couldn't have seen it was her, she'd made sure of that and, besides, he was new to the village, wouldn't have any axe to grind. She thought about the photographer again. No, he wasn't like him either, more squat, fatter, no not Jim, but the camera man was key. Perhaps the emailer wasn't a she, perhaps Kay was a pseudonym? After all, who would use their real name for such a thing?

Cordelia got up and stood by the window, looking out across the valley, the scenery was tranquil, green rolling hills, a glimpse of water in the distance, perfect. Could she see a way to tell Gerald? She shivered, not only did she know how he felt about personal betrayal, she'd seen how he'd reacted to dishonesty, within the business he was a partner in, and it was with an uncomprehending and implacable anger and a complete disassociation from the perpetrators, despite mitigating circumstances.

Had she been careless of her carefully constructed life? She shook herself, that carefully constructed life included many little services to the community, and if she didn't get her act together the Art Fair, and the charities it made money for, wouldn't be getting anything. She changed her clothes, opted for jeans and a favourite long-sleeved tee-shirt embellished with sewn-on slashes of colour, and, dressed in this new armour, headed back downstairs to finish work on the art display.

She was engrossed, using her visual talents to walk herself through the exhibits one last time. The view of the Medusa's head should be stunning as it would be revealed standing in its own white alcove as viewers came to the far end of the exhibits. It would also be an exception, an exhibit with no price on it. John, completely bemused, had agreed to show the exhibit as for sale only at Fraser Kane's London art emporium and Fraser had agreed to give a donation to her charities out of his profits when it sold. It was a joy to see John's face, though funny to see him struggle to believe her, even when she pointed out his cut would only be half of the £20,000 price tag.

The email noise alerted her, her phone was nearest so she picked it up and almost dropped it as she saw the name Kay.Dee again. It was a reply – it answered the email she should not have sent. The words dripped venom, and menace. The 'for now' rang in her head. This person obviously hated her. Why? Why? Surely anyone could see she wasn't like that? Not stuck-up, not supercilious. She sank down finding herself shaking. Her throat felt tight and sore, her mouth dry. She re-read it. It hadn't changed. It was still threatening. She fumbled as she made to forward the message to Max.

> Hi Max,
> Sorry, I had already replied – asking who and why … just got this back.
> Sorry. Dee

She would not respond again. Her whole body wanted to scream 'Why?' but she would not respond, that was what she, or maybe he, wanted.

Ping – email again, from Max;

> Hi, Not good, sounds vindictive. You must have really upset someone, any idea who?
> Just don't reply again – just leave it.
> See you on Tues – Max

Email to Max:

> Not sure who it could be, though may be a man, not a woman.
> Remember seeing that bloke on Kit Hill? He had to be the one who took that picture.
> I'll keep thinking. Love Dee

Keep thinking, she told herself as she prepared a light lunch. There had to be a clue somewhere. Man or woman. The heart was fanciful, a bit feminine, but the photographer was definitely a man. She gasped, could there be two of them, a husband and wife team? Somehow this felt worse than just one person with strange ideas, the thought that there could be a pair who were feeling vindictive towards her was quite frightening.

After a tense day she felt relieved when Gerald came home, and glad to hear that he was feeling fine and had been all day. This, at least, was good news. All evening she struggled to keep her voice light and her attention on the programme they were watching, it was exhausting, yet when they retired to bed she was unable to sleep. Those words kept running around in her head, 'never mind who – for now', 'just to see the supercilious smile slide off your stuck-up face.' Her face burned in the darkness, was that what people really saw, really thought about her?

Next morning she felt as if she had not slept at all, but managed to go through their usual routine without Gerald asking her what was wrong. As soon as he left, however, she felt insecure and decided that a walk might put a better perspective on things. Almost by habit she set off on the route that would take her towards Downham farm, along Zaggy Lane and eventually around past the Church and pub to home. As she strode out she breathed deeply of the still cool air, yet to be warmed up by what promised to be a sunny day, and could feel the tension slipping from her shoulders. Zaggy Lane was even cooler, shadowed as it was by over-arching trees, but as she emerged from the other end into the full sunlight she felt the warmth on her cheeks and let a little joy slide into her mind, pushing away the darkness.

She glanced at her watch as she passed the Church, would it be too early to call on Marian? She turned down the cul-de-sac and rang Marian's bell. There was no reply, though Marian's car was in the drive. Cordelia wondered if she was in the workshop already so took out her phone to call Marian's mobile, but there was an email waiting there, and it was from Kay.Dee. Standing on Marian's doorstep Cordelia opened the email – it said 'nice pic' and had an attachment, she opened that. The screen filled with a photograph, a close up of Max through his windscreen, obviously turning the car in Zaggy Lane. She felt her inner core shrinking, her skin sensitive to the breeze, her hands felt heavy, as if movement was too difficult. Where was safe? The little peace she'd gained while walking drained away, the openness suddenly felt oppressive. Cordelia looked around, there was nobody in the cul-de-sac, no one looking from a window, hiding behind a curtain, but how could she tell, if somewhere like Zaggy Lane was being watched? She looked at Marian's closed door again and with a huge effort started to move away, heading home. As soon as she reached the main road she started to run, by the time she reached The Old Chapel she was in tears and gulping for air.

Chapter 35

I am so close, I can almost smell the end. The Puppeteer is ready for the show. The Ambassador's wife is his, she cannot back out, she has been bent to his will. If the reader is not turned on by this stage then they are made of wood.

I read and re-read the last chapter I wrote, trying to find the words that will start the final one, but nothing came. Surely I am not so dependent on the adrenaline surge I get from taunting that woman? She hasn't replied to my last email. Although, as I hadn't sent a question I suppose she could think she was safe not to reply. Well, that will never do.

I opened my account, used the Saren web address and sent an email, I labelled it 'Masquerade'

> How does it feel to know that I know what you really are?
> You think you can fool the world? You cannot hide from me, I know you.
> Answer me ... or else the photos can find their way into dear Gerald's inbox as easily as yours!

I found that I actually had a hard-on by the time I had finished typing, the image of her on her knees had returned to me. That was a good one to remember if I needed to ramp up the hints about the sender of these emails. As for the moment, I soon channelled that energy into the words for my last chapter, not coming up for air until I had reached the climax and the end.

My cigarette had long died, I was ravenous and thirsty. Somehow the deprivation had entered into the soul of the writing, and I was certain that when I looked over it the next day it would reverberate with the pressure my mind and body were under as the words flowed through me.

I decided to reward myself with a trip to the pub for my meal and to unwind. It was only seven so I grabbed a small torch and set off on a very pleasant stroll up the lane. I took the Chapel route, of course, and enjoyed myself envisaging her receiving my emails. I wish I could eavesdrop, watch even; I am sure it would be very educational.

Once in the pub I was surprised to see the corner stool at the bar empty, my usual bar crony was not there. Regardless I pulled out the one next to it and picked up a menu. My mouth was fairly watering as I read through, scenting the aromas wafting out from the kitchen as other diners were served. I had just given my order and picked up my glass of Proper Job musing that I shall have to find a pub up in the smoke that sells this one as I've grown to like it, when Dave walked in.

He gave a swift grin and circled to his usual seat, acknowledging with a nod that I had left it for him. 'Evening,' he said to me, 'Pint of Tribute, please,' to the girl behind the bar.

'On me,' I added to the girl. She looked up and nodded, coming to me for the money as she put the glass down.

'Cheers,' Dave said.

'Cheers!' I grinned over my glass at him.

'You seem cheerful?'

'Darn right, just about finished.'

'Ah! Marking, all done? Guess the poor buggers'll be getting their results soon then.'

I took a long draw of my beer, shit, I'd almost forgotten I was marking exam papers! 'Yeah,' I said, placing the glass down, 'and I'm glad it's done, been a bit of a drudge, shut up with sheets of paper every day.'

He gave an amiable grunt.

After a while my meal came and I wolfed it down and treated myself to a dessert, piled high with ice cream and clotted cream, I was going to miss the abundance of clotted cream too, they fairly chuck it on anything here.

I don't know where the time went, Dave was in an affable mood, I got introduced to another couple who came in with their huge lurcher and shared dog talk with them, I used to have a dog - though the wife took the dog when we split. There was a pleasant buzz of busyness and enjoyment, it being a Saturday night and, as it was my turn to get the pints in again, I turned to the bar just in time to see Kevan ushering Marian through the lounge part of the pub. Jim gave me the mental equivalent of an elbow in the ribs and I watched covertly as she, all smiling said something to him, left and took a seat out of my sight, while he came to the bar. The lounge and the saloon bar share the same actual counter, though in different rooms connected by an open walk-through that, at one time, might have actually had a door in it, so when Kevan looked in my direction, at the barmaid who was by now serving me, he smiled and raised a hand. With Jim gritting my teeth in a facsimile of a smile I gave a nod in return. I handed Dave's beer to him and turned back for my own, noticing that Kevan was ordering a couple of Southern Comforts.

They left the pub before I did; I didn't like the look in Marian's eye, she looked too sparkly. She didn't see me, or if she did she didn't acknowledge me there; bitch. It put a bit of a downer on my evening I have to say, and I left the pub maudlin in drink rather than merry. I walked past the Chapel on my way home. In fact, I relieved my bladder in the darkened corner of the hedge beside their car park area.

I wouldn't be around here much longer, what did it matter who Marian went with? I wandered all across the road, staring up at stars, wondering how come they could be so very brilliant and so many! Once into Zaggy Lane, where the trees meet overhead and block out even the starlight, I switched on my little torch and wavered my way through the dark until I reached Hideaway.

I woke late in the morning, my head giving me plenty to think about, but no space to actually think. How much had I drunk? I could recall about six pints, but to end up with my round it must have been seven. I hadn't drunk so much beer for years; G&T being my preferred tipple in my real life.

After downing a few pints of water and spooning in a bit of cereal I had just begun to feel a little better when I heard a vehicle outside. It took me half a minute, and the time it took to drag myself through to the living room window overlooking the drive, to remember that Kevan was coming today to tidy the garden. He turned the van and climbed out immediately going to the back doors of the van and opening them. I retreated upstairs and pulled jeans on, over the boxers I'd slept in, struggled into yesterday's tee-shirt and went out to see him. He'd already got a professional looking strimmer out with a vicious looking blade on it. My author mind logged that; an interesting weapon.

'Morning,' I said as cheerfully as my aching head would allow, while the Jim side of me wondered how Kevan had spent last night, I answered him with, can't have been that great or he'd not be here this early.

'Hi, I hope it won't bother you too much, it'll be a bit noisy though.'

'No, it's fine, I've finished my marking and if it gets to me I may just go off for a while,' I said, thinking of my thumping head. He nodded and went back to preparing the strimmer.

It did get to me, so after a shower I took myself off out in the MG. I decided I'd go up Kit Hill legitimately and sat there enjoying the peace and quiet for quite a while. I even dozed, waking feeling ravenous and refreshed. I recalled the tea-rooms nearby that offered all-day breakfasts and feeling ready to tackle something just like that headed back down the hill. It was getting on for four when I set off back to Hideaway. Kevan had left and the garden looked bigger now that the grass was short and some of the bushes had been cut back, it also looked forlorn and scalped, the pale stalks sparsely covering where the long grasses had lain lush and haphazard as the wind and my walking had left them. There was a note under the knocker which I opened as I went in. It was on his headed notepaper but he must have rested on his knee or something as the words looked like a childish scrawl;

Jim, Can do 1 hr Weds.
Will still need to do nex Sunday to. KD

The English teacher in me mentally corrected the spellings as I read it; ignoramus. I tossed it on the table and I settled myself down to re-read my final chapter and make corrections and edits. An hour later and I was feeling happy. I was home free. I'd use the rest of the week to read and brush-up here and there then send it off on the promised day. I realised that I had not checked my emails the whole day so clicked on and opened them up. Immediately I saw she had replied; I couldn't resist smiling at the feeling of triumph it gave me.

Chapter 36

Cordelia struggled to unlock her house door, her hands shaking and her breathing ragged. She staggered in and headed straight to the downstairs toilet where she retched. Her face felt slick with sweat and her head had begun to ache. She had to tell Max, who else could she confide in? She splashed water on her face and, drying it with the hand towel, went to her iPad on the kitchen table and opened it, calling up the email again. She sat and immediately forwarded it to Max with the message. 'And now this?' not daring to watch the clip again. She sat there waiting, almost expecting him to reply at once. She became so agitated waiting that she sent him a text, saying 'look at your emails' and waited again. She'd just about given up when an email appeared.

> Hi Cordelia,
> Weird. Seems very organised to have got that. Don't like it. I wonder, should you just tell Gerald and then this person will have nothing to hold over you? Think about it. Talk on Tuesday.
> Max

Tell Gerald? Was it at all possible? She couldn't think in the surroundings that they had made together, everything in the building said that any explanation would be seen as a betrayal, that he would not understand at all, any of it. She dressed for a proper walk and headed out to the car and took herself off to the coast.

Walking beside the sea had changed her mood as she drove back safe in the knowledge that Gerald would be home shortly after she got in. She parked the car and let herself into the house. She checked her iPad, no more emails from Kay.Dee, and no other emails she cared to deal with.

As she packed everything she thought she might need for their weekend trip to Berkshire, for the christening of Gerald's great nephew, she kept up her usual pattern of chatter and observation; while Gerald meticulously packed his bag in silence. Throughout, however, she was still listening for the tell-tale sound of an incoming email, and finding some innocuous reason for going out of the room to check it. By the time it came for them to go to bed Cordelia felt exhausted, but sleep wouldn't come. Eventually, slipping out of bed carefully so that Gerald wasn't disturbed, she took a couple of paracetamol, which usually made her sleepy even if she didn't need them for a headache.

The morning was bright and Cordelia made an effort not to look at the iPad or phone at all before breakfast. They ate briskly with Gerald scanning the newspaper and Cordelia writing a couple of birthday cards that she needed to send that week. As soon as Cordelia had tidied up the kitchen and Gerald had put the cases into the car they set off. Cordelia recalled how she'd been a little annoyed that it was so close to the Art Fair, as she was often so busy that weekend, but now she was only too glad to get away from Hingsbury. They'd booked into a hotel Gerald was familiar with in Ascot, and would take their time getting up there, the christening being on Sunday morning with a lunch to follow.

So it wasn't until after they'd had dinner at the hotel that Cordelia allowed herself to checked her emails. As she opened them and saw one from Kay.Dee she almost wished she had left her phone at home, yet, when she read the new message she was glad she hadn't. What could have happened if she had not got this one? What did she do now?

It was obvious she would have to reply, she thought as she sat on the edge of the bath reading the words 'How does it feel?' So many replies flooded into her head, dirty - not because of anything I am doing, but because of what you are doing. Hurt, misunderstood, targeted, scared - but she wasn't sure what to actually say. She left the bathroom and decided to think about her reply, yet she sensed she couldn't leave it too long, in case the Kay person did as they threatened.

The next morning, after a sumptuous breakfast, they set off for Gerald's nephew's house in Sunningdale. She still hadn't formulated her reply yet, but was acutely aware of time passing.

Just twenty-eight and a commodity broker, Gerald's nephew's four bedroom house just off the A30 in Sunningdale had cost him over a million two years ago and he was quick to point out to Gerald that he'd bought at the bottom of the latest market crash and it was already worth two hundred thousand more. Side by side you could see the family resemblance and they had a head for figures in common too. His wife was pretty, sharp and a PA in the trading house where he worked. Cordelia had only met Gerald's nephew twice before, once at his own christening and then, two years ago, at his wedding, so when they met the other godparents, all young friends, Cordelia wondered if they'd just asked Gerald to be one because they reasoned he had no one else to leave his estate to, then chided herself for being cynical.

All through the service her mind kept wandering to the email and how to answer it. Despite her resolution, despite what Max had said, she had to answer this one otherwise she was sure that the pictures would be sent. There was something gloating about the words. Something that told her this person would be happy to send them, happy to see her life shredded. As soon as they reached the restaurant where the luncheon was being held Cordelia excused herself and slipped off to the ladies. Once in a cubicle she called up the email and replied. She'd decided to keep it simple, not to inflame the Kay person, not to give them too much to work on. Acutely aware that she was spending too long away from the others, she typed her reply:

> How do I feel? Upset and worried. There, that's what you wanted, isn't it?
> You have no idea about me really, please just leave me alone.

She had spoken to Gerald's sister earlier and was re-introduced to his nephew's wife's parents too but, unusually, she had found it difficult to get into conversation with the people at the lunch. The rest of the group consisted of younger people, friends of Gerald's nephew and his wife. Gerald had been sat next to his sister and they had conversed most of the mealtime. Cordelia had been placed across the large circular table from Gerald, between one of the other godparents, another commodity broker, and a young woman who chatted on incessantly about fashion to the woman the other side of her. Cordelia felt it just too much effort and had just eaten, with the occasional smiling glance at anyone who caught her eye to say, yes, I am enjoying myself, though inside she was churning over the past.

After the lunch and the giving of gifts they made their excuses, citing the long journey home, and left.

'Are you all right?' Gerald asked as they started their drive.

'What?' Cordelia had been re-running her reply to the email, how would it be read and received by the Kay person.

'Are you all right? You've been very quiet, and you were quiet at lunch too.'

Cordelia hadn't realised that Gerald had even noticed her over lunch.

'Just a bit tired,' she said, 'I didn't sleep as well as usual last night.'

'Ah, me too,' he said, 'I never sleep as well as I do in my own bed.' He seemed satisfied with her reply and left the topic alone, turning on the radio to listen to classical music as he drove.

It was late when they arrived home. Soon after unloading the car Cordelia made them each a cup of hot chocolate and they set off for bed. She couldn't resist a last look at her emails, all quiet from Kay.Dee, just one from Marian inviting her to pop round for a coffee in the morning, with a sigh Cordelia went to sleep.

Coffee with Marian was a beacon for Cordelia in the morning. As soon as Gerald was off she tidied and cleaned the kitchen, dusted and ran the Dyson around the main room and got the washing machine running. There was no reply from the Kay person and she felt hopeful that there would not be.

Marian greeted her at the door as she arrived. 'Saw you coming,' she said throwing the door wide. Cordelia went in and straight through to the kitchen. Marian peeled back the top of a packet of an all-chocolate biscuit collection, pushed it towards Cordelia and soon busied herself with the coffee machine. Cordelia noticed Marian was particularly bouncy and bright-eyed as she got the coffees ready, speaking rapidly, asking about Cordelia's weekend, as if to get it over with quickly. When she sat down she positioned herself opposite Cordelia and leant both elbows on the table, steepled her arms, clasped her hands and almost rested her chin on top of them, eye's twinkling she said 'Guess what?'

'What?'

Marian quickly tilted her head on an angle and back again. 'Kevan,' she smiled.

'Oh? Kevan? Do tell?' Cordelia could tell now that her friend was both excited and pleased with herself.

'Well, we went out Saturday night, had a great time at the jazz night, a couple of Southern Comforts at the pub on the way back then,' she paused, 'we went back to his place. Oh,' she flashed one hand like a stop signal, 'very discreet, do you know where he lives, no? It's all on its own, past Downham Forge on the lane towards Ashton. Parking out of sight of the road, no neighbours.'

Cordelia smiled, she understood her friend's need for discretion, word travelled like wildfire in a village. 'Well?'

'He's a lovely man,' her eyes widened a little, 'in every way,' she was positively grinning.

'Lucky you, and who would have thought it?'

'Yeah, he's so much nicer than any of the blokes I've been seeing, and that includes Jim.'

'I thought you were seeing him this week?'

'Yeah, and it seems rude to just cancel? What do you think?'

'Depends? Will he have bought tickets already? That would be a bit off if he has.'

'Bugger, you are so reasonable, and right. Yeah, if he's forked out already I better go along. It would be mean to leave him to go to the theatre alone.'

On her way home, feeling happier than she had for a long time, Cordelia felt her iPhone signal the arrival of an email. She slipped the phone from her pocket and opened it up. She stopped walking. It was from Kay.Dee again. She tried to put it back in her pocket, but couldn't. She had to know right away what it said. She glanced around, there appeared to be no one on the road. She could see her house and Kevan's van parked up outside it ahead. She hesitated, then broke into a trot to get home as quickly as possible.

Kevan was nowhere to be seen, so he was probably round the back of the house working on the terraces. She hurried straight in and sat down in the kitchen. She placed the phone on the table and flipped open her iPad instead and opened the email.

> Really? You didn't seem upset when I saw you last week.
> You like to give orders, don't you? Like to have people at your beck and call, is that what turns you on?
> You think I have what I want?
> NO, YOU HAVE NO IDEA WHAT I WANT.
> Go on ... ASK ME!

Cordelia sat very still, her core felt cold and solid. She noticed the attachment icon and swallowed as she clicked on it. The picture was of her own bedroom, with her in it. She pushed the iPad away, rising so fast that the chair toppled over, ran to look out the kitchen window, fingers clenched. Logically, the photograph had to be taken from over the other side of the valley but as she looked it was clear that the land over there was all lower as the other side of the valley was a lower hill than the one The Old Chapel stood on. How could that picture have been taken? The flicker of a memory of the 'toy' they thought they saw on Kit Hill, a remote controlled helicopter or something, whizzing fast up the front of the car, too fast to focus on. Could a picture be taken with something like that? Was nowhere safe? She thought of her bedroom, it had felt like her sanctuary, she shuddered.

She had to get out of the house. She'd go into Plymouth and meet Gerald for lunch. She ran upstairs, glancing at the window half afraid to see something there, grabbed her bag and ran down again. Out and round to her car. Damn! It was blocked in by Kevan's trailer. She stalked round to the back of the house calling his name.

He suddenly appeared behind her, 'What's up?'

'Kevan, you've blocked me in, I need to move, I need to get out. Now!' she sounded sharp even to her own ears but fear was driving her.

'Sorry, I'll just go and get my keys,' he said and headed towards the mower shed. She went back to where his van was parked, standing waiting for him, she glanced at his van, subconsciously read the name, 'K.D. Garden Services'. Her mouth went dry, and her skin prickled before she had consciously made a connection, and he was there opening the van door, jumping in, turning the ignition and still she hadn't moved. Kay Dee.

Chapter 37

The van and trailer pulled past her and broke the spell; she moved, ran to her car and got in, reversed it out quickly and turned to go back down towards the village. As she passed the van Kevan gave her a little salute; she shuddered. She had intended to drive into Plymouth but she suddenly remembered Marian. Should she warn her about Kevan? How could she without telling her everything else? She'd slowed the car to a crawl. She had to. She had to warn her. As she drew up opposite Marian's cul-de-sac she hesitated then turned in, pulling up sharply outside Marian's house but, before she turned the engine off, she was filled with such dread that she accelerated away again making a hash of turning in the banjo end of the road, revving the car far too much as she flew up to the junction and headed off to Plymouth.

Gerald was busy when she arrived at the offices, but calmer now and putting on a great performance, she said she'd wait and smilingly sat in the conference room where she had been shown. When Gerald's PA, Jenny, brought her a coffee after a few minutes, she seemed totally composed.

'Cordelia?' Gerald came into the room where she sat, a cold coffee in front of her.

'I, I just came into town, I wondered if you'd like to do lunch?'

Gerald looked at her as if inspecting an unusual line of figures. 'Oh, that's all? Yes, I can be free for lunch,' he smiled. Not for the first time Cordelia felt glad of Gerald's lack of interpersonal perception, in this case it made it easier not to break-down in front of him.

By the time they were sitting in a small restaurant they liked down on the Barbican, Cordelia knew what she wanted to say.

'I've been thinking,' she started, he looked at her, waiting, 'I'd like us to change gardeners,' she went on quickly, 'perhaps even with fewer hours, I can do more and it really doesn't need so much time or money spent on it now.'

'Well, you may be right, but we can just tell Kevan we do not need him for so many ...'

'No!' the word was out before Cordelia had calculated the effect. 'I really want a different gardener.'

'Why?'

'Perhaps with new ideas?' Cordelia tried to get her plan back on track.

'I don't see that, you have always directed ...'

'No. It has to be someone else.' Her eyes began to fill despite her fingernails digging into her palms, hidden beneath the level of the table.

'What's wrong?'

'He was very rude to me today when I asked him to move his trailer ... I just don't want him working for us again.'

'Why didn't you say so before?' Gerald appeared to physically expand as he understood the situation.

'I, it felt silly ...'

'Nonsense, I'll cancel his employment right away.'

On the way home Cordelia tried to decide whether she ought to warn her friend, whether she could. In the end she decided to sleep on it and decide in the morning. The garden was looking perfect as she surveyed it before she went in but it now seemed filled with opportunities for a gardener to spy on her. She wasn't sure if she ever wanted someone else working for them.

She sat in front of her iPad and challenged herself to look at the last email from Kay Dee; Kevan. She opened it and read it with new eyes. 'You like to give orders, don't you? Like to have people at your beck and call, is that what turns you on?' the clue was there, there was no one else that they employed on a regular basis, and, as Gerald had said, Cordelia had guided the overall design of the garden. It was the next bit that snagged her attention; it was true, she had no idea what Kevan wanted, she hadn't really even known until that morning exactly where he lived, though she knew it was out of the village on the Downham road. Then there was the threat, 'Go on ... ASK ME!' - what if she didn't? Last time he'd said he'd send pictures to Gerald if she didn't reply, was that still hanging over her? She hit reply, typed. 'What?' but hovered the cursor over 'send' wondering whether to add that she knew who he was. In the end she hit send without adding anything; she was too frightened to provoke him.

To her great relief there was no reply when she woke up on Tuesday and, as soon as Gerald had left for the office, she began to get ready to see Margo and Max that afternoon. She replied to Margo's email that she'd sent saying she had arrived and was fine, she sent an email to Max arranging to meet in the foyer of the Holiday Inn at two o'clock. She checked on her final arrangements for the Art Fair and was just closing down all the various pages she had open when another email came through from Kay.Dee. Immediately she saw Kevan's face in her mind's eye, somehow darker and looking malicious. She opened the email.

> I knew you'd ask.
> I want you
> – just as I saw you a few weeks ago - on your knees!
> Now we only have to work out when.

She couldn't breathe, her face suffused with heat as the memory of another time flooded back. She slammed the iPad shut, but could not shut out the memories or the mutating images flaring inside her head. The urge to be sick overwhelmed her as she stumbled to the cloakroom, shaking she stood over the toilet pan, wondering what to do. One thing was for certain, she had to warn Marian before she got further involved with Kevan, he might be seriously disturbed, the word 'psychotic' came into her mind and it seemed to fit. Psychotic, delusional and frightening, somehow she was going to have to talk to Marian.

<c...># Chapter 38

Screw this, checking and editing is boring stuff. I so much prefer the creative bit, but I know it will save me more time later if I hand in a decently tidied piece of work. I have spent most of the day and have only checked just over a quarter of the manuscript, on the other hand I am more sure than ever that I have got another winner here. It sings. It trembles. It turns me on. And talking of turning on, I realised I needed to get those tickets booked so looked up the theatre. As soon as I got to it I saw the production had been cancelled. What? Why did the fool theatre not have 'cancelled' put over their posters too? Damn them. Now what? I tried to see if there was anything else on instead and the only thing was a matinee performance of 'Epiphany' in something called The Drum. What to do?

I checked that tickets were still available then rang Marian and asked if she was able to go to the theatre in the afternoon, explaining that they'd just contacted me to say the main show had been cancelled, but I could transfer the tickets to the afternoon. She was very hesitant. I waited for what seemed to be an age after she'd said 'let me see.' To push it I said we would be able to still go to the restaurant I'd booked, only after the theatre instead of before. This was all guff, of course. I hadn't got round to booking that either. It worked, she came back brightly with a 'what time?' and I arranged to pick her up at one to get there for a two-thirty start. As soon as I put the phone down I started researching a restaurant where we could eat early. I was in luck, there seemed to be a quality bistro-type place down on the Barbican within what looked like a reasonable walking distance from the theatre. Well pleased with myself I booked us in for five-thirty and left it at that.

Cordelia hoity-toity Steadman has replied. Still sounds haughty, just as I expected; time to bring her down a peg or two. Thinks I should leave her alone and that I have what I want. Oh no, I don't think so. I could feel the smile as I sent her a reply that would get her hot under the collar and dump the blame on Kevan at the same time, unless she was stupid. On a whim, I attached a still from the video taken through her bedroom window ... it was meant to be suggestive, as I pressed send I realised it was also pretty threatening. Never mind, perhaps it would soften her up.

I got plenty of revision done on the Tuesday morning and still had time to have a decent shower, shave and get spruced-up. I was determined to play the suave alternative to the rough and ready that Kevan was offering her, after all, this was an educated woman; my tactics were to win her with my mind and a few glasses of booze, I already knew what she liked. I was prompt to pick Marian up, she looking feminine in what I guess they'd call a summer dress, and we were swiftly off to Plymouth. I really don't know the place so I let myself be guided by her as she suggested we park in a car park behind the theatre.

'Not sure what this will be like,' I said as we entered The Drum, appropriately named I thought as I felt cordoned inside a drum shaped box.

'I looked it up,' Marian said, 'it's by the Youth Theatre here, even worked on the script collaboratively.'

'I mean, it's not quite what I had invited you to - a professional outfit,' I extemporised, hell, I hadn't realised it was the youth group – what rubbish were we in for?

I sat through it. Marian seemed entranced as the disparate characters, far too many for my liking and scattered around the world, made their decisions, their epiphanies, that would change their whole lives. In my experience it doesn't happen like that, decisions either creep up through events until they become a fait accompli, or jump on you when you least expect them requiring spit-second choices; none of this pondering and careful weighing up of ways to change your future, no, none of that unbelievable stuff. Marian gave them top marks for enthusiasm as we left.

I glanced at my watch as we walked towards the wide boulevard that joins the Hoe with the city centre, four-fifty – plenty of time to reach the Bistro.

'Shall we walk via the Hoe?' I suggested, 'We've time.'

'Good idea,' Marian gave me a welcome smile, the first true one from her this outing. I was beginning to think she'd rumbled me, or Jim, that she had somehow sensed I was leaving soon. Rubbish, I know, but women can be extraordinarily perceptive sometimes. We crossed the road and were sauntering towards the Hoe, the Holiday Inn Hotel was ahead of us on our left when two people exited together. They walked away from us, but I was sure that one of them was *her*, Cordelia. The other had to be him, her mystery man, and leaving a hotel together to boot. They stopped and faced each other, we were gaining on them now, I had to risk it.

'Isn't that your friend from the village?' I asked Marian.

'Where?'

'Right ahead, by the road, talking to that,' I hesitated, 'younger man.' I dropped in the thought with the words.

'Oh? Yes, certainly looks like C'delia?' at which point the two of them turned and walked swiftly away in different directions.

As we reached the spot where they had been standing we both turned and looked the way Cordelia had gone just as her car drove past us, no doubting that registration. I'm not sure if she saw us though, her eyes never faltered from the road ahead, and we soon saw why, as she approached a silver car with its indicator flashing she slowed and let it out, his car, and they drove off in convoy.

We walked on across the road and up to the Hoe without saying anything about what we had seen. I didn't want to push it as I had that warning shot about being interested in Cordelia from Marian before. It wasn't until we were sitting with a nice glass of Medoc having ordered our meal that Marian said anything.

'Fancy seeing C'delia.'

'Hmm, do you know the man?'

'No,' she said slowly, as if thinking.

What was she thinking? I'd like to know. Was she thinking what I was, that we'd caught them after an afternoon tryst? A bit careless I thought, especially when her husband worked in Plymouth, but who knows what mad decisions people make in the grip of lust.

I made sure of three things, one, that Jim was his usual friendly, open self with lashings of wit and funny anecdotes that I keep up my sleeve for special occasions. Two, that I kept topping up her glass every time it sank below half. I only had one small glass of wine, which I kept topping up with water, I was driving; it was an easy excuse. Oh, yes, and three, my back-up devise, a tiny pinch of Valium. Yeah, I had a few tablets left since my depression after the divorce, and one thing I'd discovered back then was a small dose made a glass of wine feel like a bottle. It wasn't for me this time though, only if things weren't going well. They weren't, she wasn't laughing at the jokes and she wasn't even trying much herself, just being polite.

By the time we left the restaurant she was leaning on my arm to help keep herself steady. I'd proffered my arm and she'd taken it willingly and tucked herself in tight for maximum stability. I was not about to complain. Her voice was louder than it usually is, and I smiled as Jim whispered that he might be in luck tonight after all. The evening was beautiful, warm and light, we strolled along the Hoe and then dropped back down into the town and along to where we'd left the car.

'What do you fancy?' I asked. She giggled, something that seemed slightly out of sync with a woman in her mid fifties. Yes, that was something she'd let slip near the end, both she and C'delia were the same age, fifty-five you'd never have known, for either of them. It wasn't putting Jim off. I mentioned that I was only forty-five and it set her off in peals of laughter. 'Ooh! Does that make me a cougar?' she asked. Not thinking of myself as toy boy material I replied, 'Hardly,' and she thought my reaction just too funny.

'I mean, shall we go back to my place for a nightcap?' I suggested, Jim nudging me into his plan.

That seemed to sober her up a little, at least, she paused. 'Not sure...' she let the silence drag on, 'not sure I should go back to your place.'

'But you said your place was under observation by the village Gestapo,' I quipped, my jokes were funny now too.

'Hahahaa, you are so right – lets go and hide away in Hideaway, hahahaa.'

I turned down Hideaway's lane and soon brought the MG to a gentle stop in front of the cottage. I managed to get round to her door before she'd opened it and helped her out, offering my arm again. As soon as we were inside I guided her to the sitting room and fetched a couple of tumblers and the bottle of Southern Comfort, from the kitchen.

'Little snifter?' Jim said, waggling the bottle before her.

'Ooo, my favourite.'

'Fancy that, mine too,' he grinned as he placed glasses on the coffee table and screwed off the cap, splashing plenty in each glass. Sometimes being an observant bugger comes in useful. He sat down beside her, handed her a glass and brought his up to touch it with a satisfying ring, 'Bottoms up,' Jim said, looking into her eyes, his other hand coming to rest gently on her thigh.

Chapter 39

Cordelia shook as she speed-dialled Marian's number. It went to answer phone. She looked at the phone, it would have to wait, it was bad enough that she didn't know how she was going to explain everything but she needed time to do it and she had to get a move on if she was going to meet Max at two.

Max was waiting in the foyer by the time Cordelia had found somewhere to park near the hotel. She hurried over to him, smiling yet finding it difficult to unclench her fists, it was all she could do to keep herself from trembling.

'What's wrong?' He'd noticed despite her efforts.

'I've had more emails, and, and I know who is sending them.'

'Who? Who is it?'

'Err, well, you won't know him, he's no one, just our gardener, well was. I've got Gerald to sack him already.'

'You told Gerald everything?' They waited by the lift.

'No! No, no, I told him, that he'd been rude to me,' she shrugged, 'true.'

'And you don't think he'll do anything?'

Cordelia stared at Max as the doors to the lift opened, he started forward; she stayed put. What might Kevan do in response to being sacked? Send the pictures to Gerald? Oh, she'd been a fool! Perhaps Gerald hadn't told him yet, perhaps she could get him to change his mind.

'Cordelia?' Max flicked his head to indicate that she should join him.

What is it that they say - keep your friends near and your enemies nearer? She stepped into the lift and Max pressed the button.

Margo opened the door with a flourish. Cordelia knew to expect nothing less.

'My dears,' she said. Cordelia couldn't help thinking her mother had aged a lot in the three years since she had seen her last. Her usual eyeliner was now too dark for her papery skin, in her late seventies she was beginning to show her true age for the first time. Yet, Cordelia knew she shared her mother's fortunate genes in looking younger than her years as she aged, the reverse of when she was in her teens, where her height and attitude had made her seem older. Old enough to know what she was doing, what the hazards were.

Margo gazed at Max as if he were a star. 'You were a beautiful baby,' she said. 'It is a pleasure to be able to meet you.'

'Likewise,' Max said, but his face showed he was not easy. 'Cordelia has told me how it happened that I was ... taken away.'

Margo turned her head dramatically as if avoiding a blow. She glanced back then, looking down, said in a small soft voice, 'I was wrong to ignore your mother's pleading, but, please, understand, Johnny was dying, and he was everything to me.' She shook her head, then slowly looked up at him, 'Dee says your – adoptive parents were nice, kind?'

'Yes, my parents were very good people, this is why I have only looked for Dee, and you, now, since they passed away.'

'Good,' she sighed, 'come and sit down. I understand you have children?' and proceeded to extract so much information about his family, his wife, her parents, the children and their likes and dislikes, she should have been in the inquisition. Cordelia gratefully absorbed any new information as part of her mind constantly worked over the problem of Kevan and his threats. Would it be best to explain everything to Gerald? Could she ever prepare him enough to understand?

It was about a month after the parental tea at the Ritz. They were were sitting in a small restaurant and had eaten a light meal and shared a bottle of wine, when Gerald looked at her intently then glanced away.

'What?' she said.

'Would you say you are a truthful person?' he said turning back and leaning towards her.

She smiled before she said, 'As much as the next person.'

He didn't smile back. 'I've never understood lies,' he said. 'Even the ones mother calls white lies. She says it is to be kind, but it is still a strange thing to do. So when you say 'as much as the next person', do you mean like that, only white lies?'

'Oh, I don't know, sometimes they are needed, but, I try to tell the truth.' She hadn't crossed her fingers as she said it, but she should have done.

'Did you know I was engaged once?'

She was startled by the change of direction, 'No? You haven't said anything about it.'

'Well, I was. I met her at university, she was ... very lively, liked to talk, liked to party. I was dazzled.' He gave a small rueful laugh shaking his head. 'She said yes when I asked her to marry me ... but a couple of months later I was told she was seeing someone else, at the same time. I asked her and she told me absolutely clearly that it wasn't true, asked me how I could think it. I believed her then - but it was a lie. I found out later. I'd asked a mutual friend to be my best man. We were already at the stage of discussing a reception venue, when I found out that she was sleeping with him, although we were 'waiting for the wedding night'. It destroyed my trust in everyone. For years. You are the first person I have placed my trust in since. Now do you understand?'

She sat in shock. Her whole persona, everything he knew about her was a lie; but he'd never want the person she really was, would he? What else could she do? She wanted Gerald, his stability and ordered ways, his predictability and the life they could have together.

'Oh, Gerald, how could she?' she said while determining that she wouldn't let him down ever, she wouldn't betray him, and she'd never tell him any more lies, though she couldn't change those she had already told, those would have to stay; that was her truth now.

When they left Margo's suite they travelled down in silence. As the lift reached the bottom Cordelia said, 'I need to talk to you about what I'm going to do about these threats.'

'Sure, when?'

'Now, if you can?'

'Let's get out of Plymouth first, how about we get over the bridge and meet up at the Waitrose car park?'

'Good idea, before the traffic builds up.' They had reached the road, 'Where are you?'

'Just up there,' he said indicating to the right. She could see his silver car, 'Fine, I'm just back there – I'll see if I can follow you, otherwise find a space and text me.'

Inevitably she lost him at the Carkeel roundabout, but caught up with him as he drove slowly into the car park. It was busy at this time of day, but he headed for the most distant area from the shop doors and found a double space. She pulled up beside him and he climbed out of his car and into hers.

'Do you mind that Margo is going to come and see us before you have been able to?' he asked. Margo had coaxed an invitation out of Max to go and meet the family at home.

She did, but she wasn't going to make a fuss, Margo was only over for a short time. 'No, that's fine.'

'Only you didn't look happy while we were in her room.'

'I was listening, but I was also trying to work out what to do. Whether I can talk to Gerald, it would solve a lot of our problems if I really thought I could.'

Max raised his eyebrows, Cordelia knew he didn't really see the problem, for all his understanding of the Asperger personality.

'This is my problem, and yes, I'm jealous of Margo seeing the children before I do, but she is only here for the week, let her see them. How will you explain her to them?'

'It won't be too difficult, I hope, I've been talking about family history research,' he said. 'Now, what are you going to do?'

'I think I'll have to confront ... Kevan.'

'Really? Do you think that's a good idea?'

'What else can I do, he seems to think I am doing something terrible, seeing you. And, because he thinks I'm already being unfaithful to Gerald he seems to think I can do the same with him.'

'What?'

'That's what he's suggesting in his last email,' she said, an involuntary shudder running through her as she remembered the words he'd used.

'But if you see him, he'll think you've agreed.'

'Then I need to make sure that I see him in a way that it can't happen, I'd like you to be with me.'

He looked startled but Cordelia swept on. 'If we arrange to meet him at a place of our choice, we can go prepared, with your birth certificate, explain that Gerald and you are estranged – that our relationship is nothing but mother and son. That ought to put him straight.'

She could see that Max was thinking through the possibility of it working, in the end he gave a short nod. 'Okay, we'll try that, but it will have to be soon as we're off on holiday at the start of next week.'

'Oh! I had forgotten that, and I'm tied up from tomorrow with the Art Fair, full time. Perhaps an evening – ask to meet him at a pub or something? Perhaps over your way?'

'We can try that, see if he'll bite.' Max said glancing at his watch.

'Oh, it's getting late,' Cordelia said, noticing the time, 'Better get back - I'll be in contact.'

He leant forward and kissed her cheek, 'Take care,' he said and left the car.

She lifted her hand in farewell, but it came to rest on her cheek, covering the place he'd kissed, the feeling of love was almost too much for her to hold, her eyes filled as her memory poured out images of him as a baby in her arms. 'Oh, Max,' she sighed.

Chapter 40

I woke with a thick head and a tongue like a budgie's jockstrap, but no actual hangover. Downstairs I plucked the glasses and the nearly empty bottle from the coffee table and pulled it back to its usual position in front of the sofa. A two-seater sofa is just no good for shagging, she'd had one foot on the floor and my blasted knees kept slipping with nowhere to put my feet. It hadn't been elegant last night; the shuffle off the sofa onto the floor, but once down on the carpet I could really work it. Oh, and it had been too long, so it was quick, but I don't think that bothered her, she wasn't exactly participating.

Afterwards, as I lay there a moment catching my breath, she'd tapped me on the shoulder. I'd pushed myself off, sat back on my knees and glanced at my watch. I couldn't have her staying over, she might stumble on something that told her who I really was, I really hadn't tidied stuff away, just closed the door to the room I used for writing. It was a quarter to twelve, I said something about the village Gestapo all being in bed by now and I'd run her home and reached behind me, picked up her knickers and dropped them by her hand. She'd looked at me as if she didn't know who I was. As I stood and straightened myself up, she started to struggle into them. Not a pretty sight. I went and picked up her handbag from the floor and brought it over to her where she was, perched on the edge of the sofa, putting her shoes on. She'd stood, but only with my assistance.

I all-but carried her out to the car, shovelling her into the passenger seat and struggling to fasten the seat belt. The four or five Southern Comforts were really hitting home now, and I knew I oughtn't be driving, but I had to get her back to her place and I reasoned there'd be no one on the road between here and there, especially if I avoided the pub. I drove carefully though, aware that I was not on top of my game. When I turned into her cul-de-sac I coasted down to make the least noise possible, turning in the circle so the passenger door was closest to her house. I took her key and opened her front door then went back and helped her out. We struggled to get through the door together as I supported her in. I couldn't face carrying her up the stairs and opted to settle her on her sofa in the silver and purple front room. She sat and flopped back. I scrambled upstairs and dragged a duvet off a bed in the first room I came to, returned and pulled her legs up onto the sofa, her dress riding up, her head flopping down onto the sofa arm. I threw the duvet over her, then something told me to change her position. I turned her and placed her in the recovery position, just in case, and tucked the duvet round her so she'd stay that way. I was feeling fine just then, fine about everything.

Revision, revision and bloody revision, the thick head was turning into a dull ache. I wish I felt I could give it a miss and go out, but I can't, really, I can't. I think I need to get out of here before the weekend. I replayed last night in my head again. It wasn't good. It really wasn't. Fuck it, what does it matter? Just as well get out of here now.

Yet still there is this itch. That bloody stuck up woman. I want her. Not Jim, me. It's eating at me, the way she remained aloof all the time regardless of what she was doing. Sneaking around behind her husband's back, just like Angie. Two-timing bitch. If I could have her, just like my Puppeteer did, then I'd be satisfied. I decided to send her another email; my demands and ultimatum.

I looked up the Holiday Inn and rang them, checked on vacancies, they said it would be no problem so I booked a room using my personal bank card, not my author one. I dialled again.

'Hello, Sean?' William answered sounding as nervous as usual. Was it only with me? If not, how the hell did he make it as an agent at all?

'Yes, of course. Just to let you know I'm moving out of Hideaway today,'

'Today? Coming up to London?'

'No, moving into a hotel for a few days, then I'll be back.'

'Oh?'

'Look, I've upset a few of the locals, they really must not find me, so I'm disappearing.'

'Oh really, why? What ...' he started in aggrieved high tones.

I dropped my voice to a hoarse whisper, 'Never mind what, this is serious, just remember, I was never here, no one must ever know I was here. Lives could be at stake.' I was amused and gratified when he responded in the same tone.

'No. Of course not, wouldn't dream of it.'

'And a word to the wise,' I continued, 'the people here, very cliquey, and they don't like the fact you bought a place a local couple wanted. If I were you I wouldn't want to tell anyone I was the owner, get me? If it was mine I'd get shot of it.'

'Oh!' His voice rose again within the one syllable.

'I'll be available on my mobile again after lunchtime,' I said in my normal voice and cut the call.

It is amazing how much you can inhabit a place in a short time. I would have thought I could pack everything up in half an hour, in the end it took me nigh on two hours to make sure I had everything with me that I had brought or acquired. I stashed everything in the car then went back in again. I started at the top and worked my way down. I had to make sure there was nothing left that could identify me, the only things left were foodstuffs and I couldn't be bothered with sorting that lot out.

I was poised to leave, keys in my hand, just glancing round one last time when the phone rang. I didn't want to answer in case it was Marian, but I stood there and listened as it went to answer phone, the standard recording asked for a message after the tone, the tone sounded and there was a moments pause before Kevan said, 'Ah, I, um, seems I can do the extra hour a week that your landlord wanted. Will Monday at ten suit you? Let me know.' The phone clicked off, I smiled and left the cottage for the last time.

I couldn't help myself, I drove past The Old Chapel on the way out of the village, one last look, even though it would have been safer to go the other way.

An hour later and I was comfortably ensconced in my room at the Holiday Inn. I logged on to their internet and opened my special email account.

Chapter 41

Cordelia was distracted in the morning, she had lain awake half of the night worrying about what Kevan was going to do now he had been sacked. Gerald had not been for turning, even when she had said she'd been too hasty and that everyone needed a second chance. Gerald was not the man to offer second chances; he saw them as a weakness.

Then, this was the first of her busiest days of the year. All the other events she organised or helped with paled in comparison with the Art Fair. This morning she and a team of local volunteers would set up the Hall to take the artwork. She had worked out the plan and the lighting but it was a huge village effort to get it into place, she was almost impatient for Gerald to leave for work, wishing it were any day but Wednesday, his late-start day. She cleared the table round him and eventually he folded the paper and rose from the breakfast table. At the door he wished her good luck for the setting up day, and left.

She dashed upstairs and changed into an old pair of jeans and a tee-shirt. Grabbed her keys, her basket of goodies and her plans and was out of the door. She arrived at the same time as the first of her helpers and unlocked the hall.

'Nice day for it,' Gill said.

'And what's even better the weather's set to hold for the hanging this afternoon and tomorrow,' Cordelia smiled, when it was wet so many of the artists delayed coming in, hoping for better weather later and making it all a bit of a scramble as time ran out.

They were soon joined by others, armed with step ladders, screwdrivers and cable ties. Cordelia tacked her layout design to a board and rested it up against a wall so everyone could access it. The next two hours passed in a whirl of activity and friendly chatter. At eleven Cordelia made everyone a cup of coffee and brought out a selection of cakes and biscuits she'd made; this too was a tradition that had built up over the years. She looked around, how had she not noticed before? Marian was not there, she always came! Cordelia reached for her phone to give Marian a call, only to find she'd left it at home in her rush to change and get out. Lunchtime would have to do.

They'd finished in record time, well, they laughed, at least before one o'clock. Cordelia thanked everyone and said she'd be glad to see anyone free in the afternoon or evening to help with the hanging. With the genial chatter that comes from a group of people who know they have done a good job, the volunteers left the hall. Cordelia stood and looked around, in her mind's eye she could see the pictures and sculptures in the places she'd planned. She walked slowly up the central aisle, stepping out into the space beyond and glanced left to where the Medusa would be placed for maximum effect, she turned, looked the other way, to where she was placing a sinuous and lithe wooden sculpture in juxtaposition, yes, it would work, she smiled to herself.

As she drove down from the Hall she decided to just drop in and see if Marian was there, rather than go home and phone. She pulled up outside Marian's place; her car was in the drive so it looked as if she was home. Cordelia rang the doorbell and waited. There was a sound of water running, then it stopped and she could make out a shadow pass the narrow obscure-glass panel in the door. Marian was home. She waited a bit more, then, somehow feeling foolish, rang the doorbell again. After a moment or two Marian opened the door, immediately turning away mumbling, 'Come in.' and leading the way through to her kitchen. The smell of coffee was strong and Marian looked very pale.

'What's up?'

'Pff,' Marian huffed then looked at Cordelia, 'me being a bloody idiot, that's what.' Her lips were turned down and showed she was fighting back tears. Cordelia went to her and opened her arms, gathering her in.

'What's wrong. Oh, Marian? Come on, what is it?'

'Stupid, bloody stupid,' she said through small sobs.

'What's happened?'

Marian sighed deeply, 'Nothing, really, I just, I just let myself be made a terrible fool of and that is not me, not me at all.' She inhaled deeply and pushed away from Cordelia and sat herself down on a kitchen stool at the breakfast bar, pulling a large cup of black coffee towards her, 'Oh, and I have the worst rocking hangover I have had since I was – dunno, since I was a teenager I think.'

Cordelia didn't say anything for a moment, fearing it was something to do with Kevan, that she was somehow to blame as she'd not warned Marian in time. 'I'm sure it's not as bad ...' she started.

'Oh it is as bad!' Marian sighed again, 'Look, I was a fool, I was so bored listening to that prick Jim, huh, that I drank too much.'

'Oh! Jim?'

'Yeah!' Marian spat, 'Remember, he'd asked me to the theatre and I went, as he'd got the tickets already.'

My fault then, in a way, Cordelia thought.

'Then supper afterwards, and he is such a bore, thinks he's funny I suppose, but just couldn't stop, I know I should have kept an eye on the wine, but it disappeared so quickly. Then I compounded my idiocy and agreed to go back to his place for a nightcap. Under the influence by then, I suppose. Huh! Stupid or what?'

'So, a bad hangover ...'

'Bad hangover, yes, worse, bad sex.'

'Wha ... you mean he ...'

'No, not exactly. Oh God C'delia, it was just ... shameful. Not good at all,' she pulled a tight smile, 'and he was like, ok, done, go home, here's your knickers, slag!'

'He said that?'

'No! For heaven's sake, C'delia, it was how it felt. I feel like I can't ... look at anyone. As if they'll see what happened, just by looking,' she said one hand on top of her head as if holding it down.

'He can't treat you like that.'

'Already bloody done it.'

'I mean, he needs to apologise at least!'

'Oh, forget it, I'll probably pull through once the head has cleared, been through worse,' Marian said, looking straight at Cordelia, 'Don't say anything, please. I really don't want to think about it, and certainly don't want anyone else to know about it. I should have skipped seeing him - Kevan's a much nicer bloke.'

Cordelia felt a sonic wave shake her core as Marian said Kevan's name. She had to tell Marian, she had to warn her. 'About Kevan,' she started, 'I need to tell you something, he may not actually be as nice as he seems.'

'You *are* joking?'

'Wish I was. I've been getting weird emails, threatening, um, suggestive even and with photos ... like one taken through our bedroom window ... and they were sent by Kay Dee. That's K A Y D E E, so I didn't put it together until he wrote something that only Kevan could know and then I put it together with his initials.'

'Really? Really! What does Gerald say?'

'I didn't tell him about the emails, but I got him to sack him anyway.'

'What? Why didn't you tell him about the emails?'

Cordelia swallowed, she'd made a mistake and hangover or not Marian's analytical mind was still operating. 'There were some things in the emails I didn't want Gerald to see.' Cordelia bit her lip.

'Go on?'

'Marian,' she closed her eyes, 'it is such a long story, I really can't tell you now, I - no, we'd need some time, right now I've got to get back for the hanging.'

'Oh! I'd forgotten that!'

'But I promise I'll explain it to you. I really want to - it'll be good to share it with someone.'

'But not Gerald?'

'You know what he's like, besides, when I tell you, you'll understand.'

'When then?'

'Umm, hanging today and all day tomorrow, preview evening tomorrow night. It will have to be Friday morning, before the Art Fair opens,' Cordelia said, sounding worried, concerned her friend might just think she was stalling.

'You certainly know how to string it out,' Marian said, but cracked a smile, before placing her hand back on top of her head and closing her eyes momentarily.

'I know, I'm sorry. You're not seeing Kevan again before then?'

'Don't worry, oh, I really need to lie down.'

'Drink plenty of water,' Cordelia said with a smile, 'it's better than coffee.'

Marian raised her eyebrows, 'I know,' she whispered. 'I know.'

Chapter 42

I took time writing the email. I wanted to imbue it with a sense of control and command and, without saying anything more than I already had, the poised axe of the consequences of disobeying.

I smiled at the thought that I would be having her in the same hotel she'd chosen for her tryst. The fact that I knew that, had to be conveyed, as it may well prove to be the clincher.

The timing of when I wanted her to be here was trickier. Part of me wanted to get this over and done with, get it out of my system, but I also wanted to finish my re-draft before I left as the energy of the game was powering my work so well at the moment and I was certain I would be checking out of the hotel immediately after I'd had her.

This was my final chapter, the denouement - I wasn't hanging around after she found out who Kay Dee really was, just in case.

Chapter 43

Thoughts of Kevan, Jim, Marian or anyone else were driven from her mind as she met artist after artist arriving for the hanging. Those who abided by the agreement were no problem, they'd brought the artwork at the sizes they'd said they would, she took their hanging fees, found them on her charts and sent them off to find a volunteer with hangers to fix the paintings up. The ones who turned up with 'I swapped one large one for two small ones, they work out the same size', or 'I brought a different one, it's a bit larger but that will be okay, won't it?' were more of a headache. By five o'clock she had four oversized paintings propped by her table awaiting her decision as to how and where they could be fitted in.

For her it wasn't enough to have them hung, it was as much about presentation. It was what made the Hingsbury Art Fair more like an art gallery and less like a jumble sale, it was part of the atmosphere that she strived to create, and it worked, the pictures looked great and they sold well at good prices for both artist and buyer. At five she locked the hall and set the alarm, she was tired, more tired than she usually was, and there was still the evening session to come.

By the time Gerald arrived home she had supper ready.

'That smells good,' he said as he walked through to the study to put his case away.

'And it's all ready to eat, so we can be back at the Hall at seven.'

'Oh, yes. Though you'd think someone else could do a stint on this hanging lark.'

'They all do, besides it's only once a year and you know it is easier to get it right first time rather than upsetting people by moving things around after they're hung.'

Gerald harrumphed, Cordelia sighed; Gerald never would understand the vagaries of delicate artistic egos and it didn't matter unless it prevented her getting up to the hall on time.

One thing about Gerald, he was very good at being precise when it came to helping with the hangings. He would always be careful to make sure the distances from one to another painting were maintained, even going to the bother of adjusting previous hangings by a few millimetres to even out the spaces. What he didn't realise was the effect that his meticulousness had on the artist whose work he was hanging, they all thought him wonderful as he hung, stood back, adjusted, adjusted neighbouring pictures, stood back, checked. Each artist felt as if they were being afforded special treatment and he'd often have a few waiting for him to hang their work, rather than grabbing the nearest volunteer. Cordelia was glad of it too, as otherwise she would spend precious time after everyone had gone moving pictures to give them their own space, to create the right shapes of space between the works.

It was quite late when they got home. Gerald suggested a glass of wine as they settled down to watch the ten o'clock news and Cordelia was happy to agree. She rested back on the sofa, legs crossed, glass of wine in one hand, iPad balanced on one knee and flipped through to emails. She suddenly sat bolt upright almost spilling wine as she jerked forward, the iPad skidding off her knee onto the floor. As it landed Gerald looked up.

'You all right?' he said, looking at the iPad on the floor not her.

'Oh, nothing. It just slipped and I couldn't catch it without spilling the wine everywhere,' she gave a tight half-laugh to suggest it was just fine. It wasn't. Carefully she set the glass down and picked up the iPad again. The email was from Kay.Dee.

Somehow during the day she'd managed to forget about Kevan and his suggestions. Now, here it was; a demand. An awful demand. She felt herself go cold, and hoped it didn't show. She stood and headed for the kitchen. Gerald looked at her questioningly.

'Splashed wine on my hand,' she said, trailing the iPad in her other hand as she shielded it from his glance with her body.

In the kitchen she read the email again. Kevan knew about the Art Fair, couldn't fail to, knew that she was at her busiest just now, bastard.

> It is time for you to deliver.
> Follow these instructions to the letter – otherwise it will be my regretful duty to deliver the photographic evidence of your infidelity straight to Gerald.
> Meet me at the Holiday Inn on Saturday afternoon. Arrive at 2pm.
> Do not go to reception, walk in as if you are staying there, you'll be familiar with the place after your recent assignation there, won't you?
> Go straight to room 209.
> Knock twice, pause, knock three times.
> Be sure you 'dress' for the occasion – you would be advised to humour me.

It left her feeling breathless, hardly knowing if she was angry or frightened. Probably both. The only time she'd been to the Holiday Inn was on Tuesday. He must have been following her when they went to see Margo. She shivered. Saturday afternoon? Normally she would be taking the payments for the artwork being purchased, carefully wrapping it and sending it off with its new owner, followed by a quick check through her 'waiting' lists to find one of a similar size. Then she'd contact the artist and have them bring it in for hanging - they were always quick to oblige

– meaning the Art Fair always maintained a strong exhibition of a wide range of art. Could someone else do this? Of course, if they had to, it was a well tried system; she'd been doing it for years now.

How could she explain leaving the Art Fair and disappearing for hours on the Saturday afternoon to Gerald though, without ... without telling him lies, or the truth. She breathed in quickly in a shudder that threatened to turn into a sob. No, crying wouldn't help. There had to be a way. She rested her head in her hands, her elbows on the countertop, trying to think.

'You all right?' Gerald said from the doorway. She snapped upright.

'Yes, bit of a head, but okay, thank you,' and gave him a bright smile.

'Good,' he said as he took a glass to fill with water.

As soon as Gerald left on Thursday she forwarded the email from Kay.Dee to Max, under the subject line 'final demand' and said she'd ring later.

Cordelia arrived at the Hall just on ten o'clock and already there was a short queue of artists standing outside waiting, which was odd as Gill had offered to open up to let people in.

'Hi!' she said, 'I'm sorry you've not been let in yet,' and fished the spare hall key from her pocket.

After a bit of shuffling the first artist settled their hanging fees and looked around for a volunteer. At that point two had arrived, but still no Gill. Cordelia made a mental note to see if she was okay, it was so unlike her.

By eleven the first wave had all been hung and there was a lull.

'Linda, would you mind putting the kettle on, I think we can all do with a cuppa, I'm popping over to see how Gill is.' In response Linda smiled and went into the kitchen area. 'If an artist turns up,' Cordelia added to Joan, 'see if you can get them to hold their horses until I come back,' she noticed the retired scientist raise her eyebrows, 'or, or well, I'm sure you'd find them on the chart, where they are and how much they owe, it's all written down,' she smiled, of course Joan could cope with that, in fact Joan could cope very well with that.

Cordelia rang Gill's doorbell and waited. No answer. She stood back a little and glanced down the side of the house in case she could see Gill out in the garden. No sign of movement from the garden, but then, no car either. George could just as easily have taken it out, that wasn't evidence, but when there was still no answer from the door Cordelia had to conclude they were all out, Gill, George and Walter too.

At one o'clock Cordelia scanned her artist list. The afternoon was reserved for sculptures, unless brought in already by artists who worked in multimedia. Those stood labelled in a safe position off to one side waiting to be placed later. In fact, when she checked, there were only three artists to come with their works that afternoon. She took a moment to look round before locking up - the effect of brightness and light, colour and space was as she'd imagined and she left feeling as if something in her life was right. Before getting in her car she tried Gill's bell again - still no answer.

Within moments of being home the good feeling drained; it was as if her lovely home contained all the anxiety that had built up since Kay.Dee, Kevan, started messaging her. She stepped into the main room and just seeing the sofas recalled her shock at reading the last email. Until then it had been a threat, but vague, now the demand was there it seemed too real. She turned back to the kitchen, grabbed an apple, took herself into the conservatory and called Max.

Chapter 44

The Medusa was the last sculpture to go into place. She had reserved a white space so that it had the maximum impact but had 'hidden' it around a corner, so that it also caught the observer unawares. By four, everyone else had left and she took a quick walk around the gallery as if with fresh eyes. She stopped to adjust a couple of paintings that were a little too close to each other then shook herself, she could play with millimetres until the cows came home, but she had to get organised for the evening preview, so she mustn't. The renown of the Hingsbury Art Fair, her Art Fair, brought a paying clientele from all over the country who came for the pre-view evening, almost all buying works on the evening yet agreeing to leave them on display at least until midday on the opening day, by which time she would have the replacements lined up.

By six thirty she, and the host of helpers, were back in the hall. Glasses were set out on a tray, bottles of wine stood ready and trays of canapés were delicately covered with a cloth. Gerald was dressed as if going to a black tie do, she was in a pretty blue dress just the right side of formal, and most of the others had made an effort too. She had already checked at Gill's house and even rung her mobile; there was still no answer to either.

Cordelia spent the evening chatting to people about the paintings, escorting the purchasers to the desk and noting names and details while Joan took the money, in cash or by card using a phone app, before happily going back to place the red dots on the frames to indicate that they had been sold. Marian came in late, looking tired, took an orange juice and came to stand near Cordelia while she chatted. As soon as the couple moved on to look at the next painting, she turned to Marian.

'You okay?'

'Yeah, though I'm still not feeling quite right. Went running but it was like I had lead in my legs.'

'Still, from Tuesday?'

'Yeah, perhaps ...'

'What do you think?' Cordelia asked, tipping her hand out towards the exhibition in general.

Marian gave a small snort, 'Brilliant, as usual, I don't know why you worry.'

'Well, it's not for me, is it? It's for the charity.' She smiled, 'Have you seen the Medusa I told you about?'

'Not yet, where is she?'

'Head on down that aisle, let me know what you think. Oh, I'm needed over there,' she said, nodding towards a couple she didn't recognise who were about to lift a painting down, 'see you tomorrow morning,' and moved off. 'Good evening, are you interested in buying this one?'

She had just handed the customers over to Joan, had picked off another red dot and was poised to stick it on the frame when Kevan came in. Wearing a tracksuit and running shoes; he wasn't dressed for the occasion. He spotted her and came straight for her, she glanced round but Gerald was nowhere to be seen.

'Excuse me, Mrs Steadman,' he said, his eyes flashing, 'but you can hire me or sack me, that's your business, but you have no right to bad-mouth me in this village!'

'I don't know what you mean?' she heard herself say, though her mind was a whirl of images she didn't want to see.

'Oh, you don't, do you? Well, you can stop telling people that I'm sending you dirty emails for a start,' he growled.

'I, I'm not, I only ... '

'You told Marian that!' his voice rising.

'Kevan?' Marian said, running from behind the exhibits. 'Kevan, I said I'd talk to her.'

'It's not enough, she needs to apologise and take it all back.'

'No one else knew, until - you, oh stupid!' Marian took him by the arm and pulled him out of the hall. The shocked silence gently gave way to murmurs. Cordelia stood stock-still, her cheeks flaming. Gerald came and put his hand on her shoulder.

'Didn't take kindly to being sacked then?' he said.

Cordelia sighed, at least Gerald hadn't heard everything Kevan had said.

Next morning Cordelia took her iPad along with her to see Marian, she felt she needed the proof of the emails as Marian obviously hadn't believed her, and it was going to be difficult enough as it was. Marian opened the door and led the way through, saying coffee was ready and to go into the lounge.

Cordelia settled herself on the sofa and opened the iPad and her email account.

'Here you go,' Marian said, placing two mugs of coffee down on the table. 'Sorry about Kevan last night. He'd rung and I made the mistake of asking if he'd been sending you emails and - well, sorry, I told him I'd be talking to you today, but, men, eh? Come on, tell me what this is all about.'

'Shall I show you the emails? The ones from Kevan, first.'

'No,' Marian said, 'I think you need to start at the beginning, because you said you couldn't show Gerald the emails because he wouldn't understand, but I would when I heard this long story of yours. So let's have it.'

Cordelia clasped her hands between her knees and stared down at them. 'Long story - but this is the short version. Okay, when I was sixteen I had a baby.' She heard Marian give a small gasp. 'But he was taken away from me when he was six months old. He wasn't hurt or anything – it was just because of where we were living. I wasn't allowed to know who adopted him or where or anything, because I wanted him back.' She puffed out a breath, glanced quickly up at Marian; she had her hand to her mouth, her eyes fixed on Cordelia. 'Okay, then I had a bit of a breakdown, I guess, ran away from ... home, etcetera, etcetera, pulled myself together, pretended to be someone I wasn't, met Gerald and the rest is as you see it.'

'Oh! C'delia, a baby, but that's not the end of ...'

'And Gerald doesn't know any of this. And, and you know what he's like.'

'Yes, but ...'

'And my son has found me,' the tears were sliding out from under her lashes, she looked up through a haze, 'and we've been meeting, and, and, Kevan must have seen us, and thought – thought he was ... a lover or something. That's when the emails started. He's got pictures, he's threatening to send them to Gerald. He'd never understand – he doesn't even understand why you'd say you were fine when you weren't.'

Marian slid along and hugged her friend. 'Come on, show me these emails.'

Cordelia had filed all the emails under the name DEE, she opened it and passed the iPad over 'Here they are – you can just go from one to another – Kay.Dee, clever, I was always called Dee when I was young. Made me think it was someone who knew me by that name at first.'

Marian took it and began reading, after a moment she was shaking her head.

'I don't think this is him, I don't think it is Kevan.'

'But it must be! You just like him, you just don't want it to be him!'

'Well, look at the language, Kevan doesn't talk like this! And then, well, not a spelling mistake in the lot! I told you he was dyslexic.'

'That's nothing, there's spell checkers on emails.'

'I've seen his writing – it would have grabbed the wrong word somewhere, I promise, especially if he'd tried to write some of this - elaborate stuff.'

Cordelia blushed, 'Well, what about this one then?' she opened the email that referred to her on her knees, 'He was the only person who saw me like that, I was scrubbing the tiles in the porch.'

'Well, I don't know. Maybe someone else did, who you didn't see or something.'

'Or this picture – has to be taken from our garden and he's the only one who's in our garden without anyone taking any notice.'

'I'm not sure about that one, but why?'

Cordelia felt as if she were about to cry again. 'Look at the last two emails.'

There was a small silence while Marian read.

'Oh God!' Marian sighed, 'Well, if it is or if it isn't him, what are you going to do?'

Chapter 45

I ate an early lunch out, at the place on the Barbican I had gone to with Marian, and strolled back. I was feeling confident yet on edge with excitement. All my luggage was packed and loaded in the car in the underground car park, all I had left to do was to check out. After.

The half an hour before two o'clock dragged. I sat looking out of the window for much of the time, carefully and casually dressed in all black; shirt and trousers, so looking smart but – yes – sinister.

The knock came, a double rap, I was on my feet in an instant, my heart thumping. Three raps on the door, firm and sure. I imagined her angry and frightened. I paused for just a second to un-tense my shoulders before I laid hands on the door handle and began to open it.

The door burst open into my face, sending me reeling back. A man barged into the room. I scrambled to my feet, backing off as it was obvious he was not happy. He slammed the door closed behind him. Jeans and a tee-shirt, taller than me, I recognised him - her lover. Damn! Why hadn't I thought of this?

'Kevan? Or Kay Dee - whatever you like to call yourself?' he said pacing towards me as I walked backwards across the room, nearly back to the window. I felt like a parody, I couldn't stop my hands waving around, patting the air, but I had caught the question in his voice.

'No, no, you must have the wrong person,' I said.

His eyes narrowed but he stopped advancing on me.

'You were expecting Cordelia - weren't you? I saw the email,' his fists clenched at his sides.

'No, who? No.'

He looked at me, as if trying to assess whether I was lying or not. I tried a smile. 'Are, are you sure you have the right room?' I said in a placatory voice, 'Two, oh, nine.'

He glanced round the room and I saw the tension go out of him, perhaps this was going to be okay after all. He took another step toward the window, looking out of it now. He pulled something from his pocket, turned, aimed it and snapped my picture.

'I said, I've seen the email and this is the right room, time and date. And now we know who you are. So leave my mother alone! You have nothing to blackmail her with,' his measured words and voice carrying all the weight of a physical threat.

Before I could take in this last snippet of information or react he turned and was heading out of the room. I followed reaching the door just as he pulled it shut. I snatched it open again. 'Don't you believe it,' I spat after him, holding the door with one hand, ready to slam shut if he turned. He turned, but only to snap another picture on his phone.

Shit, shit, shit! So he has a picture of me. Is that a problem? What good will that do him? Can't trace the emails back to me, I made sure of that. And, when all is said and done, I really don't look like myself at the moment. The sooner I am back in London and the sooner I go back to my usual style the better ...

I checked out and drove. I tried to listen to the music, I tried to concentrate on the driving, but all the time the questions, the accusations and the possible repercussions were flying round my head. He did say 'mother' didn't he? It wasn't my imagination. Was it possible – well, I guess, Marian had let slip how old they were, possible I guess. Was there something of her in his face? Could be. But why the shenanigans? That was too suspicious to believe he was just her son – there is still a sordid secret there, the stuck-up bitch is still hiding something.

She isn't going to make me look a fool. Or a coward. I saw my panicked hands flapping, felt the sick sinking feeling in the pit of my stomach. I never did like violence. Real-life violence. I should have thought about him, I should have had a decoy room and watched from further down, I should have thought she might involve him. He's got my picture. Is there anything he can do with it? I glanced at my eyes in the rear-view mirror, would the essential me still be recognisable? Had I covered my tracks well enough while I was down there? I had to get to William, get him to get rid of the house. Would that help? Would he do it?

I arrived back at my London flat tired out from the drive and from running scenarios around in my head. The place was stale and dusty; where does dust come from when there is no one at home and all the windows are shut? Though early evening I threw the windows open and lugged my bags through to the bedroom of my one-bed flat with a mortgage big enough for that whole house down in Cornwall. I tossed the clothes out over a chair. Took my laptop out and returned to the sitting room. Ducked into the kitchen and looked in the cupboard for a drink. Nothing, shit. But then, I'm home and there's an Oddbins on the corner, I smiled, grabbed my keys and set off.

I treated myself to a bottle of whisky and a takeaway pizza from the Domino's just along the High Street, and returned with them. Put some rock on to listen to and settled myself down for the evening. Later, I don't know how much later, let's say halfway down the bottle, I sent the email. Good riddance.

Chapter 46

Cordelia woke with a twisted feeling in her stomach and a sour taste in her mouth, her mood anxious. On the way to the Hall she called in at Gill's again. She knocked and waited. At first there seemed to be no one home again even though the car was there, but then she heard a shuffling noise and the door was opened by George, wearing his dressing-gown, and he looked dreadful.

'George, what's happened?'

'It's ...' he started then just shook his head. 'Gill's in hospital.'

'Oh no?'

'With erm, cracked skull, and erm, not, not doing so well.'

'Oh George, why didn't you call someone?'

'I didn't know what to do, I only got home last night, been sleeping there, on the chair in the hospital, didn't have Gill's phone, didn't know any numbers off the top of my head.'

'George, is there anything I can do? Right now.'

'Erm, I don't know, you, you're busy.'

'Nonsense, not too much to help, come on, have you had breakfast?'

'No, just woke up sorry.'

'Sorry? I should be sorry, I woke you up! You're probably beat! Let me cook you a quick breakfast, what do you like, porridge or fry?'

'Oh, a fry sounds good,' he almost smiled.

Cordelia shooed him back inside and followed him. A quick look in the fridge showed she needed to get some bacon. 'Go get freshened up George, I'll be back in two minutes.' She left the house dialling Marian's number 'Marian, got a bit of a problem, can you open up the Hall and get it started for me?'

'Sure, I'm on my way already, just walking up the hill.'

'And I'm just driving down.' Cordelia said jumping in her car and making a swift U turn. As she saw Marian she pulled up, 'Gill's in hospital, not sure of any details yet, George's in a bad way and I'm just getting him some breakfast, will be over to the Hall as soon as I can, here's the key.'

'Gill? What happened?'

'Don't know yet,' Cordelia said pulling away.

Later, as George sat dressed and nursing a mug of tea while Cordelia finished cooking him bacon, eggs and tomatoes she asked, 'So where is Walter?' trying not to imagine Gill being beaten over the head by her own father as George had just described it.

'Secure psychiatric hospital – it's the Alzheimer's you know, he was never violent before.'

'I know. It's frightening.'

'If I'd been home, if she hadn't fallen, I don't know, it wouldn't have been so bad.'

'No point blaming yourself, George, you've got to be strong for Gill when she gets better.'

George put his cutlery down as he finished his breakfast, 'That's better,' he said, 'feel like a new man now I've been fed and watered.'

'What are you going to do now?' Cordelia asked. She had noticed the broken ornaments, the blood and the general disarray in the sitting room.

'I'm going back in, I want to be there for her when she wakes up.'

Cordelia nodded, 'Would you like me to tidy up a bit,' she nodded towards the sitting room door, 'in there? So it's all done?'

'Oh? Erm, I can't ask you to do that.'

'Nonsense, anyway – you're not asking – I'm offering.'

'Then, yes, thank you. Best be sorted, really?' he offered a lopsided smile.

'Yes, really. You go, please do send me a text when she wakes.'

'Thank, yes, I'll do that,' he said, checking his pocket for the phone. 'Thanks, yes, just pull the door shut on the Yale, I've got my keys.'

'Go on. Don't worry, Gill's strong,' she smiled and shooed him out of his house, turning immediately to get started on the cleaning up.

It was nearly lunchtime before she had finished cleaning up properly and returned to the Hall. Everything was fine there except there were gaps on the walls where paintings had been sold and replacements not yet called in. As for the rest of it, Marian, Joan and Harold were running the show and, apart from Harold, were used to it. They'd called him in as an extra steward and he sat imperiously on a chair at the far end watching the end sections and being watched by the Medusa. Cordelia started calling artists immediately after she had filled everyone else in about Gill's condition.

It was only as she drove home, to get a quick lunch with Gerald, that she realised she hadn't thought of Kevan and his terrible demand. She thought of Max and physically crossed her fingers, hoping that nothing would go wrong. It seemed the simplest way to defuse the matter. To explain that he was her son, that there was nothing for her to be blackmailed with, that he was all wrong about her and Max.

The afternoon had been incredibly busy and she was having trouble getting the pictures in quickly enough to fill the new gaps. One more day to go, and a couple of the artists had even run out of suitable works. However at half an hour to closing time the Hall was looking resplendent again. She'd called in extras from all the artists and they'd brought them, got them catalogued and hung or stood resting against the wall in the store room on stand-by for the next day.

It gave Cordelia a shock when Max walked into the Art Fair, but almost as quickly she reasoned that there were many strangers coming in and out, no one would remark on another. She was standing at the far end of the hall where Harold had been stationed earlier and where she could see the door and at the same time see the 'blind spots' that those on the door could not. Max gave her a quick glance then picked up the 'Guide to our Artists' and began wandering along gazing at the displays, moving towards where she stood.

'Hi,' he was grinning, 'Can you tell me about that sculpture?' he said quite distinctly in an actorly voice and obviously for the benefit of those in the hall.

'Oh, yes, she's wonderful isn't she?' Cordelia began as they moved behind the screens and towards the Medusa, 'But I'm afraid she's the only exhibit that is not for sale here.' By then she had stopped moving and her eyes were searching his for an answer to her unspoken question.

'I don't think we'll have any more trouble from him,' Max whispered. 'He was ... terrified,' he grinned again, obviously pleased with himself, 'though he pretended it wasn't him, that I had the wrong room, I'm sure it was him.'

'Did you check the name with the hotel, Kevan Doige?'

'No, but I got a photo of him,' he slipped his phone out of his pocket.

'It's by a local artist,' Cordelia said brightly as a couple entered the aisle leading to the Medusa. She smiled brightly at them, Max, standing in the Medusa's alcove held up his phone for her. She took a step forward, then reached for the phone and pulled it towards her. 'But? That's Jim!'

'Not who you thought?'

'No, not who I thought,' she felt the heat suffuse her face, 'I've made a bad mistake.'

'Who is he?'

'Shhh!' she indicated that they needed to move away as the couple were approaching the Medusa bay. 'Follow me,' she said, leading him through to the back of the hall to the store room.

'I should have thought, I mean I knew he'd seen us ... but really, nothing else added up,' she started, her voice low.

'What? Who is he?'

'Shh! The guy walking along the lane, you know that time. And we saw him at the end of the lane once. But he's just a visitor - just renting a house for the summer. I don't understand it. And ... there were things in the emails. How did he know those things?'

'Friends with the bloke who you thought did it?'

'Oh!' Cordelia looked at him.

'Yes?'

'No, no, more like rivals. They both fancy my friend Marian. Both went to Harriers with her.'

'There you go then, motive for passing the blame off on the other one.'

'Max! That's brilliant. Yes, and, yes, Jim turned out to be a bit of a shit to Marian too, so, perhaps it fits.'

'Mission accomplished! And now I must get home and give Heather a hand to get ready – we're off on holiday tomorrow, remember?'

'Yes, and thank you and thank Heather, and when you come back perhaps I can get over to see you all?'

'No problem. The hard bit is over, the explanations all done before they met Margo. Have to say she won the children over in a trice.'

Cordelia raised an eyebrow, 'Margo is good at that,' she said, her smile not really reaching her eyes.

Cordelia reached out tentatively and touched his hand, he clasped it, then pulled her to him for a hug. '

'We've done it, Cordelia,' he said and parted from her.

'Dee, please call me Dee.'

'Dee, see you soon, take care,' and he returned to the main hall and left.

Cordelia stayed put, feeling his hug, hearing his voice.

'You okay?' Marian said from the door, looking at her standing there hugging her own arms.

Chapter 47

'Marian, I was so wrong.'

'What about?'

'Kevan. It wasn't Kevan. Oh dear God! And I sacked him, and it wasn't him.'

'So who the hell was it?'

'Jim! Max showed me a photo of the bloke waiting at the room. It was Jim!'

'The sod!'

'Sorry.'

'What for? The more I think about that ... bastard, the more I wonder how come I got so drunk so quick. It's not really like me.'

'How do you mean?'

'Plus a few odd side effects that weren't just hangover, I know how my body works. I think the bastard slipped something in my drink.'

Cordelia looked at her friend.

'No, I'm not making excuses,' Marian said, 'really not – I mean – you know I told you about Kevan, hey, no complaints there.'

'Yes, yes and that was fine wasn't it. I hope I've not ruined that for you?'

'No. You know I talked to him about it, because, well he got upset and came to find you didn't he, idiot, but you know I wasn't convinced, you know the words, the spelling, something felt wrong. Now we know, I can see it – English teacher, fancy words, precise punctuation even in an email? Giveaways when you know, eh?'

'When you know,' Cordelia whispered.

'Come here you,' Marian gathered Cordelia to her, 'you weren't to know. What are you going to do now?'

'How to you mean?'

'Are you going to tell Gerald?'

'No! No, I can't.' Cordelia said, pulling away from the hug.

'Surely you can't keep this pretence up though?'

'Can't I? I've had plenty of practice.'

Marian looked at her, and shrugged. 'Was that him, by the way, your son?'

Cordelia felt herself break into a smile, 'Yes, yes.'

'Good looking young man.'

'Yes, again, yes he is. Come on, we'd better get back in there,' Cordelia said in a bright voice, and headed back into the main hall.

Later, after the others had left, Cordelia locked the Hall and double checked it, and turned towards Marian waiting for her.

'I've been thinking,' Marian began.

'Careful,' Cordelia said, recognising in herself a release of the pressure that had held her for so long.

'Ha ha! I think we ought to pay Jim a visit, you, me and Kevan. I want to see that bastard's face when we all turn up on his doorstep and confront him with what we know.'

'Oh! Do you think that's a good idea, wouldn't that make him do something else?'

'No! Best to confront that type, they are usually cowards, besides we'd have Kevan with us and I am sure he'll not be taking any nonsense. After all, he's suffered too.'

'True, I feel awful, I hope he'll understand.'

'I'm going to talk to him this evening, I'm sure I can get through to him,' Marian gave a wicked smile.

'Then let's do that. When?'

'Well, tomorrow morning. Early, sounds good to me. Before the devil's even got up, wake him up, shake him up.' Marian had a gleam in her eye.

Cordelia bit her lip, 'Okay, let's say ... eight?' thinking that she could be back and getting Gerald's Sunday breakfast ready for nine, just about.

'Not quite early enough, I think it has to be seven, half past at the latest. Catch him napping.'

'Oh, all right. Shall we walk?'

'I'll let you know, after I've talked to Kevan,' she said as they reached Cordelia's car and got in for the short journey home.

Cordelia's phone vibrated under her pillow telling her it was a quarter to seven. She slid from the bed and taking her clothes slipped into the bathroom, hoping Gerald would recall her saying that Marian had persuaded her to go for a run with her before breakfast. Ten minutes later, freshened up and dressed in her jogging clothes she tiptoed downstairs and made herself an instant coffee. She gulped it down quickly before she left the house at a quarter past, jogging towards Marian's house.

Marian was waiting by her car, as she saw Cordelia approach she slid into it and Cordelia jumped in just as Marian started the engine.

'We're picking Kevan up at the end of Zaggy Lane,' Marian said as she trundled the Berlingo past Cordelia's place and turned towards Downham Farm.

Kevan was waiting, looking bright and fresh for that time on a Sunday morning. Cordelia got out and climbed into the back seat allowing Kevan the front seat. Within minutes they turned down the steep narrow lane to Hideaway Cottage. Cordelia was aware she was holding her breath as Marian steered the car between the stone gateposts.

'Huh, his car's missing,' Kevan said, throwing open the door. Cordelia climbed out, Marian stood, leaning on her open door.

'Seems quiet,' she said.

'Always quiet down here,' Kevan murmured and began to walk towards the door. Marian and Cordelia followed him, catching him up by the time he rapped on the door.

They stood and listened to the silence that followed.

Kevan knocked again, shoving the old knocker down hard onto the stud it rested on. The sound echoed in the valley. 'He's gone,' Kevan said.

Marian went to a window, shielded her eyes and peered in.

'Anything?' Cordelia said behind her.

'I think he's right, think he's done a bunk. Nothing to be seen here ...' she moved round the house, peering in other windows. 'Nothing ... I couldn't have told you what was in there, but it looked lived-in, now it doesn't. Damn!'

Cordelia felt relieved, she didn't like confrontations, she just wanted everything to go back to normal. Well, normal but with knowing her son.

'He must have come straight back yesterday and packed and run,' Marian mused.

'Mmm, quite possibly, Max did say he was terrified,' Cordelia whispered.

'There you go then,' Marian said softly, then raising her voice again, 'I think you're right Kevan, he's done a bunk.'

'Huh! Well, I'll have to get on to the landlord then,' Kevan said, looking round the garden as if Jim might be hiding somewhere.

'Why?'

'He owes me, for work on the garden, and I'm supposed to be keeping it tidy on a regular basis. Now Jim's scarpered I'll have to get hold of the other bloke, that's all.'

Cordelia was glad in a way. Jim had taken fright and run. Run back to wherever he came from. That was an end to it, thank goodness. She could go back to her normal life without threats, without being scared every time an email pinged into her inbox. She almost forgot to tell Marian to drop her before they reached The Old Chapel. She climbed out, leant back in and smiled.

'Well, good riddance to him, that's what I say. See you later at the Hall?'

'Yeah, sure. And you are right. If he's cleared out it is probably just for the best. Take care,' Marian said. Cordelia closed the door and watched the car drive off. She turned and put on a spurt, jogging right round to the kitchen door. She paused there, loosening her shoes and taking them off as she stepped into the house. All was still quiet. She trotted upstairs and into their room. Gerald stirred as she entered.

'I'll just get a shower, then breakfast will be on its way,' she said brightly.

'Mmm Mm,' Gerald answered.

After breakfast Cordelia tried calling Gill's mobile, to speak to George. George, it seemed was at home, Gill being now stable and making progress, the hospital had sent George home to rest.

'Anything I can do George? Breakfast?'

'No, dear, no. I'm okay, and thank you for the cleaning-up. You'd never know now,' he said, still sounding tired.

'Not a problem. When can Gill have visitors?'

'Not yet, no, not yet. I'll let you know. Thank you.'

'Send Gill our love, won't you?'

'Of course, thank you.'

Cordelia hurried out and jumped in the car to park at the Hall. It was the last day of the Art Fair, and often one that was the busiest, though not always the most lucrative for the artists. Joan was already waiting when she arrived and as she unlocked she filled her in on how Gill was getting on.

The whole day went quickly as it tends to do when it is busy. As usual there were plenty of people popping into the exhibition to look rather than buy, and many stood chatting amongst the paintings and sculptures. It was by far the most social of days and once again Cordelia wondered if they could enhance the Art Fair takings by having a marquee to serve teas, at least on the last day.

They had the facilities to make and serve, just not the space to sit down when the hall was full of the exhibition, and the weather could not be guaranteed no matter when the Art Fair was held. She was just looking out of the hall window toward the playing field when Marian came and stood beside her.

'Penny for them?'

Cordelia smiled, 'Wondering if people would go for a cup of tea and cake if we had a marquee out there? Whether it would be cost-effective.'

'Ah! Good, not dwelling on yesterday, or this morning.'

'No,' she sighed, 'onwards and upwards?'

'Onwards and upwards!'

Five o'clock came, and as the last visitors left the Hall artists pounced to remove any unsold paintings and to see how they had done. Within an hour the hall was empty of paintings and sculptures and the boards were being dismantled. Kevan had come along for the first time too and was busy being directed by Marian. By eight o'clock the Hall was cleared, swept and ready to lock up. Everyone worked with a practised air, this was the fifteenth Art Fair that Cordelia had arranged and the atmosphere was one of a job well done especially as Joan had pronounced an early estimate as their best year yet.

Cordelia and Gerald were the last of the group to arrive at the pub, most of the others had already settled in and got their drinks. The food had all been pre-ordered, as was usual, and they only had to wait for it to be served.

'Here,' Marian said, as they arrived, indicating empty seats opposite her.

Cordelia slipped into the seat opposite Marian and Gerald went off to the bar to get their drinks, almost immediately Kevan appeared carrying drinks for himself and Marian and slid into the space beside her. Cordelia noticed the warm smiles they exchanged.

'So the Art Fair has done well again then?' Kevan said, raising his glass in a small salute.

'So it seems, it's amazing how well it does year on year. Thank you for helping.'

'Not at all, I'd have helped years ago if I'd known, proper like.'

'Known what?'

'That I'd be welcome, it always seemed a bit ...'

'He's trying to say it seemed stuck-up ...'

'Marian!' Kevan, putting his hand on her arm.

' - not you – the idea of an Art Fair. Anyway, he knows better now,' she grinned.

At which point Gerald returned with their glasses and stood stock-still at the end of the table. Cordelia looked up at him, 'Gerald? Are you okay?'

'Do you want to sit here?' he said, glaring towards Kevan. Cordelia realised she hadn't had the time to tell Gerald how things had changed.

'Yes, yes I do, um, it seems I made a mistake. Gerald, sit down, I'll explain.'

Gerald placed the glasses carefully down on the table and keeping his eyes on Kevan pulled the chair out and sat down opposite him. Cordelia touched his arm to get him to look at her.

'It was a mistake, I totally misunderstood. Kevan was not to blame and, and, I've asked him to come back to us.'

'But you said you wanted ...'

'He's going to do slightly fewer hours, as he's taken on another garden, but we'll be fine with that, won't we?'

'Oh! Hummph, fine,' Gerald pulled a smile and nodded at Kevan. Kevan replied with another glass salute.

Cordelia breathed a sigh of relief, glad that Gerald had just gone along with it.

Gerald turned his head towards Cordelia and leant in, 'You can explain to me properly later,' he said. Her heart sank.

Chapter 48

First thing Monday morning! What kind of time is that to see your agent, that's what I want to know? It sounds more like being hauled up before the headmaster.

Anyway, I got there, well, a quarter to ten, seems like first thing in the morning to me. It was too early for me to have got myself sorted out, that's for sure.

'Mr Galsworthy will see you now,' his twee little assistant said to me, her eyes raking over my face again, just as she had done a couple of times since I'd sat down. I sauntered towards his door and opened it with a flourish.

'William,' I said, my voice hearty.

'Sean,' he started. 'What, what have you done to your ...' he waved his hand to indicate the head region.

'It's not what I've done, it's what I haven't done – I haven't been to the barbers since I came back. You don't think I'm really bald, do you?' Though, as I had adopted my 'sinister' image as part of my author brand before I had found him as an agent, perhaps he did.

'No, but, well you look ... quite different.'

'Just as well,' I said, as he'd given me the perfect opening, 'Just as well it is a good disguise, I'll get it shaved today then I just need to grow my beard back and they'll not recognise me.'

'Oh yes, that's the other thing I wondered what I was missing, the little Lenin beard,' he said smiling, missing my point altogether.

'William, about your house, you know, those locals are very funny about incomers buying their houses for holiday homes. They just about accept them being lived in all the time, but they are like the Welsh back in the eighties, you know, they think these holiday-home owners need to be burnt out,' I laid it on thick as he wasn't picking up my hints.

'What's that got to do with your hair style?'

'Well, truth be told, I upset a few people there. I really do not want to be found, luckily while I was writing I had let my image go a bit, let the hair grow, shaved off the beard.'

'And what's that got to do with my house?'

'Oh … nothing, I just think you should get rid of it, that's all.'

'Seems a bit extreme, and hardly my fault if you …'

'You don't seem to get it, there could be some very bad publicity if they find out who I am, and that I am an author.'

'Haha, well you know what they say no publicity is …'

'Fuck that nonsense. This could be really bad. I mean, it's not even near the sea or anything, and you've hardly been there since you bought it.'

'No, well, hardly, you were there and forbade me!'

'And you didn't miss it – seriously, think about it.'

Willam rocked back in his chair and looked at me for a moment or two. I was just about to have another go when he said, 'The manuscript.'

Instantly alert, 'Yes?'

'Bloody fantastic,' he was beaming now. 'The characters … step off the page … come right up to you and speak.'

'You liked it then,' I knew I was beaming too.

'Can't wait to hear from the editor. I am sure they will be pleased. Chilling. Sexy. Twisted – it's got everything.'

'Fantastic, good. Now, can I go? I really must get to the barbers!'

'Go on then! Good job, Sean.'

'And I mean it about the house, it really wouldn't be good,' I fired off as I left, gratified to see a shadow of concern flitter across his well-scrubbed face.

Chapter 49

The first day after the Art Fair was always an anti-climax, Cordelia thought, as she flipped through her emails. Even more so this time as everything over the past few weeks had added to the tension and stress. Now she could relax a bit, wait for Joan's final figure and write her piece for the local newsletter. Max was away with his family, so she wasn't sneaking out to meet him, the mystery emailer had been identified and had fled, Marian and Kevan were getting along well, and he was coming back to do her garden again so she didn't have to look for someone else.

About half past ten Kevan pulled up in his van. Cordelia made sure she went out to greet him, still feeling guilty at having jumped to the wrong conclusion.

'All right?' he said in greeting.

'Yes, you?'

'Good. What are we doing today then?' as if there had never been any trouble between them.

'Thank you for being so good about this whole sorry mess, that man had me totally fooled.'

'No worries, I got the landlord's name and email address out of the estate agent this morning,' he grinned, 'against all their rules, apparently, but then I did go to school with him.'

'Oh, good.'

'Do you think I should ask about his tenant?'

'Why? Why would you want to do that?' Cordelia felt a mild panic tremble through her.

'Well, I can tell you he upset Marian. She hasn't said what he did, but it shook her up, I can tell that.'

Cordelia looked at Kevan with new eyes; he was obviously more sensitive than he looked.

'I don't think, I mean, he was just renting for the summer wasn't he? Probably through an agent.'

'Well they didn't use the one that sold the house, and you'd do that wouldn't you, use someone local, and they're the only local ones they know. No, I think he was someone the owner knew. There was something about the way he ordered the garden done, sounded too much like the landlord would do what he suggested.'

'I don't, I really don't know. I think, good riddance to the man, I really don't want anything more to do with him. I mean look at what, what bad feeling he created here,' she waved her hand to indicate them both.

'Yeah, perhaps you're right. So, what's it to be? Lawns, borders or terraces?'

'Terraces, please. I'm going to give the borders a bit of a weed myself.'

'Okay,' he smiled and set off towards the garden shed.

Cordelia spent a pleasant couple of hours pulling weeds and trimming the borders, her head amongst the flowers, her mind running over the possibilities of seeing Max and his family after they returned from holiday. She wondered how she could bring up Max's existence with Gerald, whether the only way would be to tell another big lie, to make Max out to be a nephew or something. She'd never mentioned a sister or brother, so perhaps he had to be more distant, the son of a cousin, that might work. Yes, that might work; only just found out that they live in the same area? Would Gerald swallow that one? It was hard. All of this was hard. She had promised herself all those years ago that she would never tell him any more lies. She was too much enamoured with him to risk wiping the slate clean back then, even telling him he wasn't her first lover had seemed a risk and she had the feeling that he looked at her differently for a few days after she'd admitted it.

She stood and stretched, peeled off her gloves and wandered down towards the terraces. The buzz of the strimmer had stopped about half an hour before and as she came around the end of the house she caught sight of Kevan sweeping the cut grass into piles with a lawn rake.

'Drink?' she called, miming drinking. He looked up, grinned and gave a thumbs up. She returned to the house, filled a pint glass with squash and a half pint for herself and took it back outside.

'Here you go,' she said.

Kevan took the glass, raised it a little and then took a deep draught. 'Hot today,' he said.

'Yes, certainly is.'

'I'll just pick up this grass, then I'm done.'

'Good, looks so much tidier when the edges are all trimmed. I'm in for lunch now, see you on Wednesday?'

'Yep, see you then,' handing her the glass back.

Cordelia took the glass and returned to the cool of her kitchen, wondering how long before she stopped feeling guilty when she spoke to Kevan.

She had just placed her empty lunch plate in the dishwasher when the phone rang.

'Hello?'

'Mrs Steadman?' the voice sounded slightly familiar but tremulous.

'Yes?'

'It's Jenny, from Pearn Associates?' her voice now identified still sounded wrong. 'It's about Mr Steadman, he's been taken poorly, an ambulance has just taken him into Derriford hospital.'

Cordelia heard herself gasp, 'What is it? What's wrong?'

'I, I can't really ... oh!' Jenny's voice cracked.

'Please?'

'I went in after lunch, he, he was just slumped in his chair. I think he'd had a stroke, a major stroke. I called the ambulance right away – that's what they said when they came.'

'Oh God! I'll go now, thank you, thanks.'

'How could ...' Jenny began, but Cordelia put the phone down and stood in a panic-induced freeze-frame for a moment, her thoughts whirling and preventing her getting going. She kick-started herself, she had to get together anything Gerald would need for a stay in hospital. She ran upstairs and collected his washing and shaving gear together, packed them into his travel wash bag, carefully laid a couple of fresh pairs of pyjamas, his dressing-gown and a towel in a small case. She knew that he'd be horrified at the idea of wearing hospital pyjamas or using a hospital towel if he was well enough to wash and shave. Minutes later she locked the door and ran for the car.

Chapter 50

She arrived at the hospital half an hour later and headed straight for A & E, expecting Gerald to have been brought there first. As soon as she had a chance to speak to the receptionist she was told that he'd been transferred straight to the Acute Stroke Unit on level eight.

Thanking the girl she turned and headed out of A & E deciding to go in the main entrance so she could orientate herself with the places she knew within the hospital. It didn't take her long to find the Acute Stroke Unit sign and follow it to the right area.

'Excuse me,' she said to catch the attention of the girl whose eyes were fixed to her computer screen as she flickered her fingers over the keyboard in front of her. The girl glanced at up her, it was enough. 'Can you help me, my husband has been brought in here, Gerald Steadman, he came through from A & E.'

'Hello, yes, he's in here, but I'm afraid you can't see him at the moment, they have taken him down for an immediate MRI scan.'

'Oh?' Cordelia wasn't sure whether this was a positive sign or not.

'It's all right, it is standard procedure for a stroke when there is lack of consciousness.'

Cordelia glanced around. 'May I wait ... somewhere?'

'Yes, of course,' the girl got up and came out from behind her desk, there's a day room at the end of the corridor, she said leading the way, 'please wait here,' pushing the door open, 'I'll let the doctors know you are here when Mr Steadman returns from the MRI.'

Cordelia put the bag down and walked to the other side of the room. The view was of another wing of the hospital, not very inspiring. She turned again and looked at the room, a range of blue wipe-clean armless easy chairs edged the space, a couple of coffee tables central and a couple of standard chairs, with arms, either side of the door. On the walls at each end were framed pictures, all created by students at a local school. On closer inspection two were really quite good, she thought, as she looked at them with her art-buyer eyes, either of these students could have made the cut. She should know. In the time between meeting Gerald and their leaving London for Plymouth she had become invaluable to Gallerie Giovanni. Roberto Giovanni had recognised her talent for spotting artwork that would sell, and sent her to scour the markets and art shows for unknown artists that he could promote.

It didn't take much to draw her back to those days, to her growing realisation that Gerald really liked her, that she really did have an eye for work that would sell, and that there was a whole different way of life to be lived. A respectable life; settled, educated, polite, and that she desperately wanted it, wanted that stability, that respectability, to be her life.

'Mrs Steadman?' a young-looking doctor stood in the doorway.

'Yes,' Cordelia said starting towards him as he entered the room and extended a hand to shake. She took his hand and smiled, suddenly she had a lump in her throat and couldn't speak.

'Dr Graham,' he introduced himself. 'Shall we sit?' indicating a couple of chairs nearby. Cordelia took a seat and he pulled the other chair out so that he semi-faced her.

'How is he?' she managed.

'Mr Steadman has had an acute stroke. The MRI that we have just done has shown that it is a primary intracerebral haemorrhage, which, in layman's terms means he's had a bleed in his brain.'

Cordelia nodded, she wasn't sure what to say, nor sure she could get the words out anyway.

'May I ask you a few questions?' he said.

She nodded again.

'How was your husband's health in general?'

'Good, he kept fit, he has a gym room at home and uses it daily.'

'Any recurring headaches, migraines?

She started to shake her head, then remembered. 'He had an awful headache recently, so bad he thought it might be a migraine, though he'd never had one of those before.'

'When was this?'

She wracked her brains, when was it? She'd come home to find Gerald back... when? The past few weeks, since the emails started, had seemed so long. She hadn't quite finished the Art Fair plans, she'd been working on them that day she knew, and it was the day she got the first email.

'About a week and a half ago I think. I remember I asked him to smile because he also said his face felt funny when he woke up, but it was okay, all even, but he wouldn't go to the doctors with it even though I said he should! Could we have stopped it?'

'Hmm, it was rather early if it is connected, and I think your doctor may not have recognised it anyway, so don't worry. Does he have any history of high blood pressure?'

'No, not at all? Why?'

'Only that this type of event can sometimes be triggered by an episode of high blood pressure.'

'His firm gives a yearly medical, nothing showed up last time, back in April.'

'Ah? Who does that?'

'I think the firm have it done privately.'

'Thank you, I'll get on to that in case it can help.'

'And now? What,' she swallowed trying to get the words past the lump in her throat, 'what does it mean for Gerald?'

'We have to wait and see, at least for now, Gerald is still unconscious though we are preparing to relieve the pressure by surgery.'

Cordelia felt tears spring into her eyes. 'Will he be all right?'

The doctor looked solemn, 'We will have to see, he's alive and there is a good chance he'd make a reasonable recovery. I can't say it will be the best outcome as it seems he was not found immediately the event happened, his PA says it could have occurred anytime between ten thirty when she took him a cup of coffee and one thirty when she found him. It seems she is instructed never to disturb him between those hours?'

'Yes, that would be right,' Cordelia's voice cracked as she thought of Gerald's unfailing routines.

'Well, if it was the later time then there may not be too much brain damage, if earlier ...' he let the unsaid words hang in the air, they dropped into Cordelia's heart with a thump. Gerald!

'I'll come back as soon as we know anything more,' he said standing. 'Why don't you go down and get a cup of coffee or something. There won't be any news for a while, a few hours at least.'

She knew he was trying to be kind, but she found it hard to even say thank you, as if her vocal cords had been tied.

In a daze Cordelia wandered towards the main foyer where she knew they did coffee. She felt she ought to be telling someone, but who? Gerald's sister? Yes, but she didn't have her number with her. His nephew, she shook her head, she didn't want to tell him, scared of ill-wishing. Nothing she could do right now anyway so a cup of coffee, and then she'd call Marian.

Marian answered the phone chirpily with her business name and voice, the echoey sound suggested it was on speaker and in her workplace building. 'Greenwood Organics.'

'Marian, it's me.'

'Hello me.'

'I, I'm at the hospital, Gerald's had a stroke ...' her voice choked off.

'C'delia, no! Oh, poor Gerald, when?' Cordelia could tell the phone had been snatched up and was off speaker, the quality immediately more intimate.

'This morning, they think, sometime before lunch... it all depends, how soon ... whether ...'

'I'll come, where are you. I'll come.'

'No, no need, I'll be okay.'

'Nonsense, where can I meet you?'

'I'm in the foyer, Derriford, having a coffee but I'll be going straight back up to the Acute Stroke Unit, I'll probably be there, in the day room, until I can see him.'

'Okay, see you as soon as possible.'

Cordelia sipped her coffee, it tasted strong but thin, without the body to justify the flavour. After a few more minutes she felt she just couldn't sit there any longer, left the half drunk coffee, and set off to return to the Acute Stroke Unit. She walked with purpose, fast but not running, but as she rounded a corner she half crashed into a man coming the other way.

'Sorry, sorry,' she said, steadying him, her hand on his arm, and realised it was George. 'George?'

'Oh, Cordelia,' he said, his face contorting as tears started from his red-rimmed eyes.

'What? George, has something happened?'

'Were you coming to see Gill? She's not there.'

'Oh George when, what?' fearing the worst.

'They've moved her to Acute Stroke, Oh God! She's had a stroke! She'll never live with that. She, she's always so busy.'

'Oh, poor Gill. Where are you going? Now?'

'They sent me down for coffee, fat lot of good. I need to be there for her.'

'Me too, come on, we'll get a coffee and, well, we'll talk.'

'Okay,' George said, his face back under control and almost managing a smile.

She got herself a tea and George a coffee with a large Danish pastry. George was just one of those men you knew would feel better when well fed.

'Here you go,' she said as she placed the tray down before them, 'Now tell me what happened, you said she was doing so much better.'

'Yes, they were very pleased, she'd regained consciousness, she was talking and seemed as bright as before. She was upset mind, about her Dad being locked away, but there was nothing to be done there.'

Cordelia nodded, 'Mmm?'

'Then this afternoon she seemed to be napping, but when the doctor did his rounds they couldn't wake her, it was all so sudden, bit of a panic and everything. She was taken for a scan and they just came back and told me it was a kind of stroke, something to do with being hit over the head, pressure or something, I couldn't take it in to be honest.'

'Did they say what they are going to do?'

'Not sure, I can't remember, but I know my Gill, she'll go mad if she's disabled for the rest of her life.'

'They know what they are doing, and if it was caught early then there won't be much permanent damage,' she said, parroting the doctor from earlier, as if she really knew. She reached over and patted George's arm. He looked up at her, gave a grim smile and reached for the Danish.

Cordelia realised that her own panic had been subdued by dealing with George's. 'George,' she started, he looked up at her again, chewing, 'I wasn't actually coming into see Gill today, just to let you know, Gerald is in hospital too. In the same ward, now – Acute Stroke,' she let that sink in. 'He's totally unconscious, they have taken him for surgery, I was just going back to see if there is any news.'

'Oh! Oh!' George said, his mouth making goldfish moves.

'Don't worry, don't worry. It's just I want to go back up there, now, you understand? You'll be okay here, finishing your coffee?'

'No, I'll come with you,' he picked up his coffee and started to gulp it. Stopped, nodded, and finished off the coffee; the remains of the pastry still in his hand, they left the cafeteria.

As they walked into the day room Cordelia noticed the bag she had brought for Gerald sitting on the floor. She had totally forgotten she'd put it down. She went to it and picked it up, placing it on a chair near the door. George wandered over to the window and stood there a moment. He turned.

'Funny we're in the same position, isn't it?'

Cordelia didn't know what to answer to that.

'And you were the first person to come and help me when Gill got hurt too.'

'Just the first of many, I'm sure, if you'd been at home,' Cordelia said.

The door swung open and Marian burst in. 'C'delia!'

'Oh Marian!' Cordelia felt her new-built defences slip away as tears filled her eyes and her throat constricted as Marian hugged her.

'George?' Marian said, as they came out of their hug.

'Marian,' he nodded.

'Gill's been brought to this ward too,' Cordelia said. 'Just heard about it from George.'

The door opened again, the young doctor again, he glanced round greeting everyone with a smile. 'Mr Dodman?'

George started towards him, 'Yes?'

'You can come and see your wife now,' Dr Graham smiled.

'Oh, good,' George looked back at Cordelia and Marian, 'I'll let you know how she is,' he said as he followed the doctor out of the room. Before the door swung shut Cordelia could hear the doctor talking to George and caught the words, 'early enough'.

George came back and cheerfully announced that Gill seemed fine now, everything working, no numbness that they were worried about, that they thought she would be okay - and left them to go and sit with her.

The time passed, it had grown dark outside. They'd gone down and eaten at the hospital cafeteria and come back.

By the time a different doctor came back into the day room it was so late it was early morning and even Marian had lapsed into silence, Cordelia stood immediately.

'Mrs Steadman?'

She nodded.

'Would you like to come with me to the office,' he said looking across at Marian. Marian stood too, 'You can talk here, I'll go and wait outside if you like?'

His solemn face did not change, 'No thank you, but please wait here for Mrs Steadman.'

Cordelia and Marian clasped hands. 'I'll be right here,' Marian said giving her a tight smile.

As soon as she stepped into the cramped little office she wished she had insisted that Marian had come with her. She sat in the chair at the end of the desk, the doctor sat too, facing her, and linked his hands together in front of him.

'Mrs Steadman, when your husband was brought in earlier today we recognised that he'd had a major stroke and treated him immediately. The MRI scan showed us a intracerebral haemorrhage.' He leant back and pressed a key on his computer, a picture of a slice through a brain showed itself. 'Here,' he said pointing to a different colour patch in the picture. 'We could see that there was a great deal of fluid build-up creating pressure within the brain such that it had closed down functions causing the patient to collapse.' He glanced at her as if to ascertain that she understood. She nodded. He went on 'We have now relieved this pressure by carrying out a procedure known as decompressive hemicraniectomy,' he said the words carefully as if it would help her understand them. 'We remove a piece of the skull, to relieve the pressure, and then we can drain off some of the fluid and seal the leak.'

All Cordelia wanted to know at this point was whether Gerald would be all right – she knew later she would want all the minute details, she knew he would too, but right now this was not what she wanted. 'Is he going to be all right?'

The doctor looked at the floor for a millisecond before answering, 'Mr Steadman, Gerald, is now awake, but I have to tell you that we think there may be serious damage. His responses are not good.'

Part 2

Chapter 51

I settled my black fedora tightly on my hairless head to keep out the cold and wrapped the blood-red scarf round my neck in the ends-through-loop style, hunched into my black leather jacket and set out. It had to be the coldest morning of the winter so far; frost rimed the railings and edged any plants brave enough to still have leaves on in late November. None of this mattered to me, I was on my way to Galsworthy's office and he would be in a good mood.

The twee assistant smiled at me as soon as I stepped through the door.

'Sean, come in!' The man himself came to his door and ushered me in. 'Great news eh?'

'Sure, what's the procedure now then?' I acted cool, but to be honest, to be listed, even on the long list, for the Best Reads was an honour, especially as we'd missed out on Frankfurt because I was so late handing in the manuscript. The publishers had aimed for the Christmas market instead, bringing the book out in early November and hyping it up as 'the perfect gift for your thrill-loving man' and all that trash. They had been enthusiastic enough to send it in for just about any gongs that were going for novels conceivably in my genre and position, but most had given it a miss – none of us had any real hopes with the Best Reads as it usually went to the strange, the literary or the historic. You were as unlikely to find a thriller there as you were to find a romance. Still, here we were and delighted, beyond delighted, by it.

'The reader's recommendation says "Though a thriller in outline this well written novel, with totally believable characters, brings moral questions to the fore, the reader is forced to decide whether they are with the protagonist, the first person narrative, or with the exploited in the tale.

Your literary experience tells you that you should be identifying with the first person narrative, yet it soon becomes clear that this action-man is not one you want to be inside the head of. You want to shout out a warning to the woman, to tell her his innermost thoughts that you are party to. She is defenceless, you want to become her defender, and yet, and yet... This is the exceptional element that brings this book out of the ordinary thriller genre into a suitable candidate for the Best Reads prize." What do you think of that?'

'Excellent, that Best Reads reader has captured the precise thing I was working on,' I said, loving how people find things in works of fiction that were not necessarily put there for any such purpose. I had wanted to tell the tale from the baddie's point of view, I just felt it would up the tension, it does, but I hadn't expected the morality to be a problem to the reader in a way that created another dimension to the story; that was a bonus.

'The reviews coming in from the press and the book sites are good too, the publishers say the orders are up week on week.'

'Great, but why did you need me to come in today?'

'Oh! I want us to go through a schedule for a proper book tour. Really the launch and those few London stores was a bit weak for a book of such calibre.'

'You're telling me! A launch party in a pub function room, glass of plonk and buy your own - not even a book shop, and signings in Waterstones and The Big Green in the same week. Barely one mention in the press.'

'I know, I know. So they feel it now needs to be higher profile, this is the plan, we are setting out on a book tour around the country. Every large Waterstones in the country, within two months, nearly all the cities in the UK!'

'You have got to be joking!'

'No, it's great, it means you'll have publicity in just about every local paper in the country by the time the judges read the book.'

'And I'll be dead, and I can't write a word while we are fucking around like that.'

'I know, but that is what gets you noticed. If the judges get the book and dump it and it is already a people's favourite, then there would be a ruckus. Get it popular then they will be less inclined to drop it. We make sure we suggest the morality angle in such a way that the reviewers think they spotted it themselves and we behave all modest about that so the judges don't think we have them hooked.'

'William, have you ever had a Best Reads possibility before?' I asked, doubting his plan.

He hesitated, 'No - but my uncle has, more than one, lots in fact, and he is advising me.'

His uncle? This was the first time I knew he had an uncle in the business. 'Who's he?'

He named one of the most famous literary agents in history; Clark Marcus! I was gobsmacked and acquiesced. It looked like I was going to have a busy couple of months ahead of me.

Chapter 52

'Come in, shut the door, it's freezing out today isn't it?' Cordelia said as Marian arrived. The Old Chapel was warm inside, over-warm.

'How's Gerald today?' Marian asked, almost wishing she didn't have to start every meeting with Cordelia in the same way.

'Just the same,' Cordelia's voice betrayed her tiredness. 'Coffee?' Marian nodded and they went through to the kitchen together. 'Go and say hello while I make it,' Cordelia suggested.

Marian left the kitchen and went through to what had been the gym annexe, she knocked at the door and entered. The view was the same but the room now held a high-tech bed and all sorts of lifting equipment. A large flat screen TV hung on a mobile arm and this was angled so that Gerald could see it, propped up as he was in bed. Over on the far side the wide door to the recently created wet room stood slightly ajar.

'Hello Gerald,' she said, walking into the space in front of Gerald so that he could see her. His face didn't move, he blinked a couple of times. She smiled. 'Yes, hello to you too. I've just popped in for coffee with Cordelia.'

He blinked twice, again.

She knew Cordelia was looking at getting him an eye-movement recognition system so that he could spell out words as she was sure he had complete understanding. Marian wasn't so sure. She'd said something that was pure nonsense once when Cordelia was out of earshot and Gerald had replied with just the same double blink.

'Back soon,' she said and returned to Cordelia.

'Okay?' Cordelia said as she came back into the kitchen.

'Yes, fine.'

They took their cups through to the main room and sat on the sofas.

'How are you coping? Really?' Marian asked.

'Fine, I have the carers who come in twice a day and help me with the hard stuff, the lifting, washing and … things. Feeding isn't a problem since they decided he had to have a gastric-tube, though he does seem a bit distressed when it starts.'

'I didn't mean how was Gerald coping, I meant you. You've not had a minute to yourself in, how long, nearly three months?'

'I had Max and the family over for the afternoon in the October half-term.'

Marian raised her eyebrows, 'Nice as that was, it wasn't exactly 'me time' for you was it?'

'I know, but it was so good. Joshua rolling down the terrace slopes, getting to meet Megan and Heather.'

'How about getting back to the book group?'

'Well, it's difficult. I know he'd be upset if someone else were caring for him, it's bad enough that I have to have help in, but I'm always there too. I can tell he must hate it, he was always such a private person.'

'I have a suggestion.'

'Go on?'

'How about if the book group meets here instead of at Gill's?'

'But Gill …'

'Could do with not having to have it at her house. She has made such a good recovery but I can tell she gets agitated when we all arrive.'

'I wouldn't want her to think …'

'I'll ask her. You could be here, on hand to check on Gerald, but you'd be back in the swing of things. You can catch up, chat to people. When did you last go out, even to shop?'

Cordelia looked down.

'You haven't, have you? You don't even go out to shop, I've seen the Waitrose delivery van here.'

'I can't, how can I go out and leave him here, like this?'

'He'd want you to, he wouldn't want you to stop living your life. You always did things independently of Gerald when he was ...' she caught herself, the word 'alive' wavered on her tongue, 'fit and well,' she finished.

'I know but that was different, and we did so much together too.'

'Exactly, come on. The book group will be a start, they can come here.'

'But Gerald would know they were here, he never liked people in the house when he was home.'

'We'll be quiet, it's not like a mad party is it? Or a coffee morning, we can have a quiet discussion.'

'I'll think about it,' Cordelia gave a tight smile, 'honest. Now tell me what is going on with you.'

'Ah me! Well, things are good at the moment. The new shampoo is going down a storm. I even got a review of it on one of those popular online beauty blogs, an organics one of course, but I've noticed a spike in sales from the website, so that's good.'

'And Kevan?'

Marian smiled. 'Good. It is hard to believe he was here right under my nose all that time, and he just didn't know I was looking and was too shy to ask.'

'You will think about the book group, twice a month, give your brains something to get themselves around. I mean, sorry. Just give yourself something else to think about.' Marian prompted as she was leaving.

'Of course, I'll think about it, see you.'

Cordelia closed the door and turned back into her home. It was time to prepare the Ensure for Gerald, to set the mixture into the pump and feed him. His body was wasting away even though his limbs were manipulated everyday, keeping the joints moving, trying to maintain some muscle mass and, perhaps, teaching the neurones he had left new tricks and new pathways. He sat up day and

270

night to avoid aspiration pneumonia while the bed moved beneath him to relieve the pressure. His gaze seemed to rest in the middle distance, she wasn't sure if he even saw the view that he used to love so much. As for the television, she only put on programmes she thought he would like as she couldn't bear to think of his fury if he was conscious of watching stuff he'd have hated. He blinked at her. She hoped it meant that he was there inside, that he could be released by finding some way of communicating.

She'd read up about stroke, it was so unpredictable. It seemed that the time that he had been unconscious and undiscovered had caused the wide-ranging damage. They assumed the stroke had happened in the earlier part of the timeframe because of the degree of impairment, but they hadn't given up hope of some improvement, they said.

The wet room had taken the longest to provide, three whole weeks, and no amount of money seemed to speed the completion of that, but once it was done he came home. It was only because Gerald had such good insurance that they could afford quality care in the home, some of the lifting and bathing equipment was supplied through the NHS but she'd bought in extra carers to help and a daily visit from a physiotherapist to work on his muscles. Nothing seemed to make any difference.

Later she ate alone in the kitchen, thinking over what Marian had said. Every day she looked into Gerald's ever-blinking eyes but, despite what she hoped and said, she still couldn't see him in there, no sign or flicker of recognition.

Maybe she would have the book group meet here, maybe, if Gill really was finding it a strain. It would be good to have a small focus outside of looking after Gerald. She felt herself sigh, picked herself up and went in to sit with Gerald again, talking to him and then turning on a programme she was sure he would like about the Spanish Armada.

Chapter 53

Good job I don't have many people to buy Christmas presents for, I don't think my feet have touched the ground for the past month, hotel after crappy hotel, Waterstones after Waterstones. The flat is dusty, again, without anyone being here. I should have let it out, got some income from it while I was away. Now there's a thought. I have the whole of January away, I could put it up on Gumtree – short let.

In the meantime, what is my plan for Christmas? Shit, an author's lot is a lonely one ... but not this evening, you can get a pass into some cool Christmas Eve parties if you are a Best Reads listed author.

I've got used to this appellation - I've been introduced this way twenty-nine times, I almost believe I'm in with a chance. The sales have been good, the publicity excellent. The reviews, city by city, have been coming in just as the great man suggested they would. Strangest thing of all, I've noticed William blossom, from a 'won't say boo to a goose ninny' to a 'confident swaggerer' which he just about manages to carry off without seeming camp. A surprise, but one I'm glad of if we are going to stick together.

Right, got them, tickets to a great party at the O2 arena tonight. That'll do me. Maybe I can pull too, it's been a while. A real while, Cornwall was the last time. That threw William too. I refused to go to Plymouth, Truro and Exeter. He just couldn't get it. I asked him if he'd sold that cottage yet. He'd prevaricated, I told him to get rid of it. If my face was going to be all over the media, if I won the Best Reads, he needed to have sold the place and cut any ties. He actually looked a little worried, as if he believed me at last, especially when I said I wasn't going to any Waterstones in the whole of Devon and Cornwall, just to be on the safe side. His face made me laugh, a right mixture of disbelief and of belief.

'Hi sweetie, I'm an author, wanna be in a book?' I shouted into her ear. The blasted music was too loud for my kind of chat-up lines.

'I'm nobody's bloody sweetie,' she said, 'go fuck yourself.'

'I was hoping we could do that together,' I tried.

She turned, gave me the finger, and left, wriggling her way through the crowd. One down, a hundred or so left to try.

Happy fucking Christmas, I thought as I woke, peeling open scratchy eyelids. I stared at the ceiling, perceptible in the light leaking in around the top of the curtains. It wasn't my ceiling - or my curtains! I glanced to the side. I'd pulled! Though I couldn't remember anything of it. Happy Christmas!

'Hey,' I said softly towards the mound of bed clothes beside me. 'Hey? Morning, Happy Christmas.' The mound moved, the duvet sliding round the shape, the face coming into view. It was a woman at least, but enough woman to make two women of the size I would rather be with. Shit. She smiled at me.

New Year's Resolution. No more seeing Melanie. She's very accommodating and younger than me but that's not the point. She's starting to think we have a proper relationship where we'll be going to book launches and stuff together. I can't do that, she really doesn't fit my image. I've told her I'm away on tour for the next month, that I won't be seeing her. She just assumes I'll come back to her when I return. Just as well I've kept my real address secret from her; I suspect she might turn stalker.

Chapter 54

The first book club meeting in December was held at The Old Chapel. It worked well. Cordelia timed the physiotherapist's visit to coincide with the start of the meeting so that Gerald was being looked after and there was something to take his mind off any noise he might hear. At least that was how Cordelia reasoned it to herself once Marian had explained how grateful Gill had been for the suggestion.

'Thank you for hosting the book club,' Gill said when she arrived, resting her hand on Cordelia's arm, 'You have no idea how stressful having lots of people in the house is now. It is as if I can't quite think of everything I need to at once.'

'It's no trouble, and it means I can join in again,' Cordelia said, wondering at how well Gill had recovered when essentially she and Gerald had the same diagnosis at one point.

Two days before Christmas Cordelia got Kevan to bring a real Christmas tree into the gym annexe and with his help got it set up. She liked the way Kevan talked to Gerald as if he was the same whole man he used to be. He had a kind and natural way about him. Not many people came to see Gerald now. There had been a flurry at the start, but after the first visit most just did not come again, and almost none actually talked to him as if he were still with them.

She had been disappointed that only one of his former colleagues had come to see him in the hospital and was surprised at how cold towards her the colleague had seemed at the time, and that none had come to visit him since he'd come home.

She talked to Gerald as she decorated the tree. Reminding him about some of the expensive or beautiful pairs of baubles they had collected over the years on their Christmas trips. The red glass ones with the gold-work patterns from Venice, the blue and white china ones from Delft, the painted wooden ones picked up in a market in Germany, did he remember that, an unusual impulse buy, and the Fabergé style ones from Moscow. She would miss their travels, even though it was always in winter when everywhere was less crowded, it took them to beautiful places with interesting museums, architecture and art galleries. She hung the last of the baubles and began to take out the strands of antique lametta, fine strands of real silver alloy 'angel hair', which she laid over each branch making a waterfall of reflected light.

'There, all done,' she said, looking towards him.

He seemed very still, she rushed over to him, his eyelids were still, she placed her hand on his chest, it wasn't moving.

'Gerald!' she shouted in his face, tried to find a pulse, pressing her fingers below his jawbone. 'Gerald?' She ran to the phone, dialled 999 and waited while they asked which service, ready with Ambulance and their home address. She rang Marian. She had to have someone with her; Marian came.

Chapter 55

'Back on the road again,' I can't imagine why I'm singing. To be honest I'm missing Melanie, she was a resolutely cheerful girl for all her other shortcomings, and she was comfortable to be around. Thank goodness this is only for another month. Already the publishers are asking about another book. Now, what I can't get my head round is when they think an author actually writes – in their fucking sleep? I'm out there pushing The Puppeteer as much for them as for me, the Best Reads will be a feather in their cap too. Anyway, just as well I have an excuse, I've quite lost my mojo, Melanie is too easy, no tension there at all and I'm back to having too many ideas that turn out to have little legs. Maybe I ought to write a collection of short stories, that's what seems to be popping up in my brain.

I keep thinking about her even now. Not surprising really, almost every time they ask the gathered audience at a book reading if they have any questions someone will say 'Delia is such a striking character, is she based on someone you know?' or words to that effect. I obfuscate, explain that almost no character in any fiction is totally fictional, that by describing a character we cannot but describe people by their colouring, their look, their manner, rather like putting together a photofit after a crime. However, it does not mean that the character is any one person ... I laugh ... that could be dangerous I say, feeling the thrill of it zing through me.

Occasionally it is the same question about 'The Puppeteer' himself, though that comes out differently, 'did you base The Puppeteer / Nick Typhon on yourself?' I smile my 'you caught me' smile and say of course, but only superficially and that I'm safe with that one as I'm not likely to sue myself. Cue laughter all round. It's like a travelling show!

William tells me he has put the house on the market at last and got an offer already. I asked who the potential buyer was and, as I thought, it's someone local. I hope he takes my advice and goes with the offer.

Chapter 56

The funeral had to wait until the third of January, what with Christmas and contacting Gerald's family. She thought bitterly of how they had all, one by one, come to visit Gerald after the stroke, and then never come, or enquired, again until the call to the funeral.

On the morning she dressed in a lace-covered black dress she had owned for a few years but had barely worn as it hugged her figure more than she really liked. It hung from her now, loose. Over this she wore an elegantly cut dark grey coat that Gerald had, unusually, helped her pick. She stood and looked at herself in the mirror. The reflection didn't look like her at all; it looked like a painting in gouache of a woman going to a funeral. Sighing, she picked up her small black bag and went outside; they had called to say the funeral car would be along at any moment to pick her up.

As Gerald had been a Churchwarden, the village had put on the honours. The altar arrangements were splendid, the choirstalls full. She had chosen traditional hymns that she knew he had liked to sing rather than anything modern or necessarily apt. She knew he would want a full funeral service with Communion included, and none of the modern trappings of videos and keepsakes. This was for him, a proper send off with committal to the ground to follow.

She dropped the token sprinkle of earth on his coffin and stepped back. Other family members followed. She took a moment to look around and spotted Max near the back of a crowd made up mainly of village retirees. She remained at her post as people came forward and shook her hand, muttering condolences.

Nearly everyone had moved off, chatting in small groups or wandering round to the church car park, or on their way up the hill towards the Hall where the funeral tea was to be held. Everyone, except Max and Jenny, Gerald's PA. She came towards Cordelia, but looking down at the coffin in the open grave. At the last moment she turned her eyes on Cordelia, they were full of tears. Cordelia held out her hand, but Jenny glanced at it and kept hers to herself.

'You're a bitch!' she said, her voice low and her lips drawn back. 'You killed him! I read that email - saw the picture - the very last thing he saw!'

'What?'

'You and,' she glanced over her shoulder towards Max, 'your lover – no wonder his blood pressure hit the roof.'

'I, I don't know what you are talking ...'

'You liar! You even have the gall to invite *him* to Gerald's funeral,' she turned again to look at Max who was still waiting quietly. 'Gerald was a gentleman, a true gentleman and you, you are just truly disgusting. You never deserved him,' her voice starting to rise.

'Jenny! Get a hold of yourself. If you mean him,' lifting her head to indicate Max, 'he's my son!'

'That's not true! That's not what it said – the email said "look at your perfect wife and her lover - look at the evidence!" I recognised *him* as soon as I arrived here!'

'Max! Come here please,' Cordelia said keeping her voice down. Max walked up to the pair, looking puzzled. 'Please tell Jenny what our real relationship is.'

'I'm her son, long lost son,' he said.

'No! You could have set that up.' Looking from Max back to Cordelia.

'How would I have known you, or anyone, was going to accuse me of anything?'

'No, I don't believe you. Gerald didn't have any children, I, we talked about it.'

279

'No Gerald didn't, Max was my son from before I met Gerald, given up for adoption.'

Jenny stared from one to the other for a moment. 'Oh God! Did Gerald know?'

Cordelia dipped her head, 'No, and he didn't know that Max had found me either. We were going to tell him once I had got used to the idea myself,' which was exactly how she had introduced Max to Gerald's family earlier in the day.

Jenny looked at them again. 'Oh no! I can see the likeness,' she said shaking her head, 'I'm sorry, I'm so sorry, I think I have to go and clear something up.'

'What was that about?' Max asked as she went.

'Jenny was Gerald's PA, it seems the last thing he was reading was a malicious email about us, and I am sure we know who it came from.' Cordelia's voice cracked as her throat constricted and tears filled her eyes, 'That bastard, he killed him, he might as well have just stabbed Gerald. Oh! But it's my fault too. If I'd not been trying to keep it secret, she's right, if I'd told him already he might not have had the bleed in his brain at all.'

'Shhh! Shh! Not your fault – that man, he's the one, he's just really twisted.'

'Twisted! I'd love to make him face up to this. Bastard! Fucking, fucking bastard! Sorry, sorry,' she fished a tissue from her bag and blotted her tears. 'It's no good. Come on, everyone will be there before me.' She straightened and marched off towards the funeral car waiting patiently outside the gate.

Chapter 57

How I love the spring! Full of new possibilities, especially now I am on the Best Reads shortlist. Just me and seven other wannabes and hopefuls! The man says I've to go quiet now, not to make too much of a fuss because the final judges don't like to be bullied by popular opinion, or for it to look like they are swayed by anything except their own 'exquisite' taste.

I've studied their form. A venerable retired television presenter who has had his own books, both fiction and non-fiction, in the number one slots of years gone past. His fiction solidly in 'general' puts him neither for nor against me at the starting blocks. Next, a literary editor with a feminist stance, my worst nightmare, she's almost contracted to dislike the thriller genre and the misanthropic attitude of my protagonist. I doubt my unusual twist of point of view will redeem the story much in her eyes. Last, but certainly not least, one of the leading book bloggers in the world who, for the past six months, has resolutely refused to comment on any of the books cited for the long list, but has announced that after the results are out she would be posting her thoughts on each of the short listed entries, to the horror of the Best Reads team and the other judges.

I've studied her form exceptionally hard, she'd started out when the idea of a blog was still quite new with the simple, if manic, idea of reading every one of the Best Reads long list before the short list was announced. Someone suggested she shared her thoughts on the internet and helped her set up her blog and so 'The Long-List Book-Blog' was born, and took off, now having a following numbering in the hundreds of thousands all around the world. Astonishing! Just think what power she wields, even if I didn't win, a positive review from her could make up for it anyway.

I have spent more hours than I ought flicking through the books she's read and blogged about, stopping when a book sounded like it might nudge close to my genre to check it out.

Whenever I found one in my genre I settled down and read her blog post carefully, even going to Amazon and reading the 'look inside' chapters to see if I would agree with what she said about the way the book was written or the tone it took. I really shouldn't have done this; it left me feeling more uncertain than anything.

At least I am off the book-tour treadmill, except now I am supposed to be writing the new book and that is harder than it sounds. What has happened to me? I can't seem to get my act together to move on and, even though I know Mel's not going to be good for my writing because there's no edge to this relationship, I've let her move in with me - it's all too good.

She's been losing weight too, seriously losing it, says she wants to look good for me; how's that make me feel? Too good, that's how. And she read The Puppeteer! That showed commitment. I mean she's not the brightest, she confessed early on to not having read a whole book since she left school, it's not that she can't read, she reads, but mostly magazines. And she watches films, I don't think I could name a film she hasn't watched, and remembered. I can't remember films, rarely the names of the characters, never the names of the actors - she does.

Chapter 58

'So what do you think of the idea?' Joan asked as the book group sat gathered around Cordelia's dining table. 'I've been following The Long-List Book-Blog for years but I've never taken up one of her challenges before, she has lots, usually to do with huge books that take a long time to get through.'

'Won't it cost us a lot, I mean, if they are on the Best Reads short list won't they all be taken out of the library already?' Linda said.

'Possibly, but we could reserve copies that aren't available right away and it does sound like a good idea – it would give us a new focus,' Gill added.

'It would mean having to read a book a week if we want to read them all by the time the results are announced – that's a lot of reading,' Toni said. 'What with the kids and the business I'm not sure I'd have the time.'

'That would cost us more too,' Linda said.

'Not if we shared books as well,' Marian said, 'that way even if we all had to buy books it would only be one a fortnight as usual.'

'And some of them will be cheaper on Kindle, and I have a spare Kindle that I can put the books onto if anyone wants to borrow it,' Cordelia said. There was a small silence. 'It's my old Kindle – I can read them on the iPad Kindle app instead,' she added.

'Wouldn't mind,' Linda said shyly.

'That's settled, then. Toni? Harold?'

Harold nodded, 'Alright, though there's only one I really like the look of on that list.'

'I'll read what I can, and skim those I can't, who'll share books with me?' Toni asked glancing round the group.

'I will,' Marian said.

'Great, then all we have to do is choose which pair of books we will start with first. Joan, it was your idea, which ones first do you think?'

'Well, that went well,' Marian said after the rest of the group had gone, 'nice to see everyone wasn't it?'

'Yes, doing the short list will certainly give us a focus. Do you look at that blog Joan was talking about?'

'No, but I might just take a gander. Anyway, how's you?'

'Fine, today,' Cordelia smiled at her friend. Marian had been light with her concern but she felt the warmth and knew she could turn to her if she felt overwhelmed. It happened. Though less often in February than in January and by the end of March she was beginning to wonder if she was going to be okay, then a very belated condolence card from a client of Gerald's abroad, sent via his office, for some unknown reason tipped her into anger and desolation. Marian understood the anger, only she and Max knew what had been said beside Gerald's grave and the thought of Jim and what he'd done burned in her too.

'Max is coming over later - he says he has something to tell me.'

'That'll be nice.'

Cordelia pulled a face, 'I can't think what it could be, I mean, he's coming on his own, it's not like he's bringing the children.'

'Don't worry, it'll be something nice.'

'We'll see,' Cordelia said, turning her thoughts away, wishing she'd not brought it up.

'A few people have been asking me if you are doing the Art Fair this year,' Marian said tentatively.

'Oh? Are they? What did you say?'

'That I don't know, but I thought I'd ask. Obviously people don't want to ask you directly, but you know how it is, it's your Art Fair but they want to be in it as usual or they want to know what is going on.'

Cordelia was silent, gazing out of the window towards the valley.

'C'delia?'

She shook her head. 'I'm not sure I can.'

'It might do you good,' Marian said, reaching out and stroking Cordelia's arm. 'You're not going out at all are you? I have noticed. You've only seen me, Max and the book group since the funeral, just us that come to you here?'

'Mmm. I feel ...' she couldn't explain it, even to Marian. She felt exposed, as if the cloak of respectability that she had worn for so many years had turned to rags. How could she go out when she felt that people were thinking such ugly things about her? She had sat there in front of her own mirror and seen herself as she was, as she might have so easily become, if she'd not met Gerald. Without him she was suspect, he gave her pretence substance. She had wondered if she could explain this to Marian; Marian who had accepted her story of Max and his adoption without so much as a flicker of suspicion, but she daren't, she daren't risk losing Marian too.

'If you are worried about needing help, we will all come and stand with you to hold it together, just like we did last year.'

'No, you don't understand, it's not that.'

'How can I understand when you won't say what is stopping you going out? Why you don't come to village events anymore? And you're not sitting on the Bench anymore are you?'

'Leave of absence,' she said, 'bereavement leave.'

'So you intend going back to that?'

Cordelia couldn't imagine going back to sitting in judgement on cases, on other people's lives, her skin was always a little thin for the liking of some of her fellow magistrates, now she would be positively see-through and they would all be able to see why. She shook her head.

'I know, it's hard. But you can't just shut yourself away, what a waste that would be!'

Cordelia shook her head again.

'Start with the Art Fair, it's your creation, your baby, no one else could do it as well as you do. Don't let that bastard take that away from you too.'

285

Marian's words rang in Cordelia's ears as she opened the door to Max later that evening. Here, really was her baby, and she had abandoned him all those years ago.

'You okay?' Max said, proffering a bottle of sparkling wine as he came in.

'Fine,' she said, 'Prosecco, nice,' she smiled as she took it from him. 'The conservatory is warm,' she said, diverting to the kitchen for glasses, then following him. He stood looking out at the view; she placed bottle and glasses on the table and went to stand near him.

'Lovely view,' he said.

'Yes, it was Gerald's favourite, but you didn't come to admire the view. What's up?'

'Hmm, okay, let's sit,' he said returning to the chairs, picking up the bottle and busying himself with removing the foil, wire and twisting up the cork. Its pop was pronounced but musical, a wisp of 'smoke' drifted from the open mouth of the bottle. He poured. Only then, when he'd handed her a glass, did he look at her.

'Dee, I have a confession.'

She felt as if she were standing on a precipice. Suddenly she didn't want to hear whatever he was going to say.

'No, I don't want to know.'

'But, you don't know what it is.'

'I don't want to know anything I shouldn't.'

'It's not like that, I'm confessing that I didn't do as you asked me ... I've been looking for my father.'

Cordelia gasped. She had not been expecting him to say that – but somehow she knew he wouldn't leave it alone.

'It wasn't easy, I'll not explain it all now, unless you want me to.'

She was shaking her head, she didn't want, she wasn't sure she wanted to know what he'd found either but she knew there was not point in saying this, he'd done it and now she had to know.

'Ned Silver, real full name Edmund di Silver, that's di - spelt D. I., lives in London, now at any rate.'

'How do you know it's the right one?' she snapped, eager to dismiss his story.

'Because I tracked him down via one of the band he used to play with, you know you told me about them. There's a website for memories of the free festivals. Not much used or updated now but someone keeps an eye on them. I posted some questions about the band and got hooked up with the drummer, Tim Beads. I convinced him I was writing a book about the free festivals and arranged to meet him, buy him dinner and ask questions. He was up for that, lives in Reading, says he's never sold out, that he helps out for free at the Reading Festival every year. You get the picture?'

She couldn't remember much about the drummer, dark hair, shaggy, brown, not much more, might have been nicknamed Bumble or something like that.

'He was able to give me the full proper names of all the band members. I wasn't letting on why I was looking or who I was looking for. He seemed pretty disgruntled with Ned anyway, it seems that Tim was hoping the band were really going somewhere, whereas after the end of the summer Ned packed it in to go off to university in Edinburgh and as he'd paid for most of the gear that was the end of the band.'

Max took a sip of the Prosecco, looked at Cordelia. She said nothing, remembering the band laughing and saying it was Ned's band. So perhaps it was, perhaps his parents paid for it.

'So then I wanted to know what each of them did after the band split. I got a load of rubbish, mostly about Tim's life, but he did say he thought Ned had gone 'into the law like his old man'. I asked if he meant the police and he fell about, no 'the Law' Barristers - that lot.'

Barristers? She tried to imagine Ned tidied up, hair shorn, neat white wig on his head.

'So I went on the trail of a barrister with the name of Edmund di Silver. Tim was right, they are a family firm. Father a QC, now deceased, cousins, male and female, a nephew and Ned,' Max said totally caught up in his narrative.

Cordelia felt cold. Ice cold. The glass slid in slow motion from her fingers and shattered on the tiled floor. Max leapt towards her, steadying her before she too fell foward. It brought her back to herself.

'Dee, all right? Dee?'

'All right,' she said, steadying herself against him, against the seat. 'I'm sorry, oh! Look at the mess!'

'Stay there, where's the mop, dustpan?'

'Utility room, tall cupboard,' she said, feeling as if she didn't know where she was anymore. Ned, a barrister, in London, real. She had come to think of him as not real, almost as a figment of her imagination, beautiful, gentle, loving and funny. She remembered calling the number he'd given her when she realised she was pregnant, hearing the woman with the posh voice answering, telling her that the family had moved, and no, she was not in a position to give address or telephone number. She remembered feeling cold then too, ice cold.

Max cleaned up the broken glass, wrapping it well in wads of paper, mopped up the spilt wine. 'Would you like a coffee?' he asked Cordelia, his face downcast.

'Yes please. Wait.'

He stopped, poised with dustpan and brush in hand.

'Have you contacted him?'

'No, not yet.'

'Don't, please, don't.'

Max sighed, 'I was hoping you wouldn't say that.'

She just shook her head.

When Max returned with a cup of coffee for each of them and sat down he looked at her. 'Okay, I won't. It's enough to know at the moment.'

She smiled and nodded, 'Thank you.'

Chapter 59

'Mel?' I called as I put down the phone. 'You will never guess!'

'What?'

'The movie option on The Puppeteer has just been sold!'

'Wow!'

'Wow, indeed! You have no idea, when a book gets to be a movie the sales go through the roof. Even the idea of it being made into a movie will drive sales. Oh, come here,' I hugged her, 'Let's go out and celebrate, dinner and a few drinks! We'll go to Giuliani's.'

'You are so clever!' She twirled away from me, half the girl I first met, 'I'll get something nice on.'

'Who do you think should play the lead?' I asked Mel over dessert, 'George Clooney?'

She almost sprayed the table with fruit salad, laughing. 'He's far too nice, couldn't play a nasty person like that, you need someone like Tom Hiddlestone, sexy but can play evil convincingly.'

'Oh!' That's the problem with identifying with a character; you always want the best for them. But she was probably right, this was her forte, not that we need to worry, it's not the author's place to suggest casting, though you hear of screenwriters writing a part for a specific actor.

'I wonder if they'll want me to write the script,' I mused, at least that would put off the day when I had to produce the next novel.

'Doubt it,' she sounded knowledgeable but it irked me to think she thought me not up to the job. 'I think it's a specialist thing,' she added as if she'd picked up on my pique.

'Oh really?'

'Well, only from what I've read in Film Magazine.'

'Well if Film Magazine says it, it must be true,' I said, huffily.

She smiled and rubbed her foot up my calf, 'You can't be the best at everything, you're so good at so much already. Let someone else do the rehashing.' She twinkled at me, I felt my feathers smooth and my ardour rise. Suddenly I wanted to call for the bill and leave, but in a nice way.

Chapter 60

Cordelia realised she must have dozed off, the television was on but not on something she usually watched, and there was someone knocking on the door. She got up quickly, almost tripped, straightened and headed for the door feeling a little disorientated and a bit nervous.

'Okay, just coming,' she called.

'It's only me,' Marian said from behind the thick wooden door.

Feeling relieved Cordelia opened the door, stepping back to let Marian in. 'Come in 'me'. Sorry, I think I'd dozed off in front of the TV, honestly, I don't know what's up with me lately!' she said as she led the way back to the main room and turned the TV off.

Marian followed her in and placed a book on the coffee table as they both sat down, Cordelia getting straight up again, 'Would you like a coffee? Or something stronger?' rather hoping Marian would say the latter. She was determined not to drink wine when she was on her own but any excuse seemed good when she wasn't, she certainly slept better those nights, whether from the wine or from the company she didn't really know.

'I think we'll need a glass of wine,' Marian said. Cordelia set off to get the wine and glasses before she even began to wonder what Marian could mean.

'There you go,' she said handing Marian the glass carefully so as not to spill it.

'Have you read The Puppeteer yet?' Marian said as soon as Cordelia was sitting.

'No, I've nearly finished the other one for this fortnight, the Windmill one, where all the chapters are song titles.'

'Well you need to.'

'Why?'

'Because I need you to tell me I am imagining things, and that this face,' she picked up the book and opened it to show the author photograph on the inside flap, 'is not one that we know.'

Cordelia took the book from her, leaned forward and pulled a hidden drawer out from the edge of the coffee table and took out a pair of glasses. She put them on then looked at the photograph, shaking her head even as she did so, 'No, I don't think I recognise him.' The bald menacing man with a small goatee type beard stared back at her.

'Okay.' Marian said slowly. 'Hmm.'

'What is it?'

'I think you need to read the book, let me just say that something made me suspicious and after that I could not be sure if I was seeing things or not.'

'Marian! You are making this all sound very cloak and dagger.'

Marian laughed. 'I am, aren't I? Just have a read, phone me when you are sure I am nuts. Nice wine by the way, Merlot?'

'Um, no idea. I can look if you like.'

'No don't be silly. I was just trying to change the conversation.'

'Marian?' Cordelia's hand was gripping the phone far too tightly. She had read from the moment Marian had left at ten that night, given up when her eyes wouldn't stay open at three, took up the book again as soon as she had woken and had not stopped reading until hunger drove her from bed and she had completed all but the last few chapters.

'Who else would it be?'

'I've read the book, at least I've read most of it. I don't think you are nuts.'

'Shit.'

'Yes, and the rest.'

'I mean, it is you, isn't it?'

'Certainly seems to be. The bastard didn't even bother to change the name much. Delia, for heaven's sake.'

'And the description, as it comes out over the first few chapters, every detail the same, like he had your photo and was describing you, and even the Ambassador, that's Gerald to a tee.'

'Well, in a way he didn't need a photo, he saw us around the village didn't he.'

'More – everything about you. He even described your mannerisms, some of your clothes. Surely writers can't do that? Take people's identities and just use them, can they?'

'I have no idea, I wouldn't have thought so, who knows?'

'And the photograph of him, can you see the likeness?'

'I can, once you are looking for the likeness you can't mistake it.'

'And?'

'And, what? I don't think there's much I can do. Not sure I want to finish the book though, it's vile.'

'Oh yes, you do want to finish it, I didn't mention the end.'

'Okay,' Cordelia said warily. 'If you think I must, I'll finish it, I'll ring you.'

'And I'll come round!'

Cordelia closed the book. She now knew what he'd had in mind if she had turned up at the hotel that afternoon and it made her shudder. She flipped the cover open and looked at the monochrome author photo again, beneath the picture it said: Sean Warner, author of the international best selling thriller 'The Stalker', grew up in Reading and attended university in Bristol studying English. He now lives in London.

Nothing to make him sound too nice or too human, a biography to go with the photograph, spare - no mention of wife or children, not even a dog. Nothing to go on. She turned back to the front pages. Publisher? Bantam, part of Random House. That was a lead. What else? She opened to a page where he'd put a few acknowledgements ... my editor da, da, da ...my agent, William Galsworthy. Why did that ring a bell? Oh, Galsworthy – another author. She realised she was wondering how to find out where he was, how to find him. Strange. She put the book down and picked up the phone to call Marian again.

Chapter 61

'I just feel so angry!' Cordelia said. Marian sat opposite her, cradling the cup of coffee that Cordelia had made by the time she'd arrived.

'I thought you might be. I wonder if the others will recognise you. I mean, I knew about the threats, the blackmail, but they don't so they'll just have the descriptions, maybe they'll not even think of you.'

'Whether they do or not - I want to get my own back!' her voice taking on an edge, 'I want to worry him the way he worried me. I want to send him emails or letters, something to get him anxious, make him think everything he has can be taken away.'

'C'delia? This doesn't sound like you.'

'Sound like me? I am not me anymore, can't you see. I'm back to the girl running from the chaos. I could do anything! Anything! After what he did? After what he did? He ...' her lips turned down, she couldn't say it.

'Couldn't he retaliate? Take you to court for harassment or something?'

'Let him! I've got nothing left to lose!'

'I think you should talk it over with Max,' Marian said softly.

Cordelia looked up sharply. 'Why?'

'Only because he's the other person who knows the whole story. He may have an idea.'

Cordelia thought for a moment. 'You're right, yep, good idea. Don't you worry about it, I'll talk to Max,' she smiled trying to diffuse the tension, let Marian off the hook.

'Okay, I promise, I'll download the book in a minute and start reading straight away, but I do have schoolwork to do,' Max said.

'I know, but please, do this for me now, it is important. There is only you and Marian I can even talk to about this.'

'Why won't you tell me anything then? Why must I read this book before you tell me what is wrong? I know there's something wrong.'

'I can't, I need you to read the book first. Promise?'

'Promise.'

She heard the sigh in the word but let it go anyway. He must be wondering if he found his mother only to find she's stark staring crazy.

Cordelia scoured the internet for Sean Warner. She found lots of pages about his novels, especially the international bestseller The Stalker and about The Puppeteer and its progress through the Best Reads. Then she found him, he had a Facebook page, Sean Warner Author where he expressed his thoughts on city after city as he toured them with his book, all complimentary. She set up a Facebook account, using her maiden name, just so she could 'like' his page, which made it appear on her own Facebook feed, but she was still unable to write on his page. She found that he had a Twitter account, though who knew whether he was on the other end of that or not, the tweets were mostly quotes from dead authors, wise or witty they seemed to come from a list somewhere. She joined Twitter using the Twitter-name @AvenGe, and followed @SeanWarner. She thought for a moment about using his Twitter handle to start rumours, true rumours that he plagiarised people's identities. Could you do that in a hundred and forty characters? She typed *@SeanWarner Your turn. I know who you are #liar* and posted it, understanding that it would get to his Twitter stream but not knowing if he'd ever see it. Distracted and tired, she closed her iPad and went out into the garden.

***

'It's him, isn't it? The man in the hotel room?' Max said when he phoned the next evening.

'Yes, I'm sure it is. You can see it's him in the photograph when you look properly.'

'Bastard!'

'That's my word,' Cordelia said, 'but yes. Did you have any trouble recognising me?'

'None, though I knew there was a reason for you asking me to read it. I'm not sure about anyone else.'

'Well, I'll find out soon enough. It's the book club read, we'll be discussing it on Friday and if they recognise me I want to ...'

'Sue him for libel?'

'Huh? No, I just want to get my own back, plague his life just like he plagued mine. I want him to know what he did to Gerald, what he's done to my life. I've never felt so vengeful.'

'Let me know how the book club goes, whether the others see you in there too.'

'Okay. Max, thanks, thanks for listening to me.'

'No bother, speak soon.'

Plague his life. What had Max said, sue for libel? That had to be an author's worst nightmare. Back on the internet she typed in 'sue for libel'. She instantly recognised she needed to narrow the search and tried, 'sue for libel novels'. 'Literary Libel' caught her attention and she opened it. Yes, this was about real people who had been depicted in fiction, usually in less than flattering lights, and had sued for libel. She scanned quickly, ... 'change of name not enough to escape being sued' 'the differences between the character and the real person must not outweigh the similarities' 'easily recognisable by people who know the libelled' 'award relating to loss of good name'.

She sat back and closed her eyes. She thought through the novel, thought of the possible differences between her and the Ambassador's wife. Well, she wasn't one of those to start with, but on the other hand the brief description of the Ambassador himself fitted Gerald very well, so that brought it back together again. The Ambassador's wife played the piano, which she didn't. Against that he has her being a supporter of the local community, raising money for charities with garden parties, coffee mornings and Art shows. That was it. Everything else tallied, her description, her mannerisms, her accent, her clothes, her car, her loyalty to her husband, even some of her responses to his emails were woven into the words he had written.

She shuddered, opened her eyes and read on ... 'he insisted that the publishers pulp the whole edition' this when an author had named a disreputable character after the river he overlooked as he wrote, unaware that a real Lord Derwent existed. 'Publisher pulped the lot when they realised they might be sued' *Might be?* She read that again. It hadn't gone to court, the publishers had been made aware and had made up their own minds. Would that work? If she sent the details to Random House, would they do the right thing? But this is a potential Best Reads winner – no, they'd not do that, not for her, not on a suggestion - would they?

The next morning she woke knowing her plan. It was crazy but it would be worth trying. She ate breakfast quickly and left everything where it was to open the internet again. She put in the name Max had told her. Edmund di Silver, and there he was. Images. She looked at him, older, changed, still with a certain look that she recognised. Ned. Barrister. She looked for his Chambers and found them. Looked for a private address and couldn't find that. The Chambers it would have to be. Email? Telephone? She chose telephone, jotting down the number for the Chambers, adding the email address so she didn't have to look it up again. She went back to the images, finding herself smiling, then wondering if he had family, a wife, children. She started a new search. He had children, yes, but it seemed he no longer had a wife, deceased. She paused, shook her head, it didn't matter either way.

'Good morning,' she said with her best Ascot accent, 'Would it be possible to have a word with Ned, ah, Edmund di Silver?' she thought she'd risk trying his pet name as if he were a close acquaintance and she'd almost forgotten to call him by his proper name.

'Sorry madam, he's in court this morning, may I take a message and get him to call you back?'

'Oh! That will have to do, when is he expected back?'

'By two, madam; your name?'

'Cordelia Springs-Steadman, Dee.'

'Concerning what?'

'A libel case,' she said confidently and gave her contact details.

'Very well, I will pass on the message, thank you.'

Cordelia sighed. It might work!

The phone didn't ring until nearly six oclock, she'd almost given up hoping but remembered in time to answer as if it might be him.

'Cordelia speaking,'

'Edmund di Silver, returning your call.'

'Ned?'

'Hmm, no one has called me that for a long time. Mr Hughes said that the caller seemed familiar and used the name Ned. I admit it piqued my curiosity. Who are you?'

'Dee Springs – as was. For that to mean anything you may need to cast your mind back to ...'

'Watchfield.'

'Watchfield,' she stopped, aware of how hard her heart was beating, as if it would flip right over – he'd remembered.

'Dee, Cordelia Springs-Steadman, that's you?'

'Cordelia always was my name, the Steadman I married.' A lump came into her throat, she swallowed.

'Well, amazing.'

'And you became a barrister, I had no idea back then, thought you were going to play guitar.'

'Like your father! Yes, would have been nice, but my path was already mapped out. Is he still going strong?'

'Dad died. About a year after you met him.'

'Oh, no, sorry to hear that. Dee, um, Hughes said you were calling about a libel case, was that just an excuse to speak to me through the Chambers. I don't mind if it was.'

'No, it wasn't, actually. But I am glad to speak to you anyway,' she said, wondering what to say about Max.

'You know it's highly irregular, usually you'd come through a solicitor, but fire away, what's on your mind?'

'Last year we had a man staying in our village. It turns out he was an author, a thriller writer, and he has used me, my description, my way of life, even my mannerisms to portray one of his main characters. A character who ... does things I wouldn't.'

'You say 'it turns out', did no one know he was an author?'

'No, no one.'

'How did you come across his book then?'

'It's one of the Best Reads shortlist and our book group are reading them all. A friend rang me to point out that she thought it was me - and that, only after she'd thought it, she recognised the photo of the author. He'd even been in disguise while he was here.'

'So just the two of you?'

'And my ... another friend, he's read the book too and spotted it immediately. The book club meeting is tomorrow, I'm dreading it.'

Ned was silent for a moment or two.

'You think I'm hysterical?'

'No, not at all, I am sure you do think he's picked out certain characteristics, the case would depend on whether anyone who knows you would recognise you and whether he has defamed you.'

'Ah! So, my test bed will be the book group. Perhaps it would be better if I don't go, they'll all gossip more then!' she laughed.

'Oh! That sounded like the Dee I knew.'

'Seriously, I mean, if those two things are true, is there the possibility of suing?'

'I think I'd need to read the book and I'd need to compare myself. Where do you live now?'

'Cornwall! It's a long way from London.'

'Nonsense, how about I catch a train down tomorrow evening, could you recommend somewhere for me to stay in your area?'

'The Plough has rooms - that's the pub, or there is a B&B. If you want a four star hotel the nearest would be St Mellion, it's only three miles away.'

'That'll do me. I'll call you at the weekend.'

'Ned, thank you. I don't know how to thank you.'

'It'll be enough to catch up, see you soon.'

Chapter 62

'What do you mean they are asking already?' I was saying to William, though I knew what he was on about.

'Well, Sean, with The Puppeteer in the shortlist for the Best Reads they would like to announce that you have another in the pipeline, to make the most of the publicity going. You know they have to kick money into the publicity for the Best Reads anyway, so they want to make the most of it,' William whined.

Bloody publishers, they are never satisfied, not only do I get the book finished on time but it is a winner, and now they want more!

'Well you can tell them I am working on it.'

'A working title would be good? And a blurb?'

'I'm not that flaming far down the line yet, I don't have a title,' though at that moment I did, suddenly a great title came into my head, only problem was I didn't know what the story was that it would fit. I was thinking fast, William was drivelling on about how difficult a position I was leaving him in and how much it would help when the next book came out.

'The Death Masque' I said, 'with Masque spelt M A S Q U E.'

'Oh! Oh? Really, that's good, very good. I'll tell them, they'll be delighted!'

Yeah, delighted, only now I was committed to a theme, though I knew I had a few lines of thought that could be moulded to fit this title, I was already coming to like it.

Mel arrived home from work and traipsed past me without a word.

'Hey, what's up?' I called, watching her walk by in her shapely burgundy skirt and white blouse.

'Nothing, just hot and tired,' she said as she went through to the bedroom, I got up and followed her, coming

302

up behind her just as she finished unbuttoning her blouse to wrap my arms around her and cup her breasts.

'Gerr-off,' she said wearily. I slipped one hand inside the bra-cup, she twisted away from me. 'I said, get off!' she reiterated.

'Don't be like that babe,' I said.

'Oh really!' she said, 'I've been at work all day and you come on like a dirty old man!'

'And you don't think I've been working? Books don't write themselves you know, every word has to be sweated out.'

'And that,' she said, walking off into the shower room, 'whining about your work.'

'Well, the publishers are onto me already, I can't faff around!' I retorted, but she'd closed the door and within moments I heard the shower running. I considered joining her, but thought better of it.

Chapter 63

The ringing phone woke her. 'Hello?'

'Good morning.'

'Ned?'

'Yes. Listen. Send your friend to the book group on time, make sure you arrive later. They may gossip in front of her. If they do I want you to tell her to make sure she gets them to repeat it when you get there. Once they see that you want to hear they won't keep it quiet. What you want to know is what made them think it was you being described. Don't be pleased, just curious about what, specifically, made them think of you?'

'I can't, the book group meets at my house.'

'Damn!' he paused, 'I know, go and make the coffee, or take a phone call. Leave them alone for a few minutes, it won't take more if there is really something in this.'

'Okay,' she said, feeling herself smiling.

'Marian, I need your help when we have the book group meeting?'

'Sure, what is it?'

'I'd like you to listen to anything they say about me and The Puppeteer while I'm out of the room, don't start them off, just listen. Then when I come back make sure they tell me to my face.'

'Hmm? You sure?'

'Yes, I want to know if they recognise me, I want to know everything they thought referred to me, what exactly put me in their minds.'

'You sound as if you want them to recognise you?'

'No, not really but if they did, I want to know.'

'Why? Surely that just rubs the salt in.'

'A bit, but if they do, if people do recognise me then I have something I can do.'

'Really? What?'

'I looked it up,' she dissembled. 'If someone is recognisable and they are 'defamed' by the writing then they can sue for libel.'

'Defamed? I'm not sure how it defames you?'

'The things he makes the woman do, the, humiliations, the breaking her will. And she breaks, doesn't she? Does every disgusting thing he wants.'

'But to protect her husband.'

'Will you do it?' her tone made it sound like an ultimatum.

'Yes, of course. Not lead them on, just make sure that if they say anything they say it again to your face.'

'Come in, hi, come in, do go through,' Cordelia greeted the book group as if nothing was amiss. She winked at Marian as she passed; their plan in place. Harold arrived last, he hefted a copy of The Puppeteer under his arm and looked at her hard as he arrived, or was she imagining it?

She followed him into the room and, as he settled himself down, she pressed her iPhone speed dial in her pocket, the house phone began to ring. 'Excuse me a minute, I'll be right back,' she said, heading for the kitchen. She stood there miming listening on the phone, she wished she could hear them in the other room. After a long three minutes she replaced the phone and walked quickly back to the dining area, where conversation died almost as rapidly.

'Are we okay?' she said as she sat. 'Shall we get started, which book first?'

'The Puppeteer,' Marian said, 'everyone's had something to say about it already!'

'Oh really?'

'Yes, Harold was saying that you must have known the author very well, and Toni thinks something similar.'

'Why would you say that?' Cordelia asked.

'We didn't mean it like that,' Toni said.

'Humph,' Harold grunted.

305

'Alright, but it's not just me and Harold, is it? You noticed it too Linda? Yeah? Even you Marian? Don't say you didn't,' Toni came back.

'I recognised the photograph on the back after I thought about the similarities. It's Jim,' Gill said. 'He even came to the book group. And he's written this – nasty book and put Cordelia in it. In fact, I think he's also used some other people from the village, I'm sure the butler and housekeeper are Dave and Liz from the shop,' then, looking steadily at Cordelia, she added, 'he even has Gerald as the Ambassador, but everything else is a total fiction, twisted, like he is.'

'Thank you Gill,' Cordelia said. 'What I'd like to know from each of you is exactly which bits made you think that the Ambassador's wife was based on me? It might help me build a case libel against him,' she took up her pen and looked around, more than one started to speak, one deferred to another and the note taking began.

Saturday morning the phone rang just after nine.

'I hope I'm not ringing too early,' Ned said.

'Not at all, are you down here?'

'Yes, thanks, at the St. Mellion place. Would that be a good place for us to meet?'

'Oh, yes, that would be fine,' she said finding herself relieved, she had wondered if he'd want to come to her house, and she wasn't sure how to answer that one. A neutral meeting ground was best. 'Just say when.'

'How about an early coffee, say ten-thirty, they have a coffee shop?'

'That'll be in the Brasserie, yes, I'll meet you there.'

Okay, so she changed her choice of outfit more than once. That didn't mean anything. She thought she needed to strike the right note, to say that she was not the woman who did those humiliating things that were written in the book, yet she also wanted to say, I am Dee! As she drove the few miles to St. Mellion she was rehearsing in her mind how to tell him about Max. She knew she ought to get it out in the open early because to wait would only make it more difficult, but at the same time if he was angry, or scared off, or disappointed, whatever his reaction then he might not help with her mission to bring down Sean Warner. Even as she thought of the possibility of not getting her revenge she felt a surge of anger, nothing mattered but to see him fall.

She scanned the Brasserie, knowing what he looked like from the images on the internet, and spotted him easily, even before he started to rise as he noticed her. As he came towards her, as she walked towards him she realised she was not prepared for this, so fixed on her quest she had not prepared herself to meet him.

'Dee,' he said smiling, holding out a hand to shake. She took his hand, shook and they turned back to the sofas where he'd been sitting. He raised his hand and ordered coffee for them both.

She felt as if she'd slipped back in time, her mind bringing up pictures and scenes, her body singing its own little song of delight. This is ridiculous, she thought, but said, 'It's so good to see you after so long,' and the words were true though sounding trite.

'You too,' he smiled at her again and she knew his smile was reflected in her own. After a long moment of silence they both started to speak at once.

'I need to ...'

'I read the ...'

She laughed, 'You first,' relieved that she was prevented from saying the words she was trying to get out and justifying it to herself as politeness.

'I read the book on the way down, so I know where you are coming from. Tell me how this all came about. Start from the beginning, when you first met the author.'

She began with the welcome package, moved on through each and every time she could remember talking to him or being in the same group as him. It didn't seem much without the emails, without the threats, but she was reluctant to mention any of that, that would mean talking about Max.

Ned leant back and studied her, she tried to smile. 'What are you not telling me?'

'What do you mean?'

'There is something you are not telling me, something important. Did you have a fling with the author? Don't worry it wouldn't weaken your case.'

'Absolutely not! I loved and was true to my husband!' She shuddered, 'Jim - Sean, whoever he really is was pursuing my friend, but then she's single, but not me, not in that way.'

He shook his head. 'Not in that way,' he echoed her. 'In what way then?'

Dee felt under cross examination and realised why Edmund di Silver was a top-line barrister. 'He - he sent me emails.'

Ned leaned forward, his elbows on his knees. 'Really? Please tell me you still have them.'

'Some, but it won't matter, he, they were sent from a false address.'

'Rarely can it not be traced in some way, but don't worry about that, what was in them?'

What to say and what to leave out? She jumped in with both feet. 'I was contacted by my son, my son that I had to give up for adoption many years ago, before I met my husband. My husband didn't know about my son, and I didn't know how to explain that I'd been lying to him for over thirty years, so we met in private. I so wanted to hear the story of his life - I knew it would 'captivate my ear strangely' - to paraphrase Shakespeare.'

'Hmm ... from The Tempest?'

Dee smiled, 'Yes, yes, well I wanted to get to know him and his family - and eventually work out a way to explain it all to Gerald without upsetting him too much, you had to know Gerald to understand how hard that would be.'

'And the author?'

'You know we didn't know he was an author, none of us in the village, he said he was a school teacher.'

'Yes, he writes as Sean Warner but his real name, by the way, is Sean Wilkes and he was a school teacher before he became an author. So, what did he do?'

'I think he saw us and decided I was having an affair and that he could blackmail me into ...' she could feel the heat flooding her face as her mind ran over excerpts from the book.

'Into what?'

'Doing those things he wrote about in the book.'

Ned sat back suddenly, looking at her. 'How do you know?'

'From some of the emails he sent. He even used some of my answers in the book, the exact words I wrote.'

He nodded. 'Interesting, so if I can link the emails to him we have a simple case - harassment. If we can't, it all comes down to whether your good name has been impinged on enough to cause defamation of character, and whether people in general, who know you, would be able to unequivocally read that character as you. How did the book group go?'

'Ah! Well, I have some notes in my bag,' she rummaged and passed over a notebook, he flicked it open.

'Quite a lot of identifiers!' he said. 'Unprompted?'

'Absolutely.'

'And your character, how would you say you were regarded? Before this book?'

'Well, hardly for me to say, good I hope. I try. I ...'

'Raise money for lots of charities with coffee mornings and the like, hold a successful large fundraiser annually, again for the village and charities, attend church on a regular basis, belong to many respectable groups and you have been a magistrate for a number of years.'

'Umm, yes.'

'And that's just from the internet and a records search.'

'Oh really?'

'Yes, yes, it's good. A respectable life slurred and defamed by an author who took your character instead of making up his own, plus, his half-witted attempt to disguise his template by changing the character's name from Cordelia to Delia is worse than keeping your real name – it shows he was cognisant of what he was doing, that man is an idiot.'

'Oh!'

'Now, is there any muck the defence can drag up about you? You need to be really honest with me Dee, if you hide something and they can prove it, then your good name is worthless and cannot be defamed.'

She was silent for a moment. Was there anything? Since she had married Gerald she had done everything right, before that was another story, another life.

'How far back do we go?'

'All the way, anything that might be on record. Arrested for being drunk and disorderly when you were twenty? Had up before the Magistrates for possession of weed when you were eighteen?'

A group of three people came towards their sofa and asked if anyone was sitting in the other seats around the coffee table. Ned glanced at his watch, 'Well they should be in a minute, hope you don't mind.' The people moved away, back towards the normal chairs and tables. In that time Dee recalled too many things she would rather not and was steeling herself to say something.

'However, nothing matters that is not on record,' Ned said once they were alone again.

Relief flooded through her, 'There's only Max. I didn't, I wasn't married when I had him ... he was adopted so that'll be on a record somewhere.'

'That's all right, that's not a crime and quite common, and we may have to mention him anyway, so it won't be something we are hiding. It is difficult to use something against someone's good character if the world accepts it and they are not ashamed of it.'

Tell him now, tell him now! 'Umm ...'

'Going back to the threatening emails? Obviously you didn't do as he asked, what happened then?'

'Umm, he, well, we thought he'd gone, scared off when Max went to the hotel room to confront him and tell him that he was my son so there was no hold over me, we even went down to the cottage to see if he was there. He'd gone.'

'Okay, and so he didn't do anything?'

'Yes, yes, he did!' she hissed, 'he killed Gerald! Though I didn't know until after Gerald's funeral when his PA told me what he'd had up on his screen when she found him. Warner sent his malicious email and Gerald read it, there was a photo with it so he would have seen what he was told was me and a lover and the shock burst a blood vessel in his brain. Which didn't kill him straightaway, it might have been better if it had, it left him totally incapacitated,' by now tears were filling her eyes.

'Sorry! So sorry, I didn't know this. I knew your husband died earlier this year, matter of record, but not this.'

'Which is why I want my revenge!'

Ned reached out and put his hand on her arm, 'And I'll do all I can to help.'

Chapter 64

Their plan was for Ned to meet some of the other people who could back up Cordelia's's story so after she left St. Mellion she rang Marian and Max to organise a meeting that evening, filling Marian in on who they were meeting and why. Marian said she could make it for drinks that evening and she'd see if Kevan was free. Max, however, was away with the family for the weekend, visiting Heather's family – she didn't say why she wanted to see him and afterwards wondered what was stopping her. Lying by omission, they call it, she mumbled to herself as she made a bit of lunch.

Cordelia was glad that Marian and Kevan arrived before Ned did, she didn't know why, but she knew she'd rather meet him in her own space with others around her. She wasn't worried by him, but something in her made her wary. She'd asked him before she'd left him earlier that day if he was in the habit of taking on clients at a whim. He looked at her for longer than felt comfortable, perhaps he was wondering why too, then he said something that made her uneasy 'Have you ever had the feeling that you made a big mistake at some time and all you want to do is go back and live that moment again, and do it differently?' She'd shaken her head, though there had been times, she knew. He smiled, 'Lucky you, I just like the thought of second chances, and this was one to see you again.'

'Glass of red, white? Beer?' she said to Marian and Kevan. Got their orders and brought them back to the sofas.
'So what is he like?' Marian asked.
Cordelia felt herself smile, 'He's very nice, interested, thinks I may have a case.'
'Idiot, I don't mean that,' Marian said, 'ignore Kevan, you know what I mean.' Kevan gave her a mock outraged

look and settled back into the sofa with his beer, hooking one foot up to rest over his knee, looking quite relaxed.

'Well, obviously older, but the essential Ned is still there, even the maverick bit, I think that's why he just took off to come down here, something different.'

"Lucky he's like that then, I mean, you want some weight behind this if you want to scare the publishers.'

'Well, that's true,' Cordelia said and leapt up as she heard a knock at the door.

Introductions over and glasses charged, Cordelia looked at Ned to see what he wanted to know.

'So, Cordelia filled me in on a lot of the events this morning. I spent time this afternoon writing these up to create a timeline. What I want from you two this evening is to add your comments to the timeline and any other information that you can offer. I am aiming to tie the author, Sean Warner, to this village in the time he was writing this book, regardless of the fact he was here under an assumed name – Jim?'

'Jim Menteur,' Marian said, pronouncing it in the way Jim had, with the e in men sounding throttled and the r at the end extended.

'Can you spell that?'

'No, not sure, I know I thought it was Mentor to begin with, I made some crack about it being funny a teacher with the name Mentor, as it's the same thing really, he grinned at me and said it was Menteur, but didn't spell it for me.'

'Do you speak French?'

'No? I studied German at school way back in the dim distant, why?'

'Just wondered? Dee?'

Dee shook her head, interesting as her education had been it had never included any foreign languages.

'Why?' Kevan asked, 'and no I didn't do French either, well nothing much past bonjour and au-revoir.'

'Well, your Mr Clever-author may have even been playing a game with his alias, if it was menteur – it would mean liar.'

'Sounds like him,' Marian said, 'he was an all round fraud.' She glanced at Kevan, 'He claimed to have been a bit of a runner, didn't he? Ha! And he wasn't above spiking drinks either, as I found to my cost.'

Ned raised his eyebrows, 'Interesting, character-wise, but not relevant at this point, but I may come back to you on that.' He jotted a note. 'Now, establishing that it is the same man, what do we have?'

'I have his photograph, at the hotel room where he said to meet him,' Cordelia said, 'though he had hair and no beard when it was taken and so looks very different.'

'Good, that's one thing in the bag and it doesn't matter, the technology that can prove it is him, comparing the photo to how he looks now, is very good and accepted in court, but it does not put him here in this village.'

'You could show that picture round the village and get ever so many people to swear that it was the same person who was renting Hideaway Cottage.'

'Yes, a possibility, you mentioned the cottage before, who was he renting it from?'

'A guy called William Galsworthy,' Kevan said, leaning forward and getting into the conversation.

'Galsworthy? Are you sure Kevan?' Cordelia asked.

'You know I needed to get hold of the owner as he owed me money, that was his name.'

'That's the name of his agent! I remember it as I recognised it first as an author's name – Galsworthy,' Cordelia got up and fetched her iPad and flipped it through to the acknowledgements page. 'There .. I also thank .. da di da .. my agent William Galsworthy!'

'Good, another thread to tie him to here, if we can find enough we can hang him with them,' Ned smiled, 'figure of speech, of course.'

'Not good enough for him!' Marian said with a glint in her eye.

'Anything else we can tie him to the village with, before we get onto the harassment charge?'

'Oh, can you use that?'

'If I can place him incontrovertibly here, and can prove he sent the emails, then it adds to the evidence of his bad character and can help bring about our aim, to get the book withdrawn.'

'Pulped,' Cordelia muttered under her breath.

Ned looked at her, 'Yes, same thing.'

'Oh! I think I have, hang on' Marian said, fishing in her bag for her mobile, 'Yes, I have his mobile number. Providing it's not one he just bought for being here, I called him on it, that would show up on the records, and even pinpoint to this area, wouldn't it?' She stopped, glancing round, 'Or is that only on TV programmes?'

Ned smiled at her, 'Yes, it is a possibility, though a bit extreme for this sort of case, however, I have an idea, how about I try ringing him and see if he answers. If he does, it is his phone, still, and we have another thread, albeit fine.' Ned tapped out the number as Marian dictated it to him, he was grinning as it began to ring with it set to speaker phone. The call was picked up and Ned put his finger to his lips.

'Hello?'

'Umm, who's that?' Ned said, sounding bewildered.

'Sean Warner, you called my phone!'

'Really? Sorry, I must have miss-dialled, sorry to bother you.'

'Well that answers that one, we can use the information if we need to push it. Now tell me about the emails, everything, and forward to me any you have left, or stored in the recycle bin.'

'Well, our nasty Mr Author was a busy boy,' Ned said as it neared ten o'clock and they were packing up. 'I will see who we can get to try to follow these emails back to the author, maybe we can use it, maybe not. Maybe the threat of it will be enough, adding harassment will put a whole different criminal slant on what we are seeking to accuse him of, it might frighten him a bit.

They all went out of the door, the night was clear and bright but not too cold. Marian and Kevan said goodnight, linked arms and begin to walk away towards Marian's place. Ned stood beside his hire car.

'I don't catch the train back until after lunch,' he said, 'may we meet tomorrow morning?'

There was nothing Cordelia could say against it, Ned had ridden to her defence after all these years, 'Yes, where would you like to meet?'

'You choose, this is your area.'

'Then I choose to collect you and take you to see Cotehele, it's a lovely National Trust place very near here.'

'Sounds good to me, and we can catch up more then,' he leant in and kissed her on the cheek in farewell, she went to put her hand on his arm, but he'd stepped back before she could react.

'Bye, see you,' she said as he climbed in his car and drove off.

Chapter 65

The title is the best thing so far about this new book, in fact the title has been the driving force. I have got myself an outline, I have my basic cast, motives, sub-plots and denouement. I haven't got my motivation and my edge. It is like a drug, I need that adrenaline, the buzz from living on the edge. I've tried my usual tricks on my own sub-conscious, the routine and the cigarette on the go, much to Mel's disgust. She, like every woman I've met recently has had a down on me smoking, and I'd cut back drastically, just having the occasional social smoke. Mel even grumped about that, said it made me look like a scrounger as I never had a packet to offer, just bummed cigarettes from others.

It's no good I just haven't got the edge I need and to top it all Mel is really off with me. I know I've complained in the past that Mel has been too accommodating, too easy and comfortable, but her being grumpy isn't the edge I need; that's just annoying.

'Can we go out somewhere tonight?' Mel said Saturday morning over a late breakfast. 'We never seem to go out now.'

'We only went out last weekend!' I retorted, 'we went out to dinner to celebrate the movie option being taken up on The Puppeteer.'

'Not exactly what I call a good night out,' she whined, 'I'm on a diet and you choose an Italian restaurant, I could barely eat any of the options, we sat and ate, you drank too much and we came home – big deal!'

'What else did you want?'

'We could have gone on to a club?

'They all play that interminable repetitive din,' I said, shaking my head.

'Ha, well I like it better than that granddad heavy metal you play when you say you are working.'

"I am working, it's part of my routine for writing!'

'And playing stupid air guitar?'

'When...?'

'Last Wednesday, you were so far gone you didn't hear me come in.'

'So what? I use that to celebrate a good plot line ... it's part of my routine.'

'Fuck your routine, you know, I thought it would be fun living with an author, despite your age, but it's not ...'

'Despite my age, you make me sound like a fucking pensioner!'

'Well, you are a lot older than me, really, what, fifteen years? It's a long time, you could almost have been my Dad.'

'Oh give over, now you are being ridiculous.'

'No I'm not, I'm being sensible, they said I needed to see sense, now I have.'

'Just ... What the fuck are you going on about Mel, 'cos I've got writing to do, you know it's not a nine to five and it's not a five out of seven, it's twenty-four-seven, writing, everyday, all day.'

'Then you won't miss me, I'm leaving, I'll pack my stuff,' she said standing and heading off to the bedroom.

I picked up another slice of bread and dropped it in the toaster; I wasn't bothered.

Twenty minutes later she brought the first of her bags through, bulging, and stood it near the door, she glanced at the messy table but headed straight back into the room, re-emerging two minutes later with a second bag. She picked up a cardboard box from the utility room and started putting things into it from the kitchen cupboard, still ignoring the messy table.

'Where are you going? Have you thought of that?' I pointed out, rather hoping this was a spur of the moment thing and she would relent when she realised the problem.

'I'm moving in with Tara,' she said, naming a red head she'd introduced me to a few weeks before, 'she has a spare room in the house she rents.'

'And how long will that last? Eh? Red heads are notoriously quick tempered.'

She turned and looked at me, hands on hips, 'You do talk complete rubbish sometimes,' she said, turned again and added a few more items to the box. I got up from the table and went to check the contents of the box, nothing looked like it was mine.

'Satisfied?' she said looking me in the eye, I felt cheap.

'Really Mel, you don't have to move out, haven't we been good together?' I said, not knowing really why I said these words, they sounded like they belonged in a soap opera.

'Yes, I do! I'm sorry Sean, you are not good for me, I need to move on.'

'Not good for you? You were a right lard-arse before you met me, look what being with me did to you, you have a fantastic figure now,' I knew I had blown it completely even as the words came out of my mouth - I had thought her a lard-arse and now she knew.

She stomped into the living room and I heard the recognisable sound of CDs being shuffled, I went after her, 'They're all mine,' I said, knowing she had her music on her phone.

'Except this one!' She held up the one I had given her on Valentine's day, she opened the case, took it out, dropped it on the floor and ground her heel on it. 'You can have it back now,' she added. 'Goodbye Sean.'

Her taxi came. She hauled all her stuff down the stairs to the kerb, I watched from the window. I wrote like fury that day and the next but by the Tuesday the anger was wearing thin. I still hadn't got the edge I needed and began to feel morose. Damn Mel, I was really missing having her around.

Chapter 66

Cordelia found it hard to sleep, her thoughts were filled with those few weeks back in the mid seventies, the unusual and unrestricted life she led with her parents, meeting Ned, falling in love with him within a couple of days of knowing him. Madness! If her parents had not been so wrapped up with each other they might have noticed, might have seen how her eyes tracked Ned everywhere he went when he was not by her side, might have warned him off, especially when his band followed them onto their next gigs even though they weren't on the lists to play those festivals. Maybe they would have told her some sensible facts of life, perhaps, instead of assuming that because she had seen so much of sex and love-ins she knew everything she needed to know.

What did she know? Dee knew her body was different whenever she was with him, that she felt beautiful, that she burned to be closer to him, that when he kissed her she felt a longing deep inside of her. As far as she could tell it was the same for him, so when they'd been half naked in his tent and he asked 'are you cool with this?' she was, 'and sorted?' with eyebrows raised she just pulled him to her and mumbled 'Mmm,' though she didn't really know what he was asking, she did know she wanted him, closer, closer. Cordelia sighed, turned again and tried to sleep and when it did come, her dreams were still full of Ned.

The next morning she dressed with even more care than usual and collected Ned from the hotel. A short drive took them to Cotehele, she pulled into the car park and they got out.

'Would you like to do the house, or just walk the garden?'

'House sounds interesting, I looked it up last night,' he smiled and she found herself smiling right back at him, it felt strange, it was as if she had almost forgotten how to smile properly in the last few months.

They wandered the dim and evocative rooms. A place you could easily imagine filled with people living life as they did in Tudor times and before, not so grand that it was a show place, but significant enough to make a statement about the strength and position of the owners.

They left the case alone and talked of their lives since they'd parted a month after they'd met, Cordelia carefully missing out the birth of her baby but filling the gap with the traumatic death of her father, leaping on to working at the art gallery and meeting Gerald, explaining her current interest in art.

His life had been, as he called it, predictable. He was the leading Counsel at his Chambers but was thinking of retiring soon to take up something a little more exciting. His wife had died a number of years ago, of breast cancer, his two daughters were both married and living abroad. It was becoming tedious, he wanted to travel and do something useful, he said.

She drove him back to St. Mellion, but instead of getting out he remained sitting there, she turned to him, he turned to her.

'Thank you for coming down and looking at this problem.'

'It's no problem, in fact it's a joy, something different, though I don't think it will come to court, publishers being notoriously cowardly, it would be fun if they did as I'm pretty sure we have a good case here, even before I bolster it up with some further investigations that I can instigate.'

'You have no idea how good that is to hear, besides, it has been wonderful to see you again after all these years.'

He nodded, 'Yes,' he said, but then he shook his head, 'I've thought a lot about you over the years. The summer after we met I had to work in Chambers for the family, as expected of me - general dogs-body. The following summer, however, I went to as many festivals as I could where I thought your father might be playing - looking for you - but his band had disappeared. I now know why.'

'You did? That's, that's very nice to hear.'

'Dee! Stop it. There is something you are keeping from me. All that you told me, wandering around in Cotehele and filling in our life stories. You were talking as if your life depended on keeping something secret. Every word sounded weighed, carefully selected.'

'I don't know what you mean? I always talk that way.'

'No you don't, you speak eloquently, you have a perfectly beautiful rhythm in your voice, but today you were talking like an automaton. Tell me, if it has something to do with this case I must know, things I do not know can be like trip wires for me, you might think it is a secret but if the defence found out and I didn't know then it would be me, our case, that would fail.'

'I don't think it affects the case.'

'So there is something? Just tell me – clear the air.'

'I – I, I was going to wait until you met Max.'

'Max?'

'My son, my son born in May nineteen seventy-six ...'

'Yes?'

'You were the only one - he's your son.'

Chapter 67

'Mine? That's what you've been keeping from me? All this time, you didn't think to let me know?'

'I told you, I was waiting for you to meet Max.'

'Not now, then, back then!'

'Ha! You think I didn't try? I rang your number and got some snooty woman who said your family had moved, wouldn't tell me anything else!'

'What? Oh, yes, yes, we did. They did, after I went off to Uni.' Ned looked down, stared into the footwell of the car. 'How did he come to be adopted then?'

Dee sat very still, these were the things she didn't want to say, her age when they were at Watchfield together, that the baby had been taken from her after her father had overdosed in a squat in London, that she'd been banned from any contact with Max, she didn't want to tell him, it sounded too squalid, but she did, and watched as tears came into his eyes rather than the scorn she had been expecting.

'Max only knows the outlines of all this, but he does know that I do not blame you in anyway,' she finished.

'Well, that'll be a relief when I meet him, I suppose.'

'Ned?'

He looked up at her.

'This doesn't change anything about the case, does it, can you still represent me?'

He smiled. 'I think I owe you this much at least,' he said. 'Though I admit it's been a bit of a shock.' He looked at his watch, 'I better get going now, I don't want to miss my train. I'll get in touch with Max and hear what he has to say during the week. I want to push on with this as fast as we can, okay?'

'Okay,' and she couldn't help a little smile of relief.

'Hi, it's Dee,' Cordelia said when Max answered his phone. 'I have something important to tell you.'

'Okay?'

'I followed up your lead with Ned, Edmund di Silver.' She heard him take a breath 'And he has agreed to work on a case against the author of The Puppeteer, he came down this weekend.'

'That's why you wanted to know if I could come over Saturday night?'

'Yes, and, well, he thinks we may have a case and he's going to push on with it. He wants to talk to you. Max, I told him, I had to tell him that you were his son.'

'Oh! Right!'

'I wanted to wait until we were all together but he sort of forced my hand, he knew I was holding something back. He's very good, very intuitive.'

'So he's going to call me?'

'Yes.'

'Good, let's get this bastard sorted out first, then we can look at playing happy families,' he sounded annoyed.

'Max, I told you, he never knew.'

'Yes, I know, don't worry.'

The phone rang on Friday afternoon at about three, Cordelia answered it.

'Dee, it's Ned, I have prepared our case and have sent the letter to his publisher. It calls for withdrawal of the book in its entirety, worldwide, otherwise we move to sue for libel. Keep your fingers crossed, we still do not have the key link between him and the email address he used to harass you but I do not intend to let him know that.'

'How long should it take?'

'That depends upon their lawyers, I would expect an answer within the week.'

'You know it's just two weeks to the Best Reads awards night?'

'Yes, another reason I pushed this. It would be better PR for the publishers to withdraw the book quietly before the results are announced, far less traumatic than having one of their authors proclaimed emperor - only to find he has no clothes. That alone might make them jump rather than prevaricate.'

'Oh! It's a bit nerve wracking isn't it?'

'Don't worry, we have a fairly good case, I still haven't given up hope of tracing the email IP address back to him but I am told he's used a system that pings them all around the world to muddy the waters, just like that character does in his book. However, the rest of the case is secure – and I would feel confident if we did have to go further. By the way, Max sounds like a good level-headed guy, seems quite protective of the Mum he's only just found.'

'He's a really nice person, hopefully you'll meet him someday soon, maybe at a victory celebration?'

'Now I like that talk! I'll get back to you as soon as I hear anything, bye, don't worry, bye.'

'Bye, I won't, thank you, thanks.'

Chapter 68

'So what's this all about?' I hissed at William as we sat waiting for a meeting with the publishers. William was looking a bit wan and he kept fiddling with his watch.

'I'm not absolutely sure, but I can tell you it is serious, very serious.'

'How?'

'They are talking lawyers, I did ask you on the phone, was there any reason they would need lawyers?'

'Yes, and I can't think of anything – I haven't revealed any military secrets, or anything have I? It's a thriller but it doesn't trespass into national secrets.'

'Who said it did?'

'I don't know, you said it was something that they'd called in the lawyers about. Fuck, look, it all passed when they looked at the book before publication.'

'Shh,' he hissed as the door opened and we were asked to go in.

Worse than an interview for the best job you ever wanted. They were ranged against us, the men in shiny suits in a row, on the left, my editor and copy editor and on the right, introduced to us, a publisher bigwig I had never met before and a lawyer.

'We have the sorry task of informing you both that we have received representation from one of the top barristers in the country accusing you of libelling their client. This is your chance to refute this absolutely, we have no wish to be sued,' the publisher bigwig opened.

'Sued?' I looked to William, 'Sued? What for?'

'Libel - defamation of character,' the lawyer said.

'Wait a minute, wait, who? Who is bringing this?' I said, but I had a sinking feeling in the pit of my stomach.

'One Cordelia Steadman.'

'But she can't prove anything!'

'You know her?'

'I've met her, yes, spoke a few times, perhaps. She lived in the village I was working in.'

'She claims you have used her as the perfect image of the character Delia in your book and that she is so recognisable to anyone who knows her that she is thereby defamed by what your character Delia does.'

"That's bullshit! Okay so she might be a bit like that woman to look at, but if I describe a person it's going to fit someone in the world, she's being unreasonable.'

'So you admit the character Delia's looks are derived from your association with this woman?'

'Not really, just maybe some of her rubbed off on my imagination, okay, she's the same colouring, same height, that's about it.'

One of the suits looked down and read out, 'detailed looks plus mannerisms, accent, interests, even sentences written by my client and used in email dialogue in the novel - these are quoted in an appendix, on their original emails.'

'Were they emails to me? Eh? Were they? No! Does this add up to proof? No! Just the delusions of a menopausal woman! I was seeing her friend, probably just jealous.'

'Here is the submission, send us back your refutation by tomorrow five pm, at the latest. We will consider what to do next.'

'Give it here, no problem,' I said, vindictive bitch!

'I'll take a copy,' William said. 'Get my lawyer to give it the once over too.'

The lawyer looked a bit aggrieved, but stuff him, if William had a tame lawyer then I was all for seeing if I could wriggle out of this one.

I wrote a bloody masterpiece, explaining how this whole libel stuff was just a crock of shit. I pointed out so many holes in the case that they had to ignore this bleating. I made sure it was with them well before the five o'clock deadline.

***

Two days later we were summoned back, same format, same ugly faces looking disappointed as William and I walked in. We sat.

'Sean, William, we have made our considered decision on this case, The Puppeteer by Sean Warner will be withdrawn from sale and pulped, worldwide, as from this afternoon.'

'What?' I leapt to my feet, I could feel William pulling on me to sit down, 'You can't fucking do that? Why? Why the fuck?'

'Please sit down Sean,' my editor said, I sat, perched on the edge of my seat. 'We cannot risk this company being sued, and that is why.'

'Seriously, there is no evidence she could bring and, have you thought of this, I am,' I stood again and held up my finger and thumb a few millimetres apart, 'this close to winning the Best Reads!'

'We have considered this, firstly, she has enough irrefutable evidence to worry us and in the hands of someone like Edmund di Silver that is too much. Secondly, if you won the Best Reads and then we had to pulp it would reflect very badly on us as a publishing house, if the book goes now it would be quieter.'

'You can't just pulp the book! I put over a year of my life into that book!'

'We, as publishers, are liable and therefore it is our choice not yours. We choose to acquiesce, at the moment all we lose is the value of the books already in print, you only lose your advance - if we went to court it could be so much more.'

'The advance?' William put in before I could get a chance.

'Yes, the advance was for a book, the book is now null and void and not through our making, your client should be more careful, he should not take the character of someone who can be identified and use it wholesale in one of his books, not even if they remained a nice character

328

and most certainly not if they turn out to be ... unwholesome in any way.'

I looked wildly at William again, he was fiddling with his watch.

'So ... the film rights?' I hazarded.

'I don't think so, Warner, be serious! I think you need to be glad that they are not coming after you for compensation ... we'd be looking to you personally if that were the case,' the bigwig said.

'Or the new book? The Death Masque?' I was looking at my editor, she shook her head.

'So sorry Sean, we won't be publishing you again, and I think you'll find it hard to find anyone who will.' She did look genuinely sorry. My copy editor murmured 'Toxic.' And I knew he was referring to me.

I sat down again as my world turned to ashes.

Chapter 69

The champagne cork popped, and the bubbles were captured in a glass before they could trickle down the side of the bottle.

When everyone had a glass Dee looked round her room, all the key people in her life were there. Max, Heather, Megan and Joshua, Marian and Kevan and Ned.

'I'd like to propose a toast,' she said, 'to friends and family, to all of you who have stood by me and make life worthwhile. Friends and family,' she lifted her glass and was joined with murmured words.

'I feel as if I have come out of a dark tunnel, this victory that Ned has won for me, for us, seems to have lifted the cloud, to mix my metaphors! I want to mark a new start in my life, I would like you all to call me Dee from now on.' She swept her glass in an arc to encompass them all, 'It's my new-start identity, the one where I have a lovely son and his family in my life.'

Marian lifted her glass, 'A toast to Dee ... Dee!' which everyone joined in with.

'And a toast to Ned, who defeated the might of the publishers and brought down that bastard Warner. He'll never be trusted by a publisher again, he's done for. Thank you Ned! ... Ned!' Dee finished.

After the delicious dinner that Dee had prepared for them all they began to leave, Max and his family first as it was getting late for Joshua.

'Night Dee, thank you, it was good to meet Ned.'

'You seemed to be getting on very well.'

'Yes, he's an interesting man, and he listens well too, I'm pleased to have met him.'

'I had better be going too,' Ned said, 'I need to get back to London tomorrow early. It's been a pleasure.'

'I don't know how to thank you. It has made such a difference; somehow it has shaken off the despair I was in after Gerald's death.'

'Maybe you can just see yourself as everyone else sees you.' Dee looked sharply at him, did he mean the worthless creature she had seen herself as or what? 'As a strong accomplished woman in her own right,' he finished.

'Ned Silver do you own a crystal ball?'

'No, but I think I know you, perhaps better than you do yourself. It is like I've always known you. Can we keep in touch, meet again?'

She stood motionless for a moment, 'I'd like that very much,' she said, feeling the smile rise from her toes to her lips, then leant forward to plant a light kiss on his.

'Oh yes?' Marian whispered to her as she and Kevan came to leave, and raised her eyebrows at Dee. The smile on Dee's face only broadened, 'Night Kevan, Marian, thank you, you know, thank you ... oh! Marian!'

'Yes?' she turned at the edge of the road.

'If anyone asks, yes, I am doing the Art Fair this year, most definitely and the charities will be the Stroke Association and Alzheimer's Research! There!'

'That's better! Good night - Dee!'

Acknowledgements:

To the many friends with different life skills, occupations and experiences of whom I asked so many strange questions in order to help get things right, thank you! Any remaining errors are my own.

To my gallant band of beta-readers who keep me on the straight and narrow when my enthusiastic typing fingers lead me astray and when holes appear in the space-time continuum of the story – Thank You: Stephanie Dickinson, Heather Douglas, Diana Greene, Nicky Hatherell, Christine Haywood and Dorothy Silverstone.

Thank You for reading A Respectable Life
by Ann Foweraker

I hope you enjoyed it and will feel able to put a review on Amazon or Goodreads – or both.

Reviews make a big difference to authors with independent publishers – thank you for your help in letting other readers find a good book when they are looking for one.

Other novels by ANN FOWERAKER

The Angel Bug
'These memoirs may be the only evidence left of what really happened, where it came from and how it spread.'

When Gabbi Johnston, a quiet, fifty-something botanist at Eden, was shown the unusual red leaves on the Moringa tree, she had no idea what was wrong. What she did know was that the legendary Dr Luke Adamson was arriving soon - and that he would insist on investigating it.

This is the unassuming start to a maelstrom of discovery and change - with Gabbi swept up in it. What starts out as an accident turns into something illicit, clandestine and unethical – but is it really, as Adamson claims, for the good of all mankind?

'The Angel Bug' is set mainly at the Eden Project in Cornwall, UK. This is a contemporary novel combining science fact and fiction, told by the people at the heart of the discovery.

Divining the Line

The first time it happened it felt like stumbling across another avenue to an ancient monument, but this one pulled at more than just his head, there was a tightness in his chest, the lights twinkled and flashed inside his mind, the intensity giving Perran a firework of a headache. Following the line - years later, in the early 1990s - leads him into Liz Hawkey's ordered life, and together they discover the source of the line.

A story of family, love and loss, Divining the Line brings the ordinary and the extraordinary together into everyday life.

Some Kind of Synchrony

Faith Warren, married mother of two, is a secretary in a city newspaper office in the late 1990s. It wasn't what she'd hoped for, but her dreams of university and becoming an author were lost long ago. Telling stories to entertain her lifelong friend on their journey to work and back is all that is left, until she tells The Story.

The real trouble began with the minor characters, just unfortunate co-incidences, but when do you stop calling them co-incidences and begin to wonder what the hell is going on – and how it can be stopped.

Nothing Ever Happens Here

Living in London suddenly becomes too uncomfortable for the attractive Jo Smart and her sixteen year-old son, Alex, after he is beaten up. so when they are offered the chance to take an immediate holiday in a peaceful Cornish town they jump at it. But not all is as peaceful as it seems as they become involved in a murder enquiry, drug raid and abduction.

DI Rick Whittington has also escaped from London and the reminders of the death of his wife and child, and through his investigations finds himself meeting Jo and being drawn into the events surrounding her.

This is a light thriller, set in the mid 1990s, which combines the historic Cornish love of the sea and smuggling with romance and hard faced twentieth century crime and detection.

About the Author - Ann Foweraker

I am poet, teacher, mother, author ... and each incarnation has had an ascendancy in my life – now is the time of the author.

I have to write poetry, it makes me, and stories weave themselves in my head even when I'm not writing, but from the moment I went to school I knew I wanted to teach - becoming a teacher when it was more of a vocation than an occupation - gaining my BEd degree in the seventies. Marriage took me from Berkshire, where I was born, to live in glorious Cornwall where the novel writing blossomed, while taking an extended break from formal teaching to bring up our four boys, but only came to fruition as they left the nest.

My books are all available from PendownPublishing.co.uk and are also available on Amazon for Kindle. The paperback books can be ordered from any bookshop, worldwide, using the ISBN number.

Please follow my blog on annfoweraker.com where you'll get an insight into the things I'm into, from belly dancing to sandsculpture, health and nutrition, poetry and, of course, writing.

Follow me on twitter at @AnnFoweraker for tweets on life, Cornwall and writing, and Like my Author page on Facebook 'Ann Foweraker' for more info and thoughts.